Well, I'd come this far, hadn't I?

And it wasn't as though I was going to go back and ask Jovis to accompany me into my father's lair. I'd defeated my father; I could climb into a dark hole by myself. I pushed myself back up, tucked the engraving tool back into my sash, gripped the lantern's handle between my teeth and set my feet upon the ladder.

The air felt even cooler in this lower cave than in the cavern with the pool. It had a musty petrichor scent, though I couldn't detect any excess moisture. It was a relief to finally touch ground again, to take the lamp from my jaw, which had already begun to ache.

I shook out the tension in my shoulders. There were perhaps more books down here, more notes, more puzzle pieces I could lock together. I pivoted, lifting the lamp.

And found its light reflecting from two monstrous eyes.

Praise for Andrea Stewart

The Bone Shard Daughter

"[A] richly told, emotional, action-laced debut....Readers will finish this eager for the follow-up."

—*Library Journal* (starred review)

"*The Bone Shard Daughter*...deserves as much attention as it can get."

—*Locus*

"Stewart's debut is sharp and compelling. It will hook readers in and make them fiercely anticipate the rest of the series."

—*Booklist*

"[An] action-packed, must-read epic fantasy....One of the best debut fantasy novels of the year." —*BuzzFeed News*

"Andrea Stewart's *The Bone Shard Daughter* is not just an amazing start to a new trilogy. It's likely the best fantasy novel you'll read this year."

—*Culturess*

"Original and intricately written." —*Ms.*

"*The Bone Shard Daughter* is one of the best fantasy novels I've read in a long time. With stunningly intricate worldbuilding that leaps off the page and characters who are so vibrant that you wish they were real, it grabs you by the heart and the throat from the first pages and doesn't let go until long after it's over. This book is truly special."

—Sarah J. Maas, *New York Times*
bestselling author

"Stewart etches this story into your heart, filling it with everything I love about fantasy: a well-realized world, dark magic that challenges your presumptions, and deep questions about identity. Highly recommended."
　　　　—Marshall Ryan Maresca, author of the Maradaine Saga

"*The Bone Shard Daughter* is intricate and expansive, incisive and thoughtful—a complex web of political and personal intrigue spun around questions of privilege, duty, and love. Stewart's debut is bound to have fantasy readers clamoring for the next installment."　　　　—Kerstin Hall, author of *The Border Keeper*

"A complex and dark tapestry of a fantasy woven through with brilliant worldbuilding, deep intrigue, and incredible heart."
　　　　—Megan E. O'Keefe, author of *Velocity Weapon*

"An unforgettable tale of magic and intrigue, and the start of a fascinating trilogy."
　　　　—Gareth Hanrahan, author of *The Gutter Prayer*

"This brilliant fantasy debut has announced Andrea Stewart as quite possibly the best newcomer of the year."
　　　　—*Novel Notions*

"*The Bone Shard Daughter* is an absolute stunner of a fantasy debut....Simply awe-inspiring."　　　　—*FanFiAddict*

The Bone Shard Emperor

"Stewart's heart-pounding second Drowning Empire epic fantasy expertly picks up the pace from *The Bone Shard Daughter*.... Stewart keeps the energy up across the many engrossing plotlines, with immersive battles aplenty to keep readers on the edges of their seats. This page-turning installment is sure to please series fans." —*Publishers Weekly*

"The hotly anticipated next volume in the Drowning Empire series....The twisting turns of political negotiations, the desperation of each character to do what's right, and the carefully written world building come together to power this compelling and suspenseful fantasy....Stewart's elegant planning and unspooling revelations will keep readers hooked from the first page, and fans will be impatient for the next and final volume in the trilogy." —*Booklist*

By Andrea Stewart

The Drowning Empire

The Bone Shard Daughter
The Bone Shard Emperor
The Bone Shard War

THE BONE SHARD EMPEROR

Book Two of The Drowning Empire

ANDREA STEWART

orbitbooks.net

Copyright © 2021 by Andrea Stewart
Excerpt from *The Foxglove King* copyright © 2022 by Hannah Whitten
Excerpt from *The Stardust Thief* copyright © 2022 by Chelsea Abdullah

Cover design by Lauren Panepinto
Cover art by Sasha Vinogradova
Cover copyright © 2021 by Hachette Book Group, Inc.
Map by Charis Loke
Author photograph by Lei Gong

Orbit
Hachette Book Group
1290 Avenue of the Americas
New York, NY 10104
orbitbooks.net

First Trade Paperback Edition: April 2022
Originally published in hardcover and ebook in Great Britain and the U.S. by Orbit in November 2021

Orbit is an imprint of Hachette Book Group.
The Orbit name and logo are trademarks of Little, Brown Book Group Limited.

The Hachette Speakers Bureau provides a wide range of authors for speaking events. To find out more, go to www.hachettespeakersbureau.com or call (866) 376-6591.

Library of Congress Control Number: 2021937946

ISBNs: 9780316541473 (trade paperback), 9780316541480 (ebook)

Printed in the United States of America

LSC-C

Printing 1, 2022

For John, who always makes sure I have time to write.
They say no one is perfect, but that is obviously a lie.

THE PHOENIX EMPIRE IN THE SUKAI DYNASTY

RIYA

DEERHEAD

MONKEY'S TAIL

1

Lin

Imperial Island

I'd thought I could set things right in the Empire if only I'd had the means. But setting things right meant weeding a garden gone wild, and with each new weed pulled, two sprouted in its place. It was so like my father not to leave me an easy task.

I clung to the ceramic tiles of the rooftop, ignoring the soft whimper from Thrana below. There was little privacy in the palace of an Emperor. Servants and guards walked the hallways; even at night there was always someone awake. My father had strolled the hallways of his own palace at all hours with impunity; no one had dared to question him, not even me. It probably helped that he kept more constructs than servants, and the servants he did keep regarded him with terror. I wanted to be a different kind of Emperor. Still, I hadn't counted on having to sneak around my own palace.

I wiped the moisture from a rain-slicked tile with my sleeve and pulled myself onto the peak of the roof. It seemed a lifetime ago since I'd last climbed up here, and though it had in fact been a few short months, my muscles felt the lack of activity. There had been administrative matters to deal with first – hiring servants, guards and workers. Repairing and cleaning out the buildings on the palace grounds. Reinstating some of my father's commitments and abolishing others.

And always there were people watching me, wondering what I would do, trying to take my measure.

Somewhere below me, Jovis, my Captain of the Imperial Guard, paced the hallway outside my room, his beast, Mephi, beside him. He'd insisted on taking on this duty himself, and though he did sleep at some point, he only did so after he'd had another guard relieve him. Having someone stationed outside my door at all hours made me grind my teeth. Always he wanted to know where I was, what I was doing. And how could I blame him when I'd tasked him with my safety? I couldn't very well order him and his guards to leave me in peace without sufficient reason. My father had been known to be ill-tempered, eccentric, reclusive. How could I give that order without appearing to be the same?

An Emperor was beholden to her people.

I sat on the peak of the roof for a moment, taking in the damp air, the smell of the ocean. Sweat stuck my hair to the back of my neck. Some of the rooms I'd discovered in the aftermath of my father's death were pointlessly locked. One filled with paintings, another with trinkets – gifts from other islands. These I set the servants upon to clean and to organize, to display in the newly renovated buildings.

There were other rooms I dared not let anyone else access. I still didn't know all the secrets that lurked behind these doors, what the things I'd found meant. And prying eyes made me wary. I had my own secrets to keep.

I was not my father's daughter. I was a created thing, grown in the caves beneath the palace. If anyone ever found me out, I'd be dead. There was enough dissatisfaction brewing with the Sukai Dynasty without adding this to it. The people of the Phoenix Empire wouldn't suffer an impostor.

In the courtyard below, two guards patrolled. Neither looked to the roof. Even if they had, I'd only be a dark shape against a cloudy sky, the rain that drizzled into their eyes obscuring their vision. I crept down the other side, making my way to a window I knew was still open. The night was warm in spite of the clouds and the rain, and shutters were often left open unless we were in a true gale. Only a few lamps were lit when I slid from the edge of the tiles, my feet finding the sill.

There was an odd comfort in creeping through the hallways of the palace again, my engraving tool and several keys hidden inside my sash pocket. It was familiar – something I knew.

I couldn't help but peer around the corner to see the door of my room. Jovis was still there, Mephi next to him. He was showing the beast a deck of lacquered cards. Mephi reached out with a webbed claw and touched one. "This one."

Jovis sighed. "No, no, no – if you play a fish on a sea serpent, that means you lose that turn."

Mephi tilted his head and sat back on his haunches. "Feed the fish to the sea serpent. Make the sea serpent your friend."

"That's not how this works."

"It worked on me."

"Are you a sea serpent?"

Mephi clacked his teeth. "Your game makes no sense."

"You said you were bored and wanted to learn," Jovis said. He started to tuck the cards back into his pocket.

Mephi's ears flattened against his skull. "Wait. Waaaaait."

I pulled back, keeping an ear out for footsteps. Playing cards while guarding the Emperor's room wasn't very professional,

despite Jovis's insistences that he needed to protect me. I supposed I'd done this to myself, hiring a former member of the Ioph
Carn and a notorious smuggler as Captain of the Imperial Guard.
But he'd saved hordes of children from the Tithing Festival and
earned a great deal of goodwill from the people.

And goodwill was something I had in short supply.

I made my way to the shard storeroom, ducking down side
passages or behind pillars whenever I saw a guard or a servant.
Swiftly, I unlocked the door and slipped inside. I moved through
muscle memory, taking down the lamp by the lintel, lighting it,
striding to the back of the room. There was another door there,
carved with a cloud juniper.

Another lock, another key.

I descended into the darkness of the old mining tunnels below
the palace, my lamp casting the sharp edges of the walls into stark
relief. The constructs my father had placed to guard the way
were dead, disassembled by my hand once I'd had the strength.
The constructs still scattered across the Empire were another
matter. All were commanded to obey Shiyen. And now that he
was gone, their command structure had fallen to pieces. Some
had gone mad. Others had gone into hiding. There were only
two constructs I'd considered mine. Hao, a little spy construct
I'd rewritten to obey me, and Bing Tai. Hao had died defending
me from my father. Only Bing Tai remained.

At the fork in the tunnels, I veered left, unlocking the door
that blocked the way. I'd often wondered what my father was
doing when he disappeared behind his locked doors. I still didn't
exactly know.

The tunnel opened up into a cavern and I lit the lamps scattered
throughout. A pool filled part of the cavern; a workstation was
set up next to it. There were bookshelves, a metal table, baskets
of tools I didn't recognize. And the chest that held my father's

memory machine. It was here I'd found Thrana, submerged in the pool, connected to that machine. As I did every time I entered this cavern, I checked the water. My lamp reflected off the dark surface; I had to squint past that to see into the water below. The replica of my father still lay in the pool, his eyes closed. After the first rush of relief came that familiar pang. He looked so much like Bayan – or, I supposed, Bayan looked so much like him.

But Bayan had died helping me to defeat my father, and when I'd finally taken the time to grieve, I'd realized there was no bringing him back. I was proof of that. While my father had grown this replica by submerging his own severed toe in the pool, he'd grown me from the parts of people he'd collected throughout the Empire. He'd tried to infuse me with the memories of Nisong, his dead wife. It had only partially worked. I had some of her memories, but I wasn't her.

I was Lin. And I was Emperor.

Even if I could use the memory machine to restore some of Bayan into this replica, it wouldn't be him.

I whirled, suddenly sure I'd heard something. A footstep? The scuff of shoe against stone? The lamps I'd lit behind me illuminated only stone and water; the only sound I could hear was my heartbeat thundering in my ears. In that one instant of blinding panic, I could feel everything being taken away from me – my years of hard work, the nights spent reading about bone shard magic, the courage I'd had to gather to defy my father – all of it dissolved in a moment of discovery. I was getting paranoid, hearing things where there was nothing. How could someone have followed me down here without the keys? The doors all locked again as soon as they latched shut.

Several of the books and pages of notes my father had gathered lay spread across the metal table. I was reluctant to move them to my rooms, where servants might see them. These were the weeds I was trying to pull: the Shardless Few, the sinking of Deerhead Island, the leaderless constructs and the Alanga. There were answers here, if only I could find them. It was finding them that was difficult. My predecessor's notes were scattered, his handwriting messy. In spite of the three locked doors, my father wrote as though afraid someone else might find these books. Nothing was straightforward. Often he referenced notes he'd written previously, or other books, but without naming where those notes could be found or the titles of the books. I was trying to assemble a puzzle that had no picture.

I drew up the chair and flipped through page after page, a headache forming quickly behind my eyes. A part of me thought that if only I read enough, if only I read it enough times, I'd figure out my father's secrets.

So far, all I'd been able to gather was that islands had sunk before, a long time ago. Knowing that more than one had sunk back then, and so far we'd only seen Deerhead Island fall, made sweat gather on my palms. I still didn't know what had caused Deerhead to sink, or when or how I might expect another island to drown. And the Alanga – another thing my father would have told his heir. Who were they, and if they returned, what could I do to fight them off?

My gaze strayed to the memory machine.

There had still been liquid in the tubes when I'd disconnected it from Thrana. Some held her blood and some held a milky fluid. I'd gathered her remaining blood into a flask I'd taken from the kitchens, and the fluid into another. In his notes, my father had mentioned feeding the memories to his constructs and to me. He'd seemed dissatisfied with his first attempts, reluctant to disassemble the constructs that might be carrying his dead wife's memories but unhappy with how little they seemed to understand of Nisong.

I wasn't sure what he'd done with those constructs, but the more pressing matter was where the memories were stored.

I'd corked both flasks, placing them on the table with the books. I'd gotten as far as uncorking the one with the milky fluid and sniffing the contents. But always I stoppered it again, searching Shiyen's notes for more concrete evidence that the memories were in that fluid. Was I getting that desperate, to consider drinking it without knowing for sure? For all I knew, it could be some sort of lubrication for the machine, poisonous and not meant to be consumed.

But some of that had come from Thrana. I wasn't sure of the connection — where he'd found her, what sort of creature she was. She was like Mephi, and Jovis had found him swimming in the ocean after Deerhead's fall.

There was nothing toxic about Thrana.

Ah, I was making excuses because part of me just wanted to drink it. I wanted to know. I couldn't be sure whose memories might be in that fluid, but I had an idea. Shiyen had been old and ill. He would have been trying to gather his memories, to place them within his replica before he died.

I was looking for answers, and some of those answers might be in the flask. The Phoenix Empire stood on a knife's edge. What was I willing to do to save my people? Numeen had told me they needed an Emperor who cared. And I cared. I cared so much.

I seized the flask, uncorked it and lifted it to my lips before I could change my mind again.

The liquid was cold, though that didn't mask the taste. Copper, sweetness and a strange, lingering aftertaste filled my mouth and clung to the back of my throat. I swiped my tongue over my teeth, wondering if I should have tasted it before swallowing. Perhaps it *was* poison. And then the memory swept over me.

I was here, still in this chamber, though it looked different.

Three more lamps were lit in the working area, and Thrana still lay in the water. My hands adjusted the tubing leading into the memory machine. Liver spots scattered across the backs of my palms, tendons pressing against skin. I pushed too hard; my hand slipped and hit the side of the chest. Something jolted loose.

"Dione's balls!" Frustration welled within me. Always one thing after another. Get something into place; another thing falls out of place. The only thing I had to live for were these experiments. My chest ached as I thought of Nisong, of her dark eyes, her hand in mine. Gone. I felt around the bottom of the chest, pushing the hidden compartment back into line.

My gaze flicked involuntarily to the other end of the cave.

And then I was back in my own body again, wondering if that was what it felt like to be my father. Strangely astonished that he had such strength of feeling at all. I'd always known him to be cold and distant.

He really had loved Nisong. I wasn't sure why that surprised me. Perhaps it was because, no matter how hard I'd tried, I could not get him to love me.

In the memory, a hidden compartment had come loose from the chest. Experimentally, I struck the side of the chest with the flat of my palm. Nothing jolted loose, but I put my hand where I remembered my father's hand pressing the wood back in.

There was something there. A small rectangle where the wood felt slightly raised. I struck the chest again.

This time, it came loose. A drawer slid partway open. I pried it the rest of the way out. Inside rested a tiny silver key.

I wasn't sure whether I wanted to laugh or to cry. Always my father kept so many secrets — secrets within secrets within secrets. His mind was a maze even *he* couldn't find his way out of. What if he had truly raised me as his daughter? What if he'd put aside his foolish quest to live on in another body, to bring his dead wife back to life?

The key was cold when I picked it up, the tiny teeth at the end sharp. I'd unlocked all the doors I could find in the palace. This belonged somewhere else.

My gaze flicked to the other side of the cave. He'd looked in that direction when he'd pushed the drawer back into place. I hadn't thought there was anything there, but perhaps I hadn't looked closely enough.

I lifted my lamp. Stalagmites blocked my path to the other side; I had to weave between them like a deer through bamboo.

At last, I reached a clear area against the wall – the spot I'd seen my father looking at. As I cast my gaze around, my heart sank. There was nothing here, just stone and the flash of crystal in the walls. I'd walked over here before; I wasn't sure why I expected anything different.

Secrets within secrets.

No, there *was* something here. He'd glanced at this spot, and I'd been experiencing his memory. There'd been a reason for it, I could feel it. I dropped to my knees, setting the lamp down and feeling around on the ground.

My fingers found the smallest crack filled with dirt.

I set aside the key, pulled my engraving tool from my sash pocket and used it to clear the dirt from the crack in the stone. Someone had chiseled a piece of stone away and then replaced it. There was something here; I hadn't been wrong.

The engraving tool bent as I used it to pry the stone out. My fingernails ached as I wedged them beneath the slab, pulling until it came free. Dirt shook loose, catching the lamplight. I peered inside the cavity and found a hatch with a keyhole.

What would my father have kept that necessitated a series of four locked doors? The key slid into the lock easily and turned with a soft click. The hinges to the hatch were well oiled; it opened soundlessly. When I swung my lantern over the hole, all I could see was a ladder descending into the dark.

There might be anything down there. I crouched down, lay on my belly and lowered both the lantern and my head into the hatch.

It was difficult to see very far into the cavern below with only one lamp, and upside down at that. The ladder was long, the bottom farther than I'd first thought. But I could make out shelves against one shadowy wall.

Well, I'd come this far, hadn't I? And it wasn't as though I was going to go back and ask Jovis to accompany me into my father's lair. I'd defeated my father; I could climb into a dark hole by myself. I pushed myself back up, tucked the engraving tool back into my sash, gripped the lantern's handle between my teeth and set my feet upon the ladder.

The air felt even cooler in this lower cave than in the cavern with the pool. It had a musty petrichor scent, though I couldn't detect any excess moisture. It was a relief to finally touch ground again, to take the lamp from my jaw, which had already begun to ache.

I shook out the tension in my shoulders. There were perhaps more books down here, more notes, more puzzle pieces I could lock together. I pivoted, lifting the lamp.

And found its light reflecting from two monstrous eyes.

2

Jovis

Imperial Island

I made a better smuggler than Captain of the Guard. If I'd
been smarter, I'd have kept that job and turned down this
one. But here I was, determined to save as many poor sods in the
Empire as I reasonably could.

Hopefully, I could keep my head while I was at it.

Mephi pawed at my jacket. "Take the cards back out." He
paused, then added reluctantly, "Please."

I swiveled my head just the slightest bit to where I'd seen Lin
peer around the corner. She was gone. She was good, I had to
admit that. I wouldn't have expected it of an Emperor's daughter.
But I'd heard a soft scrape on the tiles above and I'd known she'd
climbed to the roof. It could have been any number of things,
including my imagination, but I'd fine-tuned my instincts after
years on the run. I shouldn't have expected the Emperor to acqui-
esce when I'd asked to know where she was at all times.

The Shardless Few were right: she had secrets. And they'd
charged me with uncovering them. Following a young lady

around in the dark – I supposed this was how I was going to save the Empire. Not exactly worthy of another folk song. "Shh," I said to Mephi before he could paw at me again. "Lin – she's not in her room anymore."

The beast went still, ears pricked.

"Stay here," I told him. "I'm going after her." I made it as far as the corner before a horned head appeared at my side. I lifted my hands in silent frustration.

"You said we stay together," Mephi whispered. He'd fortunately mastered the ability to actually whisper by now.

I *had* told him that. I'd left him behind once when completing a task for the Shardless Few, and it had ended disastrously for me and, I'd thought back then, for him. I'd nearly died and he'd fallen into what I'd thought was an illness – but turned out to be a hibernation of sorts. I'd never felt so worried before in my life, unsure whether he would live or die. What if it happened again? "Fine," I said. "But stay quiet, and stay close."

Despite the newfound gangliness of his limbs, Mephi still moved with the grace of a serpent across the rocks. He slipped through the hallways even more silently than I did. I caught a glimpse of Lin ducking behind a pillar to avoid a servant.

I waited in the shadows, Mephi's tail curling around my leg. When she moved again, I moved. I'd shadowed people before – to find out where they'd hidden things, to obtain blackmail and to eavesdrop on secret meetings.

Perhaps smuggling and spying weren't so different after all.

She stopped at a small door, looked both ways, unlocked it and slipped inside.

"Mephi . . . !" I hissed.

He was moving before I'd even said his name, darting across the floor as swiftly as a river. I rushed to catch up to him, trying to keep my footsteps light, my heartbeat hammering.

He'd caught the door with a claw just before it had latched. I'd been able to read his moods from his face, unlike as it was from my own, and now I read "smug" in his expression. I gave him a grudging nod. Yes, I'd have been very put out if I hadn't brought him. Yes, it had been a good decision on his part. Yes, I needed him more than I thought.

Mephi gave me a perfunctory nod back before prying the door open a crack.

I watched Lin move to the back of the room, her lamp held high, watched her open a door carved with a cloud juniper. I opened the door wide as soon as she'd slipped inside and Mephi rushed forward.

There wasn't time for me to examine the room, and with the door shutting behind me, the light faded. There were no windows here, no places for prying eyes to reach. I found Mephi by touch.

We followed Lin into the darkness, the glow of her lamp lighting the way.

What was this place? The walls were stone and became rough-hewn; the floor tilted at a slope, leading us down. It took me a moment to realize we were no longer in the palace. We'd descended into the mountain the palace abutted. An old mine? I'd heard that Imperial Island once had a witstone mine, but it had been closed without explanation years ago. Judging by the vein of white I saw running across the ceiling, it hadn't been for lack of stone.

So what was Lin doing down here? The Emperor had her own store of witstone; she wouldn't need to mine any herself. She was here for another reason. Was she hiding something? Keeping someone prisoner? The place certainly felt like a dungeon – dark, closed-in, oppressive. Mephi pressed in close to me, and I found his presence more comforting than I'd thought I would.

A fork appeared ahead, the glow of Lin's lamp emanating from the left side. I crept forward, wondering how deep below the surface we were now. Even my breath seemed to echo off the walls in the quiet. And then the tunnel dead-ended. In yet another door. Lin pulled a key from her sash pocket.

My apprehension rose. I wasn't sure I understood this Emperor. I wasn't foolish enough to believe the official statement – that Shiyen had died of a long illness, peacefully in bed. There had been no construct guards manning the walls when I'd arrived at the palace. Even the front doors had been unattended. I'd run into Lin in the hall, her clothes torn and bloodied, Thrana and her construct Bing Tai flanking her.

It hadn't been a peaceful transfer of power.

And then, instead of executing or imprisoning me, she'd given me a position as Captain of her Imperial Guard. She'd explained how she wanted to make things right, how she was ending the Tithing Festival and her father's iron-fisted way of rule.

To the Shardless Few's leader, Gio, it didn't matter who was Emperor. Only that there was one. I'd thought perhaps he was wrong. That a good Emperor, one who cared about the people of the Empire, might not be a bad thing.

But now, following Lin into the dark, I couldn't help but spin tales in my mind of what secrets she was keeping, what terrible deeds I might uncover.

Mephi rushed forward as she passed through the third – and I hoped last – door. "Thank you," I whispered to him in the dark as I cracked the door open. I wedged a rock into the opening. I might need to make a quick, silent exit.

"We stay together," he whispered back, his voice fierce.

"You're right," I said. I could nearly feel the smugness vibrating off the beast. Like most adolescents, he very much enjoyed being right about things. Obviously I just didn't know better. Not until he came along to correct me.

Behind the door was another tunnel, leading down. Light flared at the bottom. I pulled my staff loose from its strap on my back, took a deep breath and descended.

The cavern the tunnel opened up into was vast – the size of the palace's entrance hall three times over. A pool filled part of it, a thick vein of witstone running across the ceiling. Lin had lit the lamps in the cavern, and the light pressed against the vast shadows. She stood at the center, at what appeared to be a workstation. There were shelves, books, baskets, chairs and a metal table scattered with various items.

I frowned. What would a person be working on in a secret cave below the palace except something sinister? There were a few stalagmites but no real cover – I couldn't sneak past the entrance and expect to remain undiscovered. So I lingered, squinting at the workstation, trying to make out something useful.

"Mephi," I whispered, "can you—?"

And then Lin lifted a flask from the table's surface and drank from it. Her whole body went rigid, the flask still gripped in her right hand.

Poison? I couldn't make sense of what I was seeing. I tensed, wondering if I should do something to help. But I was supposed to be spying on the Emperor for the Shardless Few, not helping her. Helping Lin wasn't my job. I mean, it technically was. But it wasn't the job I'd been sent here for.

But what sort of person was I? I didn't know what sort of person she was, not yet, and what if she was dying? Could I really sit here and watch?

Her hand moved, setting the flask down. I let out a breath.

Mephi, next to me, was sniffing the air, his whiskers trembling. "It smells familiar," he whispered by way of explanation when I stared at him.

"You've never been here before," I said.

His ears flattened. "I know that."

By the time I looked back to Lin, I saw something glinting between her fingers. A key. Another bedamned key. She stood up from where she crouched over a chest, and made her way to the far end of the cavern. I couldn't see what she was doing there, behind a cluster of stalagmites, though I heard scraping sounds, and then soft grunting as she lifted something.

As I watched, she crouched and then disappeared.

I gestured to Mephi and we moved into the cavern. I stayed close to the wall opposite the side with the pool, hopeful that if Lin popped back up again, I could hide in the shadows against the undulating stone. It was a risk, but I'd taken a fair bit of those in my day. They mostly worked out in my favor. Mostly.

Behind the cluster of stalagmites lay an opened hatch and a slab of stone. Light emanated from the hatch. Mephi sniffed the air, all the hair on his back standing on end. "Don't like it," he said beneath his breath. "Smells bad."

I resisted the urge to tap my staff against the cavern floor, though I could feel the sweat gathering on my palm. I wouldn't know what was down there unless I looked.

A growl, thick and gravelly, filled the cavern.

Now *my* hair was standing on end. Mephi darted forward before I could stop him, ducking his head into the hole. "Monster," he squeaked at me. He opened his mouth as though trying to form a more coherent thought, and then snapped it shut again.

"Stay back." Lin's voice, quavering.

I had two choices: to wait and see if Lin survived this, or to— Ah, it looked like my feet had made the choice for me already. The ladder was held solidly in place, which I was grateful for, because when I'd descended low enough to see the cavern below, my limbs trembled.

The Emperor stood between me and what Mephi had accurately identified as a monster. A construct filled half the space, its flashing golden eyes as big as my fists. Its maw was open, exposing multiple rows of sharp, white teeth. Muscular legs ended in claws that could end me with one swipe. I'd never seen one so large. What was it doing down here, behind four sets of locked doors?

I caught a glimpse of shelves, of something hanging on the walls, before my gaze was drawn inevitably back to the stand-off.

Lin held the lamp in one hand, her engraving tool in the other, and she wasn't budging. Was she mad? That thing was going to eat her.

And then the construct's gaze landed on me.

There I was, hanging partway down a ladder, staff clutched in one sweaty hand. My most potent trick required contact with the ground, which was . . . still a fair bit down.

"Jovis," Mephi hissed from above me, "move!"

It was a testament to my foolishness that I went down the ladder rather than back up, sliding as quick as I could manage. I felt the rush of air as the creature moved, its jaws snapping just above my head. Apparently, I looked like I made a more appealing meal than Lin. I was a fair bit larger. And she did look rather sinewy.

But I didn't have time to speculate on the culinary qualities of humans. I jumped the rest of the way, the impact from the fall jolting the teeth in my jaw. But I had my staff in hand, and the thrumming in my bones. The construct charged at me again, and I stamped a foot.

The entire cavern shook, dust coming loose from the ceiling. The monster stopped in its tracks but did not topple, did not so much as wobble.

Four legs. Right.

From behind it now, Lin rose, striking dust from her robe, evidently not the benefactor of the same sort of stability. "You're going to bring the whole cavern down on us, you fool!" she spat.

I couldn't argue with her. I'd panicked at the sight of the creature, forgetting where I was. I lifted my staff, hoping strength and speed might help me stay alive. I wasn't sure how I could kill such a creature, or if I could at all.

"You followed me," Lin said, brandishing her engraving tool. "You broke into my locked chambers. How did you even get down here?"

A thousand lies sprouted in my head, and I uprooted each of them. This wasn't the time for explanations. I eyed the beast, wishing I'd chosen some other weapon. Something sharp or pointy. Clobbering it on the head was only likely to make it angry. "Can we discuss my execution later?"

Another growl, the gravelly sound making the pit already growing in my stomach widen further. It came for me again, and this time I was ready. I brought my staff up and struck the construct on the nose, hard as I could.

It yelped and shook its head at the blow, though I hadn't done so much as draw blood. I rushed forward, trying to take advantage of its momentary hesitation.

For a creature so large, it was surprisingly quick. It ducked away from my follow-up blow, teeth bared. I caught a glimpse of Lin, stalking closer.

"Get to the ladder," I called to her. "I don't know how long I can hold it off." I wasn't sure if I could hold it off at all. Why was I sticking my neck out for her? All I knew was that I couldn't just leave her down here to face this creature alone, no matter who she was. I was getting soft. Maybe I'd always been soft.

The construct, sensing my attention had wavered beyond it, turned its golden-eyed gaze on Lin. Its irises flashed in the lamplight. Claws dug into the stone.

I should have considered making a run for the ladder myself, but instead I raised my voice. "Hey – finish what you started!" Technically, it had started with Lin, but I doubted it was going to stop to correct this mistake.

I was right.

It wheeled on me, charging like a deer in the middle of mating season. I supposed I should be grateful it didn't have horns. I stumbled back, my footing uneven on the stone floor, catching myself with the end of my staff. Did it matter if I died on my own two feet or on the ground? I lifted my staff and the creature pulled up just short of me, grunting. The nose was a pain point, then. Even the most fearsome beasts had sensitive spots. The eyes, too. I could aim for those.

I needed to bring its massive head within reach.

Mephi's voice echoed into the chamber. "Can I help?"

"You can help by staying there and being ready to close the hatch," I called back. I took another step back and felt the wall.

Great. I'd let it corner me. Amateur mistake for a smuggler and a Captain of the Imperial Guard. I much preferred fighting a dozen men in the open streets to this one beast in an enclosed cave. Always check your exits. Always leave a way out. But if some other person fell into danger, my brain became muddled as the melon pulp at the bottom of the wine barrel. I'd told myself so many times I wasn't a hero.

I lifted my staff to the side, opening my arms, inviting the construct to attack.

Maybe I *was* a hero. And heroes were idiots.

Its jaws opened, saliva dripping onto the floor. It lunged.

I brought up my staff – too slowly. I felt as though I were

watching myself from the side, everything in that moment clarified, distilled to a fine point of fear.

They didn't usually sing about the heroes' grisly deaths in the folk songs. Usually the hero swooned at the end of a battle, bleeding prettily from one wound, a single tear escaping. There wasn't going to be enough of me left for that.

The beast froze.

I came back to myself in bits and pieces. My painfully tight grip on the staff, my clenched jaw, my heartbeat kicking wildly in my chest.

The construct was frozen and I wasn't dead. Mephi? Was this some new power he'd granted me?

A soft scrape sounded from behind the construct and I nearly jumped out of my skin. Lin strode around the bulk of the beast, a few shards of bone in her hand, the lamp held high in the other.

"Would you care to tell me what you're doing down here?"

Despite her stature, there was something of Shiyen in the way she held her head, the way her gaze seemed to pierce through mine. I'd never met the man, though I'd seen his portraits. He hadn't smiled for any of them.

"My job," I answered simply.

"I didn't ask to be followed," she said. She glanced to the side, where Mephi was watching from the hatch. "And you brought him along too. That's two mouths I need to keep silent."

"So you're hiding things."

"Of course I am," she spat back at me. Her eyes flashed nearly as brightly as the construct's had. "This place isn't mine. It's my father's, and he never told me about it. I don't know all the secrets he kept. You would propose instead that I open up all his locked doors for everyone to inspect? Imagine some poor servant coming down here and falling victim to this construct."

Something about her righteousness pricked my anger. She

sounded like Gio. "*You* almost fell victim to it. What do you think would happen to me if you died? Everyone would think I'd had something to do with it — or at the very least, I hadn't been doing my job."

"No," she said. "*You* almost fell victim to it. Not me. The constructs are my domain, my responsibility. Not yours."

My mouth kept moving, my mind struggling to keep up. "And your safety is my responsibility."

She thrust her hand inside the beast and then removed it, her fingers now empty. I tensed as the creature moved again, bringing my staff to bear. So this was to be my execution? Mephi started down the ladder headfirst, a soft whine in his throat.

Lin lifted a hand to forestall him. "Wait. Watch."

Strangely enough, Mephi obeyed.

The skin of the beast sagged, fur sloughing off.

"I've broken it," she said. "I am the only one who knows how."

I couldn't quite relax, even as the construct fell to pieces in front of me. My face felt hot. Had she not needed me at all? I'd exposed myself, and for what? But as I thought back to what I'd seen when I'd looked down the hatch, I didn't think she could have gotten close to the construct if I'd not distracted it. "If you're so competent and don't need protection, why hire me?"

"You and I both know why I hired you. You lend me legitimacy with the people. But I cannot have you sneaking around after me, dogging my footsteps, demanding to know everything I am doing."

Mephi climbed the rest of the way down and wound his way around my legs as though he could protect me from her wrath.

"Are you my Captain of the Imperial Guard? Or are you a spy?"

The heat drained from my face. She didn't know — she couldn't know. I'd not given any sign. I forced myself to breathe. It was an inquiry meant to needle me and nothing more. "What will you do then, Eminence? Strip me of my title? Execute me?" She'd already admitted that she needed me. "I can't imagine the people who hold me in high esteem would like that."

Mephi patted my leg, trying to soothe me.

Lin stepped closer, and though she had to crane her neck, it felt for a moment as though we were the same height. "Are you threatening the leader of the Phoenix Empire?" The air between us seemed to vibrate. "What is it that you want, Jovis? To become Emperor yourself?"

I was so taken aback by this accusation all I could think to say was, "Why would I want that?" It was the last thing I wanted. I hadn't even wanted to be here in the palace. What an absurd idea. I would have laughed had I not been in a more dire position.

She blinked. The tension between us evaporated as her brow furrowed. "Why wouldn't you?"

Any number of reasons, and I wouldn't even have to lie about them. I opened my mouth to start listing them, but Lin's gaze went to the hatch. She sucked in a breath. I whirled.

A small creature with bat ears and a gull's wings watched us.

She grabbed my arm. "You propped open the door." She said it like I'd boiled rice in too much water.

"Yes." I wasn't sure what she was so panicked about.

"That construct isn't mine. I've never seen its like on Imperial before. It's a spy." And then she was putting the lamp's handle between her teeth, running to the ladder, hauling herself up two rungs at a time. No wonder she hadn't a moment's hesitation about climbing onto the roof. She moved quick as a squirrel.

Constructs were her purview. They weren't mine. She'd said as much. But I still found myself tucking my staff onto my back and running after her like a damned fool. What if she got hurt? What if it was blamed on me? Lies I told myself because I couldn't admit that Mephi was right – I was a person who helped. And apparently I was a person who helped even when it was incredibly stupid to do so.

"You said you were the only one who knew bone shard magic," I huffed as I climbed after her. Mephi clambered up after me, the ladder creaking beneath our combined weights.

"Yes," she said. "But after my father's death, everything went sideways." She pulled herself out of the hatch, and to my surprise, turned to give me a hand up. "I need to catch it. They are no longer bound to my father, which means they can pledge loyalty to others. I cannot believe it was here by mistake. Help me."

Any hesitation I'd felt melted away. Had she ever intended to execute me? Or was she just as foolish as I was, hoping that a single person could begin to make things right? I gave her a swift nod in response, and she ran after the construct. It disappeared up the tunnel entrance.

She was quicker than I'd thought she'd be, though my long legs and my Mephi-inspired strength made up the difference.

"Did you prop open any other doors?" she asked as we made for the tunnel.

"Just the one."

"It came in through the spy entrance to Ilith's lair, then. We won't catch it down here. We can intercept it in the courtyard if we hurry. It has wings – once it takes flight, things will get difficult."

We didn't speak after that, and I let her lead the way through the winding tunnels, the lamp jolting in her hand and nearly extinguishing more than once. Mephi ran at my side, never questioning where we were going or what we were doing. He might sass me about cards, but when it mattered, he was always there for me.

She slammed through the cloud juniper door, and then

through the outer one so hard I was sure her shoulder must be bruised. She didn't even wince, just kept running.

The entrance hall felt ominous at night, only the two lamps by the main doors still lit. It took her a little longer to open one of those, and I added my strength to hers, our shoulders touching, our hands pressed to the wood.

We both nearly tumbled down the stairs as it gave way. I forgot sometimes to compensate for my newfound strength, to pull back when the occasion called for it. But Lin caught her feet beneath her, taking the steps down two – and then three – at a time. She ran straight for the garden.

The palace grounds were dark, the lamps outside all blown out. A drizzle of rain gathered beads on my face and eyelashes. I leapt down the bulk of the stairs and followed her.

"A boulder," she called to me, her voice strangely steady. I'd thought she'd be more out of breath. "The entrance to Ilith's lair is beneath a boulder next to the cherry tree."

I didn't think I'd be able to identify a cherry tree in the dark, so I just pulled my staff free as I ran, hoping I'd be prepared.

The archway into the garden led straight into a waist-high wall of hedges, which Lin wove easily around. I vaulted over and heard Mephi do the same. The garden felt even darker than the rest of the courtyard, but I followed the sound of Lin's footsteps, nearly tripping at each step down on the path I couldn't see. The path opened into a circular clearing, a tree and a boulder in the middle.

Something fluttered up and into the night sky.

"Shit!" Lin said.

I wasn't sure why – after four locked doors, a cavern beneath the palace and a giant construct – this would be the thing that surprised me. An Emperor swearing like a smuggler.

She stamped her foot, and the ground shook. Mephi pressed

his shoulder against my thigh. All the suspicions I'd been carrying since I saw Thrana, since that first discussion I'd had with Lin when she'd asked me to be Captain of her Imperial Guard, rushed back in.

Thrana was like Mephi.

Lin was like me.

And I was like . . . ?

I'd tried not to think too much about what I was, what this magic meant. But ever since I'd fought the four-armed construct in front of the palace, I'd wondered. I'd been able to gather the surrounding water, to harness it to my command.

The tales spoke often of Alanga control over water.

I cleared my throat. "I guess we should—"

But she was off before I could finish my sentence, darting to a nearby pavilion, shimmying up the drain like she'd done this a thousand times before. Perhaps she had.

"Dione's balls!" I swore, and then followed her.

I caught a glimpse of Mephi's forlorn face as I climbed up the building. "Wait here for me – I'll be back!" I promised him. He'd be safe within the palace walls.

Lin had already leapt to the rooftop of another building by the time I'd crested the top of the pavilion. I ran after her, flinging myself to the next roof. I wouldn't have been able to make the jump before I'd bonded with Mephi. How long had she been doing this for? She practically flew across the roofs, the construct a dark, fluttering shape in the sky.

Rain stuck to my forehead, forming into rivulets as I ran.

"Take it down!" I called to the guards on the walls. Two of them heard me, startling and turning to see who'd spoken. "In the sky," I clarified. Only one had the presence of mind to lift her bow.

Too slowly. The construct would pass out of range before

she could nock an arrow, and I wasn't even sure if she saw the construct.

We reached the walls. The guards eyed us both, unsure of what to make of us.

Lin's gaze went to the buildings of the city, her expression grim. I knew what she was going to do a moment before she did it. "Eminence, it's too far. The construct is gone; it—"

She ran, leaping first to the top of the crenellations and then striking out hard for the rooftops. She barely made it. Her fingers scrabbled at the roof tiles, her feet hanging from the edge. But she pulled herself up in one smooth movement and was off again.

I knew my limits. Well, most times I did. I gave the guards an apologetic shrug and then dropped over the side of the wall.

The walls had been repaired since I'd arrived, which made them look a whole lot better but made them a lot more difficult to climb. I gave up halfway down and dropped to the ground. The fall jolted my knees and made me wince, but I knew from experience that any damage would heal quickly and the pain would fade.

The streets of Imperial City were empty this time of night, the shops closed and the people asleep. I'd been to the city a few times in my youth, back when I'd been studying at the Navigators' Academy. Imperial City was a day's trip away from the Academy by boat or by oxcart, and a popular place for students to get away and let loose. The streets were different then than they were now, but I could still find my way easily enough. And all I had to do was follow the sound of Lin's footsteps against the tile rooftops—a faint *click click click* above the dripping of rain down the gutters. The stones of the street were slippery, but I risked a glance up and could barely make out the shadow of the construct against the sky.

We still had a chance to catch it.

Lin was freshly crowned; I wondered who had subverted a spy construct and sent it to Imperial so quickly. If the constructs could be called now to other causes and other masters, that left a veritable army of them across the Empire, waiting to fall into the wrong hands.

The thought chilled me far more than the rain against my cheeks.

A grunt came from above as Lin launched herself at the construct and missed, landing hard on a rooftop and nearly tumbling down the eaves.

"You have to get closer!" I called to her. "Or try . . . throwing something at it."

"Throw what?" she shouted back.

I bit back a retort — that perhaps she should have thought of this before chasing the construct. I was running out of breath anyway. I careened down the main street of Imperial, flashes of a past life flowing past me. A drinking hall I'd been to once, where I'd sat in the corner alone, nursing a mug of wine. A shop with beautiful, elaborate maps, which I'd coveted but could not afford. The spot on a corner where a few fellow students had accosted me, accusing the half-Poyer boy of following them. I'd talked my way out of that. Eventually.

I never thought I'd come back to Imperial. Not to stay.

A loose oyster shell lay in the gutter in front of me. I scooped it up as I ran, feeling its heft. We were nearing the docks. I could smell the ocean, feel the breeze off the water, hear the waves against the shore. My feet kicked beneath me, moving faster than I'd thought possible, my breath quick in my throat. But wind and wings were faster still.

Another grunt from above as Lin launched herself at the construct. It veered as her fingers grasped at its tail and then pulled away, leaving her with only feathers and a fall to the rooftop.

The docks appeared ahead, the ocean beyond. Only one chance at this.

I focused on the construct, planted my feet, cocked my elbow and heaved the oyster shell at it. Should have kept running, looking for something else to throw, but I watched, my breath held.

The oyster shell went wide and the construct flew over the docks and out to sea. Escaped.

3

Lin

Imperial Island

I landed on the roof shoulder first, the feathers still grasped between my fingers. The fall jolted the breath from me and I rolled down the tiles, throwing out an arm to catch something, anything, that would stop my momentum. My fingers jammed into the gutter before I could fall off the edge, though I nearly tumbled over my own arm.

I lay there, breathless, watching as Jovis threw an oyster shell at the construct, missing by a wide margin. Some folk hero. The man they'd written a song about would have struck true, hair whipping in the wind, shoulders squared.

Jovis leaned over his knees, winded as an old man. They certainly never wrote about being tired in the stories.

The spy construct was gone, flying off to report to its master — whoever that might be. I tried to untangle the knot that seemed to be growing, by the moment, in my belly. I wasn't sure what it had seen down there in the caverns. Had it gone through any of the notes while I'd been fighting my father's hidden construct?

Had it seen Shiyen's replica? Either one might undo me – expose me for what I was.

Had Jovis seen?

I could speak prettily of working together, of needing his help, but my insides twisted like a pile of snakes. My rule looked fragile to those outside it, but the truth was even more delicate than they knew.

I climbed down the side of the building. Someone inside had woken up and lit a lamp, disturbed by my footsteps. We needed to go back to the palace before anyone could see us. The guards at the wall might already have questions running through their heads that I had no easy answers for. I'd felt a thrumming in my bones, strength rushing through my limbs – and I'd used both without questioning them.

Without questioning how it might look to others.

I was the Emperor, and I was throwing myself from rooftop to rooftop like I was Jovis come to save a group of children from the Tithing Festival. I needed to hold myself in check, to be discreet.

My wounds from my battle with my father had healed quickly, and at the time I hadn't thought much of it. But now the pieces were falling together, making sense in the way I wished I could make sense of my father's notes.

I touched a hand to Jovis's shoulder when I approached, eyeing the slats of light from behind the building's shutters, hoping those shutters didn't open just yet. "We'll take the alleys back. Come on. Quickly."

He heaved himself up and brushed at his shoulder absent-mindedly, as though my hand had left some impression on his shirt. His breathing had already steadied. "I almost had it," he said.

I snorted in spite of myself. "Next time, let me do the throwing. Of all the gifts you've manifested, that doesn't seem to be one of them."

Someone rattled the shutters of the building next to us and I darted back up the street, beckoning for Jovis to follow. We ducked into an alleyway. Refuse piles lay hidden in the darkness, and I found myself stepping into more than one slippery, unknown substance.

"Is this something you do often? Sneak about the city and step in garbage?" Jovis's voice sounded nearly in my ear, startling me. "You're the Emperor. You shouldn't have left the palace walls."

"And you shouldn't have followed me," I hissed back. "At all." Never mind what the spy construct had seen, what had *he* seen? He'd put me in a difficult position. Yes, he'd helped me chase down the spy construct; yes, he'd foolishly tried to save my life even though that exposed him. But he was brushing against secrets even I didn't fully understand.

Jovis didn't say anything for a while, and I waited for him to argue with me again, to justify his actions with his duty. It was an excuse – was he really that dedicated to protecting me? He was a smuggler, a man used to defying rules in order to seek out what he wanted. No matter how many children he'd saved, I couldn't expect him to suddenly turn dutiful and honorable. The question was: what had he wanted? Was he merely satisfying curiosity or did he have some other motive?

Instead of arguing, he let out a deep breath. "Thank you, by the way. You saved my life down there in that cave."

And just like that, my anger fled, even as I grasped to hold on to it. I had a right to be angry. But all the exhaustion from the fight and the chase was starting to settle into my bones. There were so many things to worry over. "My father wouldn't have."

"I know." I could barely see him in the dark, but I felt the brush of his sleeve against mine as he drew up next to me. "I didn't nose about, if that's what you're wondering. You can trust me."

I wanted to laugh. I couldn't trust anyone. "Of course I can't.

I don't even know you. And when were you planning on telling me that your powers come from Mephi?"

His step faltered. "Did he tell you that?"

"I can figure things out on my own — and it wasn't difficult to figure out." Beneath the exhaustion I could feel a tremor in my bones, waiting to be called upon. It had given me strength and speed when I'd needed it the most. Mephi and Thrana were the same type of creature. It was the only thing Jovis and I had in common, and I'd not felt this power before I'd bonded with Thrana. "What are they? And what are we?"

"I was going to tell you."

He wasn't — I could see the barest outline of his face as he lifted his chin to stare at the sky. That was enough for me to know, to read it on his face. My father had told me: "If you know a person is lying, don't countermand them. They'll dig in. Just continue on with what you know is the truth." I hated that his advice still held credence, but he'd been cruel, not foolish. I cleared my throat. "So we both have our secrets. I won't spill yours, don't worry. That benefits me in no way. And if I'm right, it benefits you to keep mine."

I led him around a corner, brushing wet hair from my eyes. We'd both be soaked by the time we made it back — soaked and stinking of refuse. Part of me yearned for the days when constructs manned the walls and I could enter and exit without wondering what whispers or gossip would follow me.

"What do you mean?" he said, his tone cautious.

"You don't want people to know that Mephi gives you your power. As soon as they know, it puts him at risk."

He seized my arm. Fear tightened my throat. We were alone and out on the streets. He could end me now and then run without fear of many consequences. With Thrana's help, I might match my strength to his, but I wasn't sure how to do everything that Jovis did – not yet. So far, everything I'd done had been accidental.

But his touch was gentle. "There's a garbage pile there. You almost walked right into it." He let go, as if suddenly realizing whose arm he held. "My apologies, Eminence."

I smoothed my tunic before continuing forward, my heartbeat still fluttering in my chest. "I suppose I can't say you are remiss in your duties."

"So that's why you hired me: to keep you out of garbage heaps," he said, a hint of amusement in his voice.

"Everyone speaks of assassins and disgruntled governors, and no one speaks of the dangers of refuse piles." Relief made me giddy. He wasn't trying to kill me, and I didn't think he'd seen much before following me down the ladder. Something told me he'd be treating me a fair bit differently if he'd seen Shiyen lying in the pool. If he'd understood what that meant.

I still didn't trust him.

"So when were you going to tell me about Mephi and Thrana?"

The moon peeked out from behind a cloud, limning his profile as he ran a hand through his hair. "I probably wasn't," he said. "It's not an easy thing to talk about. I'd just sound mad." He stopped. "Here, this way is shorter." He pointed down a side street. "I don't think anyone will be looking."

I forgot sometimes that even though he was from Anau, he'd studied at the Navigators' Academy and had been to Imperial before. There was little I knew about him except what the songs said.

I took his suggestion – it would be a bit shorter of a walk, and less filled with garbage. A couple of lamps were still lit outside shops, their owners having forgotten to put them out. They cast the buildings in a wan glow, barely brighter than the light of the moon. We'd passed a tiny pastry shop before Jovis spoke again.

"I don't know who you are either," he said. "And you hired me to legitimize your rule with the people, which means by working for you I've given you my tacit endorsement. It's a lot to put on the shoulders of a smuggler. How can I know you're not like him?"

I knew who he meant: my father. "I've halted the Tithing Festival. Is that not enough?" Of course it wasn't. First I'd sought to prove myself to my father; now I was seeking to prove myself to everyone else. The knowledge that I was still not enough stung my pride. But I thought of the paper crane, now sitting on the desk in my study. The work of Numeen's daughter, Thrana – who'd died by my father's order. No matter what I was, I'd grown beneath such a man's care. Jovis was right to doubt me. I sighed. "My father didn't care about the people. I do." I watched his face soften out of the corner of my eye and I knew what to say next. "I had a friend outside the palace. A blacksmith. My father murdered him and his entire family. I did not get along with my father." I did not tell him how I'd still yearned for his love, his approval. My relationship with Shiyen had been . . . complicated.

"You killed him." He said it casually, like we were two drunk classmates bonding on a late-night stroll back to where we were staying.

He knew I had. He'd seen me after my battle against my father. But I humored him anyway. "I did. He had a foster-son. We were friends. My father murdered him too and then threatened to kill me." All the truth, if a sanitized version of it. Officially, Bayan had returned to the backwater isle he'd come from. Officially, he was still alive. If only it were truly so.

Jovis reached out a hand as if to offer comfort and then, remembering who I was, pulled it back. "Your father was not a good man."

I hesitated, wondering how much more to say, part of me

wishing he'd had the temerity to touch me again. The last time someone had touched me in any way that wasn't perfunctory was when Bayan had held my hand before we'd faced my father. The rest of the words spilled from my mouth. "He was the only parent I knew. I loved my father, but he didn't love me. In the end, I wanted to live more than I wanted him to love me." All the old hurt welled up within me, a wound that never quite scabbed over. I wondered if I would live with that pain for the rest of my life.

"I'm sorry." He actually looked sorry too, and for some reason that made my heart ache more.

In all the letters I'd received, few had offered condolences on my father's death. Most had probed for information, wondering what I might change in the Tithing structures, wondering what plans I had for their islands. I wasn't a person to them. I blinked back tears, embarrassed to be tearing up at all. Was I so desperate for kindness? Was I that pathetic?

If Jovis noticed, it was only out of the corner of his eye. He waited, giving me time to compose myself. "You said you didn't know me," he said as we walked. "And granted, the folk song doesn't tell you much. Is there anything you want to know about me? A question for a question."

I took in his profile – the lanky limbs, the long nose, the hair curling about his ears. He stood almost a full head taller than me, and even though I knew the power he had, I wasn't afraid of him. There were so many things I wished to know about him. Was he a spy? Was he planning to kill me or take the crown? What had he seen inside the cavern? No. These questions would all widen the gap between us when I needed to close it. I needed the people of the Empire to trust me. I needed Jovis to trust me.

I swallowed my grief and lobbed him an easy question. "Why didn't you become a navigator? Why smuggling?"

He shrugged. "I couldn't find a job. No one wanted to hire a half-Poyer navigator who couldn't get a recommendation from the Academy. So I went home. And then I was offered an opportunity. I took it."

"You didn't want to be a smuggler?"

He tapped a finger against his chin, and I heard a smile in his voice. "Is that another question?"

"Yes. And so was that." I couldn't help but smile back. "Now answer mine."

His voice turned wistful. "I didn't want it. If you ever meet my mother, you'll understand why. She has a strong predilection against what she considers immoral activities. She even hates it when my father gambles at cards. But it felt like the only option for me." The smile faded. "Later on, I did break with the Ioph Carn. I had a wife once. She went missing seven years ago. The only way I could follow her trail was with my own ship, and those are hard to come by without money. So I took the one I had on loan from them. The trail eventually led me to the palace, to the construct of your father's I fought on the steps. He took her for one of his experiments and she's dead now. I suppose I knew it a long time ago, that she was gone. But part of me had to know for sure."

"I'm sorry," I said. It was my turn to offer condolences. Somehow it felt inadequate. I felt oddly responsible.

He stood straighter. "Will you ever use bone shard magic again?" His gaze flitted from my eyes to my cheeks to my lips.

I tensed. I'd let down my guard when I shouldn't have. There was only one right answer here, and I railed against it. How could I make a commitment like that without knowing what the future held? My father might have used it for ill ends; that didn't mean I had to. "Bone shard magic saved your life," I said. "Or would you rather have fought off my father's construct with your staff?"

I watched the movement of his throat as he swallowed. "That's true. It's also not an answer."

I didn't owe him anything. I was his Emperor. But my father had never bothered to justify himself either. "I don't know what will happen or all the problems my father left behind. I want to say that I will not, but I also can't hold myself to something like that."

His jaw clenched but he finally inclined his head. A nearby lamp caught the drizzle of rain around his head, haloing him in glittering gold. "Fair enough. But I don't know if that will be good enough for everyone else. They've been through a lot — children dying from the Tithing Festival, loved ones dying from shard sickness. They'll want it all dismantled."

"I'll do my best. That's all I can promise."

Jovis stopped in the middle of the street, his gaze going skyward.

"What?" I followed his gaze. "Is the construct back?"

"No," he said. "There's something I should tell you, because this concerns you too."

I'd passed his test, whatever it had been. I waited.

"When I fought the four-armed construct on the palace steps, something happened. Something new. Or, well, I did something new." He grimaced.

"Which was . . . ?"

"That thrum you feel in your bones. It has more than one purpose. That is to say, it can be used to do more than just make the earth shake."

The night was warm, but my shoes were damp and smelled like garbage. Tendrils of hair stuck to the back of my neck, rain trickling past my collarbone and beneath my shirt. I wanted to dry off, to crawl into bed, to snuggle up with Thrana and sleep. "Were you going to tell me or did you want to stand out in the rain all night?"

He threw up his hands. "This is me being honest with you.

Completely honest. Look." His expression shifted into one of concentration.

I waited. "What am I looking at?" And then I saw it. The rain around us halted mid-air and then began to move again — not falling toward the street, but swirling, coalescing.

Jovis lifted a hand, gathering a ball of water above his fingertips. He didn't spare a glance for me, his eyes focused on the water. "Does this remind you of anything?" he asked, his face grim.

I thought of the paintings of Arrimus, defending her island from Mephisolou. I thought of the tales of Dione, who could drown a city with a wave of his hand.

He let the water fall to the street. It splashed, droplets hitting my ankles. I barely felt them as I met his gaze.

"Alanga," I whispered.

4

Lin

Imperial Island

We'd returned to the palace last night to find the eyes on the mural open, staring down at us as though identifying us with their gazes. The sight had brought a fresh chill to the back of my neck. Was Jovis one of the Alanga? And if he was, did that mean I was too?

I couldn't fathom it. The way my father talked, the Alanga were a people unlike us, gifted with magic that made them more than mere mortals. They'd ruled the islands hundreds of years ago, and it hadn't always been a happy arrangement. When the Alanga had come into conflict, they hadn't just hurt one another. Whole cities could drown in the aftermath. According to the old stories, the Emperor's ancestors had driven them from our shores. My father had warned against their return; he'd said he was the only one stopping it. I'd always thought if the Alanga returned, they'd come sailing in from some unknown place, and since they looked Empirean, they'd set up roots, infiltrate my people. I hadn't considered they might *be* some of my people. If

Jovis and I were Alanga, then what were Mephi and Thrana? None of the old paintings depicted creatures like them. If we drew our magical gifts from our companions, and if this was so with the Alanga, why would their beasts never be painted alongside them?

I wanted to retreat to the caves below the palace to scour the books there to see if I could find some clue in the hidden cavern. But there were other duties I had to attend to, and too little time in a day.

The phoenix medallion sat gleaming at my fingertips, and I did my best not to pick it up, not to tap it against the table. Even the habits of one's predecessor seemed hard to break. The man who sat across from me did his best not to look at it. He'd been vetted by my guards, his background thoroughly scraped over. I'd done my own research too. The fourth son of a governor of little importance, he had an extensive education and claimed to be widely read. Servants had been easy enough to hire, and workers too. A steward was a different matter.

I'd found the phoenix medallion in one of Shiyen's drawers, wedged so far back I'd had to pry it loose from the wood. My father had gone too long without visiting the other islands, without ensuring their support. I couldn't make the same mistakes. And the spy construct had taught me: there were things going on with the constructs I needed to attend to. I couldn't do all of it from Imperial. I needed to see what was happening for myself.

"If I could gain the support of only one other island, which would you choose?"

The man was only a little older than me, with the small, wide-set eyes of a jaguar. "Riya," he said without hesitation. "After Deerhead, it has the most productive witstone mines. We need witstone to power quick and efficient trade, and keeping control of this resource keeps the citizens in line."

The teapot between us steamed, and rain pattered on the roof above in the silence. I decided that he had the wide-set eyes of a weasel instead. I held his gaze. So strong and self-assured – up until Bing Tai growled. Then he blinked, his face going pale.

"Peace, Bing Tai," I said. The beast at my side settled. I turned my attention back to the man, who was still trying to regain his composure. "Thank you for your time, Sai. We will notify all the candidates once a choice has been made. Close the door behind you."

He let his gaze slip to the medallion before he rose to his feet, bowed and left.

From behind me, I heard Jovis sigh. "And what was wrong with this one, Eminence?"

I found my fingers slipping to the medallion before I could stop myself, tapping it against the table. "Too ambitious. I need someone to run the palace for me when I'm gone; I don't need someone to run the Empire for me. That one –" I pointed one wing of the medallion at the door. "– would stab me in the back with this pretty thing as soon as he had the chance."

"Someone without a backbone would be easy for any visiting governor to bully."

I turned in my chair to look at him. "So you think I should choose someone who would instead *be* the bully?"

He pressed his lips together, his gaze going to the window, where the light was quickly fading. The darkness of the wet season was settling in, painting the room in faded hues. "I'm only saying that it's been a long day."

I couldn't argue with him on that. Neither of us had slept much the night before. Even after I'd dried myself off and had drank a warm cup of tea, it had been difficult to sleep. "Do *you* think we're Alanga?"

He looked to the window and the door, instinctively checking for any prying ears. He was right to check, especially after the spy construct we'd chased. "I honestly don't know. But it makes you wonder – if there is you and there is me . . . are there others?"

"Keep an eye out for Mephis or Thranas then," I said.

"And keep this to ourselves," he said.

I studied his face – wondering how he had so quickly become a confidant and if that had been by design. He couldn't have known about Thrana, couldn't have known that we'd share this common trait. But he hadn't hesitated to use it, either. A shared secret bound us together in more ways than just Imperial Guard and Emperor. He was right: we did need to keep this to ourselves. Jovis might be able to get away with revealing his powers, but I knew people were wary of me. And if I revealed I could do what Jovis did, someone would make the connection to our companions, putting both of them at risk. "Yes," I said slowly. "We tell no one, at least not until we know more."

I shifted the small pillow at my back, trying to find a comfortable position. I'd abandoned the Emperor's headdress after the first six candidates. We'd let Mephi and Thrana out in the courtyard to play in the rain, and if I had no cares in the world, I would be curled up with Thrana and Bing Tai in front of a fire with a hot bowl of soup. There were still more books in the library to read. So many more things to research.

As if he knew my thoughts, Jovis said, "I could tell the rest of the candidates to come back tomorrow."

How could I set things right if I didn't try twice as hard as my father ever had? I straightened and shook my head. "No. They've waited long enough. Send the next one in."

He obliged.

A young woman walked into the questioning room. There was something sharp and deliberate in the way she placed her steps, as though avoiding broken pottery. Her cloak was still damp from the rain; she must have grown tired of waiting in the hall and had taken a breather outside. She smelled of wet earth. Jovis returned to his spot behind me, his clothes rustling.

"Eminence," she said, "I am not related to any governors, but I answered all the screening questions correctly. I don't have a vast education, but I can read a book, and I've read many of them."

She settled into the chair across from me and I was reminded, for the thousandth time, of sitting across from the man who'd called me his father, yearning for acceptance and love. Trying desperately to answer his questions, to be who he'd wanted me to be. I'd never met his expectations. Now I was Emperor and he was dead.

The thought didn't bring me the joy I'd hoped it would.

I checked the list in front of me. "Meraya?" When she nodded, I continued: "The Imperial Palace is its own miniature island, with myriad tasks to tend to on a day-to-day basis." I set the phoenix medallion off to the side and she didn't look at it at all. I rattled off my pre-rehearsed list.

Her eyes narrowed only briefly before she attacked.

Neither Jovis nor I were quick enough to react. Her hand flung back and forward, something silver darting through the air. I checked myself instinctively before realizing: she hadn't thrown her weapon at me. From behind me, Jovis groaned.

I didn't dare take my eyes off Meraya. I kicked my chair back and ducked, pulling the cushion out from behind me and lifting it in front of my chest. A tiny dagger *thunked* into it. A heavy, staggering footstep sounded from behind me. Jovis. "Bing Tai!" I cried out.

My construct leapt to my defense.

Meraya seized the iron teapot as Bing Tai landed on the table, growling. She struck him across the jaw, sending the construct crashing to the ground. Hot tea splashed on the floor. I risked a glance back to find Jovis sprawled on the floor, unconscious. She must have poisoned him. He'd managed to pull the dagger free, and it lay on the floor next to him, its blade bloodied. Only then was I aware of the pounding of my heart. We were alone in this room, nothing between me and the assassin except one wooden table.

She drew a long, thin dagger from within her sleeve. "This won't be slow," she said. "But it won't be as quick as you might like." She took one deliberate step onto the table.

"Help!" I tore her poisoned dagger free of the pillow. I didn't know how to fight. This woman clearly had training. I felt like I moved through a haze, everything around me dulled; the only bright things in the room were her face and her weapon. I could barely breathe past my fear. I needed Thrana's help, but she was still in the courtyard with Mephi. "Why?" I asked her, hoping to buy myself time.

"I know the stories," Meraya said. "You won't let me live. This is the right thing to do; I know it is. This is for me. This is for Chari."

What was she talking about? She darted toward me. I lifted the pillow in a futile attempt to block the full force of her blow.

And then something *thrummed* inside me. I let it wash over me without thinking. It was stronger than the night before, like some sleeping creature had awoken, breaking bonds that had once held it captive. I threw the pillow at her with such force that it burst open, showering the table with feathers.

She advanced through the snowy cloud, her teeth gritted, blade still raised. I lifted the poisoned dagger; the thing was no longer than my palm, with no hilt to speak of. I couldn't block with it. I threw it at her like a dart. The dim light glinted off it as she batted it away with her dagger.

Nothing. I had nothing but a humming in my bones and two

empty hands. I was aware, suddenly, of how soft my flesh was, how delicate my skin.

The door burst open. Three Imperial guards charged into the room, weapons drawn.

Meraya lifted a hand. The spilled tea rose from the ground in droplets, coalescing before her.

All three guards hesitated. "Alanga" left one pair of breathless lips.

She sent globs of tea rushing at their noses and mouths. Two of the guards had the presence of mind to dodge. The third dropped her sword, choking on the liquid.

Before Meraya could regroup, the other two guards were upon her.

She pulled moisture from the air outside, tried the same trick again. But her control was unsteady and Jovis had been working with the guards. They were quicker than most and the water splashed harmlessly against their shoulders. She must have lost control of the tea she'd sent at the third guard, because the woman was pushing herself to her feet.

Meraya struck out with a foot, and one guard went shooting back, slamming into one of the teak pillars with a *crack*. The other two converged. They had a longer reach with their swords, and though Meraya was strong and quick, and had good aim with a throw, she didn't seem as skilled in close combat.

A blade sliced the flesh of her left arm. She gasped, but didn't drop her dagger. The two guards pressed her until her back was at the wall.

"Look – her wound!" one guard cried out.

Beneath the tattered shirt I could see the bleeding stopping, torn flesh closing. It was a credit to Jovis's training that neither guard fled. "She bleeds. That's all that matters," the other said, pressing forward.

The rest of the fight was quick and brutal.

They took turns striking at her. She blocked haphazardly, flinging her arm out, leaving the rest of herself open. They took full advantage of her inexperience. Blood soaked her tunic; her breathing echoed from the pillars. As each new wound knit, they scored another in its place.

I wanted to tell them to stop. She was like me. But I couldn't admit that, not in front of the guards.

And then a blade was sticking between her ribs, angling toward her heart, and another sliced at her throat.

Too late, too late.

Even then the wounds tried to knit. So they struck her again. And again. She gasped, her throat thick with blood.

At last, she stopped moving and the wounds stayed open. One of the guards leaned on his sword, sweat making his hair damp. He spat on the mangled corpse. "Alanga," he said, and it sounded like a curse.

The other guard gave me a quick glance, her eyebrow raised. While the guards were sworn to protect me, it was my duty to keep the Alanga from returning at all.

Jovis.

I whirled. His chest still rose and fell with his breath.

"A physician!" I called out. A woman in civilian clothes appeared in the doorway. I had the quick impression of iron-gray hair, stern features, a crisp brown tunic. I didn't recognize her, but she was there, a pen held tight in her hand as though it were a weapon. "Call for a physician."

She didn't even hesitate. She turned to obey without question. Jovis was breathing shallowly when I went to him. Carefully, I pulled aside the torn cloth of his jacket. The wound there was already closing, the flesh knitting together as I watched. His hands fluttered up, fingers grasping for mine. "Em . . ." he mouthed. "Ema . . . " There was something both sad and wistful in his tone, as though he'd found something he'd long wanted but knew he would lose again. And then his hands fell and his head lolled back.

"Jovis? Jovis!"

His breathing steadied, though he didn't open his eyes. I hoped his body was working through the poison.

A physician appeared in the doorway.

Jovis stirred and awakened. Sweat stained the front of his tunic, but his eyes were clear. If he was resistant to poisons, I wondered if I was as well. Not something I'd be testing out anytime soon, I hoped.

"See to him first," I said, pointing to Jovis.

Jovis waved the physician away. A trickle of blood stained his jacket, but he pressed a hand to the healing wound and straightened. "It's fine," he said. "Quite shallow, really."

The physician hesitated on the threshold.

The gray-haired woman had returned with him, and she spoke sharply at his ear. "Your Emperor gave you an order, did she not?"

He jumped and rushed to Jovis's side. He needn't have bothered. Although Jovis was unsteady on his feet, the wound from the knife had nearly closed. "A bandage and he'll be fine."

The physician went next to the guard at the teak pillar and put a hand out, checking her breath and heartbeat, performing a quick examination. "Broken neck," he said. "She's dead. I'm sorry, Eminence."

One of the remaining two guards covered her mouth while the other broke down in tears.

I searched for the right words to say.

"We'll burn her body with juniper sprigs tonight," Jovis said to his guards. "We will honor her passing."

I cleared my throat. "It seems the rumors are true. The Alanga are returning. Next time we'll be better prepared." I wasn't sure how I'd live up to that promise if I was an Alanga too. Meraya had mentioned another name. Chari? Was that a friend, a lover or a companion like Mephi and Thrana? "Take her body to the courtyard, to the garden. We'll hold funeral rites there."

Not everyone knew about Thrana yet. Meraya might not have known. Or she might not have had a companion beast. Did the Alanga have companions or did they not? I had so many questions, none of which she could answer anymore.

The physician hovered over the guard's body, but to his credit, waited for my word this time. I nodded. "You can go."

Bing Tai padded placidly back to sit at the end of the table and the physician gave the beast a wide berth as he left. The guards picked up the body of their fallen comrade and carried her out the door. I'd have to get someone to see to Meraya's body as well.

"You and you, there's another body in here, can we get that cleared that out?" The gray-haired woman directed servants to Meraya's corpse, pen still clasped in her hand. "I'm sure the Emperor will want the floors cleaned too."

The tremor finally left my bones, leaving me feeling drained in more ways than one. First the spy construct and now this. I needed to get out into the Empire, to know what was happening in it, what other surprises my father might have left behind.

"Eminence?" The gray-haired woman said. Her gaze swept over the dead assassin and she didn't so much as flinch. "Given the circumstances, should I return tomorrow? I was here to interview for the position of steward."

She'd reacted swiftly in a crisis without even being under my employ. I touched a hand to my hair, strands of it pulled free, floating in every direction. "What's your name? And your background?"

"Ikanuy," she said without missing a beat. "I've lived in Imperial most of my life, though I attended the Scholars' Academy at Hualin Or. I have seven children and run my own household, though the youngest is now grown and my house is empty. I'm not old yet, and was hoping to put my education to use." She rattled off these facts quickly. She'd rehearsed her answers. Well-prepared: another point in her favor.

"No husband or wife?" I asked.

"I never wanted one."

I picked up the steward's medallion from the table, strode to the door and handed it to her. "Welcome to the palace, Ikanuy of Imperial. We have much to discuss before I leave."

5

Jovis

Imperial Island

My arm had healed from where the assassin's poisoned dagger had struck me, but I still woke up the next morning feeling dizzy and disoriented, even with Mephi curled next to me. By noon, I was no longer dizzy, but the disorientation lingered. Or maybe it was just my surroundings and the company that left me so uneasy.

A few steps ahead of me, the Emperor sat on a bench in the palace courtyard, writing a series of letters. Every so often she paused, putting the end of the pen to her lips as she considered her words. Repairs were nearly complete on the Imperial Palace, and the intricacy of the paintings and architecture made me, half-Poyer former criminal from the tiny isle of Anau, feel uncouth and uncultured.

Servants had already begun to pack for the Emperor's diplomatic trip, though she'd not finalized the islands to visit nor had she yet obtained a ship. I leaned on my steel staff, watched her and felt about as useful as a paper sail in a storm. She and the guards had handled that assassin all on their own, while I'd lain about on the floor limp as a cleaning rag. An Alanga. But if she was like us, where had her companion been? Had she left the beast behind?

The assassin had been dead by the time I'd awoken. I wished I'd had the chance to question her, to find out where she came from, what she wanted. She looked Empirean.

I heard the whispers in the halls. The guards who'd killed the woman told anyone who would listen about her powers over water, her quick healing, her strength. There was a renewed sense of purpose and unity among the palace staff. The Empire was created to fend off the Alanga, to keep them from gaining a foothold.

The use of poisons and throwing knives showed planning, passion, intensity. I'd sent some of my guards out into the city and to the docks to question people. Who had seen the woman arrive? Where had she come from? Did anyone know who she was? I'd gleaned a few things. The ship she'd arrived on could be crewed by one, she'd given the name "Meraya" at the inn she'd stayed at, she'd kept to herself. She'd given Anau as the island she'd sailed in from at the docks, but I hadn't recognized her. Yes, I'd been gone from Anau for a long time, but the woman clearly hadn't wanted to be traced and I had no doubt she'd lied.

Had she truly been alone or had she come with any sort of companion? Any sort at all? I had to be delicate with the last, afraid of showing my hand.

No. No one had seen anyone else with her. So I was left with more questions than answers.

It was my foremost duty as Captain of the Imperial Guard to keep Lin safe, but even in that simple task I was conflicted. I'd come here ready to topple an Empire and had found a freshly crowned Emperor in place of the old man I'd expected. Rebellion didn't come with instructions. Should I have tried to help the assassin? Should I have murdered this new Emperor before she could name an heir?

Ranami had told me to send them reports. Surely killing the Emperor would be one step better. It would throw everything into chaos and leave me vulnerable, but would Gio care about that? Even as I thought it, though, I didn't think I had it in me. I'd broken the law time and time again, I'd defended myself and others, but I'd never murdered a person in cold blood.

Lin paused in writing her letters, her gaze on the burgeoning clouds. Bing Tai sat on her left, and Thrana sat on her right. Thrana had grown more since Lin had ascended to the throne, though her growth seemed to have leveled out. She was the size of a large dog now, her horns sweeping away from her face, forking into one branch at the very ends. I suspected that Mephi would always be a little smaller. He lay at my feet, belly up to the meager sun, his whiskers twitching as he dreamt.

"I have to do more than just end the Tithing Festival," she said. "It's just that everyone wants things to change right away, and I don't know if that's possible. These things take time."

I cleared my throat. I wasn't sure why she'd want to speak to me, but she certainly wasn't speaking to the clouds. "Eminence?"

She turned her head, one eye meeting mine. Her hand rested on Bing Tai's shoulder. "I've asked Ikanuy to send out posters. I'm putting a bounty on the constructs on the other islands. If they have no masters, then they're dangerous. And as long as they live, they're slowly draining the lives of my citizens. At the same time, I haven't dismantled all the constructs here. I need to show the strength of my convictions, but it's hard." She stroked the construct's fur and the creature let out a soft *whuff.* "Bing Tai hasn't done anything wrong." She spoke about him as though he were his own entity, his own living being. "He is all I have. He and Thrana."

"You have your steward."

A slight smile graced her lips before she returned her gaze to the clouds. "Yes, I suppose there's that."

"Ikanuy was a good choice. The Imperial Palace will be in good hands while you're gone." I heard the formal, distant tone of my voice and wrinkled my nose at it. This was who I was now, I supposed. Professional lackey. High-profile spy. A liar, just of a different sort than I was used to.

"She does have a spine," Lin said, and laughed.

So she did still remember our conversation, despite the chaos that had ensued. I found myself smiling. "She arrived readier to defend you than I was."

Lin lifted her legs and rotated on the bench, turning to face me. "So it seems we are both inadequate."

"I wouldn't dare comment on your adequacy."

She studied me, and again I was struck with that sense of disorientation. It was the same way Emahla used to look at me, with the same dark eyes. It wasn't fair, that her eyes should look so much like my dead wife's. "Please do comment on it," she said. "I need people to be honest with me."

I should have left it at that, should have just lived in that silence, but I was full of mistakes both big and small. "It's not always about adequacy or showing the strength of your convictions. Yes, dismantling Bing Tai will help to show your true intentions. But the assassin thought you meant to kill Alanga, like your forebears did. There will always be people who hate you," I said. "They don't need to write a well-reasoned essay on it. Perhaps they hated your father, or they lost someone because of the shards, or they just don't like the look of your face. You're the Emperor. You're powerful. People have to have an opinion on you. They won't all be good opinions. At some point you have to just do what you think is right."

The long look she gave me made me feel like she was dissecting the layers of me. She stroked Bing Tai's ears, rubbed the whitened muzzle. Then she pushed her fingers inside his chest. I watched with dread and fascination as the beast froze, as her hand disappeared to the wrist, as she pulled several shards free, rearranged them and pressed them back into his body.

"He was a good construct. He saved my life."

After a moment, Bing Tai laid his head on Lin's lap and whined. His skin began to sag. It was like watching wax for a seal melting as it was held to a flame. She held his head in her hands until the creature stopped whining, until his body was just loose flesh and fur on the stones of the courtyard. "It's done," she said quietly. "There are no more constructs under my command."

Her gaze flicked to me. "The assassin took us both by surprise. You're more than capable. But no more audiences without a more thorough search for weapons," she said. "If so many people will hate me no matter what I try to do for them, then there is no one I can really trust. The Alanga will hate me because I am a Sukai. And everyone else will hate me for my bone shard magic." Or her other magic, if they ever found out. She didn't have to say that part aloud.

She might have had eyes just like Emahla's, but I'd never seen Emahla's eyes look so sad. "I'd say you can trust me, but as your Captain of the Imperial Guard, I'm duty-bound to tell you not to."

It was meant lightly, and she took it so, her solemn expression breaking into a smile brighter than a dry season day. But my heart felt like the carcasses sunk inside crab traps. She *couldn't* trust me. I was sending messages about her and her plans to the Shardless Few. I'd already composed a letter about the cavern beneath the palace, the small glimpses I'd caught of notes and flasks and strange books, the assassin, Lin's plans to visit the islands. I'd thought when I'd come here that I'd be toppling an Empire, freeing the people from the Tithing Festival. But she'd already done that. My own convictions had scattered to the winds like seeds, and there was no fertile ground on which to plant them again. Should I still be loyal to the Shardless Few, whose leader had motives I did not know? Or should I hold myself to the oath I'd made to Lin?

When I didn't return her smile, she sobered. She rose to her feet, Thrana mirroring her movements. "We're still in the grounds of the palace, and there are no more visitors today. You don't have to follow me everywhere. Have your guards watch the walls. Do something else. Visit the city. You almost died protecting me – take a break."

I raised an eyebrow. "Is that an order, Eminence?"

"Just a strong suggestion." And then she swept away, her silken tunic rippling in the breeze, leaving the smell of jasmine behind.

Mephi let out the tiniest of snores. I nudged him with my foot. He grunted and sighed, readjusting. Despite my woes, I couldn't help the swell of affection I felt for him.

"If I slept as easily as you, I might be just as happy."

He yawned and then licked his lips, blinking as he came to. I stifled the yawn that formed in the back of my throat in response. I wasn't about to use my free time to take a nap. I tried not to make too many trips into the city. Sometimes I felt like I was being watched, though I wasn't sure how much of that was just paranoia. "I'm going out," I told Mephi. "You can stay here if you want."

That got him moving. He rose to his feet. Something rolled out from beneath him and he scrambled to cover it with a paw.

"What's that you've got?"

His shoulders shifted. "Nothing."

"If it's nothing, you won't have any problems lifting your paw."

His brown eyes went wide, his ears went up and he slowly lifted his paw. It was not nothing. So he was learning to lie now too. I supposed I hadn't been the best example when he was young. It was a round piece of jade, carved into the shape of two fish entwined with one another. I leaned over to pick it up, brushing the dirt from it. "That's not yours."

Mephi tilted his head at me. "I found it. I like the fish."

I frowned. "Found it . . . where?"

He scratched an ear before answering. "In a room."

"Which room?"

He gnawed at the fur on his shoulder as if he'd not heard me.

I sighed. The older he grew, the more obstinate he became. "I've told you already – you can't just pick up things you find in people's rooms. You're not actually *finding* them; someone has placed them there for a reason. And they're not yours." I pocketed the carving. I'd have to ask around with the guards and the servants to see if any was missing belongings. This hadn't been the first time. How did one teach a creature like Mephi personal boundaries?

His ears went flat against his head, and he bared his teeth. And then, in the next moment, he'd bounded forward, butting my thigh with his head, his tail curling around my knees.

"Whoa whoa careful." I tried to ward him off. "You're like a goat with those horns."

He bared his teeth again. "Not like a goat."

And for the thousandth time, I said, "Then what are you?"

He rolled his shoulders in his equivalent of a shrug. "Are we going?"

I checked my purse – I'd filled it this morning. I'd need it to be full if I was going to again cater to Mephi's appetite. The street vendors all seemed to know when we were coming, placing their tastiest, most fragrant morsels at the front of their stands and speaking more to Mephi than to me when they advertised them.

I scratched the beast's cheeks. I supposed there were benefits to steady pay.

At the gates, I gave the guards their orders. Keep watch, look out for strangers, know where the Emperor is but don't step on her heels. There were no more shipments or workers expected today, so it was an easy task I left them with.

I studiously avoided the gazes of the food stall merchants as we entered the city. By day it was bustling. A butcher passed me on my right with a bucket full of gutted fish, apron stained with bloody handprints. On my left, the owner of a drinking hall unfolded a couple of tables outside, taking advantage of the rare good weather in a wet season. Mephi trotted at my side, waiting for some sign I would stop. "I'll get you something on the way back," I told him. "I've got places to be."

He grumbled a little but said nothing.

The back of my neck itched, as though someone had brushed their fingers across it. I tried to surreptitiously glance back and thought I saw someone duck behind a building. Could have been my nerves – I'd just survived an assassination attempt and had chased off a construct spy after all – but I tightened my grip around my staff and put my hand on one of Mephi's horns anyways. "Stay close," I told him.

I was in a precarious position. I couldn't afford to get caught sending information to the Shardless Few. The messages were coded and stamped with what looked like the Imperial seal, only with an extra feather in the phoenix's crest. Most people wouldn't dare tamper with an Imperial letter. But if someone dug deeply enough, they'd start asking questions about why I visited the docks so often and why the Emperor might want to pass messages to a stall merchant. Lin had been kind to me, but I'd read enough to know the brutal history of Emperors. I'd lose my head at the very least, but I might lose a few parts before that.

The stalls and shops changed the closer I moved to the docks. Down here, the air was thick with the scent of brine and captive fish. Boxes of freshly caught squid nearly spilled into the street; barrels roiled with sinuous eels.

I doubled back and wove my way through two unnecessary streets before finally making my way to the merchant's stall. "Keep an eye out," I said to Mephi. A white flag flew at a stall selling bread. Steam obscured the back of her stall, rising to join the clouds above. Several large pots boiled over fires, stacks of bamboo baskets piled high next to them. A woman was using a pair of tongs to set rounded bundles of fluffy white bread onto the trays at the front of her stall. She was a thin woman, with long black hair she kept tied in a plait.

"Captain," the merchant said as I approached. She blinked and smiled.

I stopped and watched a thin trickle of sweat run from her hairline to her brow. There was something too stiff about her manner.

My gaze went to the alleyway behind her. I couldn't see anything but boxes and the wall, but I'd been known to make this mistake before. "Come out where I can see you," I called out.

Philine, the Ioph Carn's best tracker, rose from behind a stack of crates, a dagger in her hand. She took a step forward, touching the point of her dagger to the small of the merchant's back. The woman grimaced. The lid on one of the pots rattled as it boiled over.

"You've certainly risen in the world since we last met – Jovis, Captain of the Imperial Guard."

6

Nisong

The north-eastern reaches of the Empire

Wet houses were difficult to burn. Nisong found they couldn't be torched from the outside; she had to send her constructs inside, where everything was still warm and dry. She didn't enjoy the cries of the villagers as they watched their homes burn, but there was something satisfying in the flickering warmth, the pop of embers and the creak of wood as supports collapsed.

And still the governor of this island did not emerge.

He'd shut himself in his home, his guards cloistered inside with him. No walls around this palace; it was a small isle, insignificant compared to Imperial. It was more like a large house than a palace, really. But the shutters and doors were thick and hadn't given way to even the war constructs hammering against them.

Behind her, Shell stood over a cooking station he'd set up in the street, his spear leaning against a table as he chopped spring onions. "We still need to eat during a siege," he'd explained when she'd raised an eyebrow. A knife scraped against wood as he pushed the onions into the bubbling stewpot.

Coral had gathered herbs, Grass had found the table and the pot, Leaf had started the fire and Frond had picked up a piece of driftwood to carve. Nisong wondered what memories swirled in his mind. That one was a dreamer.

Shell waved her over. "Staring at the door won't make it open sooner." He lifted a bowl. "Come. Eat."

It felt somewhat odd to take the bowl from his callused hands, to hold it over the stewpot, to wait as Coral ladled soup into it. They'd done this so many times on Maila while the mind-fog had a hold of them.

"Ack," Leaf said, fanning a hand over his mouth. "Too hot! Do you need to use chili peppers in everything?"

"Do you need to have such a weak tongue?" Shell said.

Leaf tapped a long, thin finger to his chin. "I think I liked you better on Maila."

Shell snorted out a laugh. "I don't think you liked anything on Maila."

Nisong blew on her stew. "None of us did." They hadn't had enough awareness to like or dislike anything. She savored the rich, hot soup as it slid down her throat and made her eyes water. The crackle of the fire beneath the stewpot was a tiny reflection of the conflagration she'd made of the village. If that didn't move the governor, she wasn't sure what would. "We could be here for quite some time."

Frond sidled up to her, whittling the driftwood into a bird in flight. "Sand – ah, sorry, Nisong. Did we try knocking?"

Nisong gave him a dry look. He shrugged. She put down her bowl and took up her cudgel, then went to the door, lifted a hand and knocked.

No response. Which was what she'd expected.

Wind licked at the back of her neck, a hint of cold and moisture with it. Dark clouds formed a backdrop to the brightness of the fires. She wasn't about to give up, no matter how long the governor thought he could wait her out. Nisong had more patience than most.

It had taken time to ferry her constructs from Maila to an uninhabited isle, time to steal more ships and supplies, time to scout nearby inhabited islands and to gather more constructs to her cause. The last had been the easiest task. The poor creatures were lost, directionless, hiding from people that wanted them dead. A few kind words, a promise of some greater cause, and they were hers. They had a right to defend themselves. They had a right to punish those who saw them only as wolves to be hunted.

The first island had been easy. They'd stormed through, meeting very little resistance. On this one, the locals had put up more of a fight. Nisong supposed it was to be expected. They must have heard about what had happened on the first island and had told themselves they would not go down so easily. Petty island rivalries always meant that each one thought themselves better in some way than their peers.

She'd set her war constructs to round up the villagers, the bureaucrats to round up supplies and the spies to islands farther afield. The other constructs from Maila, the ones who also looked like people, took the torches to the houses. But Leaf, Grass, Frond, Shell and Coral had come out of the mind-fog first, had helped her commandeer the blue-sailed boat.

They were her friends.

She knocked again. "We know you're in there," she called out. A brief memory flickered: hiding in an empty cupboard, her older sister searching for her. Nisong blinked and it faded; the only thing lingering was the scent of old wood.

Grass, ever the practical one, took a torch from a passing construct. "Ready your weapons," she told the other three. "The walls may be stone, but the wood will burn," she said, louder than necessary.

A pair of shutters on the upper floor flew open. "Wait!" a man called. "What do you want?"

"All we want is the governor," Nisong shouted back. "The rest of you can live. Just send out your governor."

"Never!"

So she was speaking to the governor then. "We've razed this village and your people are outnumbered. There's no point in resisting. One of you can die or all of you can." She wasn't here to occupy the islands. Each one was just a stop to her eventual destination: Imperial. But she knew she couldn't leave the governor here alive to rally the survivors, to press her flank. Kill the leader, and you incapacitate everyone else.

"Who in all the ancient Alanga are you?"

"Nisong," she said simply.

"And are you here for money? Power? Or do you just want to wreak destruction?"

Nisong shook her head, sucking on her lower lip. She felt the scar across her cheek stretch. It wasn't just about destruction. It was about justice. News traveled across the Empire with the speed of witstone. The Emperor was dead. His daughter had inherited. When she'd heard, for a brief moment she'd felt torn. The Empire had moved past her memories, leaving both Shiyen and Nisong behind. Was there a place for her in this world, or should she instead fade into the background as she'd done so many times before?

And then she'd heard about the bounty the new Emperor had placed on the constructs. This, she understood. They'd created her, abandoned her and now they wanted her and her people dead.

She was happy to return the last sentiment.

"You put a bounty on our heads. What other choice do I have?" She welcomed the flood of anger, the desire for violence.

"Bounty? I have nothing to do with a bounty. I don't even know what you're talking about. How far do you think you're going to get here, even if you kill me? Imperial will come. The Emperor will come. Even a fraction of the Imperial Guard could crush you."

"Do you think—?"

Coral put a hand on Nisong's arm. "Listen."

From within the depths of the house, she heard the shuffle of footsteps. Her eyes widened and she understood only a moment before it happened.

"Ready yourselves, they're going to—"

The door burst open and guards poured out.

It seemed she was not the only one who understood that killing the leader incapacitated everyone else. They hadn't cared what she had to say; they'd only wished to stall her long enough to get everyone in place.

Shell darted in front of her, his spear held high. He struck out at the first guard, and the next, keeping them at bay.

Nisong raised her cudgel. "To me!" she called down the muddy street. How long would it take her other constructs to get to her?

Eight more guards poured out of the house. They bowled over Shell as though he were a sapling. He blocked two more strikes and then went down, trampled beneath their feet.

Nisong breathed in sharply, tasting smoke at the back of her throat. One step forward and she took a guard unawares, slamming her cudgel into the side of his head. She heard the satisfying *crack* of his skull. Blood sprayed, warm, across her lips. Cold mud squelched beneath her feet.

Leaf and Coral stepped to her sides. Grass hefted the torch

in her hand and threw it inside the house. The furniture in the entryway was made of woven reeds; it caught easily.

Clever Grass, Nisong thought approvingly.

The fire distracted the guards. Leaf was slight but fair with a sword. He knew how to turn events to his advantage. He sliced at the throat of one of the guards as she whipped her head toward the flames. She went down in a bloody heap. Six more guards left.

Coral couldn't fight, but the guards didn't know that. She held two wicked-looking knives and stood like she knew how to use them, her jaw set. The six of them circled, looking for openings.

"Your governor is breathing in smoke," Coral said. "He'll die if you don't help him."

They hesitated. Only one guard pressed in to attack, and Nisong fended him off easily. She heard a growl from behind her.

War constructs surged around them, flanking the six guards and pushing them back, snapping at their legs and arms.

Shell.

Nisong rushed to his side, shoving past the furred hides of war constructs. He lay in a bloody heap near the palace door, limbs caked in dirt. For a moment, their gazes met. She waited for him to groan, to push himself to his feet and lament his broken spear.

And then she realized: he was not blinking.

The mud soaked into the knees of her pants. She was kneeling, taking his cold hand in hers. He'd been the first one to share memories of a past life with her, though he'd said they were like a dream. Ginger. A fire. A man and woman and a child that he'd loved. She had memories of a life before too, but in this life, Shell was family. He'd taken point every time they'd disembarked on a new island, his back straight and spear held at the ready. And he'd died the same way. Around her, the war constructs tore at the guards. The men and women screamed, the constructs snarled and Nisong wondered if she, a made thing, could weep.

She touched her cheeks and felt wetness there. So she *could* cry.

Coral was the one who dared to disturb her first. "The fire — should we put it out? The governor is still inside."

Nisong had planned a quick death for the governor. No need for him to suffer. But the roiling, ugly feeling that lay in the pit of her belly boiled over. She licked her lips and tasted copper. Shell's lifeless fingers slipped from hers. "No. Let him burn."

Leaf knelt next to her and closed Shell's eyes with shaking fingers. The war constructs gathered around her. All the guards were now dead, one halfway down the street where he'd fled. Good.

Grass swept past her and returned with two more constructs to help her carry Shell's body. "We'll give him rites," she said, her voice gruff. "Tonight. At the beach. I'll have someone find juniper."

Nisong clenched her fists. "He shouldn't have died here."

"No, he shouldn't have." Grass patted her shoulder. "But he's gone just the same. I'm sorry. We all are."

Leaf rose. "The governor was right — the Empire will come when they hear what we've done. We don't have enough constructs to fend them off." He held his hands out in front of him as though they were a scale. "We cannot rally more to our cause without going to another island. If we go to another island, we have to fight, which reduces our numbers."

If you killed the leader, you incapacitated everyone else.

"Find volunteers," Nisong told Grass. "Constructs that look like us. Constructs that can fight. We send them to kill the Emperor. We send them to rally other constructs on the other islands. To sow chaos."

Grass nodded and left.

Coral was rubbing Nisong's back, soothing her. She sighed. "We should burn the other bodies too. Some of the villagers resisted."

"Not with Shell," Frond said. "He deserves his own pyre."

"Of course he does." Coral sounded offended at the thought. "But they're bodies. We can't just leave them out to rot."

The words triggered something in Nisong. The smell of smoke faded, replaced with the scent of sandalwood. She wasn't outside the governor's home anymore; she was in the dark bowels of a palace, her hands stained with blood. A warm gust of breath tickled at her ear.

"Working late again?"

"Shiyen," she said, a smile on her lips. "If I didn't, what would get done? There are too many problems to solve and only one of you."

He put a hand to the swell of her belly. "There will be another Sukai soon."

"And years before she'll be old enough to learn."

"She?"

"Just a guess."

He kissed the juncture of neck and shoulder, and she shivered. "Come to bed," he said.

"Is that a command, Eminence?" She said it teasingly, and was rewarded with the rumble of his laugh.

"Just a request. You've been here nearly all night."

She looked back at the construct before her, the shards of bone laid out on a sheet next to it. She'd grouped them in clusters of commands, taking her time carving the words, making sure everything was exact. "If the Alanga are truly going to return, as you say, we'll need more than just one old artifact."

"It's more than that—"

"I know. But we can't rely on it. We shouldn't. The constructs can bridge the gap."

He bent his head again, scraping his teeth against her skin, and all the commands she'd been holding in her mind dissolved in a rising tide of heat. "Can it wait one night?" he said, his voice thick.

She wiped her hands on the cloth and turned. His dark eyes looked even darker by lamplight. "Perhaps just the one."

A few drops of rain struck Nisong's cheek, carried by the wind. She was back outside the governor's house again, the smell of sandalwood gone. It took her a moment to reorient herself. The memories felt so real, so immediate. Even though she knew now that Shiyen was old and dead.

Had she been so long gathering mangoes on a remote island that she'd lost all ability to think? Their conquest didn't have to end here. She was Nisong. She had once been the Emperor's consort. And she had been the first one outside the Emperor's family to learn the bone shard magic.

Coral's hand was still on her back. Nisong shrugged her off. "No. We don't burn the bodies."

"No?" Leaf lifted a brow.

Nisong rose, let them carry Shell's body away toward the beach. "We've left a few houses unburnt. Line the bodies up on their floors. And have several of the beasts round up the surviving villagers."

7

Lin

Imperial Island

I watched from the window until Jovis and Mephi left the palace walls. I'd not had the chance to explore the secret cave before we'd chased the spy construct across the city. Jovis seemed happy to have a day off and I needed the day off from his watchful gaze.

Thrana brushed against my leg, her shoulders shaking. Her fur had grown back and was now thick and lush over her back, a darker shade of brown than Mephi's fur, striped with black. The wounds where the tubes from the memory machine had pierced her had healed over. The physical signs of her confinement were gone.

"I'm sorry," I told her. "We have to go back down to the room again." I started for the door.

She hesitated. "Not good," she said. Despite her larger size, she didn't have as large a vocabulary as Mephi did, nor as good a grasp of grammar. She would go anywhere for me, but she hated the cave in which she'd been confined. While Mephi was free-spirited and everyone's best friend, Thrana was shy around others, especially men. I'd noticed that when men raised their hands in front of her, for whatever reason, she shrank away.

My father had struck Bayan too.

I'd told Jovis I'd saved his life, but he'd also saved mine, much as I didn't want to admit it. Without his distraction, I wouldn't have been able to get close enough to dismantle my father's monstrous construct. I needed Thrana with me in case I encountered anything else. How long had that beast been down in that room, hungry and waiting?

The two Imperial guards outside my room snapped to attention as soon as I opened the door. They fell into line behind me as I made my way to the stairs. I never thought I would miss my days of isolation, the scattered few servants wandering the halls. Now, the palace grounds bustled with activity – nearly as much as in the city itself. Always someone was demanding my time or attention, asking questions or needing my input. A steward would help field those duties at least.

The eyes of the Alanga were still open. I stopped in the entry hall to look at them, peering at their faces, uncaring of what the guards behind me might think. The paint was faded, rendering each face in similar contours. Their eyes stared toward Imperial's harbor, as though they were waiting for someone to arrive. The servants all hurried past this mural, avoiding the gazes of the Alanga as if by doing so they could escape their wrath.

I wished I knew what sort of magic did this. I wished I knew what it meant.

Downstairs, servants dodged our party, carrying laundry and baskets of produce from the city. I could hear the bustle of the kitchen through the thin door, smell the garlic, scallions and ginger lingering in the air. Toward the back of the palace lay the shard storeroom, right up against the mountain where the palace was nestled.

"You can wait for me here," I told the guards.

They exchanged glances, and the woman on the right licked her lips. "We're supposed to accompany you for your protection."

I gestured to Thrana. "I have protection," I told them. "Besides, there is only one entrance and exit here." Not true, but they didn't know that. "Keep an eye out and I'll be safe."

Without waiting for a response, I unlocked the door and slipped into the darkness, my beast on my heels.

Thrana trembled as we went to the back of the room, all the hair on her back standing on end. Still, she set one foot in front of the other. I stopped, knelt and threw my arms around her shoulders, burying my face in her neck. She smelled earthy and sweet, like freshly turned soil. "I know you were hurt down here, but I'm here now. I won't let anything hurt you, I promise. Please trust me."

The trembling settled. "Yes."

When I rose, she followed me without complaint through the cloud juniper doors.

The cavern was as I'd left it, the hatch still open. I had to refill and re-light the lamps, and it took a little coaxing to get Thrana to move past the entrance. But it was easy to be patient for her, even when I'd never really been patient before. Maybe it was because of her absolute trust in me, or the way I thought of Numeen's daughter – her namesake – each time I looked at her. She was strong, but also fragile, and she needed me.

"Where did you live before my father brought you here?" I asked her as she stepped gingerly past the memory machine.

"Don't know," she said, her head and tail low. "Don't remember. Just dark and then him. Wanting me to be still. Wanting me to *cooperate*."

I put a reassuring hand on her head, scratched behind her ears and horns in the way I knew she liked. She leaned her head against my leg. She didn't seem to know where she came from and neither did Mephi. Perhaps buried somewhere in my father's cryptic notes was some mention of where he'd found Thrana. It would be a start, at least, to piecing together if Jovis and I were indeed Alanga. And if we were – why and how Alanga were created. Why now? Why not earlier? Had my father truly been doing something to stop the Alanga from re-emerging, and if so, what was it?

My lamp shone on a messy scene as I descended into the hatch. Thrana was too large to follow me down the ladder the way Mephi had, but she hovered at the edge, ready to leap down should I need help. The shelves I'd seen against one of the walls were covered in shattered pieces of clay. I picked up a shard and smelled it. Sweet and coppery, like the fluid from the memory machine. My father might have shattered them, or the monster had when it had awoken to face me, or Jovis when he'd shaken the cave with his magic. I tossed the piece back onto the shelf, frustrated. I'd never know now. There were no labels on these shattered flasks, nothing indicating what had been inside them on their stoppers. Would I have really started drinking memories when I had no clue what lay inside?

Then again, I'd already done it once.

I turned my attention to the rest of the cave, lifting my lamp high. My father had hidden this place for a reason. It might have been for the memory flasks, but somehow I knew there were other secrets. I scanned the dark, damp walls.

And found a sword.

It hung opposite the shelves in a sheath, a chain suspending it from a metal spike in the cavern wall. It seemed out of place here – a sword among my father's things? He was a scholar of bone shard magic and of history, a shrewd-gazed and ill-tempered old man. I couldn't imagine him wielding a sword, even when he'd been younger. The only thing he'd wielded was a cane.

In the play *Phoenix Rise*, the first Sukai had used a magical sword to defeat the Alanga. The actors always played the scenes so dramatically. Ylan Sukai lifted his sword and the Alanga were all struck down. Easy enough. Too easy, I'd always thought.

Now, in the cavern beneath the cavern beneath the palace, my single lamp shining the way ahead, I wasn't so sure. If Jovis was right, and we were Alanga, what did that mean for me? I approached cautiously. Perhaps I shouldn't have approached at all, but what was the sword going to do? Leap off the wall and attack me? Then again, what did I know of this Alanga-defeating magic? The play wasn't very explanatory. It was meant to glorify the reign of the Sukais and emphasize the danger of the Alanga, not to serve as an instruction manual on how to kill them.

I heard Thrana's footsteps pacing the cavern.

This close, I could see the wear and tear on the leather scabbard, the scratches, the frayed cord wrapped around the hilt. The scabbard was embossed in flames, a phoenix near the hilt. It was just an old sword. I had nothing to be afraid of. I reached out, hardly daring to breathe, my heartbeat pounding in my ears.

The leather was cool to the touch. No fires from the heavens, no pain of sudden death, not even so much as a tingle. I wanted to laugh. Of course a sword wouldn't work like that. The play was ridiculous – a fiction invented by a long-dead writer. Maybe it was an heirloom, a piece of the Sukai family past.

I walked my fingers up the scabbard to the hilt. Nothing changed. Feeling bolder, I lifted the sword and brought it down from the wall. It was lighter than I'd expected. I wasn't sure what I'd *been* expecting: I'd never held a sword before. But I'd held knives, and they certainly had heft. This felt . . . different. I pulled the blade loose from the scabbard.

The blade was white. Not just the bright sheen of steel, but white like the delicate porcelain teacups my father had treasured. Almost translucent where the edge of the blade grew sharp. Who had made this sword and what sort of material was it? Perhaps

Phoenix Rise was true, perhaps all one had to do was lift the blade to the sky to kill Alanga. For all my reading, I was swimming out of my depth here. I sheathed the sword again before I could be tempted to touch it, or worse, wave it about like I was some ancient warrior. I had work to do.

I slung the chain around my shoulder and climbed back up the ladder. I'd be making stops at Riya, Nephilanu, Hualin Or, and Gaelung – and there was distance between these places. I'd have the time to read on the boat, to research. I couldn't keep descending into my father's cavern, but I could bring some of his cavern with me.

Thrana wound her way around my legs as soon as I lifted myself from the hatch, her brow furrowed and the whites of her eyes visible. "Time to leave?"

The books at my father's workstation called to me. This quiet domain felt more mine than the busy, noisy one above.

"I heard something up the tunnel," Thrana said. "While you were in the cave."

That turned my attention. "Heard what?"

She rolled her shoulders. "Not sure. Very quiet. Far away."

I clenched my teeth. Jovis. Could the man not give me a moment's peace? He wasn't wrong, though. I'd have to schedule my time in my locked rooms. I couldn't expect my brand-new steward to deal with all things, and soon we'd be receiving visitors. I could understand now why my father had dismissed most of his servants, had left the governing to the constructs. There was too much to be done, and he was the only one who could work on his experiments and his bone shard magic.

"We'll have to come back," I told her. She pressed herself against my leg but didn't protest.

Thrana was right – a faint sound echoed down the tunnels, a distant rumble. I was nearly at the cloud juniper doors when I remembered the sword still slung over one shoulder. It was so light I'd forgotten it was there. I should have left it at the work-station along with the books, but it was too late now.

This close, the rumble clarified into an incessant pounding at the door.

My cheeks flushed, I marched through the shard store-room and jerked open the door, the lamp still held high in one hand. "What?"

Further harsh words died on my lips. It wasn't Jovis. He'd truly taken the rest of the day off. It was Ikanuy, flanked by the two guards I'd left outside the room. She raised an eyebrow, and her gaze flicked to the sword's hilt over my shoulder, but she did not back away or look reproached. So she did have a spine. "Eminence," she said, bowing her head.

"Ah, I'm sorry." Were Emperors supposed to apologize? The heat in my cheeks intensified, though for very different reasons. "I thought . . . Well, it's no matter."

"You are difficult to reach when necessary, Eminence." Her tone was neutral so as to avoid offending me and my shame deepened. I'd have to prop the doors open and leave Thrana by the shard storeroom door the next time I went to my father's workstation. She could fetch me if I was needed. My father had been answerable to no one. I had to change that for myself, no matter how it irked me.

"It's an urgent matter?"

She straightened. "Constructs in the north-eastern reaches of the Empire have organized, Eminence."

A cold feeling of dread rose in my chest. The spy construct. Was it one of them? "Organized how?"

"I hesitate to use the word 'army', but they have taken over two small isles south-west of Maila. They may already be on their way to conquer another."

8

Jovis

Imperial Island

Philine didn't lower her dagger from the woman's back. Around us, people either didn't see or chose not to.

I tried to swallow past the panic tightening my throat. Had the merchant told her anything? What did Philine know about me and my loyalties? Did she know anything she could tell the Emperor?

I took an involuntary step forward and heard a low growl from Mephi. "Don't hurt her," I said.

"Your pet is a lot bigger," she said, eyeing Mephi. She'd felt his teeth once when he'd been little more than a pup. Her gaze went back to me. "How did you land such a position?"

I affected nonchalance, trying not to think about the blade pressed to the merchant's back. Trying not to think about the letter in my jacket's inside pocket. "Yes, well, if you try hard and believe in yourself, anything is possible."

"I forgot that you thought you were funny. Jovis, Emperor's pet smuggler," she drawled, her gaze raking over my jacket festooned with chrysanthemums, my medallion, my golden sash.

"Look, I have Kaphra's money." I reached for my purse, grateful that I'd filled it that morning. I tossed the contents to her. She caught it in her free hand. "That should cover the balance I owe. I'm done with Kaphra and I'm done with the Ioph Carn."

She looked inside the purse, pocketed it but didn't remove her dagger from the merchant's back. "Kaphra decides when he's done with you, not the other way around."

Would Philine chase me to the very ends of the earth? I'd thought I'd left her behind; I'd thought the Ioph Carn wouldn't dare strike at me in the heart of the Emperor's power. I felt a thrumming build inside my bones, my senses sharpening until I was aware of all the water here on the street — steaming in the air, boiling in the pots, gathered between the cracks in the cobblestones. The pot closest to Philine had been freshly filled, the water close to the brim. I was Captain of the Imperial Guard, with Mephi at my side. I wasn't some wayward smuggler anymore. "He might have to make an exception in this case."

She must have heard the danger in my tone, because she reached with her free hand for another dagger strapped to her thigh.

Philine might have been quick, but I was quicker. I stamped a foot and the steaming pot next to her jolted. Water splashed onto her feet and her left arm.

It was enough. She dropped one of her daggers, hissing with pain. Before she could move, I stepped behind the stall and swept her feet out from under her with my staff. The merchant jumped back, out of the way of Philine's falling body.

Several people on the street slowed to watch, but I waved them along. It was a benefit of the uniform that they actually obeyed.

I pointed the end of my staff at Philine's head. "Threaten anyone I know, follow me, send anyone else to follow me, and I swear by all the known islands I will end you." I was surprised to find I meant it. I'd never killed unless I'd felt it necessary, but I'd spent a good chunk of my life running from the Ioph Carn, being afraid of them. I was done. "I've paid what Kaphra wanted for the boat. As far as I'm concerned, there is nothing tying us together anymore."

Philine put her hands up, gently pushing aside my staff. "I hear you and I understand." She grunted as she pushed herself to her feet. "I'd hoped I'd misremembered your abilities. It's one thing to tell Kaphra what happened and another to experience it. You know how he is sometimes. When he fixates on a thing, he figures out how to get it."

I remembered. He'd given me task after task, and always with a reason for why I'd not performed it exactly as he'd wanted. Always a reason why he couldn't release me from my debt. "And this time, it's me," I said flatly. "Again."

"Frankly, yes. You were an excellent smuggler, and now you'd be even better. You'd be an enormous asset to us — not just because of your abilities. Now you're in the Emperor's employ, one of her highest-ranking officials."

Endless Sea, did the Ioph Carn want me to spy for them too? I exchanged glances with the merchant, who only shrugged. I'd get no help from her. "What could I possibly want from the Ioph Carn in return? As you said yourself, I'm one of the Empire's highest-ranking officials. Why would I want to involve myself with a criminal organization?"

"The Ioph Carn have a lot to offer," Philine continued. If she'd noticed my exasperation, it didn't deter her. "We have an extensive smuggling network and are able to obtain goods that others cannot. Not even the Empire."

"I'm not in the market for black market goods," I said dryly. "Besides, if I'm such a great smuggler, why wouldn't I just obtain them myself?"

She shrugged, brushing dirt from her leathers. "You seem a bit busy at the moment. And you aren't looking for black market goods right now. Not to say you won't be in the future."

What was I supposed to say: I've left that sort of life behind? Things are different now? I'm not the same person you once knew? All grand sentiments I'd feel foolish for voicing. The thrumming left my bones and I leaned on my staff. "I'm tired," I said instead.

Philine raised an eyebrow.

"I'm tired of being followed by you, of being chased, of *fighting* you and your lackeys. I've been involved in the Ioph Carn long enough to know how to take it apart. If Kaphra doesn't want me to relay all that information to the Emperor, then he'll leave me alone."

"A threat?"

I nodded to the merchant. "A threat in exchange for a threat against my friend here."

"You must really like steamed bread."

"I really like keeping peace on the streets of Imperial City," I countered. "And honestly, what's wrong with you? I don't want to see people die for no reason. Is that so hard to understand? Now get out of my sight." Mephi stepped to my side, his teeth bared as if reminding her that he had them and yes, they were quite a bit larger than the last time she'd felt his bite.

"Fine," Philine said, backing out of the stall. "But, Jovis, if you ever change your mind, you know how to contact us."

She disappeared into the streets of Imperial like mist burned off by the sun.

"You have a lot of strange friends," the merchant said to me, her voice a bit tremulous. She turned back to her pots, replacing the lids I'd displaced.

I checked the streets. The danger had passed; no one was looking our way. I pulled the letter from my jacket and handed it to her beneath cover of the stall front. Without even looking at it, she wedged it beneath a jar of yeast.

"I wouldn't exactly call her a friend. More like an unwelcome shadow."

She didn't acknowledge what I'd said, just pulled another folded sheet of parchment from beneath the jar and handed it to me. "I've something for you too." She hesitated and then took two steamed buns from her trays. "This too. Thank you."

I'd brought this trouble on her; she shouldn't have to thank me. But my stomach growled, and I'd handed my purse over to Philine. So I took the buns, handing one to Mephi. I might as well have fed a sinkhole, the bread disappeared that quickly.

I tucked the letter into my jacket, apprehensive. More instructions? What did they want now? But it wouldn't do to read the letter on the street. "Sorry," I said to Mephi as we wended our way back to the palace, passing the food stalls again. "We'll get you something from the kitchens." He shouldered my leg – his silent version of an accepted apology.

A light rain began just as we made it back inside the palace walls. Lin had remodeled the Hall of Everlasting Peace, which was meant to house her officials, including me. Ikanuy had moved in, but the place was still mostly empty. I slipped into the room she'd assigned me, closing the door. It was larger than anything I was used to, especially my boat still docked at the harbor. I'd taken it on a couple of outings since I'd arrived, but I still lamented that it was no longer my home. This room didn't just feel too large; it felt too still.

The folded letter wasn't sealed. I opened it, sat at my desk and began to decipher the code. On a surface level, it seemed to be talking about the onset of the wet season, about fishing yields, about family friends. Anyone else glancing at it might think it a letter from one of my relatives on Anau.

I pulled the relevant information from the letter, writing notes on another page. I blinked when I'd finished, examining the message hidden within.

The Shardless Few were cutting off shipments of caro nuts to the heart of the Empire – Ranami and Gio's doing, most likely. Once it became clear that Imperial and the surrounding islands would not be receiving their regular shipment of caro nuts, governors would begin complaining to the Emperor. In the midst of a wet season, bog cough was prevalent. The only known cure was the oil from the caro nuts. If the Emperor could not ensure the flow of trade, the governors would lose confidence in her. And with her position already so precarious, the Shardless Few might be able to push for her abdication.

My sense of unease grew. I'd be here in the thick of it, ostensibly supporting the Emperor through the chaos.

I turned to the rest of my notes. It wasn't just an update on the plans of the Shardless Few. Gio knew about the palace, about the myriad locked doors, about how Lin, like her predecessor, disappeared for hours behind them.

Look for a white-bladed sword in Lin's possession, the letter said. *Find it and steal it.*

9

Phalue
Nephilanu Island

It was strange being the one on the other side of the bars. Phalue unlocked the cell, setting the tray on the floor just inside. Her father watched her from the cot, hands clasped. He waited until she'd locked the door again to reach for the bowl of noodles. The lamplight caught on the curling wisps of steam. Somewhere in the cellar, she heard water dripping into a puddle. It was raining today, as it usually was, and moisture seeped inside despite everyone's best efforts.

Phalue pulled a chair from the side and it scraped against the stone floor. For the first month or so, she'd had someone else bring him food. She had told herself she was too busy — and she had been. There had been records to sort through, items to sell, funds to redistribute, letters to send. If they'd done this the normal way, the transition would have happened gradually, and her father would have guided her the whole way. As it was, his most loyal supporters had fled, and Ranami was left to piece together all the scattered pieces of his governorship. And then there were the Shardless Few and Gio. Phalue had been unsure how to handle them ever since the coup. He wanted her dead. He wanted to take this island for himself and for the Shardless Few, the way he'd done with Khalute. It hadn't been part of his plan to install Phalue as governor.

Her father watched her as he ate, the smell of pickled onions and fish sauce thick in the air. He had always been gaunt, but he was thinner and paler now, his humble clothes making him indistinguishable from anyone on the street. She remembered when she was young, looking up at him as this broad-shouldered figure, his face looming like a distant mountain. Now he looked shrunken somehow, smaller.

"I'm still your father," he said when he was halfway through. "What's bothering you?"

Was it that obvious? Ranami always said she wore her emotions like she was drenched in them. Phalue hesitated before speaking, but what did it matter? He was in a dungeon – who would he tell? "I'm meeting with the Shardless Few this afternoon. I've been dividing my focus too many ways. If I can get them to leave Nephilanu peaceably, then that's one less thing I need to worry about. I don't have enough guards to clean up the mess with the constructs and to fend off Gio. As soon as I send too many out on patrols, I'm leaving myself vulnerable at the palace." A bounty on the constructs was all well and good, but Phalue felt all that did was encourage citizens to go after beasts they weren't capable of handling. There had been more than one attack and several deaths on Nephilanu since Lin had ascended to the throne.

Her father set down the bowl. "Meeting with them lends them legitimacy. Nephilanu is yours, not Gio's."

She sighed. "Technically, it belongs to the people and I am just the steward. One person can't own an island."

He wrinkled his nose, and she couldn't help but notice he reached for the mug of water and not the mug of wine. He stared into it, as though searching for poisons. "Do you truly believe that?"

"I'm learning to. What's the point of having power if we can't use it to help people? The farmers, the gutter orphans – they're no different than you or me."

He took a drink of water and grimaced. "If you're so set on helping people, what about helping me?"

And this was why Phalue hadn't wanted to come to the dungeon in the first place. She knew he would ask her this. He lobbied for his freedom each time she brought him food. And the truth was that she wanted to give it to him – that was the worst of it. He hadn't been a bad father, and she still loved him in her own way. But he'd been a terrible governor.

She rose abruptly.

"Phalue," he called after her.

She let out a long breath, trying to ease her temper, and then turned to face him. "You haven't changed. You ask to be set free every time I come to see you. What about all the people you imprisoned down here? What about all the people you executed? Did you ever consider their pleas? I treat you far better than you ever treated them, and you're still thinking of yourself and not of them. Those people you killed?" She waved a hand out in the direction of the city. "They had families. Friends."

His gaze darkened. "They stole from me."

"Some might say that you stole from them. That you had no right to own the land they worked on simply because you were born in a palace. They've suffered under your rule, Father. What would those people say if I set you free? They would say that I'm not who they thought I was. They would say I am just like you."

Something in his face shifted, his expression suddenly guile-less and hurt.

She didn't wait for a response; she left the damp, musty air of the cellar behind, taking the steps to the kitchens two at a time, breathing like she'd just surfaced from a dive.

Ranami caught her at the top of the stairs. She took one look at her face and wrapped her arms around Phalue. Phalue relaxed into Ranami's embrace, feeling her wife's cheek pressed to her chest, her heart kicking against Ranami's ear. Slowly, Phalue's heartbeat eased, the sounds and smells of the kitchen safe and familiar.

"You don't have to keep going down there," Ranami murmured.

"He's still my father," Phalue said, pulling back. "I owe him the courtesy of at least looking him in the eye. And I don't want to be like him – just pretending the people I've locked up don't exist. I want to face what I've done." She pursed her lips. "Am I lending the Shardless Few legitimacy by meeting with them?"

Ranami took her hand and they left the kitchens, escaping into the cool hallway, dim morning light creeping in through the shutter slats. "You don't need to do anything to lend the Shardless Few legitimacy, love. They're already a presence in the Empire. They're established on Khalute, and they've established them-selves here. Perhaps if they were half a world away – but they're not. They're here on Nephilanu and they've already tried to kill you twice."

"We can't be sure the second attempt was them. Or even that it was an attempt." Only a few days into her rule, a fight had broken out on the streets when Phalue had been in the city. Someone had tried to knife her in the ribs in the chaos.

"I know how they work. It was them. They orchestrated the whole thing. Are you sure you want to do this?"

Phalue had already dressed for the occasion, which meant,

for her, just adding a decorative chain about her shoulders and a cloak that was a little less shabby than the one she wore for everyday purposes. She still wore her leather armor and her sword belted to her side. No one was going to convince her she should meet Gio without a weapon. Phalue drew herself up and offered Ranami her arm. "Better to face them head on than to sit and wait for another strike."

Ranami pulled the hood of her cloak over her hair before taking Phalue's elbow. She wore a turmeric-yellow dress beneath it – a color Phalue always thought looked lovely against Ranami's darker skin. It was cut shorter than her dry-season fare, though, with knee-high boots protecting her feet from the mud.

Seven years of this, Phalue thought in dismay as they made their way outside. Rain pattered against her cloak. Ranami sidled up against her. "It will be the dry season again before you know it, and then we'll both yearn for rainy days."

So her thoughts must have shown on her face as plainly as her emotions. Ranami was the one who should have been born a politician, not her.

Ranami stopped her as they stepped beneath the arch of the gate. "Before I forget, you received a missive." She pulled an oilskin envelope from her bag and handed it to Phalue.

It was sealed with wax, the impression of a phoenix stamped into it. The Emperor's seal. "What does it say?" Phalue asked.

"It's for you, and it's still sealed. The envoy gave no accounting of its contents."

Phalue broke the seal, pulled the letter out, taking care not to get it wet, and skimmed the contents. "She's requesting to visit. She's asking for discretion until the details of her trip are finalized." Phalue could imagine the chaos if the news got out before the Emperor could put out her own declaration. There would be those who would look upon the Emperor with skepticism and others who would see any visit as an opportunity – either to attempt a coup or to curry favor. Other island governors would wonder if they were on her itinerary and would jostle to be included.

How long had it been since an Emperor had set foot on Nephilanu? Before Phalue could remember. Her father had bragged to other governors more than once about the time Shiyen had visited Nephilanu, but that had been even before her father had succeeded his mother as governor. Once, the Emperor would have regularly visited the islands, treating with the inhabitants. But Shiyen had preferred to let the constructs do that work.

Rumors swirled around this new Emperor. She'd halted the Tithing Festival, yes, but people were divided on her motives. Had she done it simply because she knew the Shardless Few had made the Tithing Festival the cause they rallied around? Or did she actually believe it should be halted?

Ranami had confided to her that the smuggler had taken the position of Captain of the Imperial Guard to spy on her for the Shardless Few, but what neither of them knew was why the Emperor had offered the position to him in the first place.

"And will you accept her request?"

Phalue tucked the letter back into its envelope and dropped it into the pouch at her belt. "Let's discuss that on our way back. It should be your decision as much as it is mine. Ranami – you're my wife. You're as much the governor here as I am. More so in some ways. You can open my letters; I won't mind. I trust you completely."

The look Ranami gave her filled Phalue's heart and spilled it over. "I know." She pulled herself tight to Phalue's side. "But others might mind, and we should keep some sense of propriety."

Phalue laughed as she strode back into the rain, gesturing

at her armor, her sword. "If I had a sense of propriety, first I wouldn't be meeting with the head of the rebellion with a missive from the Emperor in my pocket. Second, I'd be dressed in silks and carried in a palanquin. Can you imagine? Me? In a palanquin? I'd break poor Tythus's back. Third, I would have married you much, much sooner."

Her wife smiled at that, and even the overcast sky couldn't dim the brightness of it. "Well, a little propriety certainly wouldn't hurt you then."

Phalue laughed. "It wasn't for lack of trying. How many times did I propose to you? A hundred?" They'd wedded soon after Phalue had taken over the governorship, and for that one day, she'd been able to forget that the Shardless Few wanted her dead, that her father was locked in a cell, that there would be declarations to make and so many wounds to heal. There'd only been Ranami, resplendent in a gold-embroidered dress. Her words, her lips as they'd pledged themselves to one another.

She'd thought she would feel apprehensive; instead, she'd felt like a ship that had its fill of sailing, returning at long last to the port it called home.

They'd thrown open the gates to the palace, and anyone willing to make the walk was fed by the kitchens. Phalue wished they could get married every day. But, as Ranami had pointed out so many times before, Phalue had obligations, and she meant to fulfill them.

Mud squelched beneath her feet as they made their way down the switchbacks to the city. It had taken her so long to see how her people suffered under her father. And it had taken falling in love with Ranami to truly understand that her father's policies were unfair and exploited the people he ruled. That he had no idea what it was like to live as a farmer or an orphan in the city.

That she'd had no idea.

When she'd sparred with Tythus, she rarely made the same mistake more than once. She hoped to do the same now.

"You're brooding," Ranami said as they rounded the last switchback.

"What? No."

"Yes. You get this faraway look in your eye, and your brows do this thing —" She demonstrated, scrunching her brows together. " – and you go very quiet, and you put your hand on the pommel of your sword."

Well dammit, she did have her hand resting on the pommel. She shook out her fingers and let her cloak fall over her sword again. "I'm not brooding, I'm thinking. I just ... want to be better than he was."

She didn't have to say who she meant.

"You already are, by several measures."

"Even so – he's not a bad person. I know he was careless with the people of the island, even cruel, but he was a decent father. When I wanted to learn how to fight, he set me up with tutors. He never tried to make me do the things I didn't want to. Yes, he suggested that I do them plenty, but I think he knew I just wasn't the type to wear dresses and entertain dignitaries. He was kind to me. And I've repaid him by locking him in the cellar." She lifted a hand, spreading it before her from one shoulder to the other. "Is there a sliding scale of good? And if so, where do my actions fall? I'm trying to do better, but I don't quite know what that looks like."

Ranami reached up to kiss her on the cheek. "None of us does."

"That's not exactly reassuring."

The mud turned to cobblestones beneath their feet. A wet season transformed a city. Every storefront now had an overhang built around it; every stoop now had bristles one could use to brush the mud from boots or slippers. On the narrower streets, bamboo had been laid across windowsills stretching from one side to the other, and then covered with palm fronds. It gave the streets a darkened, cloistered feel, like walking through a tunnel.

A trail of gutter orphans soon gathered behind them. As was her habit, Phalue reached into her purse and tossed them some coins.

Ranami shifted beside her. If Ranami always knew when Phalue was brooding, Phalue always knew when something was bothering Ranami. "What is it?" Phalue said as they walked the street that led to the Alanga ruins.

"We should do something about the orphans," Ranami said. "There are too many of them. They shouldn't have to beg or to scrape coins off the street."

"You want to adopt? We can't take in all of them."

"That's a separate issue," Ranami said. She'd pressed Phalue on the matter before, but they'd only just gotten married. There was too much to do, too much to worry about, without adding a child or two into the mix. Phalue had always thought she'd adopt one day, but now that that day loomed closer, the idea made her sweat. She wasn't exactly the mothering sort. And what example did she have? Her father had been kind but not overly affectionate, and her mother had been only an intermittent presence in her life.

"They're especially vulnerable to wayward constructs when they don't have a place to shelter in at night. We should set up a system for them. We have the money; we just need to redistribute it in the right ways."

"We can add it to the list," Phalue said.

Both of them fell silent after that. It wasn't a short list, and it seemed to grow longer by the day. They could spend several lifetimes trying to fix the damage her father had done. One lifetime would have to be enough, though it felt woefully inadequate each time Phalue looked at the list.

Outside the city, the rain slowed to a drizzle. The forest was alive with the sounds of bird calls, frogs croaking and the steady drip of water filtering down from the treetops. Flowers and plants she hadn't seen since the dry season were sprouting from the earth, sensing that their thirst would now be quenched. She supposed there was some beauty in a wet season.

She felt less so when she stepped into the Alanga ruins. There was no roof here, only old and broken pillars and walls that held faint memories of paint.

"We're a little early," Ranami noted. "We might have to wait."

In the rain, Phalue added mentally. She actually enjoyed the rain when she could observe it from indoors, a mug of tea in hand, her oilskin cloak shed like a snake's old skin. She wiped a cold droplet from the end of her nose. Being in it was the problem.

Voices echoed faintly from the walls. It seemed they didn't have to wait after all. But as they drew closer, Phalue realized they'd stumbled upon an earlier meeting that had perhaps run long. Ranami stopped her before she could walk in on it.

She put a finger to her lips, and then her ear.

Phalue thanked her past self for marrying a woman who understood subtleties far better than she ever would.

One of the voices was Gio's. The other she did not recognize.

"So you want the Ioph Carn to stop black market trade of caro nuts to Imperial and the surrounding islands. And for what? So I can be poorer for it?"

"You're already a wealthy man," Gio said. "And you'll want her deposed too. Her father let you skim the fat off his profits because he couldn't care enough to stop you. His daughter will be another matter. She's looking to change things, to prove herself different. Think of it as an investment in your future. Do you think she'll continue to let the Ioph Carn do business unimpeded?"

"She won't have a choice."

"Don't be arrogant," Gio snapped.

A heavy sigh. "Which of us is the arrogant one, old man? You want to bring down a regime. I just want to profit off it. Speaking of which – what's in this for me? And I don't mean just as an investment. You asked me here: tell me what you're willing to pay me."

A brief silence. "I heard you've always wanted to raid a monastery. Cloud juniper berries and bark would make quite the addition to your collection. Used judiciously, they could expand your power."

"My desire is fairly common knowledge. I make no secret of it," the other man said in an easy tone. "But indulge me: how is this relevant?"

Phalue held her breath. Gio was speaking to one of the Ioph Carn. She was glad Ranami had stopped her from walking in on this meeting; they didn't need any further complications in their relationship with the Shardless Few. Then again, he might not care. Gio hadn't made many secrets of his goals.

"You don't need to engage in a frontal assault to raid a monastery. Their walls are high and they're always ready to defend against attacks. They'll use cloudtree bark and berries and your Ioph Carn won't stand a chance. But what people don't know is that there are always back ways into the monasteries."

"Be clear, old man. What exactly are you offering?"

"The isle just east of Nephilanu has a cloudtree monastery. I know the back way in. You stop the black market trading and I'll draw you a map. That's what I'm offering."

"Where did you get this information?"

"I protect my sources."

For a while, no one spoke. Phalue resisted the urge to scratch an itch on her nose, afraid the rustling of her cloak might be heard.

"Fine. I'll stop black market trading of caro nuts near Imperial and you give me the map."

"Done."

Ranami took Phalue's arm, leading her to crouch behind a half-crumbled wall. The Ioph Carn man strode out of the room he'd been meeting with Gio in soon after. He was short, young, his black hair slicked back. He hadn't bothered to wear a hood. Phalue didn't recognize him, though she hadn't expected to. The Ioph Carn kept to their own.

"Wait a moment," Ranami whispered. The warm feel of her breath against Phalue's cheek made her shiver. As much as Phalue wanted to discuss what they'd heard, she knew it would have to wait until after their meeting.

They crouched among the damp grass, waiting as the man's footsteps faded while they heard the brush of boots against foliage when Gio paced in the other room. After enough time had passed, they rose. Ranami took Phalue's arm again and they proceeded through the half-crumbled archway to the agreed-upon meeting place.

Gio was alone.

Somehow this surprised Phalue. She'd expected at least one other of the Shardless Few. She was, after all, here with Ranami and that made two of them against one. If she attacked Gio, there was little he could do to defend himself. He carried two long-bladed knives at his belt, but he wasn't nearly as tall as Phalue and was much older. She'd have reach on him, and more vigor. Why not just end this conflict now?

Ah, she needed to stop sizing up every situation as though it were a potential physical fight. Even if the other party had tried to have her killed. Even if he might try yet again. She needed to think more like Ranami. If she succeeded in killing Gio now, she'd still have to deal with the other Shardless Few. They'd find another leader and they'd come looking for revenge.

Better to deal with the known entity rather than the unknown one. Was that one of Ningsu's proverbs?

"Thank you for meeting with me," Gio said. He placed his hand over his heart in greeting.

Ranami scowled at him.

Phalue found she couldn't muster up the same amount of anger as Ranami had. But she skipped the greeting. "I won't pretend I don't know what you have planned for me," Phalue said. "It was never your plan to have me installed as governor. You prefer me dead."

She could feel Ranami eyeing her, could see her mouthing something out of the corner of her eye. Probably she was being too rash. But she couldn't be like the other politicians: saying one thing while meaning another. If she couldn't dissemble, she could at least be direct.

Gio spread his hands. "I would apologize, but this is what the Shardless Few have made their goal: the installation of a Council of representatives to rule the islands. Not an Emperor. Not governors. Rulers chosen by the people instead of by birth."

So she was simply in their way. "Then what did you ask us here for?"

"I want to propose a temporary truce. You're trying to establish your rule. I'm trying to expand the presence of the Shardless Few. We don't need to fight one another right now. We can live peaceably, under certain conditions."

Of course. Conditions. "Which are? We allow you to roam all over Nephilanu?"

"No, of course not. We'll keep to our caves and avoid your cities. We won't interfere with your rule. I'll ask you not to turn us in to the Emperor, of course."

The missive from the Emperor felt heavy in Phalue's pouch, a presence she couldn't stop thinking about. "And that's all?"

"One more condition: you halt this year's caro nut shipment
to Imperial and the surrounding islands. You can afford to put
off the profits until later in the wet season — I know your father
built quite the treasury. I intend to pressure the Emperor into
abdication. Her grip on the Empire is weak. No one knows who
she is. Unless she can garner support, this Empire will fall to
pieces, each island fending for itself. With the wet season upon
us, everyone will be clamoring for caro nut oil. If they don't get
it, they'll blame the Emperor.

"The Shardless Few is close to its goal. If we can force her
abdication, we'll be in a better position to propose a Council.
We're building an army on Khalute and those governors who
won't fall into line can be further pressured with force. We're
too interconnected to not have some centralized decision-
making power. The governors may not understand that, but
I do. Only I don't want it to be an Emperor. I want us to rule
ourselves."

She felt foolish for hiding during Gio's previous meeting now.
Of course he wouldn't have cared if they'd walked in on him;
he was asking the same thing of the Ioph Carn. Phalue met
Ranami's gaze and could see the caution behind her eyes. What
was she trying to warn Phalue about? She regarded Gio, who
awaited her response. Of course. Who would Gio turn his attention to once the Emperor was gone? "So you wish to pressure the
governors. I'm a governor. Where would that leave me?"

"As I said, a temporary truce. It may be we can find some use
for you in this new government, or make some sort of exception
for Nephilanu."

Phalue wondered if her skepticism was plainly visible on her
face. She wondered if it mattered. There were two options here,
and Gio understood that. Either she could accept the temporary
truce and continue to establish herself, or she could throw herself

into conflict with the Shardless Few under a rule that had just begun and with a list of tasks that wouldn't stop growing.

"Ranami," Gio said, appealing to her, "this was what we had worked toward when you joined our cause. I know you want this too."

"That was before you tried to murder the woman I love. You say we can have peace with certain conditions, but these aren't truly conditions. You're asking us to do what you want and if we don't, you'll kill her. It's not a truce; it's a threat."

"I'll accept your offer," Phalue said before Ranami could say anything else. "If I see any indication you've broken your side of the bargain – I know where your hideout is. I'll send the full force of my guards against you and send a missive to the Emperor telling her everything I know." It was an empty counter-threat. She didn't have enough guards and Gio had a veritable army on Khalute. The Emperor was distracted with the constructs; how long would it take her to send soldiers to Nephilanu? Long enough for Gio to clear out.

"Understood."

Phalue pivoted, abruptly wishing to be free of the looming ruins, their carved vines, the memories of a civilization that had once existed long ago but had since passed. No one spoke of it except in whispers, but the question tickled at the back of Phalue's mind too. Would the Alanga return? She'd had the fountain destroyed, but now she wondered if she should have left it intact, had someone report on whether or not it opened its eyes again. But she didn't know what ancient magic lurked in its stone. She couldn't be sure it wasn't a device meant to summon Alanga.

Ranami had to hurry to catch up with her. "It's a fool's bargain he strikes with you," she said in a low voice as they exited the ruins.

"I know," Phalue said. "But I have no better options."

"So," Ranami said once they'd settled onto the road, "the Emperor wants to visit us. Gio is threatening a coup."

"Welcome to marriage with a governor!" Phalue said. "I understand now why you wished to avoid it!"

Ranami tugged at her arm, pulling her in close. Around them, the rain had picked up again, though they were cloistered in the space between their two hoods.

"What are you doing?"

"This," Ranami said. She reached up and pressed her lips to Phalue's. The kiss was soft at first, and then more urgent, her hands sliding beneath Phalue's cloak to rest against her breasts. Or at least, against the leather that shielded her breasts. Why had she worn the armor? It seemed a ridiculous decision now. "I don't regret it," Ranami said against Phalue's mouth when they broke apart. "Not even for a moment."

"Regret what?" She'd lost the trail of their conversation. She picked it up again with a little effort. "Oh. Well neither do I. I mean, I never thought I would in the first place. Which is why I asked so many times."

Ranami laughed and kissed the end of Phalue's cold nose. "Thank you for that." She sobered. "The Emperor. Should we accept her request? Do you want to?"

Phalue took her hand, marveling at the way their fingers intertwined, the way they fit together. "I'm not my father's daughter," she said. "What if Lin Sukai is not her father's daughter either? I think we should at least hear her out."

The greenery of the forest gradually faded into city streets and tiled roofs as they walked. "And the caro nut shipment?" Ranami asked as they stepped into the shadow of a covered street. Oil sizzled at a nearby food stall as the vendor placed a whole herbed fish into a pan.

"We hold it, as we agreed. We don't know what this new

Emperor is like, and maybe we do need to get her to abdicate as soon as possible. I'm not sure what's right yet, and—"

A shape collided with Phalue, a dark, whirling, dirt-encrusted child. Phalue caught a glimpse of wide black eyes before the girl stumbled and then ran off. Instinctively, she looked for who the girl might have been running from but only saw the calm, easy traffic of an unremarkable street. No one even looked up.

"She took your belt pouch," Ranami said. Phalue grasped at her belt and found the empty spot where her pouch had been.

The Emperor's missive.

10

Lin

Imperial Island

Rain pounded on the deck above. I watched the servants and guards as they descended the stairs, water dripping from cloaks, eyebrows and beards. It wasn't the most auspicious weather for our departure. Sea serpents grew bolder in the wet season, though there hadn't been substantiated sightings of very large ones in years. Mostly they were the size of sharks, disturbing small fishing boats, making off with their catches and leaving shaken sailors with jagged bite wounds. No Mephisolous come to threaten a city, but the smaller ones could still be a nuisance to a ship like ours.

Part of me had wanted to rush to the north-eastern islands, to place myself between the encroaching construct army and my people. But I was the only one with bone shard magic, and there were too many for me to fight on my own. My father had kept a sparse army, relying mostly on war constructs. We'd need to start recruiting right away, but training an army took time. Every governor had their own guards; if I could persuade the most influential to send theirs, others would follow and I could stop the constructs before they got too far.

Ikanuy sat across from me in the ship's mess, papers spread in front of her, an abacus to her right, and a steaming mug between her hands. She'd come to the harbor to wrap up a few last items before I left. "Your father was quite prolific," she said, studying the figures she'd just finished calculating. "If we remove the constructs here in the palace, according to Mauga's notes, that leaves approximately eight thousand war constructs, three thousand trade constructs and five thousand bureaucratic constructs unaccounted for throughout the Empire. I cannot find an accounting of how many spy constructs there are."

And how many failed experiments? How many people's corpses had he dismantled and formed into constructs? Ikanuy wouldn't find the answers in Mauga's notes. "That's more than I expected," I said.

She shuffled some papers. "Yes, well, some he inherited from his father, or his father's mother. There was time before they died to make that transition in their commands – a task that was mostly left to the bureaucratic constructs. The constructs have until recently been under continuous repair. He didn't *create* all of them."

I picked up a piece of fish from one of the plates and gave it to Thrana, who was sitting next to me at the table's end. She accepted it graciously. "What I meant is that it's too many, no matter how they were acquired. Our army is several thousand strong at most. We need to recruit and train soldiers, and quickly. I know the constructs may not all band together, but even bureaucratic and trade constructs can fight."

She took a sip of tea, grimaced and set the cup down. "It's not as dire as it sounds. Some constructs have fallen into disrepair since your father died. Some have been killed by soldiers and villagers. And some killed one another. I just don't have specific numbers on that."

Guards moved past us, carrying several ornate chests to the hold. Bone shards I intended to gift back to the islands as a gesture of good faith. I lifted my tea. "But it *is* dire."

"If even a fraction of the remaining constructs organize, they can usurp a lot more territory and terrorize your citizens."

I let out a breath, blowing the steam from my mug in all directions. "Which further destabilizes my rule." I'd promoted Yeshan, one of my army's commanders, to general – a position formerly held by Tirang, the Construct of War. Yeshan had attended the Scholars' Academy on Hualin Or before joining the army and was known for her strategic mind – not that she'd been able to put such skills to use lately. "I've asked Yeshan to send a quarter of our phalanxes to the north-eastern reaches of the Empire. A few will be recalled to Imperial to train new troops. The remainder will be on rotating patrols throughout the rest of the Empire, recruiting and providing assistance where it's needed. The constructs gathering in the north-east are a problem, but we don't know yet if they'll organize anywhere else and where they might attack. We need to be vigilant."

"A quarter," Ikanuy said. She regarded me over the rim of her mug as she sipped.

I kept my face neutral. I'd had this discussion with Yeshan already. Reports coming in from the north-east were unreliable at best – varied as the tales of an old fisherman. Some made the constructs seem like a few hundred malcontents; others made them sound like an encroaching horde. And the islands there were smaller, less populated, less influential. My father's constructs were scattered across the entirety of the Empire. If I threw the majority of our army at the threat in the north-east and left the rest of the Empire vulnerable, all it would take was one attack on a place like Riya to have the governors clamoring for my removal.

A voice spoke up from behind me. "So the north-eastern isles are an acceptable sacrifice if it comes down to it."

Mephi appeared in the corner of my vision, running ahead of his master, sniffing the air. He made a beeline for the kitchen. Jovis had his hand wrapped around his steel staff, curling hair damp with the rain. He brushed droplets from his shoulders. Water spattered the papers on the table before Ikanuy moved them out of the way.

"I never said that," I said coolly.

"You've just implied it. No matter what *might* happen, the constructs have only organized in the north-east so far. The army is small enough at the moment. If you only send a quarter of them, they may be overrun."

"Are you my Captain of the Imperial Guard, or are you my general?" I asked.

He tilted his head to the side. "Sometimes, I'm just a concerned citizen."

"Who doesn't understand that I need to consider all the implications of my decisions, and how best to hold this Empire together." I could feel my cheeks heating, and I didn't think it was just the steam from the tea.

"You said I should be honest with you."

I hated that I was sitting and he was standing, and that I had to crane my neck back so far to look into his eyes. Water beaded on his cheekbones, his nose, the top of his lip. His feet shifted a little beneath him as I glared, and that gave me a small sense of satisfaction, though he did not look away. Bayan had always had the air of a wounded animal about him, ready to strike back whenever threatened. Jovis didn't feel quite the same; rather, he felt scarred, the wounds healed over but still evident in his bearing. I *had* asked him to be honest, hadn't I? But having him throw that back in my face in front of my steward only pricked my temper.

A tremor started in my bones. I had to clench my teeth to keep myself from tapping my foot, from letting a little of that energy out. There were far too many people here. "So do you see this decision as an inadequacy?"

He frowned and then suddenly seemed to remember who he was speaking to. He bowed his head, dipping his gaze away in retreat, and I wished I could take back the sharpness of my words. Long black eyelashes fluttered against his cheeks. "I only think the people of the north-eastern reaches deserve more." The words cut, and they were meant to. Not a retreat then, not at all.

Ikanuy was flicking beads across the abacus, studiously avoiding looking at both of us.

"Deserve more than me as Emperor?"

He opened his mouth to respond.

And then Mephi came bounding out of the kitchen, something metallic clenched between his teeth. Jovis's gaze flicked to his companion. "Hey now, didn't we just talk about this?" He moved around the table to Mephi, kneeling to pull a cooking pan from the creature's mouth. "You can't take things that aren't yours."

"No one said it was theirs."

"No one said it was *yours* either."

Thrana licked a paw and ran it over her ears as if to say, "Aren't you glad I'm different?" I gave her a scratch behind the horns and handed her half a scallion pancake in thanks. She might be more timid than Mephi, but that wasn't always a bad thing.

Jovis returned the pan to the kitchen, but instead of settling himself into the cabin or checking in on the guards who were coming along on this trip, he made his way back to our table, taking up position just behind my right shoulder. Did he expect another assassin? Here? I glared at him but he only shrugged his shoulders. "To Riya first then?" he asked.

Ikanuy paused in shifting the abacus, glancing at me. I hadn't explained to either of them yet my reasoning for the four islands we'd be visiting. I'd been too entrenched in packing, in reading, in trying to figure out what the sword was and what it did. I owed them an explanation; I shouldn't keep everything to myself. "Yes. It's one of the largest islands in the Empire, and now that we've lost Deerhead, it has the largest witstone mine. If I gain their support, the Empire will be well supplied with witstone for years to come and trade will flourish. Then to Nephilanu."

Jovis grimaced. "A small island."

I wasn't sure why he'd find Nephilanu distasteful in that way — he was *from* a small island. "Yes, and of little importance during a dry season. But it produces the most caro nuts, and we need those to survive any outbreaks of bog cough. We've just entered a wet season. I've had reports that bog cough has already begun cropping up. If we keep the supply of those flowing in, we can minimize the spread of the illness.

"And then we go to Hualin Or." My stomach fluttered at the thought. The home island of Nisong, the woman I'd thought was my mother. Instead, my father had built me from body parts he'd harvested from his citizens, finding people who had a nose like hers, or a chin, and then growing the rest of me in the waters of that cave. "Hualin Or has a storied history, one nearly as long as Imperial's, and is a center for cultural and artistic growth. Gaining their support would do much to legitimize us in the eyes of the Empire's citizens."

"And then Gaelung," Jovis said. He tapped his fingertips against his staff. He sniffed, as though he could smell the constructs on the winds. "North-east."

"Yes. Gaelung. It is an agricultural paradise, and its lands are large and varied enough to produce much of the Empire's crops. We can lose Gaelung, but then we lose some of the foods we love so much. The spices needed for the fish soup that visitors to Deerhead Island held in such high esteem? All of them are grown on Gaelung. We can live off rice, pork and cabbage, but the souls of all Empireans would be less rich for it. We need Gaelung. In the meantime, Yeshan will recruit and train soldiers. By the time my visits conclude, we'll have a better idea of where we need to allocate our troops and how great the threat is."

Ikanuy ran a few more quick sums. "I suspect you'll need more than what few phalanxes we'll have trained by the time your visits conclude."

"I've already been writing letters to the governors, asking for their help. If they commit some of their guards, we can increase our forces quickly."

"And have any responded?" she asked.

"Not yet," I said. They'd wait too — wait to see what the more influential islands would do. "But it's the best we can do at the moment."

My gaze went to the porthole, where a downpour obscured the sun. I'd not been able to find the spy construct that had escaped both my grasp and Jovis's. I shouldn't have expected I could. Still, I'd sent out servants to look for it.

If I'd had Hao, or any other spy construct . . .

But I'd vowed to put that behind me. No little spies outside the palace walls, bringing reports back to a monster below the palace. No other Emperor had ruled without magic. And I was already starting from a weakened position. What if my father had already completed one copy of himself, stuffed it full of his memories and hidden it away in case of disaster? I tried not to imagine where that might lead. Two warring factions. A divided Empire. And always people like Numeen and his family would suffer.

I had to deal with what was in front of me, instead of the endless possibilities opened by my father's experiments.

Iknauy gathered up the papers in front of her before pulling out a tied bundle of folded messages. "I have reports in from the envoys you sent out at the beginning of your reign." She glanced to Jovis. "Shall I?"

I waved at her to continue. There wouldn't be secrets there — nothing that couldn't be gleaned from talk and rumors.

Most of it was reporting on local events, some of which were concerning but not alarming. Attacks from constructs on citizens. Citizens hunting down constructs. Tremors on a few islands, though nothing as large or continuous as on Deerhead. She handed each message to me after she'd finished summarizing them. And then Ikanuy pulled out the last two messages.

"The caro nut shipment from Nephilanu has been delayed. Our envoy isn't sure why or exactly what's happening there. They did have a recent upheaval."

I searched my memories. I'd received a letter when the change of governors had taken place. "Yes. The father stepped down and his daughter inherited."

Iknauy gave me an amused look. "That's the official story. Unofficially, there was rioting. The previous governor squeezed the populace dry while he lived an extravagant lifestyle. He had a daughter with a commoner, and it sounds like the people have pinned their hopes on her. He was forced to step down."

I wanted to ask, "Is he dead?" but Ikanuy would have said if his daughter had killed him. Sent away, perhaps, or just relegated to smaller rooms in the palace. I shrugged off the uncomfortable parallels to my situation. "Then it makes even more sense to visit them. We can check in on the situation while we're there and make sure Imperial's shipment is still coming. The last item?"

Ikanuy unfolded the letter. "An envoy from Hirona's Net. She visited several isles there and noticed a disturbing pattern." Her gaze flicked up to Jovis again before settling back on me.

"More construct attacks?"

"No." She handed me the letter. "Artifacts on the isles. Alanga artifacts. They're awakening."

11

Ranami
Nephilanu Island

She should have known the girl was stealing something. Ranami had lived the life of a gutter orphan; you never collided with someone by accident. But life in a palace had apparently made her reflexes slow.

Phalue darted after the girl.

Ranami acted on instinct, ducking into an alley. She knew these streets the way she knew every callus on Phalue's hands. The street stalls would slow them both, but there was a clear path around the main street just behind this building. She leapt down a set of crumbling stairs, ducked beneath an overhang hung too low and lifted a lever on a gate, opening it just enough to slip past.

Someone from a window above shouted at her – she wasn't supposed to be back here – but she paid them no heed. She'd be gone by the time they tried to confront her. Her feet nearly slid from beneath her as she rounded the corner, the street made slippery with rain. She caught herself on the wall, using the drainpipe to help propel her forward.

The street opened up ahead of her and Ranami stepped out just in front of the gutter orphan. The girl skidded to a halt, her eyes darting from side to side, searching for an escape. Ranami kept her knees bent, her feet light.

She needn't have bothered. Phalue stormed up from behind the girl, faster than her broad-shouldered form would suggest, and seized her by the shoulder.

It was like watching a fish realize it had been hooked. The girl flailed, flopping back and forth, trying to shake loose. Phalue's grip was intractable, her fingers like claws. A few people glanced over, but swiftly returned to their business.

"I'd like that back now," Phalue said, her hand outstretched for the pouch.

The orphan pulled a few more times and then stopped, her breath heaving in her chest. Phalue wiggled her fingers and the girl held out the pouch. Before she could place it in Phalue's fingers, the girl went limp.

Ranami rushed forward to help, kneeling to pick the pouch up from the ground.

"I think she passed out," Phalue said, her hands beneath the girl's arms.

For a moment, Ranami thought the girl might be pretending in order to get away, but upon closer inspection, found that Phalue spoke the truth. She was dirty, small, but older than she had initially looked, her black hair tangled and unkempt. Beneath the rags, she was thin and bony, her ribs showing beneath her collarbone. Her left arm ended at the wrist, her hand missing.

"She must have been looking for money," Ranami said. Phalue had her purse in the same pouch as the missive.

"Foolish," Phalue said. "I give them coin. She could have waited."

"Maybe it wasn't enough? And she's small. The bigger children often steal from the younger ones. It's not an easy life."

With a shrug, Phalue slung the girl over her shoulder.

"What are you doing?"

"Well, I'm not going to leave her here. We're not adopting her, mind you, but she looks in a bad way, and it doesn't seem right to leave her lying in the street. You wanted to help the gutter orphans. We can start with this one."

That wasn't really what Ranami had meant, but she had the feeling Phalue knew it. And she couldn't argue with her logic. She didn't want to leave a passed-out gutter orphan on the streets either. The girl had fainted in front of them and now they both felt some responsibility for her. Funny how that worked.

Still, she couldn't help the trickle of unease as they made their way back up the street. Had the girl just wanted money, or had she been tipped off about the missive? It felt coincidental, but at the same time, Ranami remembered the things she'd done to get a bite to eat on the streets. She wouldn't have betrayed Halong, who was the closest thing she had to family – most gutter orphans still had something of a moral code – but the ones who had more than she did were always fair game. It wasn't until she'd stopped feeling quite so desperate that her capacity to trust had expanded.

"There wasn't much money in that purse," Ranami said. "She must have heard how spare it was when she was carrying it. Why not abandon it when you came thundering after her?"

Cobblestones turned to dirt, the switchbacks rising above them. Water ran down the path, carving rivulets through the mud. "What are you suggesting?" Phalue asked.

Ranami put voice to her unease. "Could she have been sent after the missive?"

Phalue shrugged her broad shoulders. "That's a little farfetched."

"People would have seen the Emperor's envoy on his way to the palace. Just because we haven't seen any more spy constructs doesn't mean there aren't spies of other kinds. We're taking her up to the palace. The fainting could have been a ruse."

The look Phalue gave her was partly exasperated and partly incredulous. "That's a complicated ruse. The girl is clearly half-starved."

"All gutter orphans are half-starved."

"Yes, and the likely explanation here is that she was hungry, saw an opportunity to get some money for a bite to eat and took it. She didn't expect us to pursue her so hard. And she put up quite the fight when I caught her. This little thing? That must have taken a lot out of her. I'm not surprised she passed out."

They climbed the path, Ranami hiking her skirts and cloak to jump over spots where the rain had made rivers. She envied Phalue her longer legs.

Phalue cleared her throat as they rounded the bend. "Ranami, when we do end up adopting an orphan, will you still feel this way? After all, any child we adopt will have access to the palace."

Would she feel this way? When she'd thought about adopting the gutter orphans all she could think about was how hungry she'd been as an orphan, how tired, how in need of a dry place to sleep and a kind word. She hadn't done much to imagine things from the other end – with her in the place of benefactor and a child she didn't know well in her home. A home that was now a palace, stuffed full of valuables and secrets. "It's complicated," she said.

"You trusted the caro nut farmers when we stole that box of nuts for them."

"Yes, but ... " How could she explain? "Halong trusted the farmers and I trusted Halong, so that went a long way for me. And, if I'm being honest with myself, I was trying to prove something to you. I was angry."

Phalue considered this, her jaw moving as though she were chewing the words. "Do you want to adopt to help the orphans, not because you want to expand our family?"

The words hit Ranami with the force of a storm gale; she could barely stay on her feet. Her boots stuck in the mud. Was it true? She'd always assumed that if Phalue and she ever did work out, they would eventually adopt. It made sense, especially with Phalue as the governor – she'd need an heir. Now, she tried to think through all that this meant. It would mean taking in a child that she didn't know, living with them, teaching them . . . loving them. Was she even capable? She'd been born to a mother; she must have had a father – but she had only vague memories of the woman who'd birthed her. Mostly her memories consisted of the streets, the other orphans, the scraping and the grasping and the hunger. She called Halong her brother, but they'd met when they were teenagers. Phalue had stopped and turned to look at her.

"I'm not sure I know what a family is," she admitted. She could barely hear her own voice above the patter of the rain. "Do you?"

Phalue took the two steps back to her. "My father was a decent parent, and he loved me in his own way. My mother, too. But I want better for any child of ours. And if my father could be a decent parent, you can be so much better. You've some sharp edges, I won't deny that. But beneath that you have the strongest, most compassionate heart of anyone I've ever known. Any child would be lucky to feel a fraction of the love I know you're capable of. We'll figure this out together."

This was a kindness she wasn't sure she deserved. "How do you say the exact right thing to make me feel better?"

Phalue smiled before turning back up the path. "I've spent enough years saying the wrong things. I've got time to make up for."

The girl stared at Ranami from Phalue's back as she turned, her black eyes nearly wide enough to swallow her face. When had she woken up? How much had she heard? Ah, she was doing it again.

"She's awake now," Ranami said.

Phalue glanced at the bundle on her shoulder. "The girl?" Ranami nodded. "Can you walk?"

"Yes," a small voice said.

Phalue set the gutter orphan on her feet. The girl swayed a little, though it seemed more like she was deciding whether or not to run than any unsteadiness. Both Phalue and Ranami blocked the path, and it became clear that she had decided against running when she planted both feet firmly on the ground. Mud obscured her shoes, but Ranami was sure she saw toes peeking out from the ends. "What's your name?" Phalue asked.

"Are you going to chop off my other hand?" the girl asked.

"What?" Phalue looked taken aback.

"My hand. Are you going to chop it off?" She spoke slowly and loudly, as if she wasn't sure Phalue had heard her the first time.

"No," Ranami spoke up. "Why would we do that?" She thought she knew.

"Trying to steal something is how I lost this one." The girl held up her left arm.

In an instant, Phalue had her hand on her sword, her shoulders squared. "Who did that to you? Tell me their name. Did my father order that done?"

The girl shrank before Phalue's anger, unsure whether it was directed at her. "Didn't happen here," she said. "On a different island. It . . . it sank."

Deerhead. Had she come all this way? Ranami wondered if the girl had once had parents who'd loved her, or other street orphans she'd cared about. All of them – gone in a moment, sunk beneath the sea. She still had trouble believing that an entire island was gone. And still no one seemed to know exactly why.

"Look: it's all right now though," the girl said, waving her arm about. "The guy who did it is dead now, if that's what you're worried about. At least I think he is. Probably?"

"What's your name?" Ranami interrupted. If she let them continue on this winding conversation, they'd never know.

"Ayesh," the girl said.

"We're not going to cut off your hand," Ranami told her. "We don't do that here."

Ayesh glanced behind her. "You're taking me there? The palace?"

"Yes, that's where we live," Phalue said.

Rain slicked the girl's hair to her forehead. She pushed it out of her eyes, regarding them both suspiciously. "Is it to punish me?"

Ranami knew what it was like to feel so suspicious, and if the girl came from Deerhead, she might not be familiar with who Phalue was or what she was like. She sighed. "No. I used to be a gutter orphan too. I know what that's like. We help people here on Nephilanu; we don't chop off their hands. Why did you take the pouch?"

Ayesh's gaze darted between the two of them. "I was hungry."

Old instincts stirred to life. The girl was hiding something. She was hungry, yes, but there were other reasons.

Phalue didn't have such instincts. "Come on, let's at least get something warm in your belly." The girl took two steps before her knees gave out again. Phalue caught her before she could fall and slung her over her shoulder again. "Easy now."

"I have to go back . . ." Ayesh trailed off before losing consciousness once more.

Ranami picked up her skirts and the hem of her cloak again, leapt over a puddle and joined Phalue at her side. "What exactly are we planning on doing with her? She said she wants to go back."

"Let's feed her, get her cleaned up. If we want to help the orphans, maybe we should start by asking them what they need. I need to redress the harm that my father and people like him have caused."

She should have known, once she set Phalue on this path, that she would take to it wholeheartedly – the way she did with everything. "Dearest," she said gently, "you can never account for all the harm."

"I should at least try."

This wasn't just about harm. Ranami had seen the look on Phalue's face when she'd emerged from the cellar where her father was kept. She still felt obligated to him, still felt that tug of family loyalty. Perhaps she was right – he hadn't been all that bad. He'd loved her. But love didn't always make a person kind.

The walls of the palace loomed ahead; one of the guards waved from the gate. Ranami lifted a hand in greeting and then leaned in close to her wife. "Even if you were able to account for all the harm caused, it doesn't mean you should let your father go."

"What about forgiveness?" Phalue bit back. "What about moving on?"

"You can't make amends for him; only he can do that. And right now, the people of Nephilanu need justice. They need to feel safe."

"No one can feel safe; not after Deerhead," Phalue said darkly. They passed beneath the shadow of the arch. "Poor girl. Having no family or parents is bad enough. Losing the place you called home is yet another way of being orphaned."

Ayesh stirred. "Not Deerhead," she said faintly. "I'm not from there. I got here this morning. Stowed away on a ship. They weren't too happy. Threw me overboard. I had to swim."

Ranami's mouth went dry. This morning? No wonder the

girl hadn't known who Phalue was. "You came from somewhere else? But you were on Deerhead when it sank."

"No." She struggled to lift her head, to look Ranami in the eye. "I'm from Unta."

"Unta didn't sink; Deerhead did," Phalue said. But she didn't sound sure.

"There was an earthquake. And then another one. And then one that didn't end." Ayesh's voice was small but clear. The soldiers at the walls must be able to hear. But Ranami found she couldn't move, couldn't hurry them into some private chamber. Dread had rooted itself in her belly.

"Unta is gone."

12

Jovis

Imperial Island

I'd burned the letter from the Shardless Few as soon as I'd finished with it. Letting someone find it would have been quite the way to get my head chopped off. I could imagine what my mother would say to that: "Careless, leaving such things lying about! Foolish boy. You *deserved* to get your head chopped off!" I peered into the darkness of the hold, the small candle in my hand lighting only what was in front of me. I didn't dare come in here with a lamp swinging from my hand. The deck rolled beneath me, though I kept my feet steady. The Endless Sea rarely rested easy in a wet season. They were burning witstone above-deck to keep the sails filled in the right direction, and both Mephi and Thrana had retreated below where they couldn't smell it. Burning witstone made Thrana as sick as it did Mephi.

I felt bad for the beasts, since they so clearly enjoyed racing from prow to stern and leaping into the waves — but Lin had made it clear: we needed to make good time on this trip. I'd wanted to argue — I'd found my distaste for witstone growing the longer I spent with Mephi – but I'd sparked enough arguments with the Emperor. I could imagine my mother watching me again, scowling her disapproval, wondering if I was *aiming* for execution or if I was just stupid.

More and more these days I felt like the latter.

If the Emperor was the mortar, then the Shardless Few were the pestle, and I was the hapless grain being crushed between them. A white-bladed sword in the Emperor's possession, they'd written. Steal it. Yes, a simple enough task for a folk hero who'd had songs written about him. I might have survived the assassin's poisoning, but I knew I was still all too mortal. My flesh might mend, my blood might purge itself, but I doubted my head could reknit itself to my neck if I was caught. Not something I was keen on finding out.

Boxes of old books met my gaze, four ornate chests filled with shards, various crates of food and sundries. I'd thought, when I'd been in that cavern below the palace, trapped with the monstrous construct, that I'd seen a sword hanging on the wall. I could have been mistaken – after all, I'd had other things to worry about. But I'd watched the servants carrying their cargo below decks and had seen another chest being brought to Lin's room. A chest I'd seen in the hidden caves below the palace. If she'd brought that, she might have brought the sword.

I couldn't help but think of the play *Phoenix Rise*, the assertion that a magical sword had helped defeat the Alanga. The troupes had only come by Anau once when I'd been young, though the thought of a magical weapon had stuck with me. I remembered it had made quite the impression on my brother Onyu as well, who at seven began carrying around a big stick he claimed was the magical sword. My father had ruffled his hair; my mother had pursed her lips and said even Alanga-slaying heroes still needed to wash their dishes.

I lifted the lid of a nearby box, running my hand across the spines of the books inside. Nothing alarming or even secret – just history books and old tales, and even a copy of *Phoenix Rise*.

"Do you ever mind your own business?"

I whirled to find Lin standing there, dressed in plain traveling clothes, her lamp shuttered. She flipped the shutter open, the bright light making me blink, casting her face in ominous shadows. How could such a small woman seem so forbidding? "Surely it's not part of your job to go poking around in the ship's hold. Or is this somehow protecting me as well? I see no monstrous constructs here."

Footsteps creaked on the deck above us and sweat gathered in the small of my back. I had to say something quickly. I lifted my hands, giving her a disarming grin. "You caught me, Eminence. I'm a spy, sent to report on your interest in –" I pulled *Phoenix Rise* from the box. "– very old plays." I hefted it. "Is there a reason no one's updated it? Seems a little silly to say the Alanga were defeated with a sword." I was skirting a little too closely to the truth, but in all my years of lying, I'd learned that absurdity could be a useful tool. "You can't expect me to spend day in and day out in my room or guarding yours. And I get in the way above-deck sometimes. I thought I could find something to read."

The tension left her shoulders, her stern expression easing. She sighed as though I were a wayward child she'd been set to mind. My heartbeat slowed in response, the heat draining from the back of my neck. "You could have asked," she said.

I blew out the candle; her lamp provided more than enough light. "Disturbing the Emperor to ask if I could borrow a book or two? The hold isn't locked and neither are the boxes. If you didn't want me in here, surely you would have locked them both. Isn't that what Emperors do?" Maybe that was too much of a dig at her similarities to her father. Fear had made me careless. I should take it back, soften the words. Only, I wasn't sure what to say.

Her eyes narrowed and she reached out. For a moment I thought she might strike me. Instead, her fingers only brushed against mine as she plucked the book from my grasp. My stomach flipped like a porpoise in the waves. There was something magnetic about her presence, even dressed as she was in a plain brown tunic and pants, her hair pulled back in a simple bun. I swallowed and had to force my words past a throat gone suddenly tight. "Or have I committed some grievous error?" I felt like I was committing an error that had nothing to do with the book or the ship's hold.

Her gaze met mine for only a moment before dropping away. Was it the lamp, or did her cheeks look flushed? "Not this one. I came here for this one. Choose another. Just put it back when you're finished."

It *had* been unfair of me to dig at all her locked doors. I'd come here to search for a sword, had lied about my intentions and she returned this all with sternness, yes, but with kindness too. She trusted me too much. Or I was too good of a liar. Or both.

I fumbled in the box and pulled out a book that I didn't check the title on, slipping it into my satchel. "Thank you for that, Eminence. I'll put it back. I promise." And then I brushed past her with as wide a berth I could manage without seeming to avoid her, the jasmine scent of her hair chasing me half the length of the hold. I needed to set Mephi as a lookout next time. I needed to be more cautious. I needed to . . . I needed to clear my head.

The air outside the hold was tinged with the scent of seawater and old wood; I breathed it in as though it were the last breath I took before a dive. I shook out my fingers. There had been a time, when I'd been young, when I wouldn't have known what I was feeling. But I was older now, and a widower, and had lived in my body long enough to know it. Lin was . . . complicated. She wasn't Emahla or even anything like her.

I opened the door to my room to find Mephi curled in my bed beneath the covers, a book beneath his claws. The Alanga book I'd found in the Shardless Few hideout what seemed like a lifetime ago. That should have been in my satchel. I felt inside the satchel anyways, even though I knew it couldn't possibly be in two places at once. "Did you take that from my bag?"

He leafed a page over with his claw. "No."

Ask silly questions, get silly answers. "Mephisolou," I said sternly, and that got his attention. "You can't go taking things just because you want to." The words sounded rich coming from a smuggler. From a spy. I'd thought, even after we'd bonded, I was taking on the care of an animal. An odd one that could talk. Now I felt like I was raising an unruly teenager. Children of my own had always been a distant hypothetical, a hazy-eyed dream that never quite reconciled with the messiness, the strangeness and the *loudness* of all the actual children I'd met.

Mephi crawled from beneath the blanket, stretched and then butted my hip with his head. "I was bored," he said.

It was the same excuse I'd given Lin. Was this what my mother had meant when she'd cursed me with children who behaved like me? I scratched the thick fur behind his ears, the soft dander there coating my fingertips. "What did you want with that book anyways? You don't know how to read this." I'd started teaching Mephi to read, but nearly the entirety of this book was written in the language of the Alanga, far as I could guess.

I plucked it from the bed, took it to my desk and flipped through the pages again. How many times had I idly examined the words, trying to discern meaning that I just had no context for? I could ask Lin — she had an extensive library and who knew what her education had included?

No. Terrible idea. All my motives were suspect now, even to myself. I might be Captain of the Imperial Guard, but we were at sea, where threats were few. Best I avoid her until the awkwardness of that encounter blew over. Bad enough that we shared a secret. Bad enough that I'd convinced her she could trust me that far.

Mephi put a paw on my leg to get my attention. "It's a journal. Someone named Dione wrote it."

The air seemed to freeze in my lungs. "It . . . What?"

"I can understand some of the words," he said.

"How?"

He tilted his head at me. "I look at them and they make sense to me."

My mind ran in circles like a dog chasing its own tail. I needed to slow down, take the time to parse my thoughts. If Mephi could understand some Alanga, that further proved my theory that Lin and I were Alanga. If Mephi could understand some Alanga, I could use his help to decipher some of the journal. Dione's journal — the greatest of the Alanga. The one I'd heard so many stories about. I could find out more about them and sift some truth from all the fictions the Empire had fed me as a child.

I lowered the book to my lap and took out a fresh sheet of paper. The ship swayed as I set a squat pot of ink next to it.

"Tell me what words you understand."

It was slow going. I'd recognized the word for "Alanga". Mephi recognized others, though his interpretations were somewhat vague. I had to pin down some words through context; complete sentences still evaded me.

I stopped to ask a servant to bring dinner to my room, as well as food for Mephi. He ate his meal with gusto and then eyed my work. "What does it say? Do you know yet?"

I pointed to a word. "This one here is 'Alanga'. And there's the Sukais, I know that much. So this talks about the beginning of their dynasty. According to what you've been telling me, this word here is 'kill' or 'destroy'." I flipped through some more pages. "Men, women, children. Hunt. Sleep. All."

Mephi lowered his head, as though expecting the ceiling to collapse. "Yes. A killing. Of everyone."

"The Alanga couldn't have killed the Sukais." I stopped myself. Of course. This was written by one of the Alanga. This wasn't about that. This was about the Sukai defeat of the Alanga. Men, women and children. Somehow I hadn't even considered that the Alanga had children. But of course they did — even if they lived for ever, they had to have come from somewhere. I'd thought of them as supernatural beings for so long, spurred on by the stories of them unleashing destruction on mortals, heedless of how many they killed. They'd had families.

"The Sukais killed all of the Alanga. You're right. A massacre." I ran a finger up and down the page, flipped to the next one, trying to pick out words I recognized. It was the first time I'd ever thought of the defeat of the Alanga as a massacre. The plays and the songs always framed it as a glorious victory. The commoners defeated the Alanga and were free to live their lives without fear of being slain by their magic.

They'd traded fear of the Alanga for fear of the Sukais, eventually.

"What else?" Mephi sniffed the pages.

"I'm not sure. I'm trying." I flipped to the end. Perhaps translating the ending of the book might help me get a better idea for the contents. I could get a sense for what might have happened to the author.

The words here were starker, the pen pressed harder into the page.

Mephi shrank back once he got a look at them. "I don't like this," he said. "It smells angry. It looks angry."

I ruffled his ears. "These words can't hurt you. I promise. They were written by someone a long time ago who is long dead." Still, my words sounded hollow, even to me. There *was* something menacing about the way the words marched across the page.

I shook my head and brought the lamp closer as I translated which words I could. Fewer of the words here made sense to me, except for the last sentences. Here, I was able to translate most words. When I was finished, I dropped the pen, my fingers trembling, dread strangling the breath in my throat.

Alanga will return. Kill. All.

13

Lin

Somewhere in the Endless Sea

I'd never sailed before. In the years since my father had created me, I'd not even been to the harbor. Something of it felt familiar, though. The swaying wood beneath my feet, the spray of the waves, the wind whipping at my hair. Those memories he'd tried to instill in me, working their way loose. He'd burned my mother's body so he hadn't been able to grow me from her flesh as he had himself. Perhaps that was why these memories lurked always beneath my surface and had never consumed me. I'd brought my father's flask of memories with me, along with Thrana's blood and the machine, though I hadn't been brave enough to drink any more of his memories, not just yet. The last view had left me feeling odd for days afterward, as if I would look down at my hands and see them at any moment become his hands, his personality layered over mine.

The curve of Riya's mountains lay ahead, and I could see buildings nestled in the greenery. The winds were favorable, the skies blessedly free of rain, and I'd bid the captain to set aside the witstone for now. We were making good time without it, and it let Thrana and Mephi enjoy some time above-deck. The two of them raced past me, diving into the ocean below. Thrana might not have sailed before either, but she took to it like a fledgling from the nest. Hesitant at first, and then bolder and bolder.

I turned from the rail to find Jovis behind me, his weight shifting between his feet, as if he couldn't decide whether he should keep walking forward now that he'd seen me here. But I was watching him, and he finally seemed to decide that retreating now would be unseemly. "It feels good to get out of Imperial, doesn't it?" He joined me at the prow, leaning on the wooden railing.

My heart leapt a little before becoming a weight atop my stomach. Finding him poking around in the hold had brought up unpleasant memories of him following me into the caves below the palace. He was too clever, too curious, too eager to bend the rules of propriety. I wasn't sure how to act around him, how much I could be myself, how much I was supposed to be the Emperor. And then there was the magic that we both shared.

He was right, though. I'd locked all the things I'd wanted hidden in my room. The white-bladed sword, the bone shard magic books, the memory machine. The cloudtree berries I'd harvested before we left lay inside my sash pocket. My father's legacy, and I was carrying it with me.

I tried to shake the thoughts loose. "It does feel good." The palace was my home, had been my home for as long as I'd been alive. But ruling an Empire meant knowing it, and even my glimpses of Imperial City had broadened my horizons. We were fast approaching Riya, and I was desperate to walk among its streets, see its people, smell and taste its food. "I'm supposed to rule these people; I should know what they're like."

Jovis raised an eyebrow. "All about duty? Are you really this boring, Eminence?"

"I should have your head lopped off for that," I said casually. "The Emperor is never boring."

He squinted at the harbor. "Should have done that before they wrote a song about me. The Empire is stuck with me now."

"A song isn't impenetrable armor. They write songs about dead people too, you know."

"But are they quite so catchy?"

I looked back to the cloudy skies, the Endless Sea and the lush green land beyond. I breathed in the scent of the salty spray and smiled. "Fine. Any trips away from Imperial were taken when I was too young to remember. My father kept me inside the palace walls. I've barely been into the city. Of course it feels good to leave."

Nails scratched against wood behind us. I turned to see Mephi and Thrana scrambling up a net and back onto the deck. Both were soaked through. Thrana looked better out here. It wasn't just that she seemed happier and more at ease. Her coat had thickened as she ate food fresh from the sea. Her eyes were brighter. Even her black horns seemed less flaky and dry and had more of a sheen to them.

"You're lighter on your feet on the ocean than most first-time sailors," Jovis said, his gaze on the sea, a corner of his lip quirked. "Maybe you should have been a smuggler."

"I really should have considered my options before ascending to Emperor," I said with a smile. I looked down at my salt-spattered tunic. "I need to dress before we arrive. Get yourself ready too, and the rest of the guards." Mephi was snapping at a squid Thrana had in her jaws. "And could you make sure they're at least dried off? I don't want them dripping onto the governor's rugs."

"As you will it, Eminence."

It was more of an ordeal to drape myself in the Emperor's vestments than I'd first expected it would be. The seas grew choppy just outside the harbor, and the three maidservants I'd brought with me struggled to tie my sash and to secure the Phoenix Empire headdress atop my hair. They swayed with each rocking wave, one of them blushing furiously as she careened into a wall.

"Never mind the conditions," I said to them. "You can straighten everything up once we're in the harbor. I won't be expected to disembark right away."

The roiling waves seemed to reflect the roiling of my belly. Yes, as I'd told Jovis, I was excited. At the same time, this would be my first meeting with any island governor. They hadn't had much contact with an Emperor recently, not since my father had been younger. And now I was asking them to accept my absolute authority.

The rocking of the boat calmed, and the three maidservants hurried to fix my hair and clothes. With the silk dress, the embroidered robe and the headdress, I felt heavy, my movements slow. I'd have never been able to climb the palace walls this way.

"The shards?"

The maidservants went to the corner of the room and hefted a carved wooden chest between them. All the living shards my father had collected for Riya. It was the best gift I could think of.

I opened the door and found myself face to face with Jovis, his hand raised to knock. This close, I could see the faint shadow of stubble on his chin, the flecks of lighter brown in his eyes. He brought the scent of the ocean with him, as though he'd woven it into his hair.

"Sorry, Eminence, I ... " Flustered, he stopped talking and stepped to the side. "We're docked and an envoy has come to greet us."

Somehow, knowing that he felt some nervousness around me made me feel less nervous around him. I stepped out of my cabin and swept past him. "Thrana and Mephi?"

"Above-deck, along with the rest of your guards."

"Then let's go meet Riya's governor."

He was not, as I'd first thought he might be, waiting at the docks. I might have thought this normal protocol, except for the clear anxiety of the representative the governor had sent from the palace. She was a tall, thin woman, dressed smartly, her long black hair braided down her back. She bowed, then nearly bowed again as I descended the gangplank, Thrana at my side.

"Eminence," she said, and then licked her lips. "The governor has sent me to greet you and to guide you to his palace."

I flicked my gaze down the docks and saw no other members of her party. She'd come alone then. "Riya's governor did not think to greet me himself?"

And then she did bow again. "Forgive me – him – Eminence. There is a hill and he has weak knees."

I exchanged glances with Jovis. He pressed his lips together, his eyebrows raised and gave me the tiniest of shrugs. So I wasn't the only one who found this all odd. I could demand the governor come himself to greet me, and wait aboard my ship, but he also had little incentive to make the trek. I had my retinue of guards, but the constructs were no longer under my control. I knew what he meant to say by this reception: we are doing perfectly fine without you, thank you.

My temper flared; a thrum started in my bones, but I tamped it down. I had to keep control of myself. I hadn't brought a palanquin, and clearly the governor hadn't sent one. He couldn't have known I'd leapt from rooftop to rooftop at the Imperial palace. I might have been dressed fit to weigh down a strongman, but I could walk.

"Very well. Lead the way, and we will follow."

The boards of the dock creaked beneath me as we walked, the dark, sinuous shapes of fish darting away at our shadows. Our guide said nothing as she led us into the streets of Riya's largest city.

The streets here were wider than they were in Imperial, the stones rougher and less worn away by time. People gave way before us, bowing as they saw my headdress. There was something perfunctory and wary in the way they did it, but how could I fault them? They didn't know me. I hadn't done anything for them yet except put a halt to the Tithing Festival, and I'd done that only a short time ago.

Thrana pressed a shoulder to my knee, and I reached to put a steadying hand on her head. Behind me, I heard the maidservants halt to switch carrying duties with two of my guards, the bottom of the chest scraping the cobblestones as they set it down.

I gritted my teeth.

There was a hill, it was true, but it was a hill that the lamest of ponies could have easily surmounted. Ahead, the rooftops of the palace loomed.

And then the rain started.

I avoided wearing all my formal clothes as often as possible, and a little rain had never bothered me in the past. My guards and maidservants murmured among themselves, trying to figure out if someone – anyone – had brought an umbrella. My court was new and untried. This was our first diplomatic trip, and after seven years of a dry season, people were still adjusting to the rain. No one had brought an umbrella.

Jovis gave me a rueful smile as if to say, "Well, it can't get much worse, can it?" One of the guards tried to offer me his jacket, but I waved it aside. I'd look even more foolish if I tried desperately and futilely to mitigate the damage. "If we track the dirt and rain into the palace, surely the governor will forgive us," I said, my voice sharp.

I heard a snort of laughter from behind me – Jovis again? – and strode up the hill with purpose. Our guide had to jog to keep up with me. I shouldn't have let my anger get the best of me, and it wasn't *her* fault we were being so ill-treated, but all I could think about was that man sitting dry in his palace, smugly awaiting my arrival.

The gates were open when we arrived, and four of the governor's guard flanked our party as we entered. The courtyard was small but well-appointed. I caught a glimpse of a koi pond, fish gaping at the surface. Rain dripped from my headdress and my elaborately tied hair. It trickled down the back of my neck, making me shiver and sticking my clothes to my back. I could thank the Endless Sea I'd not worn any makeup.

Still, I must have looked a sight as I climbed the stairs to the palace proper, my expression dark as the clouds above.

The guards flanking us hurried in front of me, opening the doors with haste. I didn't slow my pace in the least, marching across the threshold, not bothering to stop and wipe my feet. My robe, heavy with moisture, dragged behind me like a corpse. A flash of lightning lit the entrance hall, followed by the crack of thunder. The weather was matching my mood.

The entrance hall was empty, no one there to greet us either. Our guide bowed to me twice. "I'll fetch the governor. Apologies, Eminence. Things have been hectic lately."

I felt Jovis's presence as he sidled up to me. He leaned to whisper in my ear. "Your anger is justified, Eminence. Just don't . . . kill anyone."

It wasn't until he said the words that I realized I was practically humming with power, my bones vibrating. I knew if I struck a foot against the ground, if I concentrated, I could shake this palace from its foundations.

That thought sobered me.

I took in a deep breath, and Thrana, whom I just realized had a low growl in her throat, subsided. The governor meant to rile me. What did he mean to prove? That I was unfit? That I was too young? That I knew nothing of how an Emperor should carry herself?

He entered from the opposite side of the entrance hall, the woman who'd guided us following at his heels, her head bowed. He was a short man, older than I was but younger than I'd expected, and with the trim figure of someone who did not have bad knees. Indeed, his stride seemed unbothered. He wore a neatly kept beard, and had the beady black eyes of a stoat. His hair was tied back, his blue jacket embroidered with bright gold koi.

"Eminence, you do us honor with your presence," he said, giving me a short, perfunctory bow. "Iloh, governor of Riya." He glanced behind me to Jovis. "And Jovis, the hero of the people. I've heard much about you." The bow he gave to my Captain of the Imperial Guard was deeper than the one he'd given me.

I studied his face, the way he peered at me, the almost imperceptible quirk at the corner of his mouth. He thought he knew me, or at least, knew my type.

He did not.

I was not some pampered, cloistered Emperor's get. I had clawed my way tooth and nail to this position, defying my father and teaching myself his magic. I was Lin, and I was Emperor. "Riya has an interesting way of greeting guests, Sai," I said, my voice even. "Honored ones in particular."

He opened his mouth to issue some supercilious apology, and I held up a hand to silence him. I was more than a little pleased when his mouth snapped shut.

"Allow me to apologize. This is surely the fault of Imperial. Too long have we been absent from the lives of our governors.

So long that cultural niceties are no longer observed. I'll be sure to station a permanent envoy on Riya, near to the palace, so that we may keep in closer touch."

Iloh's eyes narrowed. He smoothed his expression – clumsily, I noted. "Of course. Riya would welcome such an envoy."

I kept my amusement to myself. It would not. An envoy near the palace meant eyes and ears in his court at all times. Any ill word about the Emperor or Imperial would eventually find its way back to me.

Now that we'd both riled one another and were on even ground, I gestured to the guards holding the chest. I didn't want to be this man's enemy, nor did I want him as mine. My intent was to gain his support. I didn't want to be like my father, ruling by fear. I'd feared him, and how had that turned out for him? He was dead by my hand and burned, his soul ascended. It wasn't a fate I wanted.

"I come bearing a gift," I said. "The Tithing Festival is ended. It hasn't been my intent only to end the Tithing, but to return to the Empire's citizens what is rightfully theirs." The guards set the chest down in front of Iloh, and at his gesture, opened it. "The shards of all your citizens, labeled and sorted. The time of constructs is at an end."

Iloh sucked in a breath, and I could see his surprise was genuine. The constructs were power, and those who held power tended to want to keep it.

He started to lift a hand to his head and stopped himself. Yes, his shard was in there too – I'd made sure of it. "Thank you, Eminence. This will mean a lot to a lot of people. But the time of the constructs is not at an end."

I resisted the urge to shake the rain off my sleeves. "Which is one of the reasons I'm here. I'm sure you've heard: some of the constructs have organized and are bearing down on the north-eastern reaches of the Empire. We are recruiting more soldiers, but training takes time. I need the help of governors like you to halt this in its tracks."

"You want us to send our guards away?" His voice was incredulous. I waited, knowing he'd further explain if I let the silence grow. "The constructs have gone wild – you've admitted that yourself. And you want me to send our guards to the north-eastern reaches? What if they're needed here?"

"So you're telling me that thus far you've not had the same sort of problems with the constructs?" I said through gritted teeth. "It's for the good of the Empire."

He shook his head as though he were scolding a child. "We can discuss the good of the Empire later. Fetch the Emperor a fresh robe; the rain has sullied hers." The servant to his right nodded and left. "Please, let us get you settled in for your stay. And I'd be honored if you would join me and my court for dinner. I have other guests coming in from other parts of Riya, and they are eager to meet you."

When I placed a hand on the back of Thrana's neck, I felt her raised hackles. "Thank you, Sai. We would be pleased to join you."

But I caught the glimpse of a quirked lip before Iloh turned away, and I knew: I'd not yet won this battle.

14

——

Jovis

Riya Island

I found a (person/mortal/citizen?) drowned (or drowning) on the rocks of my island. (Two sentences that might be describing the person, something about hair and a shirt. Mephi was very uninterested in this bit.) How could I leave him to die? I took him back to my (dwelling/house/cave?), (healed?) him and fed him. When he could speak, he told me he was here to talk to me, but had gotten caught in a fight between two Alanga. He'd ended up shipwrecked.

His name is Ylan Sukai.

—Notes from Jovis's translation of Dione's journal

Iloh was an ass. It didn't take me long to come to that conclusion. Some faces were worn a certain way from one too many smug expressions, their assedness carved into the lines around mouth and eyes. The lines on Iloh's face were a map leading to only one destination: the capital of asses.

His servants showed us to our quarters, and Lin walked into her rooms. "Jovis, with me, please."

I followed and shut the door behind me. As soon as it clicked closed, she whirled. "I should have expected this." She was angry, but this time her anger wasn't directed at the governor or me. It was directed at herself. "I remove the constructs and they no longer fear my position. My father rarely visited, and now they see themselves as individual islands instead of part of the Empire." Thrana dogged her heels as she paced. "They think I'm young and foolish. They think they can push my temper and then take advantage of me."

Both Mephi and I watched her, and I thought it wise not to point out that her temper had clearly already been pushed. "Sometimes kindness is seen as weakness, Eminence," I said.

"Don't tell me what I already know," she snapped. And then she sank onto the couch by the window, burying her face in her hands. "I'm sorry, you don't deserve that sort of abuse."

Except I was sending messages to the Shardless Few behind her back. I stuffed the thought away. "I do my best to be useful." To more than one master. Guilt, it seemed, was a heavy burden not easily shaken.

"I wanted to ask you . . . Everyone loves you. Did you see the way he greeted you as opposed to the way he greeted me?"

"You wanted to ask me..?"

She pinched her nose. "I'm being rude. Please, be at ease."

I settled into the chair opposite the couch. My hair and jacket were still damp, warmed by my body and making me feel like a living swamp.

"How do I get them to look at me the way they look at you?"

Mephi looked up at me, as if also curious what my answer

might be. I ruffled his ears. "I'm not sure I know the answer to that, Eminence."

She made a little sound of frustration and looked out the window. "Then at least show me how you did it."

"Did what?"

"The water. Back when we were in Imperial City. Down in the entrance hall, when I was angry, I could feel the power in me. I knew I could make the ground shake if I chose to. I can't practice that here, so show me how you made the water move."

I hesitated, wondering what Gio would make of this. I would be helping her to grow more powerful, not less. I kept things vague. "It's hard to explain. When you feel that thrum in your bones, think about the water. When it works for me, I feel suddenly aware of all the water around me, of how much of it there is. And then I sort of just reach out and move it. With my mind."

She laughed, and then, seeing my lost expression, sobered. "I believe you, I do. It just sounds so strange. They do seem like Alanga powers, just not as strong and I haven't seen you control the wind. Wait – can you control the wind?"

"Imagine that power and a good sailboat. If I had the ability, I might have turned down Captain of the Imperial Guard and stayed a smuggler," I said lightly.

She closed her eyes, and I felt something in the room steady. I never seemed to realize how much she unsettled me until I wasn't looking at her anymore. She breathed in and out, deeply, and I knew that if I placed my hand on hers, I'd feel the tremor in her bones.

Why was I thinking about touching her? I needed to stop doing this. I wasn't even sure what "this" was.

Slowly, she extended a hand, her fingers unfurling like the petals of a flower. And then a droplet of rain outside stopped in mid-air, hovering. It moved languidly but with purpose, slipping between the opened shutters and floating above her hand.

She opened her eyes and let it drop into her palm.

I could barely breathe. How had she done that on her first try? The first time I'd even felt the water around me, I'd not known what to do with it. Even when I'd been at the height of desperation, trying to defend Mephi from the four-armed construct, I'd only managed clumsy whips of water. And here she had isolated a single drop of water and had bent it to her will.

I was on my feet without realizing I'd risen.

She stood up, and her gaze met mine. "Like that?"

And with her gaze I was thrown back into the past, to the time I'd gone diving with Emahla. Even when my lungs were bursting, she'd kept kicking, her feet disappearing ahead of me and past the reefs. But when she'd surfaced next to me, after I'd long since given up, there'd not been anything spiteful in her laughter.

"You're a fish," I'd said to her, still gasping in air. "It's hardly fair to think I could keep up."

"So you're in love with a fish?" she'd said, kicking closer to me.

"Can you blame me? She's a very beautiful fish." And then she'd kissed me and I'd lost what remained of my breath. Kissing her did that to me. Every single time. My chest ached. I'd accepted that she was gone, but thinking about her still hurt me as much as it brought me joy.

Lin still looked at me, waiting. "Yes, exactly like that," I said, still startled. "But Emahla—" I heard the name leave my lips as if someone else had uttered it. My chest tightened and I had the sudden sensation of falling, as though both floor and ground had disappeared. Shit. Shit shit shit.

Lin's brows drew together. I could see the crease between them. "Who is Emahla?"

"I meant to say 'Eminence'," I said, heat rising to my cheeks. Real smooth, Jovis. Real believable.

"But you said 'Emahla'."

I didn't know why I didn't want to tell her, only that the thought of it made my insides shrivel. "Someone I once knew. I'm sorry. Your eyes – they look like hers."

The crease between her eyes disappeared; the look she gave me was sad. Not as though she pitied me, but as though she could look past my feeble words and understood exactly what I meant. As if she knew how it felt to lose someone who had defined your life. And then, suddenly, I did want to tell her, because I knew she would understand. I wanted to tell her all of it. I opened my mouth.

A knock sounded at the door. "Eminence?"

Her gaze turned from me. "Come in."

I collapsed back into my chair, wanting nothing more than to shrink into it, to make myself unnoticeable.

A servant entered, a jacket draped over his arm. "I was asked to bring you this. We're a humble island in comparison to Imperial, so I'm afraid we do not have anything to match your station, Eminence."

A lie. The man had no ability to dissemble. He held out the jacket. It was a humble thing, brown, the embroidery unsteady, as though the hand stitching it had been more than just a little distracted. It looked like a child's jacket.

Lin shrugged off her robe, the light from the window glinting off sinewy shoulders. "I understand," she said. "And please tell the Sai that I appreciate the offer. But such a jacket will clearly not do."

"It's all we have to offer—"

She broke in smoothly, talking over the man's protests. "The jacket the Sai was wearing when we met will do nicely."

The servant sputtered. "It's a man's jacket."

"And I don't have the most womanly of figures."

The man bowed as he backed out of the room, making apologies as he went. He hadn't meant to comment on her Eminence's figure — that was not his intent. And of course, of course, the Sai's jacket would do.

"Is this how you intend to garner Riya's support?" I asked when the door had closed.

She threw up her hands. "I don't know what else to do. Should I let him bully me?"

"No, of course not. Quite literally taking the jacket off his back, though . . . "

"Petty, I know. But lying down and taking his polite abuse won't earn me his respect."

I had to admit — it wasn't just the eyes. There was something of Emahla's fierceness in this woman, her determination. She was the Emperor. I had to keep reminding myself of that, for more than one reason.

"Food?" Thrana said, startling me.

"They'll feed us soon enough," Mephi said to her.

"Ah," Lin said, smiling. "Our charges. I forgot to ask for food to be sent for them. I'll ask when I get the jacket." She lifted the headdress from her brow and placed it on the table. It still dripped from the rain. "We have a good deal of time before dinner. Go get dry and comfortable and make sure my guards are alert. I'll have food sent up for our little beasts when it's time for us to eat." She gave Thrana an affectionate scratch beneath the chin.

"Or our not-so-little beasts, more accurately." I eyed them both. If they kept growing, they'd be the size of ponies before long. That was a thought. Instead of Mephi curling around my neck as he had when he'd been small, perhaps I could curl around his. Foolishness, really. His growth had slowed lately.

She waved a dismissal at me, and I retreated out into the hall, Mephi on my heels. I snagged a servant by the elbow, asking which room was meant to be mine.

It was much, much smaller than Lin's, but I had it to myself, which was more than the other guards and maidservants could say.

I shrugged off my jacket, found a piece of parchment and dashed off a quick report to the Shardless Few. I'd searched for the sword Gio wanted and hadn't yet found it. Lin was meeting resistance to her rule on Riya. The constructs were an issue, and not just in the north-eastern reaches. But when it came to her burgeoning powers, I hesitated. I'd told her we should keep this between us, but lying came easily enough to me. I'd gone to Imperial to topple an Empire. Was I backing down now simply because the Emperor made me think of my dead wife?

I pressed the tip of my pen deep into the paper. No. It was more than that. She was also toppling the Empire, just in a different way. She was dismantling the constructs, returning the shards to the people. Would it be fair of me to destroy her rule without first knowing what it would be like?

I knew what Gio would say – that the people deserved to be ruled by themselves and not an Emperor. Perhaps he was right. But I also knew how fickle people could be, how much they could bicker, how they could argue over insignificant details, letting the larger issues pass by unaddressed.

And the issue of the Alanga loomed. Who were they? Were they all like me and Lin? If they were as dangerous as the Sukais had made them sound, then this was the worst possible time to dissolve the Emperor's rule.

Damn it. This was supposed to be simple.

I didn't mention her powers. But I wasn't a fool. At some point, I'd have to make a choice; I just didn't know when that point would arrive. I leaned back in my chair. "What am I supposed to do, Mephi? What do you do when you have difficult decisions to make?"

He didn't answer at first, and I could nearly see the gears in his mind working. When had Mephi actually had a difficult decision to make, except which fish to chase? "First," he said slowly, "make sure you are not hungry."

I laughed. That wasn't bad advice, actually. And I could use a bite to eat. "Let's go out into the city. I'll buy something for you. And there will be food when we get back."

According to the letter Gio had sent, I could find a Shardless Few contact in Riya, selling tortoiseshell carvings. I checked in with the guards before I left, assigning them shifts outside the Emperor's door up until dinner. And then, freed from momentary responsibility, I left my jacket out to dry in my room and made my way into the city.

Riya's capital wasn't ostentatious in its wealth, though it was obvious on more than a cursory glance. Stone lanterns were set at regular intervals, and despite the rain and mud, the streets were surprisingly clear of debris. The buildings were three, sometimes four, stories tall, painted white with wooden accents. There were enough awnings that I could keep from getting too wet if I hugged the sides of buildings. Mephi, on the other hand, trotted in the open street, stopping every so often to shake the rain from his coat — an action that did not endear him to passers-by. He shrugged when I gave him a mild admonishment. "I like the rain," he said. I stopped to purchase dumplings for both Mephi and me, tossing them to Mephi and watching him catch them out of the air. They steamed as I threw them, the paper sack of them in my hand almost too hot to touch, the oil seeping through. In my satchel, the note to the Shardless Few pressed against Dione's journal. He'd spoken about meeting Ylan Sukai — the first Emperor. This was something none of the legends or stories had mentioned. I wasn't sure why.

The spy's store wasn't far from the palace, the door propped open. I ducked beneath the awning and felt cold water drip onto my neck.

Perhaps it was just the water, and the shiver that crept down my spine, but I had the strange sensation: I was being watched. I turned and saw only the people passing in the street. Mephi looked up at me, confused. "Everything fine?" he whispered.

I patted his head in response. But I wasn't sure it was. The last time I'd felt this way I'd been attacked by one of the Empire's constructs and almost killed.

Uneasy and unsettled, I turned back to the shop. An array of carved tortoiseshell items met my gaze. A man worked on yet another piece in the corner. He gave me a questioning look, which I waved away as I browsed his wares. Just paranoia. Still, the streets of Riya, which had felt safe just a moment before, now felt dangerous.

I picked out a comb, and slid the note to the vendor with the coin. He palmed both without even giving me a second glance.

Again, the sensation I was being watched.

"Jovis," Mephi hissed out.

I whirled, and this time, I caught a glimpse of a foot disappearing around the corner.

15
Lin
Riya Island

My maidservants had finished preparing me for dinner when Jovis stormed inside my room, Mephi bounding behind him. "Are you having me followed?" My maidservants gave him wide berth as they left the room, sensing the anger roiling off of him like a storm front wind.

"Would it be a surprise if I was?" I asked. "You act like it's within your rights to have more privacy."

"So this is what it's like to be your citizen," he said, his eyes narrowed. "Followed at every turn, every move watched. How like your father."

I was on my feet, Thrana growling next to me, before I could remember having risen. "In case you've forgotten, you *broke into* my private rooms. You seem to always find yourself in places I'd rather you not be. And now you accuse me of having you followed? Are you really in any position to accuse me of anything?"

"As I already explained, it is my duty to protect you," he said. "Who will everyone blame if you turn up dead?"

He sounded like he believed it, but all good liars believed their lies. "You're my Captain of the Imperial Guard. You're supposed to obey me; you're not supposed to be poking around my things!"

Mephi only looked at Thrana, his head tilted to the side. But then Jovis was standing before me, just as angry as I was, and I hated that I had to lean my head back to look him in the eye.

"Then maybe you should have chosen someone you felt you could *trust*," he said. "Instead you chose a half-Poyer smuggler who defied your father."

Someone I could trust? There was no one I could trust. No one who knew me, who cared about me, who understood what I'd faced. All I had was Thrana. To my abject embarrassment, I felt hot tears prickle at my eyes. I swallowed past the lump in my throat and steadied myself. "And you think these things make you untrustworthy?"

For a moment he just looked confused. And then all the fight drained out of him. "No, Eminence, that's not what I meant to say. I swore to protect you. I also swore to serve the people. If I seem overly curious, that's why. No one really knows who you are. Not yet."

Of course. It had seemed a grand gesture at the time, making that the focus of his oath. Now I was the one who felt foolish. I chose my next words carefully. "I did not have you followed. I should have led with that."

He studied my face for a moment and then let out a breath. "I believe you. And I suppose I couldn't fault you if you had. I will try to be more open with you, but I need the same back from you."

"I'll try." I couldn't try. I imagined telling this man that I wasn't actually the Emperor's daughter, that I was a facsimile, that I was a thing he'd created. Not a construct, but a person grown in the strange waters below the palace. What a stupid thought. It was like the terrible temptation to stick one's hand inside the mouth of a freshly caught shark. Such a confession would destroy me and everything I was trying to build.

Thrana settled, and Mephi cautiously approached, sniffing her cheek. She snapped at him, still riled.

I was aware, suddenly, that I was standing too close to him, that I could feel his breath tickling the hair at my forehead. He wasn't wearing his jacket, and the tunic beneath was sleeveless, revealing lean but firmly muscled shoulders. I took a surreptitious step back, kneeling to stroke Thrana's neck and calm her. She'd had a rougher upbringing than Mephi and was so much more volatile.

"I went into the city. It was a very boring trip," he said, attempting a wry smile. "No gambling, no courtesans."

I blushed to think of him with courtesans. Would he tangle his fingers in their unbound hair? Whisper jests into their ears? I brushed the thoughts aside. "Why did you think I'd had you followed?"

The smile faltered. "Because someone *was* following me, Eminence."

I almost regretted this retreat into formality, but would I really rather us be shouting at one another? "Did Iloh set someone to it, then?"

He shrugged. "I'm not sure. I only caught a glimpse, and nothing recognizable. But I've been followed before, and I know the feeling. Maybe—"

A soft knock sounded at my door. A servant peeked into the room, her gaze on the floor. "Eminence, dinner will be served shortly. It would honor us if you and your Captain of the Imperial Guard joined us in the dining hall." She closed the door behind her.

"It could have been Iloh," I said. "I'd believe it of him. He doesn't even know me, but he clearly already dislikes me," I said, rising to my feet. Thrana butted my thigh with her horns. "Keep an eye out."

Another knock sounded at the door, and another servant brought in platters heaped with freshly caught fish and squid. "The governor hopes this suffices?"

At least in this Iloh hadn't tried to insult me. I'd weather his other insults, but I'd rend him limb from limb if he thought to do poorly by Thrana. "Yes, thank you."

Both our creatures pounced on the trays as soon as they were set down. They'd be occupied while we were gone.

"Into the den of bears, then?" Jovis said.

"Fetch your jacket and let's make our way to the dining hall. You forget: I've lived in a den of my father's constructs. Surely this can't be worse."

It was worse.

The other guests had already been seated by the time we made our way to the dining hall, so that when I entered, Jovis on my heels, everyone turned at once to scrutinize me. I was glad I'd asked for Iloh's jacket. It might have been a man's jacket, but it fit me. I'd forgone the heavy headdress, but I tipped my chin up and strode to the two empty cushions, hoping I conveyed power and dignity. Jovis was seated at my right hand, and he shifted on his cushion as everyone looked at him, obviously uncomfortable with the attention.

"Thank you for joining us, Eminence." Iloh was seated across from me. "The jacket suits you nicely."

"Thank you for sending it," I said, willing myself to be gracious. I needed this man to be my friend, after all.

"Allow me to introduce my other guests." He went around the table, giving the names and positions of the seven other people seated for dinner. I did my best to remember them. There was the mining supervisor on Riya, a ceramics artist, three close relatives of Iloh, a visiting governor from a nearby isle and a wealthy landlord.

The woman seated to my left was Pulan, the visiting governor. She was soft-spoken and had a pleasant manner about her; she wouldn't meet my gaze, but smiled when she spoke. I struck up a conversation with her as the food was being served, and learned that her isle had its own, smaller witstone mine.

The supervisor of Riya's witstone mine was seated next to Jovis, and I heard him rather boisterously asking after Jovis's magic. "You set those Imperial soldiers on their heels, I heard," he said. "Gave them something to remember you by, didn't you? And now you're one of them. Hilarious, isn't it?"

"I'm the Captain of the Imperial Guard," Jovis said smoothly. "Hardly a soldier."

"Is it true you're from some backwater isle? You carry yourself like a Sai, even if you are half-Poyer."

Not really the flattering assessment the man intended. But Jovis only smiled. "I'm from a backwater, it's true, and was a smuggler to boot. Can you tell my mother I carry myself like a Sai? I'd appreciate the gesture. She is constantly disappointed in me."

The supervisor laughed and slapped the table. "Ah, so she's the Empirean one, then. You have my sympathies, Captain."

Would that I could so easily win over the table.

In Riya, food was served on large platters, placed in the center of the table for everyone to share. Servants shifted the position of the dishes every so often to ensure that everyone could have their fill. I'd researched this ahead of time, so at least I hadn't embarrassed myself by bringing a maidservant to test my food.

I followed everyone else's lead, reaching out with my chopsticks to serve myself. Mustard greens drizzled with a dark, salted sauce, steamed white fish with scallions and peppercorns, fried turnip cakes with bits of dense sausage. I had to admit: Iloh had not skimped on this dinner as much as he'd skimped on everything else meant to honor me.

Iloh's sister sat across from me, and she smiled as I set down my cup of tea. "It's been a very long time since an Emperor has graced us with their presence," she said. "The last time was after your father was newly married, before you were even born. We're grateful you're ending the Tithing Festival, but this change in regime gives me cause to ask: why do we need you?"

The corner of Iloh's mouth quirked again and I knew he'd put her up to this. She wasn't the governor and could speak more plainly while Iloh claimed he did not feel the same way she did. I found myself pressing a hand to the floor, my bones humming with magic. "You need me the same way you always have. The Empire must be united to stand against threats, including the Alanga. Give me your vocal support and the Empire will continue to stand."

"What happens if we don't?"

The table fell silent. I gritted my teeth and felt the power leak from my palm into the floor. The dishes rattled and more than one person glanced at the ground, fearing a quake. A hand touched my knee beneath the table. Jovis.

I was letting myself lose control. Before I could stop myself, I might be lifting water from teacups. I'd never forget the hateful, contemptuous look on the guard's face when he'd spat on the assassin's body. *Alanga*. I took a deep breath, lifted my hand and the dishes quieted. "We stand together or we fall to outside forces."

"Forgive my sister," Iloh broke in smoothly. "But you've begun to dismantle the constructs. You're ending the Tithing Festival. Your army is small. If the Alanga are returning, how are we meant to fight them?"

"*I* will fight them," I snapped back.

Iloh only looked amused, lifting his teacup to hide his smile. A few other people at the table stifled giggles. Here I was, a young slip of a woman, dressed in his jacket, claiming I would single-handedly fight the Alanga. I'd come here wanting to project power and grace; instead I seemed a child throwing a tantrum, making threats I couldn't follow through on. I was slipping in their regard, though I'd not been very high to begin with.

If I failed at this, if I could not win this man over, my already precarious rule tipped into unsustainable. Someone else would step into the power vacuum. Someone else would try to lead. I wouldn't just be thrown out of the palace; I'd be hunted down and killed. I could do so much good with my power – if I could keep it.

I lifted the teapot to pour myself another cup, waiting until the conversation around me had roused once more. I needed to get control of myself. I needed to find a way to charm this den of bears. I could feel Jovis's presence at my side, his shoulder warm against mine as he reached for a piece of roasted duck.

He had a disarming way about him – self-deprecating, affable. I couldn't be like him. But I had other assets.

What were my strengths? I could read stories on people's faces when I tried. I'd spent too much time talking, not enough time listening. Acting chastened and embarrassed, which was not that hard given the circumstances, I turned my focus to the faces in the room.

What I found there surprised me. They all liked Iloh. Not the way a sycophant does, but they genuinely liked him. They laughed at his jokes, vied for his attention, basked in it when it was received. And Iloh, for his part, was generous with his subjects. Had I misjudged him? If I had, why did he treat me so poorly?

And then I noticed something else. While he bestowed his favor on all, his gaze lingered on Pulan, the visiting governor. She did not seem ignorant of these looks. Her expression was hopeful yet sad, the way a pup might regard a meal she knows she will never get a piece of. I watched her swallow and avert her gaze, her fingers clasping tightly beneath the table.

"Are you married, Sai?" I leaned in to ask her.

Her gaze flicked to Iloh before she shook her head. "No, Eminence."

I stayed silent, waiting.

Like most people would, she rushed to fill the silence. "I know, it's odd for a woman my age, and a governor. I have no heirs."

"You could adopt—"

Flashes of color marred her cheeks, and she met my gaze for the first time. "If that was what I wanted." Her eyelashes fluttered as she looked away again. "Forgive me. It's just something I've heard far too often."

"It's not your first choice," I said, hoping to keep her talking.

She laughed, a little bitterly. "No. I wish he'd stop inviting me to these things." And then she lifted her mug as if to stop her words and wouldn't say anything further to me.

I caught Iloh watching us. He was unmarried as well. Pieces began to click together in my mind. There was something going on between them; I just wasn't sure exactly what.

I'd done what research I could before arriving. I knew that Iloh's father had died in a boating accident, and his mother had died on the younger side of old. Iloh had taken over the governorship before his mother's death. He had not married and had not named an heir.

At his age, he should do it soon. I knew all too well the chaos that might ensue if he died without an heir. So then why hadn't he married? And did Pulan have anything to do with it?

Dinner finished without any further embarrassing incidents, but then I'd resolved to keep my mouth shut. We were invited to walk the grounds of the palace, servants moving from room to room with sweets and freshly sliced fruits.

I tapped Jovis's elbow as we moved into the courtyard. The rain had stopped, leaving the air warm and damp. Lamps were mounted on the pillars, flickering with the wind. "I need a little space," I said to him.

He frowned. "Is that wise?"

"He won't try to murder me, not in his own court," I said.

"But you don't deny he . . . might try to murder you?" Jovis raised an eyebrow.

"Well, he certainly doesn't *like* me very much. But I need to speak to him. Alone."

Jovis leaned in before I could leave. "His mother," he said. "She was shard-sick and that was what killed her. The mine supervisor let it slip while we were talking. Iloh doesn't want anyone to know. The family hid it."

I stopped to consider this. My father knew who each of the shards belonged to. He kept meticulous notes. It was enough to hold the shards of the governors; he didn't need to use them. Unless he'd done so intentionally. A punishment. Yes, that would be like him.

No wonder Iloh hated me. "I'll be careful," I told Jovis.

I passed the ceramics artist and the landlord, and found Iloh by a pillar on the far end of the courtyard. He turned a little, saw me and his lip curled.

"I'm not my father," I said before he could say anything to spur my temper. "I don't intend to rule the way he did."

"So you say." He took a sip of his drink and grimaced, as though it were bitter. "Eminence."

"I came here in good faith."

"Your father spoke of protecting us from the Alanga too, you know," Iloh said. "The artifacts are awakening. Is this the best time to stop using constructs, to disrupt the world order?"

He didn't believe what he was saying. "There is never a good time. But it needed to be done."

Iloh looked me up and down, weighing me with his gaze. "And you were the one to do it? You Emperors, all so full of grandeur. Tell me, Eminence, how does this all help me?"

I took a gamble. "Why haven't you married Pulan?"

He took a step back, nearly spilling the drink in his hand. "How did you . . . ? Did *she* tell you?"

"Pulan told me nothing. I can see it on your faces."

He took another drink, though his fingers trembled. "I shouldn't keep inviting her to these things."

"You wanted to see her."

His lips pressed together. "I heard your father would do the same thing – just look right through a person. It isn't exactly pleasant."

Yes, though my father would have let a person sit in that discomfort and then used the information against them. "Apologies," I said. "I caught you off guard. But perhaps I can help?"

He gave me a sidelong glance and barked out a laugh. "No one but the old gods could help me, I think. My father left debts behind, and I need to marry advantageously. Pulan's isle isn't valuable enough."

"It has a witstone mine," I said.

"A small one," he said.

"I have resources. I can help develop the mine. It would give you leave to marry her."

He looked at me, a bit incredulous. "And what do you gain?"

"Your support. A higher tithe of witstone."

"I shouldn't have led with that. There are other problems." He downed the glass, his posture unsteady. "Pulan wants children."

His words settled like a stone in my belly. "You can't have them."

He swirled the dregs and eyed me over the rim of his cup, his lips pressed together. For a moment, he didn't say anything, his gaze fixed on mine. I could feel the weight of it as he judged me. And then he let out a breath. "I thought I'd have them when I was ready, when I wanted them. But I've had more than my share of philandering in my youth and not once – not once! – have I ever produced a child. Even when I stopped caring about preventing it." He raised his eyebrows. "I thought to mock you when you came here and look, now you have ample material to mock me with."

"I'm here to build alliances," I said. "I'm not here to mock you. But perhaps you should let Pulan decide if that is a barrier."

"She—"

A screech sounded from the second floor. My heart jolted. I'd know that voice anywhere.

Thrana.

16

Phalue

Nephilanu Island

Phalue would have liked to say that Ayesh cleaned up well. But all the first bath had done was to outline the painful way the girl's skin stretched over her bones. The hair was a lost cause and full of nits, though Ayesh didn't seem to mind when they cut it close to her head. She ate voraciously, and then vomited, and then tried again, more slowly. The second time she'd been able to keep the food down.

Phalue had meant to send the girl on her way after she'd been fed and cleaned and they'd had the chance to ask her a few questions. But the physician who'd looked at her said she'd be back within a day if they sent her away in her condition. Or worse – dead.

So she stayed, first one night, and then another, and when she finally was too restless to stay in bed, Ranami and Phalue brought her to their sitting room and asked her about Unta.

Reports had trickled in over the past few days as scattered refugees found their way to Nephilanu. Most had stopped at islands closer to Unta, though others had sailed farther – as though afraid that whatever had sank Unta would reach beyond the borders of the island and into the Endless Sea.

There was something quick and anxious about the girl's walk as she made her way into the sitting room; she picked her feet up soon after setting them down, her gaze darting into every corner. She sat in the cushioned chair across from them, though she checked behind her more than once, her back to the hallway door. Ranami had set the chair there, and now Phalue wondered if that had been a deliberate choice. Did she mean to make Ayesh uncomfortable?

"Can I go yet?" she asked as soon as she sat down.

Phalue picked up a tray of egg tarts and proffered it. The girl took a tart gingerly and then nibbled at the outside of it, as if afraid she had to make it last. Phalue cleared her throat while she ate. "We've heard reports about Unta, but you were there. How did it happen?"

Ayesh took her time finishing the tart, her black eyes wide. Ranami sighed. Phalue cast her a "be patient" look. After all, the girl had been through something more traumatizing than either of them could imagine.

"There were little earthquakes first," Ayesh said once she'd finished. "Some of them, people didn't even notice. There are earthquakes sometimes. But then there was a big one. I was by the docks trying to catch some fish when it hit. Traded with another kid for line and hooks." She bit her lip. "Dropped them in the water when it hit. Just the one hand, see? Everything shook. A couple buildings fell down. When it stopped, I tried to get my line out of the water with a stick. Was in the middle of that when another one hit.

"This one was bigger. And it didn't stop. Everything started creaking and rumbling and falling over. People were screaming."

"But you got off the island," Phalue said, encouraging her.

"I was at the docks," she said. "I didn't bother going back or trying to find anyone. I just went straight to the nearest boat I thought I could hide on. People were going to try and escape but I couldn't sail. It was the only thing I could think of – making sure I lived."

She looked at her fingers, rubbing off the remnant of crumbs, her lips pressed together. "I don't think any of the kids I knew did."

Phalue pressed on; she had to know. "The entire island is gone?"

Ayesh shrugged. "I was in the hold. But I heard what the people in the boat were saying – and that's what they said. There was a lot of shouting, a lot of gasps, a lot of crying. The crying went on for a long time. I'd hear them come down to the hold sometimes at night, just looking for somewhere private to let it out."

"Did anyone say why it sank?" Ranami asked.

Ayesh shrugged, her gaze tracing the beams of the ceiling. "I don't think anyone knew. Not for sure."

There was a witstone mine on Unta – Phalue remembered that much. It was the explanation the previous Emperor had given for Deerhead: a mining accident. But there were witstone mines on so many islands. Did that mean they were all at risk? Had the man been hiding something, or had he – on this rare occasion – spoken the open truth?

"Did you see anything that might tell you why it sank?" Phalue asked.

Ayesh let out a short laugh. "I'm a gutter orphan; you think I look for things like that? I was too busy trying to get my damned line out of the water. I'm not looking for explanations. I'm looking to live. Can I go now?"

Phalue exchanged a glance with Ranami. The girl had

answered their questions. She wasn't a spy; she wasn't leveraging her place here. A spy would have tried to stay, would have wedged herself into palace life. Phalue nodded.

Ayesh rose to her feet and then stopped, hesitated. She plucked at the fresh tunic she wore. "Can I have my old clothes back?"

Her ... clothes? They weren't clothes; they were rags. "What? Why?"

Ranami put a hand on Phalue's arm. "She can't go back into the city like that. The other orphans will see her as having more. She'll become a target."

The servants had likely thrown out the wet, stinking scraps as soon as they'd peeled them off from Ayesh's body. "The servants will find you something appropriate. Ranami, do you mind . . . ?"

Ranami rose to her feet and ushered the girl out of the room.

Ayesh stopped at the door. "Thank you, Sai," she said. And then they were both gone.

Phalue stretched her legs out and rolled her shoulders before getting up. She would have to deal with the sinking of Unta, with the questions, with any incoming refugees and her own frightened citizens. Not to mention Gio and the Shardless Few. She didn't trust the temporary truce. But at this moment, she had a sparring match with Tythus, and those always helped her think.

She belted on her sword, fastened her armor and made her way to the palace courtyard. It was blessedly dry today – or at least, as dry as a wet season got. The stones were still damp, the air still moist, but there was no rain at that moment, and that was a welcome change.

A shout rose from the walls right as she was stepping outside. She frowned, watching the guards on the walls ready their bows.

Tythus strode to meet her. He was a similar age, height and build as she was – which made him a perfect sparring partner. But he was also a friend, one she'd come to appreciate almost too late.

If he hadn't freed her, the Shardless Few would have found her still in the cell her father had put her in, and placed a convenient knife between her ribs. "Constructs," he said when he was close. "Harrying a supply wagon."

"How many?"

"Two. The driver is only just holding them off. Didn't think we'd need guards on the wagons up from the city. I'll have to change that. It's not safe outside the palace anymore. Not until we're able to take care of all the constructs."

Ranami was nowhere to be seen; she must still be tending to Ayesh. Phalue tapped the hilt of her sword. "Well, let's go help."

Tythus gave her a wry look. "I'm supposed to be sparring with you, not fighting war constructs with you. Ranami will be annoyed."

"Tell her I ordered you to do it." She went to the gates, Tythus on her heels. Ever since her meeting with Gio, she'd been feeling frustrated, pent up. She didn't have the numbers to fight him head on, and she didn't know how to deal with the constant, shadowy threat of assassination. It put Ranami on edge; it put her on edge.

The wagon had stopped a little way outside the gates. Two constructs stood between it and the palace walls, snapping at the oxen. The driver was shouting and had a walking stick in her hands. She swung it at them, barely keeping them at bay.

"Shoot if they get close to the gates," Tythus called up to the guards. "We'll engage them on the ground."

They approached the war constructs shoulder to shoulder, their strides matching. Both constructs were pieced together from wolves and giant cats; one had a bushy wolf tail and the other a lashing leopard's tail. Both had teeth and claws that glittered in the wan sunlight.

The constructs were so intent on the oxen and driver that they didn't notice Phalue's and Tythus's approach. They lifted their swords in unison and attacked.

The constructs whirled at the last minute.

They hadn't seemed so large back when Phalue had been standing at the gates. But each was almost as big as the oxen hauling the cart. Perhaps this hadn't been the best idea. She did have guards for this very reason, after all. But then the golden, spotted beast in front of her swiped out with a heavy paw, and Phalue had no more time for regrets.

She leapt back, the claws raking grooves in her boot, catching skin beneath. Sparring with Tythus was different than facing down a beast. Phalue slashed at it and the creature slid below her strike, its belly to the ground. She could see Tythus out of the corner of her eye faring better than she was. But he'd been in actual fights while she never had.

Phalue clenched her jaw, dodged another swipe and thrust at the construct. This time, she caught it on the shoulder. A glancing blow, which only seemed to make the creature angrier, but it was something. This could be like sparring with Tythus. The constructs were shorter, steadier on their feet, and with more pointy ends. She could adjust.

Four more strikes and her blade sank into the creature's side, scraping past ribs to find the vital organs beneath.

Tythus had already dispatched his construct and stood off to the side, watching her. Show off. He looked barely winded.

In contrast, her calf burned where the construct's claws had caught her leg. She waved the wagon driver toward the palace. "The way is clear now."

She bowed. "Thank you, Sai. I knew the constructs were out of hand, but I didn't know it was this bad." She went back to the wagon and tucked her walking stick into the back.

Phalue went to Tythus, dropping a hand on his shoulder. "Gio agreed to a truce," she said. "We need to start clearing out the constructs now, before any other people get hurt. Take all but a few of the guards and start running patrols in the city and the other villages on the island. Listen to any rumors about construct attacks. Eliminate them as quickly as possible. We focus all our efforts on that."

"That leaves the palace vulnerable. Do you trust Gio's word?"

Phalue shook her head. "I don't, but I have to hope he'll keep it." They'd been keeping the caro nuts from shipping, paying the farmers but storing the nuts at the warehouses instead of sending them to Imperial. If Gio had any honor at all, he'd halt his plans for taking over Nephilanu. "I'd meant to ask before we got distracted: how is the family?"

Tythus barked out a laugh. "The same, mostly. My youngest came down with a fever. My wife was worried for a moment it might be the bog cough, but it cleared up after a few days."

He'd always asked about her and she'd not known much about him – and she hadn't bothered to find out. It was one of the things she was trying to remedy: her awareness of her place in the world and how that affected others.

Tythus's gaze went past her. "Looks like we've been caught."

Ayesh stood beneath the archway, dressed in the hand-me-downs of a servant's child, a bundle clasped in her arms, hand curled around the top of it. She stared down at them as the supply wagon passed into the courtyard. Ranami stood behind the girl, her expression irritated. "You're a governor," Ayesh called out. "You know how to fight?"

Phalue beckoned her over. If she wanted to ask questions, she should do it up close.

Ranami crossed her arms, casting Phalue a questioning look. Phalue shrugged – what harm could it do to answer before the girl returned to the streets?

There was nothing hesitant in her step this time. She hurried over, nearly dropping the bundle. Someone in the kitchens had packed her buns and rice dumplings; faint trails of steam still rose from the package. There was a blanket too, and an oilskin cloak. "You know how to fight?" Ayesh asked again.

"I learned when I was young," Phalue said. "My father indulged me, and I never stopped practicing."

"Every day," Tythus said next to her. "And she ropes me into this torture."

"She makes you practice with her," Ayesh said flatly.

Tythus raised an eyebrow. "No, she doesn't make me. It keeps me fit. Phalue is a good sparring partner. And a good friend."

The words warmed her in a way she hadn't expected. Ayesh studied Phalue, as if trying to figure out whether Tythus was telling the truth. She skirted around them and started down the path to the city.

"Strange child," Tythus muttered as she walked away.

But before she reached the first turn in the switchbacks, she stopped, turned again. "Can you teach me?"

Phalue frowned. "Teach you?"

"To fight," Ayesh said, trudging back up the path once more. "I'm small, I know. But that's why people think they can pick on me. I want to stand up for myself. I need to."

There was something in the stubborn set of the girl's lips that reminded Phalue of a time long ago. She'd stood in front of her father in the dining hall as he lounged with a woman on his arm — one she didn't recognize — a mug of wine held in the other hand. At twelve, she was already too tall, her shoulders too broad; her hands and feet felt like oversized leaves at the end of slender branches. Around her, the sounds of laughter and revelry continued unabated. "I want to learn how to fight," she'd said. She'd had to shout it again to be heard above the noise. She'd asked once before during a formal dinner and had been denied. But, watching her father, she'd come to understand: he was a bit more lax when he was intoxicated.

Her father lifted a hand and lowered it, and the noise around him quieted a little. "You're a governor's child. You don't need to learn how to fight; you've got guards to take you into the city when you want to see your mother. You asked me once already and the answer was 'no'."

Phalue set her jaw. Visiting her mother surrounded by guards was never a relaxing proposition. "And I'm asking again."

Her father peered at her and the conversation quieted further. She'd never been so aware of being so alone. Her mother had left the palace half a year ago. It was just her and her father and always so many strangers she didn't know. She needed this.

And then he'd laughed, raised his mug and leaned back in his chair. "Very well. I'll find someone to teach you."

Fortunately, her father had been the sort of drunk who still remembered his promises.

Ayesh hadn't moved, her jaw still set, her bundle of food and clothes still clutched in her arms. She was small, no one could deny that. There was the missing hand too, but there were ways around that. These were reasons to teach her, not to deny her. It would even out the girl's disadvantages and improve her chances in the city. Wouldn't that be something Phalue could do to help? And she spent this time in the practice yard already.

If Phalue told her no, would the girl even move? Or would she ask again, as Phalue had? She had a feeling she knew the answer.

"I'll teach you," Phalue said. "Come back here every morning around this time. Every morning, mind you – this takes dedication. I'll give you lessons."

A grin broke out across the girl's face – the first Phalue had seen from her. "I will." She marched down the road without looking back.

Phalue looked up to find Ranami staring at her. Ah, she should have discussed it with her wife first. Especially after going out to fight the constructs. She knew she often acted impulsively; it was one of the things she was working on. Tythus sheathed his sword and they went to meet Ranami at the gates.

Phalue might have worn her feelings like a second skin, but Ranami, when she was upset, didn't do much better.

"Dismissed for the day?" Tythus asked.

Phalue nodded to him and he retreated into the palace. She wished she could do the same. "I should have asked," she said to Ranami. "I didn't think she would take 'no' for an answer."

Ranami closed her eyes. "You're the governor. You shouldn't be battling constructs or teaching street orphans how to use a sword."

"I'm also someone who was once a girl and wanted to learn how to fight."

"She'll be in the palace every day. We can't afford to bring in new people right now, not with the Shardless Few at odds with us."

"Then how will we ever adopt anyone?" Phalue asked. "You have to trust someone, dearest."

"I trust you," Ranami said.

"Then trust me on this," Phalue said. "The girl is harmless."

She hoped she was right.

17

Nisong

An island in the north-eastern reaches of the Empire

Her spy construct had returned from Imperial after they'd conquered the third island. "There's a man in a cave below the palace. He sleeps in the water," the gull said, perching on the windowsill of the governor's suite.

It was a third-level construct, not complex enough to relay much more than the words others had spoken. Nisong pressed it for a description. The description was sparse, but she knew: it was Shiyen.

Shiyen was dead, but then so was Nisong. He'd created her — why not create an approximation of himself too? Something swooped within her, filling her with yearning. In her memories, he'd loved her. In her memories, they'd been happy.

But that wasn't the only information it brought. The Empire had arrived.

The soldiers stole onto her island under cover of nightfall, emerging from the darkness with the howling winds. The spy construct had been right about the attack. Nisong could only see flashes of lamps and torches from her vantage point in the palace, hear the distant clash of metal against metal and the growls of her beasts. As much as she wanted to be out there in the thick of it, she had more important tasks to attend to.

Five villagers knelt before her, their heads bowed. Blood ran in rivulets from behind their ears, gathering at their chins and dripping onto the wooden floor. All but one trembled. There hadn't been time to find opium to ease their pain. A small regret, one she could live with.

She sifted the shards in her hand, blood and hair and pieces of scalp still attached. "Let them go," she said to Leaf. "Bring in the next five. I'll need more."

Two bodies had been laid on a blanket by the bed. A better ratio than was usually had at the Tithing Festival. They could be a little pleased about that at least. Her constructs had steady hands and a good deal of strength. The process had been quick. Why use soldiers? She would have to suggest this method to Shiyen when—

Ah, of course. Sometimes it felt like she was living two different lives, split across two different times.

The shards clinked to the bottom of the clay bowl when she dropped them into the water, blood clouding it like red fog. Nisong turned to the shards she'd already cleaned and, while her constructs marched the villagers out and brought in a fresh batch, began to carve.

She knew the commands; she knew the method to reach inside dead flesh. Bureaucratic constructs could perform minor repairs on other constructs. So she'd realized from a logical standpoint, there was nothing stopping her from creating them.

Three of the five next villagers screamed as the chisel was applied, one grunted, the last one whimpered. Nisong gritted her

teeth through the noise, concentrating on her task. These constructs needed to fight for her, and to do so with some proficiency.
She'd written out commands on sheets of paper before creating
the first of them, trying to find a balance between complexity of
commands and using as few shards as possible. And the gaps in
her memories frustrated her – there had to be other, better commands but she had no memory of them. She had to be ruthlessly
efficient or this wouldn't work.

Her gaze flicked to the window again as the roar of fighting
drifted above the sound of pounding rain. The villagers knelt
trembling on the floor, their shuddering breaths like the sound of
waves inside a seashell. She held out a hand and Leaf deposited
the shards into her palm. "The next ones."

The shards had cooled by the time she scooped them out of
the water and replaced them with the fresh ones. She picked off
the skin and hair, dried them on her already bloodied skirt and
carved them too.

"So what – you'll drain us twice as fast?" called out one of
the villagers as Leaf and the beasts escorted her from the room.
"You monster!"

Nisong didn't respond. If their first shard was already in use,
then she supposed she would be doing that. But how much could
she care for the shard-sick when she had her own people to protect?

The gull construct landed on the windowsill. It shook off the
rain, sending droplets scattering across the floor to mingle with
the blood. "The invaders have taken down the largest barricade
and our archers are out of arrows."

"How long?" Nisong said, judging her pile of carved shards.
It could be enough. It might be enough. If she sent out too few at
once, they'd lose any numbers advantage. The constructs she was
creating wouldn't be Tirang, or even second-tier war constructs.
They'd be something a little less than third-tier. Skill wouldn't

be on their side. The previous isle had been small; even after her constructs had rounded up the corpses of the people they'd killed, there weren't enough. She needed more dead flesh to make enough constructs to defend against the Empire's soldiers.

They'd had to create more bodies on this island.

The gull tilted its head, as though that might help it peer through the rainy streets below. "Not long. We put the most time into the first barricade. They'll be at the palace walls soon, and those are more decorative than defensive."

"Quickly," she said to Leaf. "Fifteen more, all at once."

He raised an eyebrow and leaned in. "Nisong, is that wise? If they choose to resist, that's more than we can reasonably handle. I know we're desperate, but so are they."

She closed her eyes. "Bring the children."

To Leaf's credit, he hesitated only a moment before leaving the room. She didn't want to tithe the younger ones; she'd argued before against putting children through the Tithing. But their doom was fast approaching and regrets could be addressed later. Shiyen had said the memories of children were duller so it was doing them a favor. And it had always been done thus. She reached reflexively behind her right ear. The skin there was smooth, no soft spot she could feel. He'd repaired the blemish before placing the commands and memories within her body. She wasn't sure why he'd bothered doing that and then hadn't added back the missing two fingers of her left hand. Or perhaps she'd lost those later and had forgotten.

She had no memories of the Festival. Her fingers ached as she carved the next five shards, as the children were brought in, shaking and crying. A few reached new hysterical heights as they entered. Oh – the bodies next to the bed; she should have at least hidden the bodies. Too late for that now. Better to be done quickly than to drag this out. She signaled to Leaf, who took the hammer and chisel in hand.

They cried, yes, but they didn't scream. One casualty of the fifteen – a girl who wouldn't stay still when she was asked to. Her shard would be useless.

The gull called from its perch at the windowsill. "The soldiers are at the gates."

No time to debate ethics. Nisong gathered the last fourteen shards, cleaning and carving them as quickly as her shaking hands would allow. She thought the lettering was still accurate enough to work. There was only one way to find out.

Outside, she heard a crack. Lightning? But there'd been no flash. The gates – they must have found something to batter them with. The soldiers could climb the walls, but she supposed they didn't know what was waiting on the other side – not for sure.

"Everyone to the gates, including the prisoners," she said. "Now."

Constructs were better than people this way. They moved quickly to obey – no confusion or questions or hushed whispers.

In the courtyard, the rain hammered at the paving stones. Every footstep seeped moisture into her weathered shoes. Strange, that even now, she could still be irritated at the feeling of cold water between her toes, at the squish of wet fabric. The commands clacked together in her three separate pouches, barely audible above the sound of the storm.

Something pounded again at the gates.

The villagers she'd taken prisoner huddled in a group, hands pressed to wounds, arms wrapped around hurting children. Surely some of the attacking party had family or friends on this isle; surely if it came to it she could use them as hostages. But then the crowd behind the gates roared, and she knew: they would not stop to ask questions or to hear any negotiation attempts.

To them, she was just a monster, mindless and hungry.

The bodies were piled in a corner of the courtyard. Someone, she wasn't sure who, had gathered juniper to burn with them. A kind gesture, but a waste of time. She darted to the bodies as the din outside the gates rose.

Coral knelt next to her as she worked. "They'll breach soon."

"Get a weapon." She took Coral's arm, guiding her toward the palace. "Keep yourself safe."

Frond stepped away from the constructs lined up by the gate, knife in hand. He still held the carving he'd been working on — a bird in flight, the feathers almost complete. He looked at it as though he'd forgotten he held it, and then knelt to set it on the ground. "I'll be your weapon," he said. "Someone should protect you while you work."

She wouldn't have chosen Frond, but there wasn't time to assemble constructs to guard her. And would it even make a difference once the soldiers broke in past the gates? Frond was a carver, not a fighter. He was short, his hair constantly in his eyes, his gaze always distant. He didn't belong on a battlefield; she'd dragged him on to one. She would have chosen Shell, who was at least competent with a spear.

But Shell was dead.

"Thank you," she said. She took a deep breath in, trying to center herself despite the shouts. It had taken her a few tries on the last island to create constructs from the villagers' bodies. She'd been more than a little out of practice. There, she'd done it while the world around her was calm. Here, she was trying to create constructs to stave off an attack already underway.

There was a place for her in the heart of the Empire. It would be worth all of this.

Nisong tried to hold on to that thought as she palmed the commands — her and Shiyen, together and unbroken. She tried to drown out the crack of wood breaking, the sobs of children.

Only her body, the shards of bone and the body in front of her, his face still wide-eyed in shock.

She reached for his chest, her mind calm. Cold, dead skin met her fingertips.

"They have broken through," Coral said breathlessly, back at her side once more. "They have axes. They are taking apart the gate."

Nisong had died once already, her memories showing her sickness, flashes of nausea and weakness. That had been painful enough: she wasn't ready to die again. She wasn't ready to give up.

Coral seized her arm. "You've told me of your memories. Go back earlier," Coral said. "You were never able to center yourself around the Emperor. Think of your sister."

"She dismissed me too," Nisong said, shaking off the woman's soft hands.

"Not always. And that was enough. Here." Coral seized a branch of juniper and shoved it beneath Nisong's nose. Behind them, she heard the creak of wood as the attackers pried boards loose, growls and metal clashing as her remaining constructs did their best to defend the courtyard.

They were going to die. She might as well humor her. Nisong breathed in deep.

And was transported. She stood at the stairs in the entrance hall of the palace on Hualin Or, watching her servants load her things into a palanquin.

"It should have been Manlou from Gaelung," her sister, Wailun, said from behind her. "Not you."

Nisong only shrugged one shoulder. She'd heard as much from the servants' gossip, from whispers in the streets, from her own parents. She was to be the Emperor's consort; the words couldn't bother her anymore. She'd outrank all of them.

"He doesn't care about you," Wailun said.

"That doesn't matter," Nisong said. "I am now his most advantageous match."

Wailun let out an amused snort. "And I suppose you had nothing to do with that scandal, just as you had nothing to do with Enara's on Deerhead. Attempting to coerce the Emperor's steward into poisoning you — that was not something a potential consort should be caught doing."

"She let fear rule her actions," Nisong said. "She saw me as a threat and sought to solidify her position. If she was caught, that's no fault of mine."

"And you had nothing to do with it?"

"I didn't say that either." She clenched her jaw. "You are the one who always tells me to use my mind to my advantage." So many light manipulations, so many deeper ones, so many favors bought and paid for. She'd earned this.

Wailun lifted her hands. "I'm not here to scold you."

A lifetime of hurt welled up within her. But Wailun had scolded her, many times. Always in front of their parents or their friends, or her friends. Foolish, plain Nisong, who showed up where she didn't belong, who spoke up out of turn. When they were alone, she could be kind. When they weren't, she treated her with disdain. All Nisong wanted was for someone to believe in her, to hold her in some sort of esteem. When she was alone with her sister, she felt that maybe Wailun did, only to have her hopes dashed over and over.

She'd closed off her heart to Wailun long ago. Sometimes, though, it felt as though all she'd done was close the shutters to a window behind which a storm raged. The water still seeped in and rotted the wood. "What are you here for then? To expose my crimes? To confront me? It couldn't wait until tonight?"

Later, her family would send her off with a formal dinner.

Her mother and father would praise her – yes, she was worth something to them now. She'd been both looking forward to and dreading the event. The praise would be empty. She wanted, more than anything, to leave this life behind and to start anew.

"I wanted to warn you. You've won a battle, but things won't be better as the Emperor's consort."

It was Nisong's turn to snort. "They couldn't possibly be worse."

Wailun only regarded her, her expression solemn. "I know what you're capable of. I know that you're more competent than others think you are. But Shiyen has lived his whole life knowing who he is and who he is meant to be. He has been taught and groomed and tested. He won't see you as a consort; he will see you as an asset, but one less than what he should have received."

Nisong lifted her chin and pressed her lips together. "I am not less. I will show him."

Before she could react, Wailun glanced about and then enveloped her in a hug. "Just be careful." She drew away and retreated up the stairs.

For a moment, she couldn't move, caught by her surprise. It hadn't occurred to her until this moment that Wailun might also have suffered pressure from their parents and others to be a certain way. That maybe she did love her in her own, flawed way.

Wailun left her with the scent of juniper in her nostrils and with the storm behind her shuttered heart briefly calm.

Rain soaked her hair in the courtyard as she came back to herself. Coral was still kneeling beside her and miraculously, they were not dead yet.

"Now," Coral said. "Now try."

Without even thinking, Nisong pressed her hand into the dead body's chest. Flesh became incorporeal. She set the shards into their places and withdrew. The man sat up, awaiting a command, his flesh animated once more. He was a pitiful thing, the gaping wound in his belly weeping fluids. But Nisong didn't have the time to sew that shut, to refine him, to make him any more complex.

"Destroy the attackers. Protect the constructs."

He moved to obey.

She went to the next body, and then the next, centering herself around the scent of juniper. She didn't dare waste time by watching the battle, though Coral gave her small updates. Frond stood over them, heading off attackers that made it past their initial defenses. Once she thought she felt the rush of air from the swing of a sword. There wasn't time to worry about it, because if she stopped she would die. They would all die.

"Hurry," Coral said into her ear. "We need more."

How could she hurry when she needed to concentrate? Nisong dared a glance at the battle and quailed. The constructs she was creating had helped, but she wasn't moving quickly enough. Bodies littered the paved courtyard. She made brief eye contact with a woman in a torn soldier's jacket, her face a fierce grimace. Nisong's stomach flipped.

The woman rushed at them.

Frond stepped to meet her without hesitating, blocking her sword with his knife, pushing her back to give them space to work. Nisong's breath caught as the woman sliced at Frond, heedless of his counterattacks. He was too slow, too timid. She tore her gaze away: watching wouldn't help him.

Nisong took Coral's hand and pressed the pouches of shards into her palm. "You have to pull one from each pouch and hand them to me when I need them."

Coral's brow furrowed. "But what if I make a mistake and—"

"Please. Or we'll die." And then Nisong turned away before there were any further protestations and plunged her fingers into another chest.

Coral worked alongside Nisong, their hands moving in unison. Reach for more shards, place them inside a body, give the command. The shambling constructs marched into battle, small pieces of them falling by the wayside.

Her hands ached, her back ached, and all she could smell was juniper and all she could hear were screams. But she could feel a change in the pace as they worked side by side, a turning of tides.

At last, only three bodies remained. She reached back and no shards met her palm. "Coral?"

"I've no more."

Nisong dared to turn. The first thing she saw was Frond, laid out on the stones of the courtyard, his knife still clutched in his hand. An arrow was embedded in his chest. Nisong crept to him, exhausted, already knowing what she would find and dreading it.

Rain dripped onto his sightless eyes, running into the furrows by his eyes. He'd not carve any more figurines. She'd promised him freedom and a life outside of Maila and had brought him death instead.

She pushed aside the guilt. They'd already suffered losses on this march toward Imperial; they would suffer more before the end. Nisong scanned the courtyard.

Only a few scattered combatants remained, cornered into the walls by the constructs. The rest of the soldiers had retreated.

She sagged to the paving stones, her hand still on Frond's chest. They'd won.

18

Lin

Riya Island

Thrana screeched again and fear lanced through me, white-hot as a lightning bolt. I barely felt the ground meeting my feet as I ran to the entrance hall and up the palace stairs. I wasn't sure what I'd do when I got there; I carried no weapons. I just knew that I couldn't let anything happen to her.

I burst through the door to my rooms. Something struck me on the side, carrying me to the ground. Someone was on top of me, his face swathed in dark cloth, a knife glinting in his hand.

My bones hummed with energy. I slammed a hand at the assassin's wrist and saw the blade go skittering away.

And then Jovis was lifting the assassin off me, his face enraged. He threw him to the side and his body struck one of the chairs in my sitting room. The assassin groaned but rolled to his knees.

Thrana.

I caught glimpses of movement as I thrust myself to my feet. One more assassin, circling Mephi and Thrana. Only Mephi was fighting back. Even though Thrana was larger, she shrank away, letting out pitiful shrieks each time he tried to strike. Mephi's muzzle was bloodied, though I couldn't be sure if that was his blood or one of the assassins'.

I kicked the door behind me shut. "I can help," I said to Jovis, my voice low.

"I'm the Captain of the Imperial Guard," Jovis said. "I'm supposed to protect you."

I flexed my fingers, thinking of the power I'd demonstrated earlier when I'd pulled the water droplets inside. It had surprised him that I'd been able to do so much. "You can't protect me if you're dead. And I'm not as helpless as everyone thinks I am. Besides, you *really* shouldn't be trying to tell me what to do."

He'd seen me in the hallway, bloody from the battle with my father, but victorious. He knew, better than anyone, that I could hold my own.

Jovis gave me a quick glance, then pulled a dagger from his belt. He tossed it to me, and I caught it by the hilt. "I'll take the one on the right," he said. "Can you handle the other?"

I felt the strength flow through my limbs, stronger even than when I'd eaten the cloud juniper berries. There was no one here to care if I let loose with my newfound magic. All the fear I'd felt turned to molten anger. "Yes."

They dared to come here, and to attack *Thrana* instead of me? My fingers tightened around the dagger. I lifted it. But instead of charging at the assassin on the left, I let my awareness sharpen. I felt the moisture in the room and outside the window. It was as easy as it had been when Jovis had first shown me. I gathered the droplets, felt them coalesce into a pool at my feet. And then, just as the assassin charged at me, I lifted it to slam into his face.

The assassin choked, nearly dropping his weapon.

I stepped inside his guard and sliced my dagger across his ribs. I'd cut enough flesh when I'd been learning my father's bone shard magic. This felt no different. Only the blood was warm this time. He leapt back, pressing a hand to the wound.

Jovis had broken a chair leg clean off and was using it to bludgeon the assassin on the right. My opponent had underestimated me but was quickly recovering. Jovis's opponent dodged his attacks, keeping his blade at the ready.

I backed away, looking for a defensible position. So it was I found my back against Jovis's, my dagger raised, Thrana at my side. She'd found her courage again with my presence, and I felt the rumble of her growl as she leaned against my knee.

Both assassins attacked.

The Alanga that had attacked me back on Imperial had been relying on the element of surprise. These two men were well-trained fighters, moving with the fluidity of dancers. The man I faced bobbed and dodged, unwilling to engage me directly. He knew my strength and speed now. Instead, he searched for an opening, feinting with his blade.

I felt Jovis's presence at my back as he swung, his shoulder brushing briefly against mine. I gathered more water from outside as I ducked a blow and Thrana snapped at the assassin's heels.

The assassin eyed the pool of water I'd gathered. I knew what he thought: that I'd throw it in his face again, choking off his breath. Instead, I sent a small flick of it toward his face, and the rest hurtling toward his knees in a wave.

He dodged the water aimed at his head but overbalanced and fell as the wave struck his legs. Thrana darted forward, burying her teeth in the man's arm. He dropped his blade, trying to break Thrana's grip.

Jovis grunted.

I whipped about to find the other assassin's blade embedded in Jovis's chair leg. Before the man could recover, I crouched beneath Jovis's upraised arm and cut a slit up the assassin's abdomen. It was easier to kill than I'd expected. It was still just flesh, waiting to be carved.

My blade dripped onto the floor. "As I said—"

Jovis's eyes narrowed and he turned, nearly knocking me over. He swung his makeshift club and the embedded dagger caught the other assassin in the face. The hilt slammed into the assassin's temple with a *crack*. He'd shaken off Thrana, though his arm was limp, and his blade was in his other hand. He'd been about to stab me in the back.

My heartbeat pounded in my ears, echoing the drumming of the rain on the roof. Jovis and I stood there for a moment, shivering, our legs entangled from both our hasty pivots, our shoulders pressed together. My gaze met his, our breathing evenly matched. I found myself fixated on his parted lips. I'd once thought him unremarkable and now I couldn't look away. I wasn't sure what I wanted more – for him to step away or for him to stay. His free hand reached out, covering mine. I held my breath.

"The dagger," he said, his words warm by my ear. "Someone will come."

It took me a moment to register what he meant. Of course. I wanted to sink into the floor, into the floor below that, and then into the cold, wet earth. I was Lin, I was the Emperor and I was an idiot.

I loosened my grip on his dagger and let him take it back.

And then I remembered Thrana and Mephi and felt even more the fool. I took a few steps back from Jovis, giving him space. Both of our beasts were on their feet, blood marring their fur but their eyes bright. "Are you hurt?" I asked them.

"No," Mephi said.

"No," Thrana repeated.

The door burst open. Five guards marched into the room,

Iloh following them. They quickly surveyed the room, the two dead assassins.

"You're well?" Iloh asked.

"Jovis is a competent captain. He took down both men."

The infuriating man had the temerity to smile at the praise as if he deserved it. Even his posture changed, straightening as he wiped his dagger clean and slid it back into its sheath. "Yes, well. It *is* my job."

I'd never quite wanted to punch anyone so much before.

"I'm not sure how assassins broke into the palace," Iloh said. "I assure you, we took every precaution before your visit. My guards should have taken care of them before they could ever make their way to the guest quarters. I owe you my deepest apologies. Please forgive me."

Iloh wouldn't have sent assassins after me in my rooms: he would have waited until I was out in the streets so he could deny any responsibility. I waved him off. "Jovis was followed when he was in the city. I should have brought this information to you."

"Even so, Eminence, I swear it won't happen again." Iloh took another glance around the room. "Did the roof spring a leak?"

The water. Heat crept up the back of my neck. The floors and rugs were soaked, pools of water gathered where I'd thrown it at the assassins. I was supposed to be keeping my magic secret, and here I was, leaving evidence of it everywhere.

"You should probably check. It was like this when we got here," Jovis said smoothly.

Maybe I didn't want to punch him. I wasn't sure. "Wait," I said as the guards started to drag the man away. "Is he still alive? I want to speak to him."

The guards looked to Iloh, who nodded. They propped the man against the wall and I approached. He was neither young nor old, with the sort of bland face that would be difficult to pick out of a crowd. His eyes were still closed, his breathing steady. I knelt by his side and patted his cheek until he started to awaken.

"You're in the guest rooms of Emperor Lin Sukai," I said. I knew how a knock to the head could be disorienting. "You tried to kill me. Who sent you?"

"Your father abandoned us. You left us all alone," he said, his gaze bleary.

"Abandoned who? I did no such thing."

"What is he talking about?" Jovis, at my shoulder.

"I have no idea."

"Why leave us alive? Why command us to do the same things every day?"

"Who sent you? Why are—?" I stopped, the rest of my words drying up on my tongue. I hadn't known what my father had done with the failed constructs – the ones he'd made before me. He hadn't destroyed them. Pieces began to fall together in my mind.

Slowly, his eyes focused on me. "I have no answers for you," he said.

If only there was no one else here – I could reach inside him, modify his commands until he spoke the truth to me. If I could get him onto my ship, get him alone, I might still have a chance.

He laughed as if he knew what I was thinking. Before I could ask another question, he cracked his skull against mine. The world tilted around me. Vaguely, I was aware he'd gotten to his feet, and somewhere in the distance Thrana growled.

And then something warm spurted over me. Blood.

For the barest moment, I thought it was my blood. So this was how I ended. Not by my father's hand, but by the hand of one of his wayward constructs. The room started to settle. Jovis stood over me, his dagger buried in the man's chest.

Not my blood. His.

I reached out, trying to steady myself, and found Thrana's fur beneath my fingers. She bolstered me as I stood. "You didn't have to kill him," I hissed at Jovis. "I never ordered that." My head was beginning to ache. I looked down to find blood staining Iloh's jacket.

"Your jacket." I turned to Iloh. "I'm sorry." I wasn't sure what I was saying. As soon as I'd stood, the room had started to spin again.

I tried to focus on Iloh's face and only got a glimpse of his baffled expression before Jovis's face swam in front of mine. His brows were drawn together in a dark line. "What was I supposed to do? Let him kill you? I don't think that would have worked out well for either of us."

"I am the Emperor," I snapped back, indignant. I buried my fingers in Thrana's fur, trying to make the room stay still. Pain drained away my flash of anger. There were too many people. "And . . . and I could use a bath. Please."

Everything moved quickly after that. Jovis stalked out, taking his place by my door. Servants swarmed in and out, cleaning up the water and blood. One led me to the baths, Jovis trailing behind. He waited outside the door.

The bath steadied me. And then all I wanted was sleep.

I crept back to my room like a scolded dog. I'd failed. I needed those four islands to support me. And Iloh hated me. The people hated me. I curled into the guest bed, Thrana next to me. I buried my face in her shoulder, taking in her scent – like woodsmoke and damp earth. "I don't know what to do. They don't want me as Emperor. How do I keep fighting for that if I'm the only one doing it?"

Thrana's cold nose found my ear. "I'm here. Ikanuy is helping. Jovis and Mephi are helping."

Jovis. Was he really helping me? I couldn't be sure. "Thank you," I whispered into her fur.

Her chest rumbled as she sighed.

I woke to a knock on my door. Still drowsy, I rose. Thrana mumbled a little in her sleep as I moved her aside and found my slippers. I tightened the sash on my sleeping robe, ran a hand through my hair and opened the door, expecting to find servants or Jovis.

Instead, Iloh stood in the doorway, smartly dressed and much more awake than I was. Was he wearing the same jacket from the night before? "I owe you an apology."

It took me a moment to arrange my thoughts. The air still smelled faintly of copper. "The assassins? You already apologized."

"Although I still think that was a vast oversight on the part of my household guards, that's not what I came here to apologize for. I've treated you unfairly."

My thoughts finally fell into line. "Your mother," I said. "I know my father used her shard and killed her. I had no power over the things my father did; I wish I had. Suffice to say, we rarely saw eye to eye." I thought of Shiyen's temper, of my desperate attempts to please him, to be who he wanted me to be. And I thought of the day I'd killed him.

"I always thought the Sukais cut from the same cloth," he said.

I was not a Sukai, not truly. But I let him continue.

"I spoke to Pulan. I took your advice. We talked all night. If you keep your word and send resources to develop her mine, she will marry me. The children . . . we'll figure that out later. Together." He seemed more sheepish than he had last night, without the benefit of drink to bolster his courage and honesty.

I let him swim in his discomfort for a moment, just because he'd let me swim in mine for so much longer. And then I did the gracious thing. "I'm glad to hear it. And I'll keep my word. We can draw up the documents before I leave, if Pulan will stay long enough to sign them. I'll ask her for a slightly higher tithe in exchange." I slid that in at the end, hoping he was in a good enough mood to agree. Once they were married, their households and rules would combine.

"Of course, that's only fair given your investment," Iloh said. He bowed, and for the first time, it felt genuine. "I'll distribute the shards to my people. It will go a long way to healing the rifts your father created."

"And the guards to help with the constructs in the north-eastern reaches?"

My heart sank as he shook his head. "I have to look after my own first. I received a report this morning of a construct attack on a village just east of here. If I send guards away now, they'll see me as abandoning them. These are hard times, with constructs attacking, Deerhead sinking and the bog cough on the rise. The bog cough has already begun to hit Riya, and caro nuts are expensive. I can commit some of my guards, but not as many as you would probably like."

The construct assassins and an attack on one of Riya's villages at the same time? I had the feeling these things were related. "And if this attack originates from the group in the north-east? You'll just be swiping at the legs of the beast instead of cutting off the head."

He spread his hands. "The fact of the matter is that I am responsible for Riya. You are responsible for the Empire. The constructs are the purview of the Emperor. I'm sorry."

The floor felt like it was dropping, my stomach going with it. He couldn't do this. I could order him to commit all his guards. I could take back his shard or the shards of his family, use them to threaten him until he did my bidding. It wasn't for me. It was for people like Numeen and his family, who needed an Emperor who cared about them.

My senses sharpened, and I was aware of the tea steeping in the next room, the moisture gathered on the roof, the sweat beaded on Iloh's forehead. I might not have constructs, but I had other powers.

Thrana nudged her nose into my palm. I thought of the crane Numeen's daughter had folded, wet with her blood, the way my father dealt with the people who he felt had opposed him. I took in a deep breath.

I was not him.

But then I studied Iloh's face. He wasn't shutting me down, not completely. He was waiting.

He wanted a counter-offer.

My mind raced over the words he'd said. *Ah.* "You need caro nuts." Imperial had a store of oil. Nephilanu's shipment to Imperial had been delayed – I wasn't sure why yet – but we would be receiving more. "Let me solve another of your problems. I'll have my steward send you some of Imperial's store of oil. It should arrive quickly." I ran some mental calculations. Considering how many people usually got sick with bog cough, there'd be enough left over for Imperial in case anything went wrong.

"That would put my people much at ease," Iloh said. "And it would save my coffers. I'll be able to hire and train more guards in the interim. In the meantime, my guards are at your disposal."

He might have driven a hard bargain, but I'd made an ally instead of an enemy.

So I allowed myself a smallest bit of smugness when our visit concluded, the papers for the development of Pulan's witstone mine signed. I'd sent a copy to Ikanuy so she could handle the administration of resources. But Jovis followed me through these negotiations, always standing a step behind, his staff tapping gently against the floor.

Finally, once we were back aboard the ship, watching the workers undoing the docking lines, I rounded on him.

"Out with it. You're not still troubled by my admonishment last night, are you? I understand now why you killed him, but I'd also had my head nearly caved in and I was in the middle of questioning him."

He only frowned, his gaze on the Endless Sea. "I shouldn't have called you foolish. You are the Emperor. I shouldn't have forgotten."

Why was he telling me this? "And how should I remind you?"

He looked to me, his expression solemn. "You already have. Eminence, Deerhead sank into the sea. Why? I've been thinking about it."

"You believe the theory about the witstone mines."

"I don't know what to believe. But should we really be developing new mines when we don't know why Deerhead sank? Which island is next?" Jovis said. "Which of us will drown? Unta? It's not anything like Deerhead, but it also has extensive witstone mines."

I couldn't help but remember my father's edict – that the mine on Imperial should never be reopened. Did he know something I did not?

"It's the only lead we have," Jovis said. "And you just agreed to help develop a mine on Pulan's island. Will hers be next?"

I wanted to snatch that staff from his hands, to stop that infuriating *tapping*. "Do you think it's so easy to be Emperor? Do you think I don't consider these things? I have to gain the support of these governors, or my rule teeters on a knife's edge. How can I deal with the larger problems right now? How can I think about the sinking islands and the Alanga if I don't have the power to do anything about them?"

He didn't look away, meeting my gaze as though we were

equals. "So you would sacrifice the lives of everyone living on Pulan's island so you can accumulate power?"

Why did he insist on seeing me in the worst possible light? "You think this is about power? Alanga artifacts are awakening. The constructs are wreaking havoc. We need to have a united Empire. Am I intentionally sacrificing Pulan's island? No. You don't know that her island will sink, or even that it will happen anytime soon. We don't even know if it's the mines that are causing it."

"I was on Deerhead when it sank," Jovis said. "Sometimes I still dream about it – the buildings collapsing, the people trapped inside their homes as the island carried them into the depths." He stopped, swallowed. "Nothing is worth that. *Nothing.*" If he were Bayan, this would be a contest, each of us vying to be the last to look away. But I could see the fear in Jovis's eyes, the tightness around the corners of his lips. This wasn't a contest, not to him.

"Eminence!" a servant ran up the docks, her face flushed. She stopped at the edge, bowing to both of us.

I leaned over the rail, glad for the interruption. "Did Iloh have something else to say to me?"

"We just received news from the south," she said, "and he thought you should know before you left. It's Unta."

My lips went numb, my arms and legs prickling as though a thousand spiders climbed my skin. "There's been a disaster," I said, echoing Ilith's first words regarding Deerhead Island. I didn't need the servant to tell me, yet I did, because I needed to hear it from someone else's lips.

The servant blinked, wiped the sweat from her forehead. "Yes. Unta has sunk. It's gone."

Thrana wound about my legs, thrusting her head beneath my hand. "Not good," she croaked out. "Not good."

19

Phalue

Nephilanu Island

The girl was quick on her feet, Phalue had to give her that. She moved in light steps that were difficult to follow and to predict. Rain filtered through the fronds above, falling every so often in cold droplets on Phalue's cheeks. Ayesh carried a wooden practice sword, though even the lightest one they had was still a bit too large for her. But that was one way to build strength, and she could lift it – which surprised them both.

Phalue watched Ayesh's steps, dodged and struck the blade from her hand.

The girl hissed in pain, shaking out her wrist as her sword clattered across the cobblestones. She didn't stop to rest though, chasing down the blade and lifting it. "Again. I can do better."

"Is there someone in particular you're trying to kill? Or just yourself," Phalue said.

Ayesh scowled and rushed at her.

She'd have to put an end to this eventually – it was something she'd learned from their first lesson, when the girl had worked herself to literal exhaustion. Despite Ranami's misgivings, Phalue had given the orphan free rein in the kitchens and a cot in a small room she could take some rest in.

"This is how it starts," Ranami had said. "We can't watch her all the time. I thought she wasn't a spy when she wanted to leave so quickly, but now she's here so often. I wouldn't worry so much except that it puts you in danger."

"I can take care of myself."

"You can take care of yourself in a battle – I'll give you that. This is politics." In the end, she'd caved, because she'd wanted to help the orphans, after all. But maybe Ranami was right. Phalue just didn't have an eye for deception.

She parried Ayesh's frenzied attacks. "Shoulder back," she instructed. "Don't face me head on. Make yourself a smaller target."

"I'm already a smaller target!" the girl grunted.

Well, she was right about that. "You could be an even smaller one," Phalue pointed out. "And what is your first goal in a fight?"

Ayesh sighed. "Make it more difficult for my opponent to hurt me."

"And sometimes that means running away."

The girl rolled her eyes and Phalue laughed. There was something charming about being treated with such irreverence. Ayesh didn't seem to really care about Phalue's position as governor. She did care what Phalue could teach her, and that was refreshing. With everyone else she was more than an instructor. She'd been doing her best to project calm, as Ranami had suggested. The sinking of Unta had sent emotional ripples outward, and Nephilanu was not immune.

There was no witstone mine on Nephilanu, which helped a small measure. But most people didn't trust the explanation that mining accidents were causing the islands to collapse. Still, at

Ranami's urging, Phalue had planned an escape route from the palace down to the docks using the hidden Alanga entrance in the walls. They had a store of witstone in the palace. It was a precautionary measure.

Three nights ago, there had been a small tremor, and Phalue had woken bolt upright in bed, sweating and trembling, unable to get to sleep even after the tremor had long since faded and no others followed. All she could think about were the people trapped on Deerhead and Unta as their islands sank, dragging them all down, down into the Endless Sea.

The slap of a sword against her thigh brought her back to the moment. "Hah!" Ayesh crowed. "Look at how good I am. Got one on you!"

"I was distracted. Don't get ahead of yourself," Phalue chided.

"Sai." Tythus strode up, interrupting their session. "Someone's here to see you."

Something in his tone made her sheathe her sword. "Someone."

He nodded. That could only mean one person: Gio. She wasn't sure why he'd be visiting. They'd only just established a truce. More conditions? She hoped not. The patrols were doing what she'd intended and were slowly eliminating the constructs on Nephilanu. "Let him in and then fetch Ranami, would you?"

Tythus moved to obey. Phalue glanced back at the orphan. "I'm not sure how long this will take. You're welcome to wait, though."

Ayesh swung her sword experimentally, checking her stance. "I'll wait."

The girl's stance wasn't bad, and she only needed one hand to wield her weapon, but Phalue pursed her lips. She'd been teaching Ayesh the way that *she* fought, and she was much larger than Ayesh would ever be. There had to be something they could do to adjust, a way of fighting better suited to the girl's stature and speed.

"Am I interrupting, Sai?" Gio approached, his oilskin cloak drawn up over his head. He'd done something to his nose so it didn't look like his, had covered the milky eye with a patch. It was something of a disguise, Phalue supposed. He still looked foreboding with the scar peeking through, as if he were one of the old Alanga from the tales, come to avenge a broken pact. In the rain, most people wouldn't give him a second glance, which was lucky for him. There were still posters about, offering a reward for his capture. But then, there were still a few errant posters of Jovis, too. No constructs worked to replace them.

"Yes," Phalue said, unwilling to engage in niceties. "But you're here and I have a moment." She beckoned him to follow her between the pillars so they could have a little more privacy. And away from Ayesh. Not that she thought Ayesh might actually be a spy – but Ranami would appreciate it.

She stopped where the old fountain used to sit. Gio eyed the spot, the stones there unweathered. "I'm not here to break our truce, if that's what you're wondering."

Someone touched her elbow. She didn't have to look to know it was Ranami. "Is something wrong?" she asked.

Gio shook his head and then stopped. "You appreciate directness," he said to Phalue. "I've heard that you received a missive from the Emperor asking for a visit. Did you intend to grant that?"

Well, that was a surprise. She hadn't told anyone about the missive except Ranami and her father, and her father was imprisoned. A servant had taken her response to the Emperor's envoy, but that was it. Ranami clutched Phalue's arm a little tighter, her posture stiff. Phalue knew what she was thinking: Ayesh.

They hadn't been in complete privacy when they'd discussed the missive. They'd been beneath the arch of the palace gate. There were other explanations.

Ranami must have looked to Ayesh, because Gio followed her gaze. Ayesh was still swinging her wooden sword, darting forward and back, fighting off invisible enemies. He watched her for a moment. "Is she yours?"

"No," Ranami said quickly. "She's from the city. Phalue is teaching her to fight."

"A distant relative of yours or the governor's?"

This was going on an odd tangent. Did he know the girl? Either way, he was asking too many questions. "It's not really your business," Phalue said. "And neither is our decision whether or not to accept the Emperor's request."

He finally turned his gaze back to Phalue, his brows low. "I had one condition of the truce, and that was that you not send the caro nut shipment this year. Isn't whether or not you fulfill that my business? Isn't it the business of all the Shardless Few?"

Annoyingly persistent, this one. Phalue could see why rebel leaders always had enemies. "I already agreed to the terms. That should be enough for you."

"Do you intend to keep them?"

"I do."

"Then if you do allow Lin to visit, if you hear everything she has to say as she lobbies you for support – what will you tell her when she asks why the caro nut shipment hasn't been sent?"

Who was the governor here? Her or Gio? He might have preferred that it be him, but that wasn't the way things had ended up. "I won't lie, if that's what you're asking. I'm sure we can speak of things peaceably, even the caro nuts."

"So you are intending to have her visit?"

And this was what she hated about politics – the wheedling, the insinuations, the need to always be careful exactly what one was saying lest it be misinterpreted. Why couldn't everyone just have their cards pinned to their shirts instead of holding them close to their chests? They'd certainly get a lot more done, and faster, that way.

Phalue had already sent her response to the Emperor; she'd announce the visit once she was sure the letter had reached Imperial. She needed to know more than what the envoy could tell her. Who was this new Emperor? What was she like? She'd ended the Tithing Festival – why? Phalue couldn't just blindly follow the Shardless Few, no matter their stated goals. No matter what threats they made. Yes, she wanted a fairer and more equitable society too. But there was something about Gio that never seemed quite true. Perhaps it was the stories – the myths – built around him. Had he grown up on Khalute? And had he truly taken the island singlehandedly? She'd never believed it, but now, looking at him, she wasn't sure. Even disguised there was an air of imminent threat about him, like storm clouds lurking on the horizon.

She stared him down and refused to answer. He could find out when the announcement went out, not before.

He shook his head, water flinging from his hood. "Refuse the visit. Deny her."

"He does have a point," Ranami said. "Inviting her here only invites confrontation."

And when had Phalue ever backed down from a confrontation? "It's not about that. When we agreed to a truce, you laid out your terms. None of that involved you having a say in how I govern Nephilanu. You wanted the caro nut shipment halted? It's halted. That's all I owe to you, Gio."

He glowered at her from beneath his hood, his one black eye like a sinkhole in the crags of his face. "Deny the visit," he said again.

"I will not."

For a moment, she thought he might attack her. She would

have welcomed that – the clash of blades, his strength matched against hers, the simple arena of a physical fight. Let that decide the matter.

But he took a step back, his lip curled as though he'd tasted something bitter. "I won't break the truce. But you're making a decision you'll come to regret. And it won't be me making you regret it. The Sukais have never been a peaceful people. They have never in their long history looked out for the interests of others. They murder those that oppose them, they hoard their magic and they seek out power no matter the cost.

"A Sukai might convince you they care, that they have some grander motives, but they are always lying. Always."

20

Jovis

Somewhere in the Endless Sea

I'm surprised to find Ylan is good company as he recovers. I keep mostly to myself, but having someone else around is comforting, and I find we have much to talk about. He is a scholar, and well-read. He walks with me sometimes as I tend to my island, and we speak on the natures of beasts and men. He has made the study of ossalen (??) his life's work, and I add my own thoughts to his observations. But we don't always get along. He says the Alanga are too powerful. What counts as a small squabble (conflict?) between our people can upend boats and flatten farms. When I point out that the Alanga pay a damage price (restitution), he snaps that some of us do. (Mephi was unclear on the wording in the next lines. Something to do with doubt and questioning and guilt.)

I ask that we speak on other subjects and he relents, but always we end up circling back.

What if — he asks me — there was a way to keep
my brethren in check?

—Notes from Jovis's translation of Dione's journal

Unta was gone.

I wasn't much in the habit of making prophecies; that
was more my mother's discipline. "If you keep that up, you'll
break a bone." "You'll burn yourself if you're not careful."
"There will be times you regret speaking your thoughts aloud,
Jovis." I knew the sinking of Unta wasn't my fault, that it had
occurred long before I'd singled the island out, but nothing could
change the queasy feeling that I'd named Unta as the next island
to sink, and it had.

It felt like a lifetime ago that I'd been paid to drop a girl and
a boy off at Unta, putting them in the care of the Shardless Few,
saving them from the Tithing Festival. Mephi had liked them.
I wondered if they'd made it off the island before it sank, or if
I'd saved them from one ill fate only to subject them to another.

"This doesn't change anything," was the first thing Lin had
said, though her face had been pale. "We have to move forward
with expanding Pulan's mine. I need Riya."

"For what? Moral support? Iloh's guards won't make enough
of a difference." And there was the instant regret for speaking my
thoughts out loud. My mother really *was* a prophet.

"See to your duties, Captain," she'd said, her chin tilted, her
words crisp. "And leave the politics to those who understand
them." We'd barely spoken since.

I glanced out the porthole of my cramped room, watching
the clouds roll over the waves, the Alanga book in my hands.
I'd launched an investigation into the assassination attempt at

Riya – or what investigation I could. I'd taken the weapons they'd used, pieces of their clothing. Their clothing was plain and dark, but the similarities ended there. The outfits were pieced together from disparate parts – some items looking new, some old and patched. When I'd brought these findings to Lin, she'd seemed surprisingly unconcerned, eager to be rid of me once more. There was something she wasn't telling me. Secrets lingered around the woman like fish scales wedged beneath a butcher's fingernails.

A knock sounded at my door. "Nephilanu's been sighted," one of my guards said.

I closed the Alanga book and stowed it back within my bag. "I'll be up to the deck shortly."

Mephi was already up there with Thrana, after having sighed and moped about my cabin for the better part of the day. Finally, as we approached, they'd stopped burning witstone above-deck. He hated being in confined spaces, but loved being out on the Endless Sea.

I made my way to the deck only to run into the one person I'd been wanting to avoid.

"Eminence," I said. She was dressed in a simple tunic with only light embroidery at the collar. Her sash was the same color, blending in. Her hair was pulled back in a tail, a few strands having worked their way loose in the wind. And then she fixed me with those dark eyes and I felt lost all over again.

"Jovis," she said.

I was angry with her and she was the Emperor – I had to remember both these things, because part of me wanted to apologize for my harsh words. "You look nice," I said, and cursed myself for speaking. Never could just let a silence sit.

She looked down, as if unsure what she was wearing that warranted such attention. She grinned. "In this? Should I meet the governor of Nephilanu this way?"

"Why not? You might start a new trend. After all, if the Emperor does it, it must be fashionable."

"Ah, fashion. The only power one really needs to rule an Empire."

Ruling an Empire. Yes, that's what she was trying to do. Even if that meant putting people at risk.

Something of my thoughts must have shown on my face, because she went still and formal once more. And, curse me, I wanted to make a joke, to make light of the situation, just to feel that ease between us once more. But that would be the coward's way out.

"The witstone mines . . . " I said, trailing off. I wasn't sure what more to say. I'd stopped using witstone after Mephi's poor reaction to it. The thought of more mines being developed filled me with a terrible dread. "You should close them. At least until we know for sure what's causing the islands to sink."

"Are you my adviser or my Captain of the Imperial Guard?"

I didn't bother answering, because I knew a trap when I heard one. She glared at me and I glared right back. "I am a concerned citizen," I said, wishing I could have instead kept my mouth shut.

"I've told you already: this was the best solution. I have a whole Empire to consider, not just individual islands or people. Do you think I should always do the righteous thing? The righteous thing isn't always the *right* thing. So until you come up with something better . . . " She waited, giving me full opportunity to provide a solution. And – Dione's balls – I had none. She nodded. "Then I will continue to do as I see fit for our Empire. As is my right and my duty."

She swept past me to the cabins below.

It was better this way – when we didn't get along. But somehow, I couldn't shake the feel of fighting the assassins with her at my back, when it felt like for a brief moment we'd both set aside our roles. It had felt like we could take on an army and come out unscathed. I shook my head and went to the railing.

Mephi and Thrana swam alongside the boat, chasing one another in the wake. I called to them and waved them up. We'd be making landfall soon.

They scrambled onto the deck and I had to leap back to avoid getting drenched as they both shook off seawater. Mephi bounded to me, demanding his cheeks be scratched. I obliged with a laugh. Thrana hung back, her head low, ears back. She didn't quite trust me. Lin had said her father had experimented on the creature, and this torture had left its mark.

It was strange to return to Nephilanu. The last time I'd been here I'd been a smuggler, searching for my lost wife. Now I was Captain of the Imperial Guard, a lofty position I wasn't even sure I wanted. And I knew something about the island that Lin did not. The Shardless Few had helped depose the prior governor, and even now they were probably strengthening their foothold on the island. In the jungle to the east of the city was their hideout, where I'd found the Alanga book. I pushed away the trickle of guilt. By all rights, I should have told her. I was her Captain of the Imperial Guard and she was setting foot on an island with a significant Shardless Few presence. But I was also a Shardless Few spy.

I needed to go back. The more I thought about it, the more I knew there had to be other hidden doors in that dark hallway. The hideout had once been home to Alanga, their murals gracing the stone walls. What better place to find answers about the Alanga than in a place they'd once lived?

We docked at the main city and I caught a glimpse of the palace on the hillside above the rooftops. Ranami knew well enough she should pretend not to have met me – we'd met while she'd been working for the Shardless Few. Hopefully she had briefed Phalue.

Lin reappeared on deck, resplendent in her Emperor's phoenix robes, headdress firmly in place. The maidservants had carefully dried and restored the clothing after Riya. Painted flames licked the hem, fading into a deep blue at the shoulders. She didn't speak to me or even glance at me. Thrana crept to her side and leaned against her thigh. Only then did her expression soften, her hand coming to rest on the beast's head. Mephi, much as I hated to admit it, was very much like me – brash, not good at listening, thought he was funny. Lin and Thrana were an odd pair. She was bold, sharp, compassionate yet ruthless. And Thrana crept through rooms like a shadow, flinching whenever someone turned their full attention on her. I'd found Mephi as a baby, and I wondered if Thrana would have behaved differently if she'd had a kinder upbringing. Still, she seemed to grow bolder in Lin's presence. And Thrana smoothed Lin's harsh edges.

This time, there wasn't a lower-ranked envoy waiting at the docks. Both Phalue and Ranami stood there, arm in arm. Ranami wore a simple silk dress with a high collar and square neckline, its green surface unadorned with embroidery. Phalue hadn't changed a whit even after becoming governor. She wore leather armor that had seen more than just a little use, her sword strapped to her side. Their two guards had brought a small curtained palanquin for Lin. No one else attended them.

I took my place at the Emperor's side, but just a little behind her, my gaze fixed on the shining mass of hair her maids had bound up in various buns and braids.

Mephi and Thrana joined us, and together we strode down the gangplank. Phalue put a hand over her heart in greeting and bowed to Lin. "Eminence, we appreciate your visit, especially in this time of crisis." I wondered how many blamed Lin for all this new upheaval. The constructs gone wild, the sinking of Unta.

The harbor was nearly full of boats. Some must have come from that doomed island.

The trembling earth, the sun hot against my neck, the screams of people buried in the rubble. I shut my eyes tight, trying to chase away the memories.

"And I appreciate you receiving me," Lin said. Her voice was low and even, giving no indication of the terrible reception we'd received on Riya. She looked to the palanquin. "Will the three of you be riding with me? There doesn't seem to be enough space."

"We're humble people," Phalue said. "I've often walked the way up and down from the palace to the city. It wouldn't make sense for me to change my habits now."

Lin considered for a moment. "Then let me walk with you. We have much to speak on, and I'd like to see your city from the ground."

I stifled a smile. Context meant the world. Making her walk had been an insult in Riya. Here, she could gain favor by walking. And Lin seemed to grasp for any advantages she could find. I couldn't help but admire her cleverness.

Her handmaids descended from the gangplank with the chest of Nephilanu shards.

"As a token of my appreciation for receiving me," Lin said, her voice raised, "I give you the shards of all your people. I have halted the Tithing Festival and dismantled my father's constructs."

The people gathered near the docks to watch were listening. Oh, well done. They'd carry that info through the city even ahead of our entourage. She'd find a more pleasant reception from the people here, at least.

Phalue motioned for the two guards with her to take the chest. They loaded it onto a compartment at the back of the palanquin, along with a smaller chest of Lin's belongings for her stay. "We thank you for returning what belongs to us. This will go a long way to mend any enmity between Imperial and Nephilanu."

Interesting.

But then Lin turned to the men and women following her. "The streets are narrow and our party large. I trust Nephilanu's guards to protect me. I give you leave for the rest of the day."

I might have thought this was just a generous gesture, meant to mirror Phalue and Ranami's lack of attendants. They'd have more privacy, more intimacy. But her gaze landed on me and I knew she didn't want me dogging her steps. "Jovis, you too. But please join us for dinner."

She knew as well as I did that I'd been avoiding her. "Is that wise," I said beneath my breath, "given Riya?"

"I can handle myself," she said, and without waiting for a response, followed Phalue and Ranami, Thrana on her heels.

Why was I even arguing with her? I'd already wanted to find a way to the Shardless Few hideout. This gave me the opportunity. Still, I couldn't help but watch as the crowd parted and she and Thrana made their way to shore. She could handle herself? She was new to her magic; she didn't have complete control yet. She was so sure of her cleverness that she would let her anger with me get in the way of her safety.

Ah, but what did I know either? I still didn't understand this power running through my veins, where it came from, what my limits were. And she'd shown herself more than competent with water.

The three maidservants, smiling at one another in delight at this unexpected day off, strode down the docks and toward the city. The guards I'd assigned to accompany Lin looked to me and I waved them toward the shore. They could use a bit of time off too. Time that wasn't spent rocking on the waves. Mephi watched my face and gave me a querying chirp.

I was tapping the bottom of my steel staff against the worn wooden boards of the dock. I stilled my hand. "She'll be fine," I said, and it sounded like I was trying to convince myself. I needed to give the maidservants and guards a head start so they wouldn't see where I'd gone. I checked my purse. "Want to sample the foods of Nephilanu?"

I'd only just eaten breakfast, but Mephi was more than game. I bought him a serving of fried fish and crispy noodles from a young man who was more than a little awed by both me and Mephi, and had to be reminded to take my money. "I have one of your old posters," the young man said as he passed over the food, "from when you were wanted as a smuggler. I kept it."

He sounded proud, like he'd found a pearl in an oyster someone else had thrown away. "That's ... very nice." I'd paid to have those damned posters tossed and now people were keeping them? I wanted to slink away into an alley and cover my face with grime. But I supposed there was no hiding now that I was Captain of the Imperial Guard.

"It's strange times." I checked around me and saw none of the men or women from the ship. He kept talking as I tried to edge away from the stall without being rude. I needed to get out of this conversation, for more than one reason. "A little spy construct bit one of my brother's fingers clean off when he was checking his traps at the docks. He didn't do anything. The creature just attacked him. And Unta ... That's two islands now. Makes you worry about which one of us is next. I keep thinking I feel the ground shaking."

"The Emperor is doing her best to ensure the safety of her citizens," I said. It felt like a lie.

The young man grinned. "And we've got you, of course."

His confidence only made me feel ill. "Yes, you've got me. Jovis from the song. Saving children and now saving the Empire."

"They'll have to write another song for that. Ah, no no!" His noodles, left too long unattended, had begun to burn and he whirled to attend them. I took the opportunity to flee. Sweat dampened the small of my back as though I'd been engaged in battle rather than friendly conversation. Once I'd been just a smuggler, trying to find his missing wife. Now I was a spy, an Imperial guard, a folk hero — and these things didn't always run in agreement with one another. I couldn't have known exactly where my path would lead back when I'd accepted the magic that Mephi had given me. But now people *relied* on me. They looked to me for hope and safety.

I couldn't shake the feeling that they were about to be very disappointed.

Mephi hurried to keep up, a few stray noodles still hanging from the corner of his mouth. "Going to see Gio?" he asked hopefully as we strode into the jungle.

"Hoping not to run into him, actually. You might like him, Mephi, but I don't trust him."

"He's not a bad person."

"Most people aren't. But do I trust most people? Not at all."

It had been a while since I'd last been to the hideout — and I practiced what I would say. There would be a guard at the entrance, but the Shardless Few knew me. I could tell them Gio had sent for me, and that would buy me a little time, at least. But I had to know: were there more doors in those corridors, and what lay behind them? Was there something that could help me further decipher the book? Some artifact that might help defend against Alanga with sinister intentions?

There was so little about them that we understood. Did Alanga arise in cycles? Did the old, dead Alanga come back to life, or just new ones like me? They lived for such a long time; were they like the creatures that only lived in a wet season, waiting for the rain to hatch their eggs? And the question that still haunted me: if Lin and I were Alanga too, what had happened to the creatures the old Alanga had bonded with?

The entrance to the Shardless Few caves was where I remembered it. A crack in the cliff face, mostly hidden by vegetation. I gestured to Mephi to stay close behind me. He'd slid past me easily when he'd been smaller; now he would barely fit through.

I took a deep breath, my mouth dry. I hated this part. Turning sideways, I wedged myself into the crack. I swore it was even smaller than the first time I'd slipped through. It smelled like damp earth and rotting leaves.

I made it to the other side and found a blade at my neck.

"Who are you and what are you doing here?" A lamp swung out of the darkness, flaring orange in my eyesight. I squinted.

"It's Jovis — or don't you recognize me now the posters have all been taken down?"

The blade withdrew. "We weren't expecting you." The man holding the blade peered at me suspiciously.

"Ask Gio," I said. "He sent for me."

He gave me another long look, as though I were an ox he wasn't sure he wanted to buy. "I'll take you to him then."

Not what I'd wanted. "Yes, of course, lead on."

As soon as he'd turned, I took a step swiftly toward him and wrapped an arm around his neck. I hadn't had the time to learn much when I'd been with Gio, but I remembered this. I applied just the right amount of pressure, and within a few moments, the man was passed out on the floor.

Mephi wove around my legs. "Not very nice," he said.

"Oh, he'll be fine," I told him. "You don't seem to worry very much when I spear a few fish. That's not nice either, is it?" I picked up the lamp from the ground and made my way further into the caves. The walls smoothed out a little farther in, becoming more like hallways than tunnels. I'd have to hurry even more; that fellow would wake up quickly and I still had to make it back for dinner.

The hallway I'd wandered into the last time I'd been here was still dark and empty. It stretched long, the walls blank. I put a hand against the cold stone, trailing my fingers along the passage.

"The door was here," Mephi said, stopped in front of a blank section of wall.

"I remember." I pivoted and tapped my staff against the opposite wall. I wasn't sure, but I thought it sounded different. I pressed my palm to the stone. What had I done last time to make the door open? I'd been angry, about to shake the foundations of the caves. And then I'd pulled back at the last minute, sending only the barest trickle of magic into the wall.

I wasn't good at precision. But I'd have to do my best. I concentrated, feeling the trembling build in my bones. Out of the corner of my eye, I saw Mephi crouch, his ears flattened, eyes on the ceiling.

Controlling the flow of power was like trying to dam a river with my hands. No wonder Mephi looked skeptical. I felt a surge flow through my arm and then managed, at the last moment, to slow it. And then I pulled back before I could bring the cliffs down on our heads.

Something clicked open.

The stone swung outward, revealing a door where there had been none. I slipped inside, Mephi rushing ahead of me into the dark. "Mephi!" I called out exasperatedly before giving up. There was no point in scolding; the beast never learned.

I swung my lamp out ahead of me, trying to figure out what this room was for. It was mostly empty, a well-preserved rug in a style I didn't recognize stretched across the floor. Mephi had already made his way to the corner, sniffing the intricately carved table there.

"Can you tell what they ate?"

"Smells like wood," he said, disappointed. He pawed at the rug, getting his nose beneath it, rooting around for things he could take.

I pivoted to the opposite wall and saw the sword. It hung on two hooks embedded into the wall, the blade bare and the sheath laid behind it. Perhaps it was the lamplight, but it didn't look like it was made of *metal*. I frowned as I closed in on it. The cord used to wrap the hilt was frayed and dark, as though it had seen use. I touched it, the cord still silken beneath my fingertips, and felt a tingle run up my arm. He'd asked me to find a white-bladed sword in Lin's possession. A sword like this one.

"You are, by far, the worst spy the Empire has ever seen."

I whirled to find the doorway no longer empty. Gio stood there, arms crossed, and he did not look pleased.

21

—+—

Lin

Nephilanu Island

Perhaps I shouldn't have let my temper get the better of me. I couldn't avoid Jovis for ever; I'd appointed him my Captain of the Imperial Guard after all. But every time I thought of his righteous indignation, his surety that he spoke the truth, a shiver of anger ran through me once more. According to him, I was supposed to leave that mine underdeveloped, leaving Iloh unable to marry, and me unable to garner any support from Riya.

Part of being a leader was making hard choices. He'd said so himself: someone would always hate me for each decision I made, one way or another.

I just wished it wasn't him. But that was foolish. Just because we shared this link between us, the same sort of magic, didn't mean we had to be friends. Just because he was my Captain of the Imperial Guard didn't mean we had to be friends.

I didn't *want* to be friends.

"Eminence?"

Phalue had said something, and I'd been too muddled in my

own thoughts to notice. We walked through the streets of the city, people peering at us from shop windows, gutter orphans peeking around corners to catch a glimpse of the Emperor. They seemed more friendly than standoffish, as they had in Riya. Announcing the return of their shards probably helped a good deal. If I was to win Nephilanu, I needed to put all thoughts of Jovis from my mind. I could handle him later.

"Apologies, Sai," I said, inclining my head. "What did you say?"

"I was saying that the last time an Emperor visited Nephilanu was when I was a little girl. I have a few memories of your father. He was a foreboding man."

Indeed he had been, even in his older years. I remembered his phoenix-headed cane rapping against the floors, his stern disapproval, the smell of sandalwood swirling after him like mist in the wake of a ship. "He did not often mince his words. And he could see through a person to the heart of them beneath."

"A difficult man to have as a father," Phalue said.

"Yes." I hesitated. Ikanuy had briefed me on the situation in Nephilanu – how Phalue had deposed her father and taken control. "It's a misfortune we do not get to choose our parents."

Her lips pressed together, twisting into a half-grimace, and I could see her feelings on the matter weren't as clear as mine. Her decision to depose her father had been harder. I tucked the information away. But this was a common thread to build upon, to form connections. "I've heard you've made changes." As I had made changes.

Her expression brightened, and she and Ranami exchanged glances. I felt a pang of envy at her hand on Phalue's arm, the joy in their eyes when they looked at one another. It was clear that theirs was a marriage born of love.

Would I ever have that choice?

"As I said before, we are more humble than my father was. I don't mind it and neither does Ranami. Nephilanu has been prosperous because of its caro nuts, and this is a prosperity that should be shared with her people."

"They seem to love you," I noted. Indeed, Phalue's presence was met with smiles from her citizens. I thought of my father walking up the road to the palace and knew he would only inspire fear. I didn't complain as we climbed the switchbacks – I'd done more than that when I'd been trying to defeat my father – and I could tell it raised me a little in the governor's estimation. She was someone who appreciated hard physical work – I could tell by the armor she wore and the easy way she wore her sword.

Ranami showed me and my guards to my rooms, and I reserved the room next to mine for Jovis. The palace wasn't what I'd expected, despite my envoy's reports. Although the paintings and murals were elaborate to the point of being gaudy, the furniture was simple, the hallways bare.

An odd place, where the governor considered herself humble, her wife had once been a gutter orphan, and even the palace had been stripped.

"I'll let you rest," Ranami said, "and we can speak of Nephilanu's support for Imperial at dinner, as well as the state of the Empire."

I wouldn't like what she had to say, I could already tell. There was something prickly about Ranami, and I suspected much of it had to do with who I was. I wasn't sure how to gain her respect, though I thought I might need it if I was to win over Phalue.

I took the time to bathe and to read. The books I'd brought with me from my father's laboratory were filled with observations, notes scratched into the margins.

I skimmed, looking for mentions of islands sinking. I didn't find any, but stopped at a passage that hinted at it.

*Fifty years ago, my grandfather hypothesized on the islands'
stability. They quake — all islands quake — but they stay afloat.*

His grandfather. There was a book that contained the notes
Shiyen had taken when power had transferred from his mother
to him. There must be a book that had his mother's notes from
her predecessor's lectures.

I sifted through the books in my chest, their spines and covers
blank. The second book I found that was not in Shiyen's handwriting proved to be the correct one. Did she mention anything
about the islands' stability?

Outside, a light pattering of rain had begun, the overcast skies
threatening heavier fare. Steam still rose from the bath Phalue's
servants had drawn in my room. I curled my feet below me on
the cushion and searched for any mention of stability.

*My father thinks the witstone forms a sort of scaffolding, that it
is what keeps the islands afloat. Witstone moves our ships; why
would it not also move the islands? Pure conjecture.*

The last bit was sharply written and underlined. It seemed I
was not the only one with a complicated parental relationship.

But something Shiyen had seen or researched had convinced
him this wasn't just conjecture. He'd shut down mining on
Imperial. I picked up another of his book of notes and read,
looking for information I could use. He'd been busy in his time
below the palace. The pool in that cave had special properties,
he'd claimed. As did Thrana.

Dread filled the pit of my stomach as I read the words. Her
blood, mixed with the ashes burned from witstone and his blood,
made the liquid I'd drank to experience my father's past. My
father had told me he'd burned his wife's body before he'd made

these discoveries. What, then, had he burned to create the memories he'd stuffed into my body? I flipped the pages, searching for an explanation.

I found instead the description of how he'd made me.

Pieces gathered from various citizens he'd kidnapped, pieces that resembled my mother. A nose here, a pair of eyes there, the arms of some hapless young woman from Deerhead. All sewn together and placed into the pool to heal and grow.

I shut the book tight and had to stop myself from throwing it across the room. It made me want to claw my own skin from my bones. I couldn't help what my father had done to create me. I had to remind myself of that.

Thrana padded over and laid her heavy head in my lap. I rubbed the soft fur of her cheeks. "Where did you come from? Why did my father capture you?"

She began to shake. "Dark place," she said. "He made me stay in the dark place. He *hurt* me."

"I know." I kept my voice low, soothing. "And that will never happen to you again. I promise."

She huffed out a breath, her shoulders still shaking. I waited, stroking her forehead, sensing she would speak if I just let her.

"I came from the dark place. But I was looking for light. I found the door and then your father found me. He put me in a cage. And then he put me back in the water and there was pain."

I'd thought I could never really hate my father, no matter what he'd done to me. Now I found this was not true. Thrana had been helpless, a creature seeking love and care, and he'd given her suffering. I cradled her head in my hands, bringing her up to look me in the eye. "I will always take care of you."

"I know," she said with a sigh.

By the time dinner had arrived, Jovis had still not shown up, and the intermittent flashes of anger I'd felt at him before turned into a torrential lightning storm. What could possibly be keeping him? Was this his petty way of getting back at me for sending him away?

Ranami came to fetch me, peering into my room as if looking for someone. "Your Captain of the Imperial Guard? I knocked on his door but no one answered, Eminence."

"I sent him on a task," I lied. "He may join us later."

Now I was beginning to wonder: had something happened to him? All the anger turned very quickly to worry. I hadn't solidified my rule yet, and the constructs were doing their best to end that rule. No doubt whoever was sending them would count hurting Jovis as hurting me. To be fair, I'd thought about hurting him myself, more than once, but the thought of him lying somewhere, bleeding out from an assassin's blade, made my throat clench. I couldn't wish that fate on him, even if he did have an eminently punchable face.

We followed Ranami to the dining hall. She was wearing a green dress, bright against her skin. She hadn't bound her hair up as was the style, but wore it half loose, the shining waves falling past her shoulders. I was short and wiry; she was tall, rounded and graceful. I'd never before wished for that sort of beauty, but she did make it look very nice.

Phalue stood to greet us in the dining hall. I was relieved to find no surfeit of invited guests, no extra faces to decipher. Just me, the governor and her wife.

Thrana lay down next to my designated cushion and shot me a look that said "look at how well-mannered I can be". Back at the palace, she would have been bounding out into the courtyard with Mephi, chasing butterflies after eating a hearty meal of freshly caught fish. I had to admit she'd been tolerant of this trip.

"Eminence, thank you again for joining us. I trust your stay has so far been comfortable?" Phalue said.

"Yes, thank you, Sai." I sat, and Phalue and Ranami followed.

The servants brought the food as soon as we'd all seated ourselves. Two different curries, rice and a noodle soup. Again, we served from communal plates and bowls. Only a few islands, it seemed including Imperial, served separate plates.

Someone brought a plate laden with fish, which Thrana accepted graciously, eating with the same delicacy as Ranami.

We made small talk for a brief moment – remarking on the weather, the growth of wet season crops and the size of Thrana's teeth. And then Phalue sat back, regarding me. "You'll be wanting to know why the shipment of caro nuts has been delayed."

"I appreciate your directness," I said. And I did. If she were Iloh, we would have been dancing around the subject throughout dinner, and she'd only get to the heart of the matter when she was drunk in the courtyard. "And yes, I was wondering that. Imperial and the surrounding islands have always received a hefty shipment from Nephilanu, and apart from the regular tithe amount, has been well-compensated for it. We're at the start of the wet season, and we both know the bog cough will be more prevalent. Has there been a problem with this year's crop, Sai?"

Ranami set down her chopsticks. "No problem."

They exchanged another glance, this time serious. "We want you to abdicate," Phalue said.

I barked out a laugh and seized another piece of goat meat, lifting it halfway to my mouth. And then I stopped, put it back down and read their expressions. "You're not joking. Why accept my visit then? Why not write me back and turn me down?"

"We thought these things best discussed in person, Eminence," Ranami said. Her tone was respectful, yet in spite of the title, I could tell she didn't see me as an Emperor. "The fact is, the people don't know you."

Again, that accusation. It irked me more hearing it from yet another island. "A problem I'm seeking to rectify through these visits. My father kept me in the palace most of my life and stopped visiting the islands when I was young. It is through no fault of my own that no one knows me."

"Be that as it may," Phalue said, though her tone did nothing to reassure me that she felt this was not my fault, "we've been without direct guidance from Imperial for some time. Your father's reign was disastrous by most measures, and now you're here, telling us that your reign will be better. That you're the one best equipped to clean up his mess. Deerhead and Unta have sunk. We're currently taking in refugees from Unta and trying to find places for them. The constructs are attacking the citizens and organizing into an army in the north-east. You bring us back our shards and that's wonderful, but, Eminence, you can't ask us to trust that you'll fix everything."

Now I understood something of my father's anger. Why did they think we had an Empire in the first place? I picked up the piece of meat again, chewing slowly to give myself time to think and to calm down. I had to make them understand that the Empire needed a leader. If we did not stand together now, we might fall.

I set down my chopsticks. "I've read my share of history. The islands were once independent. Back in the era of the Alanga."

My words had the intended effect. Ranami went pale and Phalue looked disgruntled. Phalue leaned her elbows on the table, the weight of her shoulders making it creak. "We don't intend to return to the era of the Alanga."

"And yet . . ." I folded my hands.

"The islands would rule the islands," Ranami said.

"Alanga artifacts across the Empire are awakening," I said, keeping my voice low and steady. "From everything we know of them, they look human even if they're not. The fact is: they are living among us and waiting for a chance to strike. Would you be able to stop them?"

"Would you?" Phalue asked.

"My father did not pass the secret down to me," I admitted. I couldn't admit that I had Alanga powers myself. "But he left notes and books. I believe that with time and effort, I will find a way to stop them. No matter what the method is, I'll need the support of the islands. I'll need your support. This means we stick together, we stay strong. And part of staying strong is not getting sick. We need those supplies and we need them circulating."

Ranami fixed me with a level gaze. I wondered whose idea this was: hers, Phalue's or both? I couldn't tell. "Imperial will receive caro nuts when you abdicate."

I did my best not to clench the chopsticks in my fist. "And who will replace me?"

"A council of island representatives," Phalue responded. "One from each island, formed to make decisions pertaining to the health of the Empire as a whole."

So they wanted the same thing as the Shardless Few? Or perhaps the Shardless Few had put them up to it. "Really?" It was hard not to keep the incredulity from my voice. "And what of the larger islands? They won't complain that they only get one representative? Will everyone agree on the decisions that need to be made or does nothing get implemented until everyone agrees?"

"We can deal with these things," Ranami said.

"Just because one Emperor has been succeeded by another doesn't mean it's time to throw out the whole process," I said. "I want the same things you do – a better, fairer world. Give me a chance. I'm not my father."

But they didn't know that. I could make gestures, throw kindnesses their way, but they would be watching me, wary of the next move I might make.

I would never be enough. Just as I was never enough for my father.

For a moment, the hopelessness of it all swallowed me. Why was I even trying? Thrana, next to me, pressed her cold nose against my elbow. And then I remembered Numeen and his family, and his daughter's bloody crane. I could be a better Emperor than my father, and I could unite us against what was to come. There was no one else.

They didn't know me and they didn't trust me. All my attempts at convincing them would just sound like begging. I had to show them I was worthy.

As I'd done with my father.

"Have you thought about the people this action will harm?" I said.

Both Phalue and Ranami blinked. Oh, they'd been so caught up in their ideals that they'd not thought through the consequences.

"Say you don't ship the caro nuts. Not now, not ever. Nephilanu is not the only island in the Empire that grows them. People around and on Imperial may still find ways to get them or have their own stores. But when the supply is low, prices go up. It's not the wealthy who will suffer."

"You could prevent that by stepping down," Ranami said.

"And if I did," I said slowly, "would I not be exactly the kind of Emperor we need? The kind who cares? Who is putting the lives of everyone at risk here: you or me?"

We stared at one another, gazes locked, Phalue's jaw working.

A knock came at the door. Without waiting for a response, Jovis entered, Mephi on his heels.

"Eminence," he said, his face pale, "there's been an attack."

22

Jovis

Nephilanu Island

Ylan has a clever mind. He follows one logical thought to another, stringing together conclusions as easily as a fisherman strings up fish in a line. And he tinkers, fiddling with things until he can make them work better. He's shown me an improved pulley (Mephi said circle-rope-thing — but I think this is what he meant) he made for hoisting sails. And he's come up with a clever contraption that traps fish in the water. It works without fail. I delight in these inventions and his explanations of how he created them. But there are other, darker things he's learned.

"The Alanga language has power when combined with the right substances," he tells me. "Let me show you what I can do with it. Help me and together we can perform miracles."

—Notes from Jovis's translation of Dione's journal

I still had the sword in my hands when I turned to face Gio. "Just thought I'd visit," I said.

"Knocking a person out that way doesn't last very long," Gio responded, his arms crossed. I noted the daggers at his sides. "Blood flow returns to the brain once you take your arm away, and they wake up a short time later with a headache." He took in my Imperial uniform, the staff and the sword in my hands.

Was he going to fight me?

And then Mephi, the idiot, bounded over to Gio, butting his thigh with his horns. Gio's stern face broke into a smile and he scratched the base of Mephi's horns. "Yes, well, it's nice to see you too."

For a moment I thought I knew how Lin felt to see me greeted with smiles everywhere while she dealt with suspicion.

I tried to give a nonchalant shrug, though that was difficult with both hands full. "The Emperor is here to see the governor, and I thought you might have missed me. Formed a real bond last time, didn't we? Storming the palace together, deposing a governor – quite the adventure."

The frown returned as quickly as it had disappeared. "And you render my guard unconscious. An interesting way you have of saying 'hello'. It looks like you came here to steal."

"This?" I hefted the sword. Gio flinched. "Does it belong to you? Did you even know that your hideout had secret doors?" I thought of the other secret room that looked like it had seen some use. "You told me you'd not found any Alanga artifacts in the tunnels, that there was nothing here you could use as a weapon. You sent me a note that Lin has a similar sword in her possession and you wanted me to steal it. Are you collecting these artifacts? Why? What do they do and why do you want them?"

The sword was lighter in my hands than I'd expected. It felt like it was made of wood rather than metal.

"Put the sword back," Gio said.

"Is it yours?"

Mephi glanced between me and Gio, finally seeming to notice this was not a friendly reunion. "Jovis, can we just talk?" Mephi said. "Do we need to fight?"

It always hurt me to feel like I was disappointing him. "No," I said, but kept the sword raised. "We don't need to fight. Again, is it yours?"

"No," Gio said.

I tucked the staff beneath my arm, took the scabbard and held it out for Mephi to take. "Well then," I said cheerfully, "I suppose it's mine now. Whoever owned this is obviously long dead. You weren't aware of these hidden passages, which I've kindly revealed to you. And I was lucky enough to find this sword."

"Jovis," Gio said, hands raised, "you don't know what you're doing."

"I'm walking out of here with this sword," I said, starting toward the doorway.

His daggers were out in a flash, catching my blade between them. He twisted. The old bindings on the hilt slipped beneath my fingers. I tightened my grip and the sword stayed put. He was strong for an old man, and quick. For a moment we stared at one another, and I had that feeling like I had the last time Gio and I had nearly come to blows – like we were standing on the edge of a precipice with only rocks below to break our fall. He jerked back and darted in again.

I wasn't a swordsman. I managed to knock his attacks to the side just barely. He whirled with the momentum and came at me again. I danced away. One of his daggers snagged in the hem of my jacket, catching the skin beneath, and sending a quick blaze of pain across my belly. The other I ducked under. My bones thrummed. I didn't dare cause a quake this deep underground;

I'd been foolish to do so in Lin's underground caverns. Moisture here gathered in small, distant droplets. I had only my strength, my speed and my wits.

If I'd been less stubborn, I'd have let him have the sword. But I was tired of secrets, of people who sought to use me without first laying out their truths. I wasn't a tool to be wielded by those in power, kept in the dark about their secrets. If he wasn't going to tell me why he wanted these swords, I was going to find out myself.

I struck back.

My first blow was clumsy. Gio sent it glancing away, darting in with his other dagger. I tried to lift the sword to block, too late. I felt the shock of the slice across my arm, followed by the sting and warmth of blood. I pushed it aside and brought the sword back to bear. He couldn't move out of my longer reach quickly enough. The blade grazed his thigh as he leapt back.

Gio stumbled and fell. He dropped one of his daggers with a clatter, pressing a hand to his injured leg.

"Age catches up to all of us," I said. I stepped around him, Mephi at my heels. But all it took was one look at Mephi's face, his brown eyes forlorn, to make me stop. I pivoted. Gio still knelt on the floor, his breathing heavy, palm against his wound. Ah, I wasn't as callused as I wanted to believe. "Are you badly hurt?"

"I'll live," he said, his voice dry. He looked up at me, his teeth clenched, his milky eye reflecting the lamplight. "But where do your loyalties lie, Jovis? With the Emperor or with the Shardless Few?"

Why was he so invested in making me choose sides? My loyalties lay with my family, with Mephi, with the people I could help and save. It was a truth that burned brighter than a thousand torches in the night. That's why I'd started down this path. Not for the Shardless Few, and not for an Emperor. I opened my mouth to tell him this; instead, all that came out was, "She's not a bad person." I wasn't sure why I was defending her. It wasn't as though we were friends, or even on particularly decent terms at the moment. All I could think about was how she was *trying*, and that mattered more than her station.

"Good people can still do terrible things." His eyes darted to the blade before returning to my face. "Do you think, with the power of the bone shard magic at her fingertips, she'll just give it up? She may be returning the shards to people, and she may be dismantling the constructs, but what do you think will happen when she faces an immediate crisis that can be solved with her magic? You've been around her: you know her better than any of us Shardless Few. Do you think she won't use the power she has at her disposal, even *just this once*, to handle it?"

I thought of the way she'd so cavalierly offered money and workers to develop the mine near Riya when we weren't even sure what was causing the islands to sink. "She wouldn't," I said, and made myself believe it.

"You're choosing the wrong person to be loyal to. She won't be Emperor for long, not when the supply of caro nuts dries up."

He said it like he knew. "You. You've had something to do with that, haven't you? There are other islands that produce nuts, and the Empire's coffers are deep enough to procure them. When there's enough money, someone is always able to provide." It was the same with witstone. He knew this; everyone did.

Unless he'd brokered a deal with the Ioph Carn too. I narrowed my eyes as I regarded him and he didn't waver. He had, hadn't he? But this wasn't my fight. Lin would have to find a way to deal with both the Shardless Few and the Ioph Carn. I brushed past Gio, Mephi on my heels.

"Jovis," Gio called after me. I didn't turn or stop. "Keep hold of that. You don't know what it does."

"You don't either," I called back to him. "And don't expect to receive any more letters."

No one bothered to stop me on my way out.

It had started to drizzle by the time I made my way back into the forest. I felt lighter than I had since I'd begun this whole endeavor. No more lying to Lin, no more secret letters. Mephi handed me the scabbard; I slid the sword into it and strapped it to my back. He shook his head like the scabbard had tasted bad.

"Don't like it," he said. "Or the sword."

I couldn't say I liked it much either, but I certainly wasn't going to leave it in Gio's keeping. I checked the position of the sun on my way into the city – setting quickly. I was running late. I had to take the sword back to the ship; I didn't dare bring it to the palace. Too many questions. So I rushed back to the ship, nodding to my guards, and stowed the sword in my cabin beneath the thin mattress in my berth. I could still make it to the palace in time for dinner if I hurried.

But I re-emerged on deck to the sounds of an argument.

"Well, if I can't get on the ship, send someone to Jovis and tell him I'm here."

I froze, my heart caught in my throat. I knew that voice. Mephi gave me a questioning look, but I didn't have the breath to answer. I made my way to the gangplank.

There, on the dock, was my mother.

Seven years – and they'd changed her in all the ways that didn't matter. Her hair was streaked with silver, her cheeks just a shade more gaunt, the wrinkles around her lips more prominent. But her stance was one I'd recognize anywhere: hands on hips, head lowered, as though she were about to charge through any obstacle, her skull leading the way. She often looked at me that way when she was frustrated – when I'd told one too many stories, or when I'd not heard what she'd said for the third time. She wore a cloak over her clothes, her pants tucked into her boots and a satchel at her side.

"Wait!" I put a hand on the shoulder of the guard. "I know her. That's my mother."

"She said as much," the man said, "but we couldn't be sure."

I gave him a pat to let him know no harm done, slipped past him and descended the gangplank on shaky knees.

"Hey," I said, unsure of what to do. Was she angry with me? *I'd* be angry with me. I'd disappeared for seven years.

She reached up, seizing my face between her palms. Her black eyes searched mine, wet with tears. I thought my heart would beat out of my chest as I waited for her to say something. *Anything.* "Jovis," she said finally, her voice shaking, "you foolish, *foolish* boy. The Ioph Carn? How could you?"

I was a grown man with a lofty position. But I wilted beneath her glare, feeling like I'd never left Anau, like I was still a child. "I'm sorry. I had to."

She seized my hair in her fists, shook me a little. "You never *have* to do anything. You *chose* to. Don't lie to me and don't lie to yourself."

The knot in my throat unwound, tears pricking at my eyes. "I missed you."

And then she was wrapping her arms around me and I was burying my face in her shoulder, still damp with the rain, smelling all the things that reminded me of home: scallions, ginger, sesame oil and that musky scent beneath I couldn't describe but knew it meant I was in my parents' house in Anau.

"Seven years and you never wrote." Her voice was muffled against my shirt. "Not until now, and only the one letter."

"I'm sorry," I said again. I could apologize for several lifetimes and it still wouldn't make up for what I'd done or the hurt I'd caused. "I didn't want to draw attention to you. I didn't want the Ioph Carn to seek you out."

She patted my back the way she always used to when I was sick. "Fine," she said. "Fine. I'm still mad." She drew back from me, sniffed, wiped her eyes and seized my shoulders, took in and released a deep breath. "Captain of the Imperial Guard. I told both your aunties, you know. And Eina, who makes the scallion pancakes. Can you believe she said I was lying? When the news came through by other means, she was very embarrassed. Wouldn't say a thing to me, though. No apology!"

"How excessively rude," I said. My heart felt both full and hollow. "Emahla . . . she's dead, you know."

My mother took my hand. "I know. We all knew, Jovis. When you're young, you think you can change the world. You think you can bend it to your will. When you're old, you learn to change your small corner of it and live with the rest."

"So am I old now?"

She gave me a narrow-eyed look. "Old*er*."

Mephi nudged my elbow. "I can meet her?"

My mother's face went pale as she regarded this speaking creature. But I'd learned one thing from all my days of smuggling: if you acted as though something were normal, everyone else would start believing it was so as well. "Uhhh, yes. Mephi, this is my mother. Mother, meet Mephi."

Mephi sat on his haunches, placed a paw over his chest, and inclined his head.

My mother, bemused, did the same. "It's good to meet you, Mephi." She turned her questioning gaze to me. "I heard stories that you had a talking pet, but wasn't sure what to believe. Like the old sea serpents in the stories, hmm?"

"He's not a pet. He's a friend I picked up," I said. "Near Deerhead. I've raised him since he was small."

She finally regained her composure. "I hope he's given you as much trouble as you gave me."

I laughed. "Oh, that he has." I searched behind her. "What about Father? Is he here with you?"

Her smile slipped.

"Is he well? Is he safe?" I was squeezing her hand too hard. I let go. How many years had I woken up at night in a sweat, thinking of the Ioph Carn bursting into my parents' home?

"He's fine," she said. "Don't worry."

That never boded well. What reason would I have not to worry? As if worry were a thing I could sheathe and put away.

She took in a breath. "The bog cough—"

"What? He's sick? Why are you here? Who's taking care of him?"

"No, stop! Let me finish." She waved her hands as though trying to ward off biting flies. "He's fine; he's not sick. But the bog cough is spreading on Anau. Emahla's mother caught it, and then her father. He's helping their daughter take care of them."

My mind raced. Emahla's younger sister would be grown now, too. I couldn't wrap my thoughts around it. "He's not young anymore. He needs to stay put in the house."

"What would you ask him to do? They're practically family. Everyone is falling sick and someone needs to take care of them."

"The Emperor is here to ask about the caro nut shipment," I said. "She'll make sure some gets sent to Imperial and the surrounding isles. Anau is close by. You'll get some."

And I hoped it would be quickly. I couldn't see the sun behind the clouds, but the light around us was fading. Lin would have my head for being late to dinner, folk hero or not.

"Can you watch over my mother?" I asked the guards at the gangplank. "Find her a place to sit and have some tea? I need to get to the palace."

Somewhere beyond the docks a commotion had started. Raised voices, a woman's sobbing.

My gaze focused over my mother's shoulder.

Two of Lin's maidservants were dragging the third woman between them. Their deep blue dresses were dark with blood, their faces spattered with it. I moved as though through a nightmare, my footsteps pounding against the dock yet never feeling quite quick enough. The handmaid they carried was limp, her dress torn in the middle. I couldn't make sense of the flesh beneath, couldn't tell exactly where the gashes began and ended. It looked like a piece of meat a dog had been given to gnaw on.

Her blood dripped onto the cobblestones, mingling with the mud.

"What's happened?" I took over from one of the maidservants, whose left arm was lain open.

"A group of war constructs," she said, tears cutting trails through the blood on her face. She pressed a hand to her wound. "They came running through town and went straight for us."

23

—

Lin

Nephilanu Island

"Where have you been?" The words left my mouth before I could stop them, filled with the worry I'd been trying to suppress. I'd told Ranami and Phalue that I'd sent Jovis on an errand. Now they knew I couldn't even keep track of my own Captain of the Imperial Guard. How could I claim to be a competent Emperor? And then his words filtered through my mind. "Wait. An attack? Where? In the north-east?" Had the constructs made their way closer to Gaelung?

"Here." The cuff of his sleeve was stained with blood. "Your maidservants were attacked by a group of war constructs." His lips pressed into a line. "One of them is badly injured."

They were young girls, all pleased to have found employment with me, all of them well-read and accomplished. I'd chosen commoners instead of governors' get as had been done in the past.

I'd thought I was doing them a favor.

"And the other two?" I asked, breathless. "Are they all right?"

By his grimace I could tell they were not. "One suffered a bite to the arm. It's bad. The other has a few scratches but is otherwise physically unharmed."

I looked at the governor and her wife. Both were on their feet. I'd risen without realizing it, my fingers clutching at my skirt. My handmaids had helped me dress just this morning, had braided and styled my hair. "I have to go," I said.

The servants had begun to clear the dishes, the faint smell of curry lingering in the air.

Phalue frowned. "I want to assure you that we sent guards to hunt down any war constructs left on this island. There shouldn't have been any more. Certainly not a group of them. We would have warned you if we'd known."

War constructs were conspicuous and Nephilanu was not that large. I believed it. "Someone sent them," I said. "Of all the citizens in your city, they attack my handmaidens? Someone is leading the constructs, and they are bearing down on the heart of the Empire."

"Then you'd best go see to the heart of the Empire," Ranami said.

"I'm seeing to my maidservant," I shot back. "You think the constructs will be satisfied with just taking a few islands? You think they won't eventually attack your people?"

Ranami lifted her chin. "We can manage on our own."

I was dealing with this the way my father might have. I needed to back down, to work collaboratively, to soothe both my anger and my pride. "You might be able to. But is it so wrong of you to work with me until the crisis has passed? See how I handle this. See how I handle other problems. I'm a capable leader and I do only want what's best for this Empire. I am not my father. I don't want anyone to suffer. Think it over. Messages can be sent through my envoy stationed by the docks."

I looked to Jovis, who waited at my elbow with Mephi. "Did anyone call for a physician?"

"Yes, Eminence, although I don't know how much she can do for the girl who's the worst off."

I placed my hand over my heart and inclined my head to Phalue and Ranami. "I'm sorry to leave so abruptly."

Jovis, Mephi and Thrana followed me out of the dining hall.

Rain began to fall by the time we made it into the courtyard, though I couldn't bring myself to care. I'd suffered the damp before and I was just . . . tired. I shook wet hair from my eyes as we took the switchbacks down to the city; it had started to come loose from the elaborate knots. Despite my exhaustion, my bones hummed. The war constructs could still be out there. I felt each droplet of water in the air. I'd put the power of bone shard magic behind me, but now had magic of an entirely different kind.

I wondered if this one had consequences, too.

We reached the edge of the city, the street opening up at the harbor. I was eager to get back to the ship, to find out how my handmaidens fared, to offer them what comfort I could. But then, without warning, Mephi dashed off to the right.

"Mephi!" Jovis called after him.

Thrana followed soon after, like a dog that scented a rabbit. "She'd behave better if it weren't for him," I said.

Jovis only rolled his eyes. "I think we're both at fault here. Come on."

We hurried after them. They wove between people like they were swimming through the waves, and we had to dart past startled city inhabitants to keep up. They both slowed and stopped just a short way off the main road. There was a refuse pile there, which both beasts were sniffing at happily.

"He's not usually *this* disobedient," Jovis murmured. "They must be really hungry."

But Thrana had eaten dinner with me. And then I saw something in the pile. A chunk of white stone. A face.

I crept closer, peering through the rain, something in my bones telling me that this was important. Mephi and Thrana both sniffed at it. I knelt, my robe muddied, trying to ignore the stench. An Emperor and a refuse pile once more – who would have thought? But then I got a closer look at the face.

It was the remains of some statuary that had been hacked to pieces. A woman's face, her eyes wide open. My fingertips tingled when I touched it. I thought of the white sword, and some recognition flickered in me. The sword wasn't made of some strange metal. It was *stone*. The same stone as the remains of this statue. "I'm taking this," I said, pulling it free. Half of a fish carcass slid from the face as I lifted it.

I didn't have any place on my person to store it. It wouldn't fit inside my sash pocket.

Jovis noticed my hesitation. "Here." He put out his hand. "We'll have to get it cleaned off and then I'll put it in your cabin. I promise." I let him take it, shivering as the rain began to soak through my robe. He slipped it inside his satchel, next to a book I didn't recognize.

When I looked up, I found myself meeting the gaze of a man on the other side of the refuse pile, his cloak shadowing his face. He had a heavy bag around his shoulder, lumps pressing against the cloth. He'd been collecting something here, just like I had. There was something rough in his demeanor, the short stubble on his chin. Even through the pouring rain I saw: he only had one eye. The other was covered with a patch.

His face looked familiar, but then he turned and disappeared down the street.

"Mephi. Thrana. Let's go."

This time, they obeyed.

The rain had increased to a torrential downpour by the time we made it back to the gangplank. A silence hung over the ship and that made me more apprehensive than anything else.

"She's in the servants' bunk," one of the guards called from the deck. "Eminence," he added belatedly.

We hurried onto the ship and below-deck. Servants and guards hovered outside the door to the servants' bunk, crowding the narrow hallway. They pushed up against the walls as they saw us coming, though my shoulders still brushed against more than one of them.

"Go to the mess hall," I heard Jovis saying to Mephi and Thrana. "Go get some food."

The servants' bunk had been cleared of everyone except the handmaids and the physician. The physician knelt next to the lowest bunk on the left; the other two handmaids hovering over her. Both look disheveled. One had a bandage wrapped around her entire forearm.

The porthole had been opened to let in some light. The maidservant lay on the bunk, swathed in bandages, red seeping through the cloth. The war constructs had torn at her torso. I knew what my father liked in a war construct: big teeth, even bigger claws.

The girl was breathing, though barely. I wished I hadn't been detoured by Mephi and Thrana.

I knelt next to the physician, an elderly woman who startled when she saw me. "Eminence," she said, blinking furiously. She moved her medicine bag over, trying to give me more space in the cramped quarters.

"How is she?"

The physician regained her composure. "I've done everything I can for her. The wounds are deep and she's lost a lot of blood. All you can do at this point is give her broth and rest."

I read between the lines. The situation was dire. No physician wanted to admit to the Emperor they could not perform miracles of healing, not after what had happened to my ostensible mother and all the physicians who'd failed to cure her illness.

I hadn't thought about sending guards with the maids when I'd given them the day off. I'd thought of my own needs for protection, yes, but not theirs.

And this was where it led.

The physician licked her lips. "I can recommend another physician on Imperial who has experience with these sorts of wounds. If you have witstone, you might make it."

I took the girl's hand in mine and struggled to remember her name. Reshi. I'd been so involved in the larger things, the bigger picture, that I'd forgotten to think of the smaller things. And sometimes these were the things that mattered the most.

She didn't respond; her hand was cold.

I rose, peering past Jovis and picking out one of the guards in the hall. "You there. Fetch my things from the palace. We leave for Imperial. Now. Burn as much witstone as we have."

The servants and sailors scattered to obey.

"I'm so sorry," I told my other two maidservants, and felt tears pricking my eyes. "This is my fault."

They only stared at me, unsure of what to say. That made three of us.

I whirled, ducked out of the servants' bunk and almost collided with an older woman in the hallway. She was nearly as short as I was, her graying hair pulled back into a bun, her tunic and pants simple but clean.

"Oh!" She patted my shoulder. The contact shocked me. I didn't know this woman. Few dared to touch the Emperor without permission. "I didn't see you. I was looking for my son."

Jovis, at my shoulder, sucked in his breath.

The woman peered past me. "Jovis, there you are." And then she looked at me again, as though seeing me for the first time. "Is this . . . the new Emperor?"

"Yes, Mother," Jovis said from behind me, his voice strained. "That's her. You're meant to call her Eminence."

She looked me up and down. "You're completely soaked," she said. "You'll get sick if you stay that way. I'll make you some hot soup. It always helped my boys." And then she turned and strode down the corridor with purpose.

I watched her go, a little flabbergasted. "Your mother is here?"

Jovis coughed. "I didn't really have the chance to tell you. It's what kept me from making it to dinner."

"And your father?"

He grimaced. "Being an idiot on Anau. There's an outbreak of bog cough there. It's put my friends and family in danger, including him. I don't suppose you can . . . ?"

I shook my head. "I sent most of Imperial's store of caro nut oil to Iloh on Riya. I didn't think Nephilanu would withhold their shipment. I can ask Ikanuy if there's any to spare, but I left only enough to hold Imperial over."

He seemed to deflate, his head bowing. "I thought as much."

"I'll do what I can to procure caro nuts from somewhere else. Your mother can stay in your room and charter a ship back home once we reach Imperial."

Jovis screwed up his face. "Thank you. And don't mind her manners, please – Anau is very small and she knows everyone there."

I watched her back disappear around the corner. "No, it's fine," I said, and found I meant it. There'd been something familiar in the way she'd treated me, and it made me think of Bayan. We'd been friends so very, very briefly.

My meeting with Ranami and Phalue, and the attack on my

handmaids made it clear: I had work to do. "You're scholar-trained," I said to Jovis. "Meet me in the mess hall. I have orders to write and I could use a second eye on them."

I gathered pen and paper from my room. Above, footsteps pounded as the ship was made ready for departure.

I found chaos in the mess hall. Jovis's mother was in the kitchen, ordering the cook about as though he were her assistant. And the cook, to my surprise, went about meekly gathering the things she said she needed.

I raised an eyebrow at Jovis.

"She's a cook too," he said, as though that explained everything. "A good one."

I wasn't going to stop her. Indeed, I wasn't sure she *could* be stopped.

One of my servants passed me a sealed letter. The phoenix seal was unbroken. There were only a few people who had access to the phoenix seal. Ikanuy was one. My general Yeshan was another. My heartbeat quickened as I slipped a finger beneath the seal and broke it.

It wasn't good news.

The soldiers I'd sent to the north-eastern reaches had been forced to retreat, letting yet another island fall to the constructs. Nearly all of the men and women I'd sent had been killed. Reports from the battlefield spoke of monstrous war constructs, of the dead joining in battle. The few soldiers who'd returned all said the same thing: the construct army was growing.

Two more islands and they'd be at a good jumping-off point to attack Gaelung. If Gaelung fell, the Empire would be irrevocably weakened.

I swallowed as I settled onto the bench at one of the tables, my throat aching. I couldn't just concern myself with guarding the people who saw themselves as important. I'd made that mistake here and my handmaiden was paying the price for it. I think that was the worst thing about being Emperor: I never seemed to be the one my poor decisions cost the most. I folded the letter back up and laid it on the table. "I shouldn't have kept soldiers in reserve. We need to send the rest of our army to the northeast. Now. I'll write to Ikanuy and to the governor of Gaelung. Gaelung is large enough to host them and we have an established trade route there. Supply lines will be easy to maintain."

"And Unta?" Jovis said, his voice deceptively light. "People will panic – more than they already are."

"You were right." I hated to admit it. "We need to shut down the mines. My father's notes imply there's a connection to the sinking. He shut down the mine on Imperial once he realized what might happen." How like him not to care about the implications for the rest of the Empire. I stood at a tipping point. The mines provided a large source of income for many of the governors. I needed their support to push back the construct army. And witstone facilitated trade among the islands. Without continued mining, everyone's stores of witstone would eventually run out. Trade would grind to a halt. Caro nuts would be even harder to come by.

At the same time, the sinking of Unta had sobered me. "Scaffolding" the old Emperor had said. If what he'd suspected was true, then we were slowly chipping away at the very foundations that held us afloat in the Endless Sea.

"I'll send out a proclamation telling everyone to halt production of witstone and any further mine development. That the witstone keeps us afloat and mining it is what's causing the islands to sink." I had to speak with authority, or no one would obey.

"They won't be happy with that," Jovis said. "People will want proof. They'll say you're making it up. They won't want to believe it."

All I had as proof were my father's disjointed notes. I gave him an exasperated look. "Since when has anything I've done made anyone happy? We'll resume production as soon as we figure out how to stabilize the islands. It's the best I can do. I'll keep my promise to Iloh on Riya, just not right now."

Wood scraped as a steaming bowl of soup was set in front of me. "There," Jovis's mother said, a self-satisfied smile on her face. "Now if that's not the best, most invigorating soup in all the isles, you can close my shop down. I'll take some to your maidservant too. It'll help."

It did look good. But there was so much more work to do, and never enough time to do it in.

She saw my glance, set a hand on the papers and moved them just out of reach. "You need to eat, and you need to stay healthy."

She sounded like she actually . . . cared? But she couldn't care; we'd only just met one another. Without warning, feelings I hadn't known I had came welling up from inside me. Sometime far in a past life, I'd had a mother, or at least, Nisong had. Despite her position as a governor's wife, she'd liked to cook and by Nisong's journal, it had comforted her.

I'd wanted a family so badly – I'd clung to the idea that perhaps my father could love me, if I only tried hard enough. And now this woman was treating me more kindly than my father ever had, and I'd done *nothing* for her.

The soup blurred in my vision. But I picked up the spoon and ate. It *was* good, better than anything the ship's cook had made. Thick noodles swam in broth, a sheen of black sesame oil on top. It was slightly spicy, the broth flavored with some herb I didn't recognize. Had she brought her own herbs? "It *is* the best," I said, trying not to cry. "And I wouldn't shut down your shop if it wasn't."

But I took back the papers and started writing out my edicts again. I needed to finish this. There was still research to be done, a whole Empire to hold together.

Jovis's mother sat next to him on the bench. "Does she have any relatives?" she said in a whisper I could hear. "Or is it just you, the guards and the maidservants?"

I could almost hear his jaw grinding. "Her Eminence is *right there.*"

I stood abruptly, almost tipping over the bench. "I'm going to finish this in my room. Thank you for the soup . . . "

"Ongren," she said. "But you can call me 'Auntie'."

"Thank you, Ongren," I said. I gathered my papers and fled. I was halfway down the hall before Thrana caught up.

"She was nice," Thrana said, looking up at my face.

I let out a shaky breath. "She was." Thrana wound around my legs as I let myself back into my cabin.

Thrana leaned against my hip. "I wasn't used to kindness either."

I didn't want Ongren to pity me. I didn't want anyone's pity. I was the Emperor and not to be pitied. I needed them to love me, to exalt me.

I finished writing the orders and set them aside. I turned to the crate at the foot of the bed. My father's books, the vial of memories, the sword. I'd been puzzling over his books for so long, trying to decipher what exactly he meant by some of his notes. I couldn't find any mention of the sword, which left me frustrated to no end.

Two islands I'd visited, another had sunk, and I was only a little closer to unraveling the secrets I needed.

I picked up the bottle of memories.

"Lin, are you sure . . . ?" Thrana said.

I didn't respond. I uncorked the bottle and let the liquid slide past my lips.

The world around me dissolved. I was in the cave below the palace, the memory machine in front of me, my nostrils thick with smoke. "This has to be enough." My father's voice emanated from my throat.

The brazier in the memory machine was filled nearly to the brim with blood. A chunk of witstone sat in the middle, an island in a sea of red.

My gaze flicked to the side. Bowl after bowl of blood, lined up next to the memory machine. And all I could feel was my father's grief, his hope. I pulled two rubbery ends of tubing out from within the chest, placed them in the brazier and opened the valves on them.

"Nisong," I whispered, and then lit the witstone ablaze.

24

Ranami

Nephilanu Island

The visit could have gone worse, though when Ranami imagined what "worse" meant, all she could imagine were farfetched scenarios in which Lin had marched an army to their doorstep and had demanded Gio's head. They'd kept to their side of the truce, but at what cost? The wet season was in full swing now, and people were starting to die of bog cough. Ranami had expected that sacrifices would have to be made in their quest to take down the Empire, but she had expected those to be made on the battlefield by an army of the Shardless Few, each member ready and willing.

Not by people coughing into the dark, drowning in their own fluids as they waited and hoped for a cure that would never come.

They'd thought they'd hunted down all the constructs on Nephilanu. Clearly, given the attack on the Emperor's maidservants, that wasn't the case. Phalue had insisted on sending the guards out on patrol again. If they started shipping caro nuts, the Shardless Few would redouble their efforts to take Nephilanu. To take Phalue's life.

She lingered on the steps to the cellar, one foot up and one foot down.

"You've stopped drinking wine," she heard Phalue say.

"I don't really see the point in it down here," her father responded. A pause. "I appreciate the books and the lamp you brought me. I know you didn't see me read much when you were a child, but I did when I had the chance."

"When you weren't busy." The words were flat. Ranami knew that tone – Phalue only ever used it when she was disappointed in someone.

"Yes, well I didn't use my time the way I should have. I can see that now. I should have . . . I should have spent more time with you." He coughed.

She shouldn't be listening in on this. Phalue had invited her down to these visits more than once, but Ranami couldn't quite gather the courage. Not to face Phalue's father – she had no fear of him – but to see the pain on Phalue's face. Much as she hated the old governor, she understood that Phalue's experience of him had been different. Ranami only knew the effects of his actions: the increased caro nut quotas, the harsh punishments, the lack of any system to give back to the farmers. She didn't know him as a person. She certainly didn't know him as a father.

"There are a lot of things I should have done differently," he was saying. "I won't say I regret everything. And I can't agree with how you're running things. Are you really thinking of sending caro nuts to the poorer islands? You'll be breaking your truce and you won't even be paid that well for it."

"You're sick," Phalue said. "I'll have a physician see you, bring you some caro nut oil. And there has to be a way we can make it a little less damp down here."

For a moment, Phalue's father didn't speak. "That's more kindness than I would have shown any of my prisoners. Thank you."

"You're still my father. You just . . . Ah, why didn't you think for just a moment about what you were doing? You lost sight of everything except your own vanity."

"I can try to do better, if you'd just let me prove it."

"It's too late for that."

Ranami backed up the stairs. She didn't want to walk in on this conversation. Maybe another time she'd visit Phalue and her father, but this felt too personal.

The smell of the kitchen wafted over her as she climbed — onions and ginger, mingling with the pot of seafood stock bubbling over the firepit. The servants moved around one another with the grace of dancers, narrowly avoiding collisions, plates and vegetables clutched in their hands. Even after they'd married, even after she'd moved her paltry things into the palace, it was difficult for her to believe she lived here — that everything here was now hers as well. She still woke up sometimes from dreams where she was back on the streets, hunting for scraps to eat, trying to piece together enough things to sell. When she was in those dreams her life in the palace seemed an imagined thing.

Someone scurried among the servants, her head just below their shoulders. Ranami froze on the steps as she recognized the girl. Not some kitchen servant's wayward child. Ayesh.

Ayesh had been at the palace this morning — and though Phalue had given her leave to eat at the kitchens and to sleep in the room they'd set up for her, Ranami had watched her leave. What was she doing back here?

A couple of the servants glanced at Ayesh, but they'd seen her here before and they were busy preparing the evening meal. Dishes scraped against one another, knives chopped and always they talked — gossiping about Unta, about the Emperor and her visit, about the Shardless Few. Ranami had listened in on these conversations more than once, eager to know what was being said among the commoners. They paid the gutter orphan little mind.

And as Ranami watched, cloaked in the darkness of the cellar stairwell, Ayesh took full advantage of their lax attention. She went to the pantry, peeled off a banana and began to eat it. While she ate, she surreptitiously pilfered a whole leg of cured pork, three mangoes and a jar of dried fish. These went into a bag she carried at her side – one she didn't have when she'd been there for lessons in the morning.

Ayesh slung the bag over her shoulder and made for the door.

Swiftly, Ranami crept up the rest of the stairs. She might not have been small like Ayesh, but she'd spent enough time creeping around city alleyways to know how to make herself unseen. She strode along the walls, keeping servants between her and the girl, ready to duck behind one of them if Ayesh turned around.

She waited just a bit after Ayesh left the kitchen to follow her. A glimpse of short black hair and brown tunic disappeared around the corner. Ranami frowned. The girl wasn't headed in the direction of the gate.

When she peered around the corner, she saw Ayesh lingering near a door, her fingers stroking the surface of one of the few tapestries Phalue hadn't sold. The woman had stripped the palace near bare before Ranami had stopped her. They had enough in the treasury to enact the policies they wanted to; there was no point in being overly austere. What they needed most was time, and that couldn't be bought with artwork or baubles.

There was a conversation happening behind that door between two servants, though Ranami could only hear bits and pieces of it.

" . . . think I've not noticed . . . other ways out. And how . . . not everyone can . . . we'll drown!" The last word was thrown with vehemence. Someone else was speaking in a low, soothing voice. Ranami couldn't make it out.

Some of the servants knew about the old Alanga entrance in the wall – the one leading straight down the slope. Ranami and Phalue couldn't keep all things secret, and they'd needed help to prepare for the possibility of Nephilanu sinking. She was certain some of them had pieced together what the preparations were for.

There had been no easy choices – should they have been open with the servants about their plans? Or should they keep them quiet and project the confidence that the island needed? After lengthy discussions, they'd decided on the latter, but the decision hadn't rested easily with either of them.

Ayesh continued down the hall, gazing at the painted beams, the carved doors, her hand trailing along the wall. At last, she turned.

Ranami ducked back into the kitchen. Phalue hadn't finished her conversation with her father, which Ranami was grateful for – she wasn't sure how to explain why she was skulking around as though she didn't own the place.

When she thought Ayesh might have passed, she cracked the door. The girl's back retreated down the hall, disappearing behind the archway that led to the courtyard.

Ranami hesitated on the threshold of the kitchen. Phalue liked the girl. But Phalue liked her father too. She liked damn near everyone, and fiercely disliked the few she didn't. It would hurt her if the girl was a spy. But it would hurt her even more if she never found out and Ayesh carried information to the Shardless Few.

What the girl had overheard about the preparations to flee could come back to haunt Phalue. It was bad enough that it was a source of palace gossip. What if Gio found out? All it would take was one well-placed rumor to undermine Phalue's place as ruler. It would stir unrest and foment panic – exactly what they'd been trying to avoid. Ranami knew the ways words could be used against people. If Gio had a source of information in the palace, he could twist what happened inside it, the decisions that were made. And then, no matter Phalue's intentions, no matter how hard she tried, there would always be those who saw her as they'd seen her father.

The people of Nephilanu loved Phalue, but love could quickly sour under the right conditions.

She slipped from the kitchen and made for the courtyard. Ranami believed in the Shardless Few; she believed in what they wanted for the Empire. Phalue had shifted her position to better align with their goals. And still that was not enough for Gio. If Phalue would not protect herself, Ranami would do it for her.

She took her oilskin cloak from the hook by the door, swung it around her shoulders and stepped into the courtyard. The rain had broken, but there was always the chance for more. Ayesh disappeared beneath the arch of the gateway and Ranami hurried after her.

The vegetation outside the palace walls had grown thick and lush since the wet season had begun. Bushes that had once seemed brittle and dead sprouted fresh green leaves. Grass and ferns grew past Ranami's waist. She had to duck and sway to avoid the reaching branches.

Ayesh trudged ahead of her, bag slung over one shoulder. Ranami lingered behind, keeping her footfalls light. Despite Phalue's admonition that she would need to learn to trust an orphan if they were to adopt, Ranami wasn't sure she could trust this one. How much did they know about the girl really? She was clearly a gutter orphan and yes, she'd been in a bad way when they'd found her. Her story about Unta had seemed real enough. But Ranami knew what desperation was like.

When the bookseller she'd eventually apprenticed with had realized she knew how to read and had offered a place in his home, she'd pretended more knowledge than she'd actually had. She'd been convincing at it too. Ranami had picked up bits and pieces from before her mother had died, but it wasn't any impressive amount. Whenever the bookseller had left, or had his back turned, she'd thrown herself into the task of learning, filling in the gaps of her knowledge until she met the standard she'd first pretended to.

What were a few lies when you could fill your belly at night and lay your head somewhere safe?

And then, when Ranami had grown older, there had been the touching. Brushes against her shoulders and waist, lingering looks. She'd hated it, hated the way he cornered her so there was no way to get around him. Others she'd known on the streets had been through far, far worse, so who was she to complain? By then, the bookseller was getting old, and would soon die, so she'd gritted her teeth and waited it out. She wouldn't go back to being a gutter orphan. Not ever again.

Ayesh glanced back and Ranami ducked behind a bush. The girl's gaze searched the path but, finding nothing, she continued on her way.

She was the wife of the governor now, Ranami reminded herself. And she was hiding in the bushes. Not exactly a turn of events she'd ever anticipated. It seemed she could marry into power, she could wear the well-tailored dresses and sit at Phalue's side – but a part of her would always still be a gutter orphan.

The greenery faded into the cobblestone streets of the city. Ayesh took one last look back and darted toward an alleyway.

Ranami swore, untangled herself from the brush and followed.

Spying would have been easier than teaching oneself to be a bookseller's apprentice. It would have been easier than collecting trinkets to sell for bits of coin. It would have been easier than stealing purses. All it meant were a few lies, two open ears and a tongue willing to speak.

She turned the corner after Ayesh and saw only a heel disappear around the next corner. Had the girl spotted her? She wanted to know — where was she taking the information she'd gleaned? Was it to Gio or some third party?

And why the food? Phalue told her she could have all she wanted to eat when she was at the palace. Did the girl mean to sell them? Skim a little extra money where it wouldn't be noticed? It was something Ranami might have done. Or perhaps she was being uncharitable. Perhaps Ayesh had friends she wanted to care for.

She rounded the next corner onto a busy street, filled with stalls. No sign of Ayesh — only merchants hawking their wares, the smell of onions thick in the air. Steam rose from pots, rising to the bamboo and frond ceiling above. Ranami squinted into the crowd, trying to see to the end of the street. She couldn't shake the feeling that Ayesh had turned onto this street on purpose.

Perhaps Ranami *had* lost something of her old self.

The rain began again, pattering against the palm fronds above. People around her drew up their hoods or lifted umbrellas. Her feet were already damp. What was she going to do? Search each street for a sign of the girl? She should be in the palace, sipping a cup of tea, going over their treasury and allocating money for the items on their list. Ah, maybe she *had* gone soft. She turned around to make her way back up the switchbacks.

She arrived back at the palace to find Phalue in the courtyard in the shadow of the second-floor balcony, conferring with Tythus. "That was quick," she said, holding out a hand. Tythus handed her what looked like a small, pointed shield. Phalue inspected it, lifting it, checking buckles. Even in spite of what she'd seen and the news she brought, Ranami's heart still swooped when she looked at her wife. There was both strength and kindness in the way she handled herself and the way she handled others.

Phalue looked up to meet her gaze, smiled and beckoned her over. Ranami went, rehearsing in her head what to say.

But Phalue had other things on her mind. "Look at this," she said. "I had a blacksmith in the city make it."

"A bit small for you, isn't it?"

Phalue gave her an amused look. "Of course it's not for me. It's for Ayesh. The girl is small, but she's quicker and stronger than she looks. A shield can be a weapon too, as well as providing defense." She held it up against her arm like a vambrace, the pointed end over the back of her hand. "She can't fight like me and expect to win. I'm bigger than most of my opponents, except Tythus. With her speed, two small weapons would be better suited to her. But without a hand, she can't wield a dagger with her other arm. But this?" Phalue flipped the shield over, showing Ranami the straps, the cap at the end meant to go over Ayesh's wrist. "This becomes an extension of her arm. The end is sharp, as are the edges close to the point. So now she has another weapon as well as something she can use to defend herself."

"That's clever," Ranami said, all of her rehearsed words falling to dust in her mouth. This was one of the things she loved about Phalue: when she decided on something, she leapt in headfirst without reservation. When their relationship had begun, Ranami had marveled at Phalue's openness, her willingness to share, to be vulnerable and to love recklessly. Ranami had always been the more cautious of the two of them.

She looked to Tythus, leaning against one of the pillars. "Could you give us a moment, please?"

He nodded, uncrossed his arms and retreated inside.

Phalue frowned. "Is something wrong?" She tapped a finger to her chin. "You were going over our accounts, yes? Did you find a discrepancy? Some item on the list that will require more funds than we first thought?"

"I . . . " There really wasn't a good way to say it, was there? "I saw Ayesh in the kitchen."

"And? What does that have to do with anything? She's allowed to be in there."

"She came back after she left the palace. Why would she do that?"

"I told her to," Phalue said. "I knew the shield would be coming today. She must have come back, realized I was still busy and then left again."

Now Ranami was doubting herself – was there an easy explanation for everything she'd witnessed? But she'd learned to trust her instincts. Ayesh was hiding something, and neither Phalue nor she knew what it was. "She stole food from the kitchen. I don't know what for. And I caught her in the hallway, listening in on a conversation between servants. They were talking about our contingency plan."

Phalue tilted her head, her brows knit. "Were you following her?"

"No. Well, yes. Fine. I tailed her into the city and lost her. I wanted to know if she was taking that information anywhere and, if so, who she was taking it to. Phalue, if that got to the wrong people, they could use the information to damage you. Things are hard enough as it is."

"No one seems dissatisfied with my rule," Phalue said.

"No one says it to your face," Ranami said. "But there are whispers. And it is so easy for whispers to become shouts with the right provocation. The stories may say that Gio took Khalute single-handedly, but I doubt they're true. It's clear he knows how to gather people to a cause. Look at how the Shardless Few follow him. I worry he'll undermine you and try to take over."

"He can try."

"All it takes is one mistake, one misstep he can use against you. He'll drive a wedge between you and this island."

"Ranami, please." Phalue set the shield against a pillar and took Ranami's hands. "You're right – I do need to be careful. And I appreciate you're here looking out for me. But sometimes there are reasonable explanations for the shadows that you see."

Maybe Phalue was right – maybe she was seeing sea serpents in the fog. She took a deep breath. "I don't know who the girl is or what she truly wants."

"Why don't you talk to her? Get to know her? I won't scoff at you or tell you you're being ridiculous. If it makes you anxious to have her around, we can take more precautions. You said before that I'm one of the few people you trust. I may trust more easily than you, but there is no one I trust more deeply. I'll ask the guards to keep an eye out. They can track when she leaves and when she comes back and what she takes with her. Would that help?"

Some of the tightness in her chest eased. "Yes, that would help."

"I'm the governor now. I saw how quickly my father lost his position and how easily the Shardless Few incited a riot. This isn't something I take lightly." Phalue cleared her throat. "Speaking of things I don't take lightly ... I think we should send out the caro nuts. We don't have to send them straight to Imperial, but the Emperor is right. If we do what Gio wants us to, people will suffer and die. People who have already suffered under the Empire."

Ranami clenched her hands, the knot in her chest growing tight again. "If Gio finds out, we don't have enough guards here to fend off an attack."

"Just a little at a time," Phalue said. "Hidden among other goods."

"You want to smuggle them?" Ranami said. "We're not the Ioph Carn."

"Smuggle what?"

Ranami whirled to see Ayesh emerging from behind one of the pillars. She hadn't heard her approach. Hadn't she just been here? The bag Ayesh had been carrying was gone.

"Ah. Nothing," Phalue said. And then she was sweeping up the shield, a grin on her face. "Here's the surprise I was promising you."

The girl's black eyes focused for a moment on Ranami. She could have been imagining it, but for a moment, she thought she saw the flicker of acknowledgement. Again, that tug of instinct.

Ayesh had known Ranami was following her.

25

Jovis

Somewhere in the Endless Sea

Ylan insists that he can use the power of the Alanga language to keep the Alanga in check. "You are granted long life (immortality?) and powers over wind and water," he says. "What can the rest of us do in the face of that?"

What he shows me isn't a pulley or a fish trap. It's an abomination. I cannot even commit some of the things I've seen to paper. It's too much. He means well, I know he does.

He asks me for my help. I deny him. He pleads. He argues.

And then, at last, he says he must return home. He says it's been years. Has it? Days and years have little meaning to me; I measure the time in seasons.

I wish he wouldn't go, but I'm too angry to tell him so.

—Notes from Jovis's translation of Dione's journal

L in's maidservant died two days later, in spite of my mother's soup, in spite of the physician's care, in spite of all the witstone we burned to get the ship to move faster. Lin ordered the ship put to port at the next island so we could give the girl a proper funeral.

And I did my best to keep my mother in check, unobtrusive. It was not a task I was very successful at.

"She's the Emperor," I said to her for the thousandth time, watching her roll out dumpling wrappers in the mess hall. She was always moving, rarely still.

"An Emperor can't enjoy my dumplings?"

It wasn't that – she *knew* it wasn't that. It was the way she insisted on telling Lin what to do, ask when she'd last eaten, point out that the dark circles beneath Lin's eyes indicated not enough rest. It simply wasn't done. I stared at her until she felt my gaze, and she set down the rolling pin to stare right back.

"Jovis, she has no family except people she's never met. Her father is dead. Her mother is dead. She seems lonely."

I remembered when I'd spoken to Lin in the streets of Imperial City, when she'd seemed more like a person and less like an Emperor. And then there was that time we'd fought side by side against the assassins. There had been a moment . . . But that was foolish of me. "I don't think she wants your pity," I said. Why were we talking about Lin? I hadn't come here to talk about Lin.

She frowned at me. "Is this just the way young people are? I don't pity her. I see someone who is sad and I want her to be less sad. What's so wrong about that?" She waved her hands at me. "Bah! Get out. I'm busy and you're bothering me."

I found myself walking out of the kitchen before I could stop myself. Habit. I glanced to the side and found the mess hall cook, forlornly playing a game of cards against himself. Ah, so I wasn't the only person to be successfully banished. Somehow that made me feel better.

Mephi greeted me when I went above deck, rising from the measly patch of sunshine he'd found.

"You're worried," he said as he joined me by the railing.

I stared out at the Endless Sea, unable to put aside what Philine had said to me back on Imperial. We were arriving at a port soon, just to stock up on supplies and send Lin's letters.

Lin hadn't been able to secure caro nuts from Nephilanu, and she didn't have enough oil left on Imperial to give to other islands. My father was on Anau in the midst of an outbreak, caring for a sick family. Was he sick, even now? Neither my mother nor I had brought it up. He'd always avoided the bog cough, but at his age, he might die if he caught it.

Seven years and I'd sent one letter. I knew he wouldn't scold me for it. But he'd look at me with love and disappointment, and it would devastate me for the pain I'd caused him. Yet I wanted that feeling more than anything, because it meant he would still be alive to *be* disappointed in me. I could get in contact with the Ioph Carn. I could ask them to smuggle something.

"I'm not sure what to do," I said, running my hand through my hair. I'd let it grow a little longer again. "I can do something, but I'm not sure if it's the right thing. It could be a very good, or it could be a very bad – but most likely it would be both."

If I sent a message, if I told them I'd be willing to do something for them, I'd be putting myself back in the same place I was seven years ago – beholden to the Ioph Carn. I'd thought I'd finally escaped that. How much would Kaphra ask of me? What did he want?

But if I never did anything to help, what sort of person would I be?

"If you don't do the thing?" Mephi asked. "What is it then?"

I sighed. "It's very bad. It's only very bad." I had to stop telling myself I didn't have choices. I did, and I'd have to live with the consequences of whatever I decided. The task the Ioph Carn set for me might not have anything to do with Lin. It might not hurt her at all. I couldn't know yet.

"What's very bad?" Lin appeared behind me, dressed in her traveling clothes. I hated it when she was dressed that way. It made her feel too normal, too approachable.

I calmed my fast-beating heart and squinted at the clouds in the distance. "The weather. I think sometimes that the spots of sunshine we get are only so we can remember how much nicer it was before the wet season started – and be all the sadder for it."

She laughed. "And everyone is always so excited at the first wet season rain. It wears off too quickly." She fished around in her sash, pulling out something that fit into her palm. "There's something I've been meaning to give to you."

I held out my hand and she dropped a shard of bone into it.

"It's yours. I found it when I was sorting through the shards to return to the islands. You and I both know I'd never use your shard, but I thought it would be a nice thing to do, seeing as—"
I wound up my arm and threw the piece of bone into the ocean.

She frowned. "Well, that's one way to keep it from being used, I suppose."

"It's not mine." I still remembered the soldier's breath against my ear as he told me he'd spared me. "Probably a chicken bone or something. You would have found out eventually if you'd tried to use it." I leaned down to show her the scar behind my ear. "Here. Feel."

Her fingers were cold against my skin, her touch gentle and probing. "No piece missing. Hm."

I swallowed and moved away. "The soldier took pity on my family. My older brother died during the Tithing Festival. I was all my parents had left. So he left me the scar and left me my skull intact. Whatever shard he turned in was a false one."

The sun hot against my scalp, my knees digging into the ground, the pain and the blood trickling down the back of my neck. I'd never forget those sensations, even as I'd forgotten the soldier's face.

She touched the spot behind her ear absentmindedly.

"Surely your father didn't . . . ?"

Lin shook her head. "No. The Sukais never tithed their own." She pushed away from the railing. "I need to find some juniper to burn with the body. The captain said there should be some aboard." I watched her go, wishing I could have made her laugh another time. We could all have used more laughter.

We made landfall at the port later that morning, and Lin gave us leave to stretch our legs. "Be back after lunch," she said, "and quickly, or I'm setting sail without you."

"You're not going ashore?"

She shook her head and gave me a wan smile. "I'm helping to prepare Reshi's funeral." Thrana followed her, though she threw us a regretful look over her shoulder.

Lin had already sent her uninjured maidservant into the portside town with her letters and orders, so I had nothing else to do except find the Ioph Carn. Mephi trotted alongside me as we descended the gangplank, and I could feel his hopeful gaze on me.

And feed the beast, of course.

I wasn't sure what island we'd stopped at, but the town was small, nearly engulfed by a thick rainforest on all sides. Mountains rose sharply from just beyond it, looming over the buildings like jagged teeth. Mist lay heavy over both mountains and forest. "Don't wander off," I said to Mephi as we walked into town. "This is a less populated place than you're used to and I don't know what sort of creatures live in the forest here." I'd heard stories, and had even seen a trophy or two from some strange animal. Wasn't keen on meeting one in the flesh.

I'd never been to this island, but I knew how to find the Ioph Carn. Their network was extensive. If there was an island in the Empire untouched by them, I hadn't heard of it.

I wandered through the streets, stopping at one of the few stalls to purchase steamed fish in a black bean sauce for Mephi. He sat on his haunches to eat it, picking through it with his paws as though they were fingers. The vendor gave him a curious look and then cast me a raised eyebrow. I only shrugged and continued on my way. I didn't owe him answers.

It took me only a little longer to find it. A doorway carved in an intricate pattern. But hidden in the pattern was a symbol. I glanced down the street and then, spotting none of Lin's maidservants or guards, knocked softly on the door.

Footsteps creaked from inside. "Who is it?"

"Just a midnight songbird, looking for a roost."

For a moment, I thought the password might have changed. I tightened my hand around my staff, wondering if the person behind the door was readying an attack. And then the door cracked open. A short old woman peered at me. It took her only a quick glance to assess me: my uniform, my staff, Mephi at my side.

"Jovis," she said. "I've been told to expect you."

"You . . . what?" There was no way Kaphra could have known I'd stop at this particular island and come looking for the Ioph Carn. She gestured me inside and I followed, a bit bemused.

She shut the door behind me. "Kaphra sent missives to all the islands. It came in two parts: one telling us you might come to us, and a second with instructions for you." She went to the desk by her window, opened a drawer, opened a false bottom and pulled out a piece of parchment. I caught a glimpse of silver darts before she let the false bottom fall back into place. Not as defenseless as she looked then.

"Here." She proffered the paper to me.

I was tapping my staff again unconsciously so I stilled my hand. "I never said what I was here for."

She only smiled at me, her teeth small and crooked. "You tell me what you want, and it's done. But this is what Kaphra wants in return."

The letter had no teeth that I could see, but I knew there'd be teeth in the writing of it. There always was a catch with Kaphra. Never could be a simple job. I reached for it hesitantly, afraid of its bite.

She pulled it back. "Ah-ah, what did you want done?"

I sighed. "A month's supply of caro nuts, smuggled to Anau."

She considered, doing the mental math. "Difficult, but consider it done." And then she placed the letter into my outstretched hand.

I unfolded it and Mephi crouched next to me, his ears flattened against his skull. I needed to relax. Kaphra might just want me to influence Lin to leave the Ioph Carn alone, or to bring some proposition to her attention.

The Emperor has a white-bladed sword in her possession. Steal it and bring it to me. You have thirty days.

—Kaphra

My heart kicked at my ribs. This wasn't something simple. What sort of foolishness was Kaphra asking of me? First Gio, and now Kaphra. The swords were Alanga artifacts, they had to be.

If I did what Kaphra asked, if I stole an artifact from Lin, she'd find out it was me. I had no illusions about any camaraderie we'd formed. She'd execute me. I'd have to run to avoid punishment. And then the only way I'd be able to live was by smuggling again. Was this what he was aiming for? Get an Alanga artifact and have me back under his thumb again?

I clenched my jaw and tucked the letter into my sash pocket.

"A fair bargain?" she asked.

"It never is with Kaphra." I swept from the house, my mood darker than the burgeoning clouds.

Mephi jostled me as we walked back toward the ship. "Is it bad?"

"Very bad," I said. I had to find a way around this. I still wanted to make sure Anau got its bog cough cure, but how could I manage what Kaphra wanted without playing right into his hands?

The sword – the one I'd found in the Shardless Few hideout. It was a white-bladed sword too. Perhaps I could substitute it out. Gio had warned me to keep hold of it, but hadn't bothered to tell me why. If I could even catch a glimpse of the one Lin ostensibly had, I could tell if it was similar to the one I'd taken. I'd not seen any such weapon in the hold, but perhaps she was keeping it in her room. There had to be a way I could check.

Mephi and I were the first ones back to the ship.

I made my way to the Emperor's cabin, trying to think of excuses to linger, to look around. She might not have brought the sword with her, but I had the feeling she liked to keep her secrets close. Like her father had.

The guard I'd assigned to the door nodded to me, and I waved her away, dismissing her from her post. I rapped on the wood. No one responded. I frowned. She'd said she was staying behind to help prepare for Reshi's funeral, and the guard hadn't indicated that Lin had left. "Mephi, check the mess hall just in case, would you?" He bounded down the hall and returned only a moment later, shaking his head. I knocked again, louder. Nothing.

A thousand possibilities ran through my mind. She was sleeping, she was dead, she'd been taken captive. I pounded on the door loud enough to wake the dead. "Eminence?"

Still no answer. She wasn't sleeping.

I rattled the knob, found it locked. The air in my throat felt like a solid, twisting thing. I'd agreed to steal from Lin and now something had happened to her. I shoved a shoulder against the door. It bent with my weight but didn't give way.

The thought of someone holding a knife to her throat, of someone cutting her, filled me with a dread I couldn't name. They were impossible things. I *needed* them to be impossible things. If she was dead, she'd never give me one of her wry looks again, her sharp retorts, or laugh at one of my jokes as though I were *actually* funny. What if one of those assassins was – right now – holding a blade above her chest?

I took a step back and then rammed into the door, hard. The wood around the latch cracked, the door gave way.

Lin sat on the edge of her bed, a flask in her hand, her gaze clouded. Thrana cowered at her feet, something between a whine and a growl in her throat. I lowered my hands so the beast wouldn't feel threatened and tried to make sense of the situation.

She wasn't dead. She wasn't under attack. She wasn't asleep.

"Eminence?"

Lin didn't respond. It was as though she couldn't hear me at all. She stared at the wall, her lips slightly parted, her hands limp at her sides. She'd done the same thing when I'd seen her in the cave below the palace – drinking from a flask and then going blank. I took a hesitant step into the room and reached for the flask. It looked like one of the clay containers the cook kept fish sauce in. Nothing overly strange about it.

The Emperor blinked. Her gaze focused on me. "Jovis?" She frowned and looked at the broken door. "Is something wrong?"

"You didn't answer when I knocked. I thought . . . " It sounded as foolish to my ears as it must have sounded to hers. "What were you doing?" I didn't have the right to ask such a question, especially not of the Emperor, but her face flushed.

"Studying," she blurted out.

I looked to the flask, to her empty hands, to the spot at the wall she'd been staring at. "Yes, wood grain can be quite fascinating," I said lightly. "And helpful when it comes to solving an Empire's problems."

"I've been trying to figure out all the mysteries my father left behind," she said, waving an arm to encompass the whole of the Empire. "What he knew, what he didn't know. The notes he left might as well be encrypted. He never told me anything; he only ever gave me the information he thought I needed in the moment. And now he's gone and I'm just . . . " Lin stretched out her hands, grasping, as though trying to capture a breeze through her fingertips. "You have no idea what that's like. So yes, I may seem distracted."

I knew a deflection when I heard one. In the past, I might have poked and prodded. Perhaps if she were someone else. But finding her safe and whole just made me feel tired and relieved. "I thought you might be dead. Or injured. When I saw the flask, I thought someone might have poisoned you. There are people that want you dead, Eminence."

"You were worried about me?" She placed it somewhere between a statement and a question.

Her dark eyes met mine. Even the Emperor's cabin on this ship was small; she sat a mere step away from me, so close I could smell the scent of jasmine wafting from her hair. My mouth went dry. I wasn't sure if I should answer that or how. I wasn't sure what answer she wanted.

Thrana had calmed, and she rested her big head in Lin's lap. "You should tell him," Thrana said. "He might be able to help."

Lin stroked Thrana's head, her expression softening. "Shut the door. I'll show you. Just . . . keep this to yourself." She rose without waiting for confirmation, brushing past me as I turned to shut the door, her sleeve grazing my arm.

She knelt to open the crate at the foot of the bed. A small chest lay within. The rest of the contents were covered with a blanket and try as I might, I couldn't peer beyond that. "My father had a memory machine," she said simply, gesturing to the chest. "He left notes on it and I've been figuring out how it works. It stored memories in liquid. In here." She tapped a fingernail against the clay flask.

It seemed too fantastical to be real – but then, so did bone shard magic. "So do you just . . . ?" I mimed uncorking the flask.

"I drink it. And then I live out the memories he's stored. Witstone ashes are involved, mixed with other things – his blood, for one. Thrana's blood for another." She saw my grimace. "It's not pleasant. But then, neither were most of the things my father did." She curled her fingers around the base of one of Thrana's ears, her voice soft. "I don't want to keep things from you, but you must understand there have been few people I've ever been able to trust."

"I know that feeling too."

"You could injure me in a thousand ways with the secrets I've told you." She rose and I felt my knees wobble. Her lashes fluttered against her cheeks. "Do you still not trust me? I want you to trust me."

She wasn't lying or trying to deflect. She told me the truth, and it made my heart ache. "You're the Emperor. You have your father's power." I could feel the wall the words put between us, and wished that I could take them back – just as much as I knew they had to be said.

"It's who I am. Would you rather I be someone different?" The hint of sharpness beneath that was so very, very Lin.

Yes. No. I closed my eyes, trying to think clearly.

Mephi pressed against my leg. What would he want me to do here? According to him, I was the one who helped. My satchel swung loose against my side, the book inside its only weight. I cleared my throat, lifting the bag between us as though it were a shield – the only thing between me and my doom. There was no reason I should keep this from her, and she'd spent long hours of study. Translating the book with Mephi's distractible help was slow going. Perhaps she'd seen this language before. A question for a question. A secret for a secret. It only seemed fair.

"I found something," I blurted out, reaching into the bag and pulling out the journal. "Back on Nephilanu, in some Alanga ruins near the city. It was like the statue's face," I lied. "It seemed to call out to Mephi. It's in a language I don't recognize and I've been trying to translate it – with only a little luck. I think it's an Alanga book. Your father's libraries are extensive. Maybe you've seen this script before?" I shoved it at her.

She took the book from my hands, opening it and leafing delicately through the pages, her curiosity taking over. "It *is* an Alanga book." Her gaze raced across the words, her lips parting in surprise. "Dione's journal – the last Alanga to fall to the Sukais. He and the first Emperor were . . . friends?"

"You can read it? You've seen this language before?"

Her trembling fingers trailed over one page, pressing the paper flat. "I've not just seen this language; I've spent long, lonely nights learning it."

Of course the Emperor would keep old, forbidden Alanga works. It made sense. "Why didn't you tell me you knew the Alanga language?"

She turned the opened pages toward me, her expression grim. "Because I didn't know I knew it. This isn't some lost language. It's the same script used for bone shard magic."

26

—

Lin

Somewhere in the Endless Sea

The Alanga language and the language of the bone shard magic were one and the same. Had the Alanga used bone shard magic too? Although I could decipher pieces of Dione's journal, my understanding of the language was imperfect, and the easy, conversational structure of the journal was so very different from the stark commands carved onto bones. Jovis hadn't given over full custody of the journal to me; instead, he would bring it to me and sit to the side as I read, a comforting presence I wasn't ready to dismiss. Besides, he'd offered suggestions every so often that had proved helpful.

At least that's what I told myself.

We were making landfall at Imperial to briefly regroup before going to Hualin Or and then Gaelung. My ostensible mother had come from Hualin Or. Her family would be there. I wondered what they would make of me. At least Hualin Or's witstone mines were small. My order to halt witstone production wouldn't affect it as much as some other islands. We'd be landing at Imperial soon, where I knew I'd be busy seeing to the needs of the Empire. I had only a little time left on the ship that I could devote to my research. I opened the crate at the foot of my bed and took out the sword.

"Careful," Thrana said.

I looked at her. What did she mean by that? "It's a blade. Of course I'll be careful."

"Not just that," she said. "It smells strange."

A bit unnerved, I set it back down and instead lifted out the statue's face. And nearly dropped it back into the chest. Sometime while I'd stored it away, the eyes had closed. I suppressed a shiver. It made me think of the mural in the palace at home, the Alanga lined up, hand in hand, their eyes closed. Until, one day, they'd opened.

They'd opened the day I'd fought my father. The day Jovis had appeared at the palace steps. The day I'd bonded with Thrana.

I set the face in my lap.

Thrana sniffed it, her whiskers and wet nose tickling the back of my hand. "Smells strange too."

"It's an Alanga artifact. Like the sword," I told her. I couldn't believe it was a coincidence that the mural's eyes had opened on that day. I doubted it was my bonding with Thrana that had done it: the eyes had opened several times since. That left Jovis's appearance at the palace steps.

A knock sounded at the door.

I hastily put away both sword and flask but kept the statue's face in my hand. "Come in."

It was Jovis, Mephi on his heels. He strode into my room, the journal in his hand. My two handmaidens passed behind him in the hall, giving him sidelong looks as he shut my door. We'd been spending quite a lot of time alone together. They would talk. The guards would talk. I couldn't bring myself to care. I was Emperor. Let them talk.

"He never says how Alanga are created. All he talks about is Ylan Sukai and their philosophical conversations. It's as dry as the historical textbooks I had to read at the Academy. Ylan is angry about the Alanga's conflicts causing collateral damage. Dione likens their conflicts to storms – things that cannot be contained or stopped. They eat, they go fishing, they drink tea and they talk." He tossed the journal onto my desk. "If I flip through farther, it seems like Ylan changed Dione's mind somewhat. They work on something together – I can't tell what. And then there's a betrayal." He tapped his staff on the floor – a gesture I'd come to associate with his agitation.

I curled my fingers around the statue's face. "When you first arrived in Imperial, did you use your magic to fight off my father's construct?"

Jovis blinked. "What?"

"Did you use your magic to fight my father's construct?"

He shook his head as if to clear it. "Yes, of course I did."

I looked to the open porthole, the light rain and sea spray dampening the wall. My thought, half-formed before Jovis had walked in the door, solidified into a theory. I lifted a hand, felt the tremor in my bones, my awareness of the surrounding water sharpening. And then I crooked a finger, lifting a sphere of water from the ocean and bringing it floating through the porthole.

Jovis frowned. "Why are you—?"

I hefted the statue's face and let the water splash onto the wooden floor of my cabin. Nothing. The eyes stayed closed.

Jovis fidgeted. "Were you in the middle of researching the applications of Alanga magic in cleaning floors?" He gestured at the door. "I can go if you're busy."

"I thought maybe—" My breath caught. The eyelids of the statue moved, as though the carving were alive. Slowly, as I watched, they opened, sightless white orbs looking into mine.

I forced myself to keep a hold of it instead of hurling the thing across the room. I turned the carving toward Jovis. "The mural in the entrance hall of the palace is from the Alanga era. After you used your magic, all the eyes in the mural opened. The artifacts are awakening because Alanga are near and using their magic. It's not just a sign the Alanga are awakening; it's a warning system."

Jovis pondered this. "Artifacts have been awakening on other islands; ones we've not been to. And I didn't use my magic on Nephilanu. Did you?"

"I didn't. Which means two things: there's at least one Alanga on Nephilanu that isn't one of us. And there are more on other islands. We don't know who the others are, if they know what they are, or what they want. We need to start figuring that out. I'll get in touch with my envoys at the islands where artifacts have awoken, see if they've noticed any other unusual activity."

Jovis looked to Mephi and Thrana. "People will find out eventually. Once more of us start appearing, they'll notice everyone else has a creature like Mephi. They'll put the pieces together. We can't control this."

I tried to force back the panic rising in my throat. I'd worked too hard for too long to become Emperor. At the same time, I couldn't give up Thrana. I didn't even know if that was possible. She felt like a part of me now, inextricable from the rest. "We hide for now. I'll do what I can to counteract my father's propaganda. If we reveal that you are an Alanga first, people will be more likely to accept this change. But if I reveal that I am . . . I know my position is precarious. It would be just one more thing the governors could use to pressure me into abdication." It wasn't fair that Jovis should have the love and adoration of the Empire's people, and I had to fight for even a modicum of respect. No one knew – or could know – what I'd done to end my father's reign and why. So they saw me as his protégé, his rightful heir, an extension of him. Bayan was dead. Numeen was dead. His family . . . dead. All I had were my title and my position.

The statue's face was cold in my hand, its eyes slowly closing.

"Someday, your secret will get out. Why not get ahead of it?"

So many secrets. I was an overfull cup, threatening to spill at the slightest mistake. "Easy for you to say," I snapped at him. "The folk hero of the people, rising from the bottom to save their children. But me? I end the Tithing Festival and return their shards and they all still regard me with suspicion. I know what they must think of me; what you must think of me. Spoiled, young, inexperienced, foolish. How can I change that?" It was more than I should have confessed to him and I felt the shame of it heating my cheeks. I understood a little why my father tried so hard to bring Nisong back from the dead. Emperor was a lofty position, and a lonely one.

"I don't," Jovis said, tucking the journal back into his satchel.

What did he mean? "Don't what? Want to be like my father either? You're not in danger of that."

"No," he said, and his eyes were as serious as I'd ever seen them. "I don't think you're spoiled or foolish. Young . . . well, there's no debating that. Inexperienced? You've only just taken your father's place. But you're brilliant, and hard-working, and kind. I didn't expect that."

Something shifted in the air between us, made it thicker, harder to breathe. That's what he thought of me?

A knock sounded at the door. I blinked.

"Eminence, we're at the docks," one of my handmaidens said. "We'll be disembarking soon."

I cleared my throat. "Of course. Come in."

She entered, followed by my other handmaiden. They spared neither of us a glance, bustling about, packing up soiled clothes and securing my crate. There was barely enough room in the cabin for two people, much less four. I beat a hasty retreat out the door and above-deck, hearing the scratch of claws and the tap of a staff as Jovis and our beasts followed.

The air was thick with moisture, though rain hadn't yet begun. The green mountains of Imperial rose above us, rocky outcroppings covered in vegetation. The city and the palace nestled by the harbor, green roof tiles an echo of the surrounding forest. I put a hand to the railing and realized: I still held the statue's face.

"I can take that if you wish," Jovis said at my elbow.

I started to hand it back to him when I caught a glimpse of the eyes. They were open again. My breath caught in my throat. "Did you——?"

He looked down at himself like that would give him a clue as to whether or not he'd used magic. "No," he said. "Not at all. You?"

"If I had, I wouldn't have asked you." Anxiety gripped me by the throat. There was another Alanga here. On Imperial. They would know I was one too. They'd see Thrana and they'd know. The only thing I might count on was that the other Alanga would be reluctant to reveal themselves too.

Jovis took the proffered piece of statuary and stuffed it into his satchel. "I can take Mephi out into the streets, look around," he said.

"After we're settled back at the palace," I agreed. "It can't hurt."

I composed myself enough to see Jovis's mother off at the docks. My father would have thought it beneath my station, but she'd been kind to me. Ongren handed me a basket before she disembarked which included salted egg yolk cookies and a packet of herbs.

"What are these?" I asked, holding them up.

She leaned in conspiratorially. "For tea. They're good for

fertility. The Empire needs an heir." She patted my cheek and smiled.

Heat flushed my chest, rising to the very tips of my ears. When did I even have the time to think about heirs? "I, uh, thank you."

"Watch over my boy," she said, and then she turned to say goodbye to Jovis.

Despite the rain that finally broke through the clouds, my mood lifted as I set foot on the cobblestones of Imperial's streets. Here, at least, was home. I wanted a couple of nights spent in my own bed, Thrana curled beside me. I wanted a bath. I wanted my favorite steamed buns the way the palace's head cook made them. Ikanuy had sent a palanquin, which I gratefully settled into, brushing droplets of rain from my cloak.

I'd intended to take a bath as soon as I'd returned, but instead found the palace in an uproar. I knew servants gossiped – it was one of the reasons my father kept so few – but even in the short walk from the gates to the entrance hall, I could hear their whispers trailing me like the waves in a wake of a ship.

Ikanuy greeted me in the courtyard, her hand drawing back the curtain of my palanquin. "Forgive me, Eminence," she said, her face pale. "But there have been a few developments since you left."

I didn't like the sound of that. "Tell me."

"Everyone knows."

The world around me seemed to stop, fear freezing my limbs. They'd discovered my father's secret rooms. They'd found I was not who I said I was. They'd found I was created, not born. Why hadn't they torn down my palanquin as I made my way to the palace? Called me out for the impostor I was?

"There are now reliable reports," Ikanuy continued, "that there are people among the construct army. Some of our soldiers claim that the people themselves are constructs. Their leader says she is your older half-sister. She says her claim to the throne supersedes yours, even though she's illegitimate. Iloh has defected and is now calling for your abdication."

It took me a moment to absorb what she'd said, the blood still pounding in my ears. It wasn't what I'd thought it was; then again, the news wasn't good. What had my father done? I couldn't believe he'd actually fathered an illegitimate daughter, not based on the memories of his I'd shared. I focused on the second part of what Ikanuy had said. "Iloh defected?" That was two islands now calling for my abdication. Two islands I needed to support me.

"I placed the letter on your desk. He says you promised to develop the witstone mine on the neighboring island."

"The ban is only temporary! Surely he can't expect—" I broke off. It was pointless to explain this to my steward, not when Iloh was the one needing convincing. With the construct army looming and the unpopular witstone mining ban, others might follow Iloh's example. I couldn't believe this woman leading the army, whoever she was, would suffer me to live if she ascended to the throne. "We'll need to send an envoy – see if we can't get him back on our side. I can't lift the ban, not yet."

"There's another thing," Ikanuy said. "There's a man here to see you. He says it's urgent. Eminence, he is a cloudtree monk."

My spine stiffened. The monks rarely left their monasteries, though they sometimes sent apprentices to nearby towns for supplies. I'd never heard of one coming here, to Imperial, to the palace. There were no monasteries on this island. "An envoy?"

"I'm not sure. He declined to explain to anyone except to you. We put him up in the Hall of Earthly Wisdom. He's there right now."

I checked my appearance. Travel-worn but not atrocious. Outside the palanquin, rain had begun to wet my hair and shoulders, but it wasn't a downpour. This would have to do. "I'll see him. Jovis, Thrana, Mephi, with me."

"Should you take a contingent of guards?" She left the rest unsaid. Considering that my father never had the best relationship with the monasteries. Considering the stories of the monks' prowess in battle.

"This is enough." I wasn't sure yet what he had to say. The fewer ears that heard it, the better.

We walked briskly across the courtyard to the Hall of Earthly Wisdom, next to the palace gardens. It was a rectangular building with an overhang running around the outside, supported by pillars. The main hall was an open space with a high ceiling, the doors to various rooms around its perimeter. Despite light filtering in from high above, the hall itself was dim.

I strode through the open doors. A couple of servants moved within, freshening up the rooms and carrying dishes away. "Where is he?" A servant pointed wordlessly to the small dining room, off to the side of the main hall.

I found a man inside, sitting cross-legged on a cushion at the table, a steaming mug of tea cupped in his hands. For some reason I'd pictured him old and wizened. This man was young – perhaps even younger than me. High cheekbones cut slashes across his faces; his nose curved gently outward like a hawk's. His hair was close-clipped and he wore simple, dark green robes.

"Ah," he said, smiling and setting his mug down. "You must be the new Emperor."

Something in his expression made me wave back to Jovis. "Tell the servants to leave. Close the door."

He moved to obey.

"I am," I said. "But I do not know you."

"You shouldn't." He folded his hands on the table. "I've lived my whole life in the monastery. My name is Ragan. Please, Eminence, sit."

As though he were the master here, and not me. "I'll sit if it pleases me."

His smile only widened. "You may want to. I bring news. Good news!"

I thought of the tasks I'd set Ikanuy to and raised an eyebrow. "The cloudtree monks have decided to conscript themselves to my service?"

"Ah. No. But I have."

"One monk."

"Eminence." He lifted a finger, his expression going stern, as though to rebuke me. "You should never turn down help. Not when you need it. News of the construct army is spreading fast. Your soldiers have done what they can, but the construct army has taken several islands. They are coming for you. And the Shardless Few lie in wait."

The instructional tone from this youth irritated me to no end. Thrana growled, her hackles raised.

He looked at her, nodding as though in understanding. "You've bonded too closely with your ossalen."

My veins turned to ice. Behind me, I heard Jovis's staff tap against the floor. Once, twice. "What do you mean?"

"History. Imperial teaches it, though even your knowledge is sorely lacking. It was the Alanga purge, you see. The Sukais destroyed not just the Alanga – they burned their books, razed many of their buildings. But the monasteries are fortresses. And we –" He tapped his temple. "– we kept the books safe." He lifted his mug and took another sip. "So you shouldn't scoff at my help. Besides, I am not simply one monk. As I said: news!"

Jovis spoke up from behind me, his tone dry. "Do your elders know you are here?"

"Ha ha," Ragan said, breaking into a smile again. "You are a funny man. Of course they know. They sent me. Yes, I know you are both Alanga."

Hearing him say it aloud made me want to stuff something in his mouth just to shut him up. Was there anyone within hearing distance?

"But!" He held up a finger again. "Here is the news: so am I."

27

Jovis

Imperial Island

I'd forgotten what it was like to be alone (or "lonely", Mephi isn't sure). Ylan reminds me of my life before becoming an Alanga. Everyone I've known from that time has long since passed away. I'd forgotten what it was like to feel like every small thing mattered.

And maybe he's right. Maybe the small things do matter.

—Notes from Jovis's translation of Dione's journal

Imperial didn't feel like the respite it should have been. Ragan had kept his mouth shut about being an Alanga at Lin's request, but in spite of the absence of a beast at his side, there was an oddness about him. A cloudtree monk out and about? In Imperial? More than one scholar had requested to meet with him, inquiries Lin had all denied.

Pressure for Lin's abdication was mounting – it was what I'd wanted when I'd joined the Shardless Few. Now, though, I found myself hovering outside her bedroom door at night, pretending not to hear her frustrated crying, but wondering if I should knock, ask her if she was all right, offer some words of comfort.

When I'd told Lin what I thought of her, I'd been thinking of my mother's hands on each side of my face. The truth.

She didn't deserve this.

I swung my staff harder than I intended, sweeping the feet clean out from beneath the guard I was sparring with in the courtyard. She fell onto the cobblestones with a grunt, the wind knocked out of her. I cringed at her gasping, and then put out a hand to help her up once she'd caught her breath. "I'm sorry, that was too rough of me."

She gave me a weak grin. "That's just how we get stronger."

No, I thought to myself, *that's how I accidentally kill you.* Around me, guards clashed with blades and staves.

"That's it," I called to them. "We're done. Keep alert. Constructs are running about wild, looking for any opportunity. And remember: some of the constructs may look like people. Don't hesitate."

Mephi came barreling out of the gardens, shouldering my thigh. I did my best not to fall over. "Hello hello hello!" he said. Some of the guards cracked grins. A wonder they still liked him; he'd rifled through their things and had turned more than one sentimental item into an impromptu toy. I was still working with him on personal boundaries.

We were leaving for Hualin Or the next day – the island Lin's mother had come from. She'd died when I'd been young, and all I remembered were the white flags being flown from the masts of ships and the eaves of rooftops. A sudden illness that ravaged her body and left her a husk in a matter of weeks. No one knew how to cure it, and I'd heard my mother and father talking in whispers — that several physicians who'd failed had been executed.

I was curious to see this place, this family. My mother was right: Lin had no one. But perhaps she could find kinship there. Surely they would support her claim? And then I wouldn't have to hesitate on the threshold of her room, hand lifted, wondering if I should knock and offer a listening ear.

I clenched my jaw. It didn't matter. I might have stopped sending letters to the Shardless Few, but I wasn't her friend. I'd poked around as much as I'd dared and hadn't found the sword Kaphra had charged me with stealing. If Lin had brought it with her, it was locked up tight on the ship.

"You're brooding," Mephi said to me as we climbed the steps to the palace.

How could I explain all the thoughts in my head to him? "I don't know how to do the right thing anymore," I said. "I came here to do the right thing, and now everything is muddled."

"Does anyone know what is right?"

I gave him a sidelong look. "Are you reading ... philosophy?"

He shouldered my leg. "There's a library here. You taught me to read — you can blame yourself for that."

Laughter rang down the hall when I entered the palace. Lin. I gritted my teeth as I heard another voice. Ragan. She'd welcomed him easily — too easily. She was so aloof sometimes, so convinced of her own intelligence. I wondered if she knew that anyone with half a nose could smell the loneliness on her. And there was something about him that set me on edge. Perhaps it was his smile, or his condescension, or the way he held up a finger whenever he had something important to say — and he seemed to think that nearly everything he said was important.

I made my way toward the voices. They sat in the dining hall, each with a mug of tea between their hands.

"Are you telling me that you have to be an apprentice until you're thirty-five before you even get to try the cloudtree bark? That seems like for ever."

Ragan held up a finger. "No. That's how long it takes for most people. I was having cloudtree bark at eighteen. But I was a prodigy. I learn quickly."

"You must be one of the youngest masters among the monks."

He let out a short, embarrassed cough. "Ah. No. I am still an apprentice. There is more to becoming a master than just fighting skills. I do excel at the martial arts, but they said I still have much to learn and that I lack the necessary temperance and wisdom. It's why they sent me. They thought getting out into the world might help me learn."

"You're young; they expect too much of you."

"I'm not that young," he said peevishly. And then he laughed. "I'm sorry, Eminence. There's that lack of temperance, I think. Youth is no excuse. I've been patted on the head since I was young, told I have so much promise. When you hear that day after day you feel you have a lot to live up to."

"You'll do your masters proud, I'm sure."

I was going to grind my teeth into dust at this rate. There was an army on their way; didn't the monk understand this? I knocked on the opened door to make them aware of my presence.

They both looked up at me, startled. Thrana lay curled next to Lin, sleeping.

"I need to speak to the Emperor in private," I said.

I couldn't help but note the disappointment that flitted across Lin's face. "Give us the room, please? Thank you for answering my questions."

Ragan stood and bowed to her. "Of course, Eminence. I hope you'll allow me to help further."

I didn't move as he came to the doorway. He smiled at me as

he slipped past, his robes smelling of pine sap. I shut the door firmly behind him.

"Where's his companion? Does he even have one?"

Her voice was cool. "You don't like him."

My chest felt like a furnace. "Of course I don't. He says he came from a monastery. Which one? Did they really send him? If every Alanga has a companion, then where is his? What does he want? He can't just want to help."

"His monastery was on Unta. He gave me a letter signed by his masters. He says he and his companion have a more mature bond and don't need to be so close. They're called ossalen. His is waiting for him in the mountains above the palace and he will call him when he's done here. And he wants to help." Steam rose from her mug, wisping into the air just below her chin. "Ragan lost everyone he knew when Unta sank, so have a little bit of compassion, won't you? You said, when you came here, that you wanted to help. And I trusted you."

And she shouldn't have. But I couldn't say that.

Lin sighed, her gaze going to the ceiling. "I can't send him away. Jovis, we need him. If he's anywhere near as powerful as we are, then we can use his help in the coming battle. I need Hualin Or's and Gaelung's support, but we're losing soldiers as fast as we recruit them. My general sent word: they'll arrive at Gaelung just after we do, and hopefully they'll be able to handle the army on their own. I'm trying to climb a muddy hill and I'm sliding back every three steps. I might need you and Ragan to fight."

A knock sounded at the door. "Eminence, it's Ikanuy."

"Come in," Lin said, her gaze still on me.

Ikanuy entered, her gaze going back and forth between me and Lin. "A representative is here to see you," she said. "From the construct army. He is here to negotiate on behalf of his leader. He is under the care of the palace guard."

Lin breathed in deeply, holding out a hand to call Thrana back
to her side. The beast sidled up to her, slipping her head beneath
Lin's hand and into her lap. "Send him in. I can receive him here.
Have the servants bring tea and refreshments. Jovis and Mephi,
stay, but send in two more guards as well."

Ikanuy left to obey.

One of my guards entered first, followed by the construct
army's envoy. He was a thin man, unassuming, in simple clothes.
He wore his black hair pulled into a bun, and his long face,
though not old, showed the signs of being lived in. I found myself
studying him for signs that he was a construct. The only thing
I could discern was the subtle shift in skin tone from his darker
face to a lighter neck — and that could have been a happenstance
of birth or sunlight. And then all I could think about was how the
previous Emperor might have hacked the head off of one body
and stitched it to another. Gruesome.

I had to admit that if he was a made thing, he was well-made.
Not the sort of thing I could compliment the fellow on. There
was something that felt oddly rude about it.

He caught me looking and cast me a quick, rueful smile — as
though he knew what I was thinking. He took the seat opposite
Lin and the two guards behind him settled into place. A slight
shift in his seat, the lift of an eyebrow — *all this, for me?*

"I know she's not my sister," Lin said, her voice flat. "She has
no claim here."

"My name is Leaf, Eminence," the man said, as though Lin
hadn't said anything at all. "And I'm here to negotiate on behalf
of Nisong."

An odd choice, to name the daughter after the Emperor's
wife, and likely not her given name. Not that "Leaf" was normal
either. Was I staring? Or was this how much I looked at people
under normal circumstances?

"I've heard the stories from the north-eastern reaches," Lin said. "If you wanted to negotiate, you wouldn't be murdering my citizens."

Again he continued as though he hadn't heard her. "Abdicate in favor of your sister, and the terror stops. The people are saved."

This wasn't the first time Lin had been offered such a bargain. I wondered what I would do if I were in her place. Abdicate in favor of the Shardless Few, in favor of this alleged sister, or keep trying to hold a crumbling Empire together? I'd thought once that I'd have taken the first option, or the second. Now, with Mephi's head beneath one hand and my staff in the other, I knew who I was. I would take the third path.

And so would Lin.

"That's not a negotiation; that's a demand."

Leaf spread his hands as though the commands were written into his shards and his words had run out.

Servants filtered into the room, stepping quickly in and out of the silence, placing mugs in front of both Leaf and Lin, pouring boiling water, bringing plates of small grilled fish and braised vegetables. Leaf did not lift his mug or take the pair of chopsticks a servant offered upon a napkin.

I might have stared at our guest, but Lin's gaze was sharp as needles, pinning him to his seat. "Is she like you?"

She'd spotted something I had not. He *was* a construct. Leaf opened his mouth as if to respond, then closed it. Took in a breath like he meant to try again, and then shook his head. I knew that look. I'd seen it on constructs I'd told stories to, lies that confused their purpose or commands. He wasn't sure what to say or how to answer. He found a response on the third try. "She is your sister." A non-answer.

Lin leaned forward, the steam from the mug below curling

tendrils about her cheeks. "Tell her to stand down *first*, and then we will negotiate the terms of peace."

"That won't be acceptable," Leaf said.

She studied him, her expression softening. "What does she truly want? Does she think that being Emperor will solve any of her problems?"

"It solves some of ours." He did not waver from her gaze. "I want to live. Can *you* offer me clemency?"

Well, I knew the answer to that. She couldn't protect both citizens and constructs alike. A person couldn't make a wolf and goat live in peace. Lin, however, surprised me. "I know you think your situation is hopeless, but I'm still learning and discovering things about bone shard magic. Give me a chance to do more research. There may be a way for us to coexist. Wouldn't that be better than murdering helpless citizens?"

Leaf lifted his hands as though they were a set of scales. "One leader promises me an empire. The other says that *perhaps* we can be allowed to live in peace. Which bargain would you take, Eminence?"

"Yes, I understand your point. But surely there are those you care about. What happens to them in a war? How many of them will die?"

A flicker of emotion crossed Leaf's thin face before his expression flattened. "I don't think feelings were written into my commands." He stated it smoothly, confidently, but I knew: he was lying. He cared about his construct companions – much more than he was letting on. It felt like the world were shifting beneath me, as it had on Deerhead Island. Could a construct have feelings? I'd only encountered lower level constructs whom I could easily confuse. I'd never met the Emperor's more complex constructs. I'd heard tales of Mauga, Ilith, Tirang and Uphilia – of their intelligence and the terror they inspired. Had these constructs had feelings? It seemed Lin thought so. Yet she'd destroyed them.

I wasn't sure whether or not she was being sincere in her offer to help.

"How much does your leader care about all of you if she insists on sending you to your deaths? You must recognize that this isn't a true negotiation. She's trying to intimidate me and wants everyone else —" Lin gestured to the guards standing behind Leaf. "— to think she has made a good faith effort so they'll be more willing to accept her rule. Of course the deaths aren't her fault. If only I'd acquiesced, they wouldn't have been necessary. I assure you, I'm familiar with such tactics. I am the Emperor's daughter. And now I am Emperor. She's manipulating all of you to get what she wants. She wants to take my place and she won't accept anything less, no matter what she loses. No matter who she loses."

Leaf only pushed himself to his feet, his face slightly flushed. "If that's all you have to offer, Eminence, I'll take your refusal back to Nisong."

Lin rose. "Tell her what I've offered. See if that gives her even a moment's hesitation."

He gave her a stiff bow and practically fled the room, leaving both the tea and the refreshments untouched. The guards followed him out.

Lin sagged in her seat once he'd gone, picking up a plate of fish and handing it to Mephi and Thrana. "He's a construct and so is his master. The Shardless Few in the south; the construct army to the north-east. And around us, the islands sink."

I shouldn't feel sorry for her. I couldn't. "Are you ... complaining about being Emperor?"

She shot me a dark look. Ah. Too far in the other direction. I'd overcompensated. But then she let out a rueful laugh. "When you say it like that, it does seem foolish." She smoothed the front of her jacket. "We leave for Hualin Or tomorrow. Hopefully we'll have better luck there."

"Hualin Or won't be enough." Were these the words of comfort I'd been thinking of offering? But I could feel the truth of it. Nephilanu had taken the side of the Shardless Few. Riya had taken the side of the constructs. Even if Hualin Or joined Lin's cause, her army was still small and untrained.

"It has to be," she said. She swept from the room, Thrana following in her wake.

When I'd let slip what I'd thought of her, had I also said she was more stubborn than five thousand mules?

Mephi butted his head against my thigh. "Long day. Tomorrow we sail again!"

"Yes." I smiled, scratching the top of his head. At least one of us had few worries. I wasn't sure what to tell Mephi and what not to. I didn't need to drag him into my problems.

I couldn't sleep that night, my mind filled with thoughts of the constructs, the Shardless Few, and that infernal Ragan. I tossed and turned so much that Mephi grumbled and leapt to the floor. Frustrated, I slid from bed and grabbed my cloak. A walk might clear my head. Or at least tire me out enough so I could sleep.

Mephi stirred a little as I left the room but didn't wake up.

A light rain pattered against the cobblestones, gathering in small puddles where the stones were uneven. The courtyard was quiet at night, though I saw a light still lit in the Hall of Earthly Wisdom. Ragan, no doubt doing something that would irritate me. I turned away and instead walked the perimeter of the palace.

The workers had repaired all the cracking plaster, replaced any broken roof tiles. The palace had looked the worse for wear when I'd arrived, but had recently begun to look new again. It might not have been my boat, or the Endless Sea, but it soothed me.

Until I noticed the broken ironwork.

It was tucked up beneath the roof, a decorative piece not meant to hold any weight or perform any function. Beneath it was an open window. Or at least, what looked like a window. There were no shutters, nothing stopping the rain except the roof.

Why, when making the repairs, had Lin not directed this piece to be repaired or removed? It could have been an oversight, but she was meticulous. I didn't think this was something she would have missed. If the oversight was purposeful, then she was hiding something.

The opening looked to be above the second floor, but I'd not seen stairs for a third floor or even the outline of a trap door on the ceiling. This place seemed unconnected.

I should go back to sleep. I should get ready for the journey ahead.

But I never could let a mystery just lie like that. To my mother's consternation, I'd climbed – and fallen from – many trees as a child just to find out if the bundle of twigs I'd seen was actually a nest. The palace was asleep and the guards at the walls faced the city. If I was quiet, I could be in and out of that opening before anyone could find out.

Before I could convince myself otherwise, I found myself back inside the palace, climbing the stairs of the entrance hall, making my way to a window close to the opening.

This was a terrible idea, it really was. But then I was climbing out the window and onto the roof. Rain had slicked the tiles and I had to struggle to maintain my balance. I crouched, crawling up the roof to the apex, making sure each hand and foothold was secure. I peered over the edge, not sure what I would find.

The opening was tucked below the roof, and from my vantage point I could see it was lined with hay. It reminded me of the nests I used to find. Was this the lair of one of the Emperor's old constructs? It didn't look to still be in use.

I tested the broken fixture. I didn't think it would hold my weight. Someone might have used it once to gain access to the lair, and it seemed that was a one-time thing. But I had strength granted to me by Mephi, and I was tall. I eyeballed the distance. If I hung over the edge of the roof, my feet would nearly reach the opening. There was an overhang below. If I fell, I'd probably break something, or more than one something. I supposed I could heal from that, as long as my head wasn't one of the things I broke.

Feeling more than a little foolish, I lowered myself over the roof's edge. My feet hung into the opening. The gutters creaked at my weight. I swung my legs back, then forward, and then let go.

I didn't swing gracefully into the den as I'd intended. My chest hit the wall and I slid, grasping at plaster for a hold. I managed to seize the edge of the opening as I fell, my cloak torn and the skin beneath scraped and bleeding, my arms aching.

I hung there for a moment before gathering the courage to haul myself up and inside.

It smelled like an animal — musty and astringent. Uphilia's lair? She'd been the Emperor's Construct of Trade and I knew she'd had two pairs of wings. What possible secrets could be hiding in the lair of the Construct of Trade? Boring secrets, probably. Secrets not worth risking broken bones for.

But I dug around in the straw regardless, searching for secret compartments.

I didn't need to look that hard. I found something hard and square, and I lifted it from the straw. I squinted in the darkness. A . . . book?

The moon was hidden by clouds, so I couldn't even make out the cover. I felt around in the darkness and found a lamp secured to the wall. There was still a little oil in it, and flint and tinder beneath.

I lit the lamp, and though it flickered, I could see.

It was a record of births and deaths here on Imperial. I flipped through the pages until I found the record of Lin's birth.

There it was: 1522–1525.

My stomach swam with unease. Surely someone had made a mistake. But it was too egregious an error. I shut the book and buried it beneath the straw, struggling to breathe past the tightness in my throat.

Lin Sukai, heir to the Emperor, had died when she was three. So who was the Lin I knew?

28

Nisong

The north-eastern reaches of the Empire

Leaf returned from Imperial with the news Nisong had expected. "She won't abdicate. Definitely not in favor of you. And she's not happy you're claiming to be her illegitimate sister."

Well, she couldn't claim to be Nisong, the Emperor's dead wife. There were limitations here she had to work within, but with the chaos she'd managed to sow, the sinking of Unta and the moratorium on witstone mining, people were looking for an alternative. They could convince themselves that she deserved to lead more than Lin did. She would make them pay and then she'd take her place at the heart of it all. As Emperor.

The army at her back certainly helped matters.

Smoke rose thick into the air, burning the insides of Nisong's nostrils. She watched the fires rage across the town, listened to the screams of people fleeing their houses or being burned alive. She thought she could smell the scent of crisping flesh on the wind.

They were lucky, she supposed, that it had rained the past few days and the wood was still too damp to burn quickly.

Coral and Leaf flanked her, though Coral averted her gaze, her hand covering her mouth and nose. "Is this truly necessary? They might have surrendered."

Nisong clenched her jaw. And then what? Did Coral not understand? "We can't take half measures. They want us all dead. The Emperor placed a bounty on each of our heads before we did anything wrong. Do you think if they were in our position they would offer mercy?"

"No, but—"

"Then we can't offer mercy either. They'll never see us as people. We're just useful monsters, discarded when they no longer want to deal with us." They'd never had a choice in this. They'd awoken from the mind-fog on Maila to find a world that was already hostile toward them.

Leaf cleared his throat. "The Emperor did offer us clemency."

Coral gave Nisong a sharp look. This was the first she was hearing of it. Nisong waved a dismissive hand. "It's not a real offer."

Leaf thumbed the hilt of his sword, running his other hand through lank black hair. He cleared his throat again. "She wants peace, Nisong."

She watched Coral and Leaf exchange glances as though they had something unpleasant to say to her and they weren't sure which of them should be the one to say it.

Leaf was the one who spoke up. "How many more of us have to die until you're satisfied?"

Shame welled within her. She'd already cost them Shell and Frond. They'd both died protecting her. Those days of them gathering around a fire, sharing food and old memories – those days were gone. They'd never happen again. But Nisong wasn't responsible for their deaths. The Empire was. Her anger was a flame that licked away the guilt. "The Emperor said she'd try to find a way for us to live without draining her people's lives. Her rule is weak. How long will everyone stand by and wait while the Emperor experiments on us? And do you want to open yourself up to her, let her reach her hand inside you and manipulate your shards? Change who you are?" No. The Emperor didn't deserve that sort of trust. The Empire didn't deserve that sort of peace. "This isn't about my satisfaction."

The Empire expected a monster? She would be the monster.

Her beasts filled the streets, growling and snapping – a tangled river of fur, claws and feathers. She'd collected more constructs as they'd swept across two more islands. And she'd continued to enact her impromptu Tithing Festival. She'd had a little more time to repair the bodies, to optimize some of them for combat. Still, she'd heard the other constructs in her army call them "shamblers". She couldn't complain; it was a fitting name for such lowly creatures. They followed behind the beasts, mopping up the stragglers.

"I'll watch over you," she told Coral and Leaf. "I'll keep you safe."

A family ran out of one of the burning buildings, leading a boy by the hand. Their gazes darted down the streets, frantically seeking refuge. The boy cried and the constructs leapt for them. One of the boy's fathers drew a sword; the other a kitchen knife. They pressed the boy between them.

"They didn't do anything to us," Coral said.

Nisong rounded on her, her temper fraying. "Shell and Frond might have something to say about that if they were still alive."

Coral shrank back.

"Ah, I'm sorry," Nisong said, reaching her hands out. Coral

took them, leaning into her touch. "I don't like this either. I wouldn't do this unless I had to, you do understand that?"

She'd realized after the battle in that palace courtyard that Coral held some memories of a past life too, though Nisong wasn't sure whose memories they were. Someone who'd once been close to her.

These people deserved what they got. They didn't care about the lives they were snuffing out when they killed constructs. Still, she surprised herself by lifting a hand and calling out. "Leave them alone. We may need them alive later for Tithing." Her constructs fell away from the family, regrouping and circling back toward her.

Nisong set her sights on the next island, visible on the horizon. That one was larger than the islands they'd conquered so far. She thought of the map and oriented herself by the sun peeking through the clouds. Ah yes, Luangon. Known for its cliffside caves and its riotously spicy eel in hot oil. They'd know the construct army was coming, and they had a larger population. And Luangon had a witstone mine − a small one, but enough to provide the citizens with a higher standard of living. There would be people specifically trained to fight, with better weapons. But Nisong had more constructs now too, with the ability to make more. And Imperial would not be able to send reinforcements in time.

She'd sent Grass on ahead in the smallest sailboat she could find, instructing her to land somewhere uninhabited and to make her way to the island's capital from there. She'd sent more than one spy construct over only to have them shot at with arrows. They were too obviously constructs and were conspicuous as spies.

Grass looked like a harmless old woman. She'd be able to get in closer, to listen in on conversations, to judge the size of the force they'd be facing. It had been more difficult than Nisong had thought it would be to send Grass away. Of the original constructs who'd helped her escape Maila, only Coral, Leaf and Grass were left. They'd lost more constructs than Nisong liked to admit during this advance.

"Some of the survivors are fleeing the island. They're taking boats from the harbor," Leaf said to her. "What should I tell the constructs?"

"Leave them alone and let them flee," Nisong said. Her appetite for violence was fading. "Someone needs to tell Luangon that we are coming and that we have no mercy. They will have seen the smoke from the fires but they don't know exactly what has happened here." She focused on next steps. "Coral, have the shamblers gather the bodies in the palace courtyard. Leaf, get the beasts and round up the survivors. We need more shards."

Coral moved to obey, and Nisong followed Leaf into the streets. She'd been able to rescue some opium from a shop before they'd started the fires. At least they'd be able to keep the people quiet as they harvested their shards. It would be easier on everyone this way. She watched out of the corner of her eye as Coral directed the shamblers. Not all of them obeyed. Nisong had instructed them to obey Coral and Leaf, but spoken commands didn't have as much staying power as carved ones. She'd have to reiterate that command later; there simply weren't enough shards to spare.

Already a few of her constructs had needed repairs, a shard or two dying out as the people who'd given them passed away. They couldn't kill everyone in the Empire and still live, but they needed to subdue them.

The streets of this city were paved instead of packed dirt, and more than once she paused to stamp out burning embers before they could reach the flowing hem of her pants. Smoke stung her eyes and she tried not to cough. Leaf sent out the beasts, rounding up survivors huddled in alleyways or staring wide-eyed at the remains of their homes.

"We'll start the Tithing tonight," Nisong said to Leaf. "The sooner we can build up our army, the sooner we can take Luangon and make it our base of operations. From there, we can—"

A crack split the air, followed by a low rumbling. The ground below her feet trembled, but only briefly. Everything in the town went silent except for one errant scream. Leaf seized her forearm.

"What was that?"

She stared back into his pale face, his wide black eyes, and didn't know what to say. She only had two experiences to compare it to – the quake she'd felt once on Imperial soon after arriving, and the moment on Maila when the world had gone sideways and the mind-fog had lifted. Even the beasts had halted in their work, the people they'd been rounding up looking about as though the sky was about to fall.

Nothing else happened. Her taut muscles relaxed, her heartbeat slowing in its gallop. "I'm not sure, but—"

Her gaze fell upon Luangon. Smoke rose from several places on the island, swirling upward to meet the clouds. "It's not us," she said, her heartbeat speeding up again. "It's Luangon."

And Grass was there.

She was running, her slippers slapping against the paving stones, jarring her teeth with each step. The beads on her tunic clicked against one another. It took her a moment to realize where she was going. The docks.

"Nisong!" Leaf called after her. "The prisoners, should we—?"

The wind whipped away his words. It didn't matter now; what mattered was getting to Grass, getting her back from Luangon. She remembered Grass mindlessly sorting through the food on Maila before she'd woken up from the fog. Before Nisong had brought her out of it. Now she had a dry wit, steady hands, an even steadier mind. Bit by bit, she was losing them again.

Not Grass too.

"Wait!" Leaf called out. His feet pounded after her. Waiting was for calmer times. She saw the island shake again before the sound hit her ears, rumbling low like distant thunder. Behind her, a burning house collapsed, sending sparks and embers flying into the air.

She'd heard whispers from the people they'd captured – that Deerhead Island was gone, sunk into the Endless Sea. She hadn't quite believed it. She'd been to Deerhead in her memories; it was a monument of an island. Gone? Vanished? Unfathomable.

But now she was living through a hazy, fire-tinged nightmare. All terrible things seemed possible.

She slowed when she reached the docks and Leaf caught up to her. "That one," he said, pointing. "It's small but quick." She didn't know much about sailing, so she let him lead her there, following as he unwound the rope tying it to the dock and leapt inside.

It rocked gently at their added weight.

She couldn't take her gaze away from Luangon, found herself leaning in that direction, as though that could make them get there any faster. Leaf darted around the deck, though she didn't pay much attention to what he was doing. Wind filled the sails, and then they were maneuvering past the other boats and skipping out into the Endless Sea.

Her breath caught in her throat as a louder rumble sounded, as more smoke and dust billowed up from Luangon's buildings. She could imagine what it was like there on the ground for Grass – the buildings crashing around her, people screaming, dust filling the air and choking her breath.

"How will we find her?" Leaf shouted over the wind.

She wasn't sure. She'd told Grass to go to Luangon's capital. Perhaps she'd gone and had gathered her information already. Perhaps she'd been near her boat, ready to return. Luangon wasn't far away; they could still make it.

Another crack sounded, dust and debris billowing out from the shoreline. The caves were collapsing. Now she could see the mountains sinking, the entire shoreline slipping into the Endless Sea. Leaf stood at the prow of the ship, his long black hair lashing at taut shoulders.

"Leaf! How much longer?"

For a moment he didn't respond, and she thought he hadn't heard her. And then he whirled and went straight to the rigging. He looked as though he'd seen his own grave.

"Leaf. Leaf!"

He stopped in his work. "We won't make it, Nisong," he told her. "I know you want to. I know you want to save her. But it's sinking too quickly. By the time we're close enough, we won't be able to get away in time. The island will pull us down. Do you understand?"

She looked to Luangon again, where Grass was. Grass could already be dead right now, crushed by falling walls or struck by loose rocks by the shore. Her heart sank. "I'm so sorry," she whispered. "It should have been different." She met Leaf's gaze. "Take us away from here."

He nodded and adjusted the sails.

She kept vigil on Luangon. Ships in the water had come to the same conclusion that Leaf had, their sails adjusting as they tried to get away. Thin white trails of smoke rose into the sky as people burnt witstone. Other boats launched from the docks. If Leaf was right, they might still be doomed. But she supposed if it were her, she'd still reach for a frayed rope. Survival was a heady instinct.

The harbors disappeared, and then some of the buildings. The creaking and groaning from breaking wood and falling stone made the island sound like a living thing, mortally wounded. Now, watching it happening, she believed the stories about Deerhead. Was this the Empire she was fighting so hard to take over? One that was slowly drowning in the Endless Sea? If another island was sinking, what was stopping the rest?

Despair was a heavy, suffocating companion, hung about shoulders never strong enough to bear its weight. It smothered her, making her breath come short.

Or maybe Grass was still alive, trying to escape before being dragged beneath the water. She had to stop thinking about it. Shell and Frond had died in fear. Was this the fate that awaited all of them?

Buildings submerged, followed by treetops, hills. The sinking accelerated until the mountains began to slip beneath the surface of the water like a whale descending after taking a breath. Birds rushed up from the island in dark, moving clouds, trying to escape. It didn't seem like it should be happening. She was watching a nightmare.

And then it was gone. Water rushed in to fill the void where the island had been. They were too far away for Nisong to see individual ships, but she could see flashes of white disappear – sails dragged under. She'd wanted to wreak violence upon them, but a violence of her making, not this massive disaster that dragged in even Grass.

"Brace yourself," Leaf called out.

She meant to ask why, but then she saw the wave, radiating outward. A wall of water, fast approaching. Her mouth went dry. The ship they'd taken was small – barely large enough for two people. Could she swim? She searched her memories and came up blank. She wasn't sure. The wood of the boat's side was warm beneath her hands; she gripped so hard that splinters drove beneath her nails.

The wave struck the boat, knocking it to the side.

She lost her grip on the wood. Cold seawater buffeted her, ran up her nostrils. All she could taste was salt and bitterness.

29

Lin

Hualin Or

Rain pounded on the deck above my cabin. I hadn't taken much with me when we'd disembarked at Imperial, aware that we'd be leaving again. I'd locked both the door and shutters of my cabin, trusting my guards to keep my belongings safe. The sword was still there when I checked, and so were my books.

Hualin Or was north of Imperial, an island known for its history and art. It was where Nisong had come from. But I knew, just because I was ostensibly related to them, didn't mean I'd have their support. I'd taken to wearing the style of Hualin Or just so I could get used to it before we landed – the elaborately trimmed robe with the long, billowing sleeves, belted with a sash. The sleeves seemed to get in the way every time I tried to eat, write or even turn around – getting caught in Thrana's horns at the slightest provocation.

I held the flask of my father's memories between my palms and looked into the open neck of it, watching the liquid swish inside.

"Are you sure?" Thrana asked from my side. "It makes you upset . . . and strange."

"Strange? Why do you say that?"

She shrank back, her ears flattened to her skull. "It makes you not like yourself."

"I don't see that I have many choices. I need to know what my father knew, and he died before he could pass on his knowledge to me." I'd spoken to Ragan, and he'd told me he wasn't sure why the islands were sinking. He didn't know who else would be Alanga nor when we could expect to meet more of them. Since he wasn't a master yet, he'd not been allowed access to the monastery's most restricted manuscripts.

I was Alanga, and I wasn't looking to crush the populace or needlessly kill them. I didn't see them as less than human; I wanted to help them. All my life I'd been told the Alanga were bad, that they only desired power. I'd seen them as a monolith, a single people. Thrana's paper crane sat at the corner of the small desk in my cabin. I never wanted to make that sort of mistake again.

If my father had lied, if all the Sukais had lied – then who were the Alanga truly? Jovis, Ragan and I were all so different.

There were answers in my father's memories.

"Make sure no one comes in," I told Thrana, and then I uncorked the bottle and took a sip. The taste of the liquid was sweet and coppery; my vision blanked to white as soon as it washed over my tongue.

I was in my father's body again, my hands pressed against the surface of a table. I recognized the questioning room where Shiyen had always asked me about my memories; I caught a glimpse of the balcony beyond where he liked to gaze over the city. But it wasn't Shiyen before me. It was his mother, a middle-aged woman, her silvering hair pulled back into a severe series of knots. She wore a silk jacket painted with cherry blossoms, the collar high and the waist long. She held a long, thin stick in one hand – a branch stripped bare of bark.

"We lived in harmony with the Alanga for a time, or at least what passed for it," she said. "But then the wars began, and us commoners were simply in the way. We say it was the Sukais that figured out how to kill the Alanga, but it was a traitor that gave us the information, who helped to create the swords. Why do you think we keep that secret?"

Shiyen rubbed one hand against the table's polished surface before answering. "Because we cannot allow any of the Alanga to be seen as good."

His mother tapped the table with her stick and Shiyen flinched. "Yes. People don't understand or grasp nuance. Can an individual? Yes. But people in general must be led. We are the ones that saved the Empire; the Alanga are the ones who sought to destroy it." She put down the stick and lifted her hands, gesturing in a circular motion to indicate each group. "What happens if we let these concepts intermingle?" She twined her fingers together.

"It becomes too difficult for people to know who is good and who is bad."

"Precisely. We are the saviors, my son. We must always be seen so."

I felt Shiyen squirm in his seat. "But are we not actually the saviors? Isn't that the truth?"

In a flash, the Emperor seized the stick and lashed it, whip-like, over his knuckles. I felt the stinging pain as though it were my own; Shiyen's movements mirroring what would have been mine. He cupped the hand to his breast, cradling it. In that moment, I couldn't separate us. I *was* Shiyen.

"The masses think we are saviors. We did what we had to. We killed them all, my son. We could not know which would hurt us and which would protect us – and they all had too much power. So we killed every last man, woman and child. All the Alanga. The traitor helped us create the swords. He helped us hunt them all down. Was he good, to turn against his own people? Were we good, to kill all of them?"

I was a wellspring of hurt and consternation; it fountained from my heart and poured into every corner of my soul. My gaze went to the Emperor's hand, her fingers tight around the branch as she awaited my answer. "We were good," I choked out. She lifted the stick. "And also bad," I finished quickly.

Her hand lowered. "Yes. And no one must ever know."

I came back to myself in my cabin, my knuckles aching with the ghost of remembered pain. Thrana had lain her head in my lap, and her eyes tilted upward as I tried to shake off the memory. "Not a good one?"

"No," I said. "They never are. But I needed to know. The swords were made to kill Alanga. I don't know how they work yet, but that was their purpose. And there is more than one. I'm not sure what happened to the others: if they're still hidden in the palace or if they made their way somewhere else. But I need to find them or they could be used against us."

Us. Already I thought of myself as an Alanga, as belonging to that group.

Above, someone called out that they'd sighted land. I'd brought a big oilskin cloak this time, and I swept it over my shoulders before leaving my cabin. I found Jovis and Ragan in the hall both dressed in cloaks, Ragan with a finger raised, Jovis scowling fit to murder someone. Ragan's companion Lozhi was small and gray, his horns still only buds, and he crouched at Ragan's feet, watching his face. Mephi watched the other creature curiously.

"There's not enough room to pass you here." I knocked on the door to my maidservants' quarters. They must have been waiting for me, because they opened the door, the chest of shards already carried between them. "You'll both have to move."

"Of course, Eminence," Ragan said with a smile. "We were going above-deck anyway."

Jovis smoothed his scowl, though it looked like it took some effort. Every interaction between him and the monk seemed to end with Ragan smiling and Jovis scowling.

"Guards, to me!" Jovis called, and the hallway became even more crowded. We all shuffled above-deck.

The rain was just as hard as it had sounded below. Mephi and Thrana darted across the deck, splashing in gathered puddles and shaking water from their fur. Lozhi ventured more hesitantly from the folds of Ragan's cloak.

The mountains of Hualin Or rose from the Endless Sea like the crooked teeth of a sea serpent. I had to squint to make them out in this downpour. My heart jumped a little in my chest. This would be where I met my ostensible family. I had to enter this with confidence, to show no hesitation. They had to think me Nisong's daughter.

Jovis sidled up to me at the rail. "We're not bringing him, are we?"

I glanced back at him from beneath my hood. "I assume you mean Ragan? Not to the governor's palace. But he will remain here on the ship. He's already been made aware of this." Silently, I fretted about leaving my room with its books and secrets locked but unguarded – I knew better than anyone that locks didn't necessarily stop a person. But it was that or take Ragan with us, and while people had assumed that Thrana had been a gift from Jovis, they might raise eyebrows if they saw Ragan with the same type of creature.

No one was there to greet us at the docks except a large

palanquin sent by the palace, four guards at the posts to carry it. There was room inside for me and Thrana. Jovis and I exchanged glances. It was an odd reception, certainly. Silent and without ceremony – although perhaps due to the downpour? No one said anything to me. Only one guard stepped to the side as I approached and opened the door to the palanquin. I accepted, graciously, gesturing for my guards and maidservants to follow behind.

Water dripped from my cloak and from Thrana's fur, seeping into the wooden floor of the palanquin. It had a musty scent, as though it hadn't been used in years. I felt safe in it, at least. I didn't know how many assassins Nisong had sent after me.

Still, curiosity overrode fear, and I drew back the curtain a little to see the city pass by – the city Nisong had come from. The main street was neatly kept, storefronts still open in the rain and mats laid out for visitors. Every building seemed to have some extra flourish – an elaborate iron-wrought lamp, embroidered curtains, painted entryways. Imperial was beautiful, but Hualin Or was exquisite. I wanted very badly to cast off my title and to sidle into these shops, to lift their perfumes to my nose and to touch all the intricate carvings.

I let the curtain fall back before I could be further tempted. I was here for one reason: to get the support of Hualin Or's governor – my aunt.

"Nervous?" Thrana whispered up at me.

I never saw the point of lying to her. "Yes."

She laid her head in my lap in response.

The guards set the palanquin down by the entrance to the palace, beneath an overhang. Jovis moved immediately to offer me a hand down to the cobblestones. I took it, feeling the calluses of his palm below mine, the tremor of his bones beneath. He let go as soon as my feet touched the ground.

The lamps in the entrance hall were unlit; rain pounded on the roof above. Tigers chased one another across wall murals, the shadows of pillars hiding faces, tails, bodies. The beams across the ceiling were carved in geometric patterns, the tiles at my feet echoing them. Something about all this sparked a sense of recognition, but it did not feel like home.

The governor and her family stood arrayed in front of me, lined up one next to another with uncanny precision. She wore the same sort of robe that I did, the long sleeves swaying with the wind from the open door. Like me, she was short, with the same thin, wiry build. I could see echoes of my face in hers – the same wide-set dark eyes, the same high cheekbones, the same small chin.

She studied me as I studied her, finally bowing, her hands clasped before her. "Eminence. Welcome to Hualin Or."

The others in the line all bowed in unison. Beside me, I saw Jovis shifting from the corner of my eye, his staff clicking against the tiles.

"Thank you, Sai," I said to my aunt, Wailun. It was a warmer reception than the ones we'd received at other islands. At the same time, it felt cold. Or maybe my expectations were just unreasonably set. Jovis's mother had treated me like family. These people were supposed to be my family. A small part of me, perhaps, had hoped for the same warmth.

But these were politics. I was not here to reconnect with long-lost family; I was here to ensure the tithes would continue, to recruit guards, to shore up defenses against both the Alanga and the constructs. No one was saying anything in response. I cleared my throat. "We have much to speak about and very little time. Even now the construct army advances."

"Over dinner," the governor said. "Please."

A servant approached her, whispering in her ear. Such was the silence that I could hear what she said. "Should we not light the lamps? The storm has made it dark."

The governor looked about, as though noticing for the first time. "Yes," she said.

The servants scurried to obey.

"We've brought you gifts," I said. "As a thank you for hosting us, and as a promise of my intentions as Emperor."

"Over dinner," the governor said again. "Please." And then she turned to the side, gesturing for me to follow.

I took Jovis and the two maidservants with me, the chest still balanced between them. Hualin Or served individual dishes, as Imperial did, and something about this place made the hairs on my arms stand on end. They were family, and I didn't feel I could trust them in the least.

The dining hall in Hualin Or was vast, and our party only took up a small section of the table. My maidservants were guided to a small, separate table behind me, and they set the chest down next to it. Both Mephi and Thrana sat in the corner, combing the moisture from their fur with their paws.

Jovis sat to my right, and to my left two men and a woman sat closely together. I'd read up on Nisong's family. The man to my immediate left was her cousin, and he was in a relationship with both the man and the woman; between them they had one child. I did the math in my head. The boy must have been ten years old by now – not old enough to be seated with his elders.

Servants came to take our cloaks and to hang them on hooks from one wall. Beneath the hooks was a drain. A clever configuration, and one my father would have envied. The Imperial palace was beautiful but had no such niceties.

I sat on my cushion, the ends of my sleeves still a little damp, and everyone followed my lead. "Sai," I said, gesturing to the wooden chest. "I have brought you the shards of your people.

Just as Imperial has ended the Tithing Festival, we will also no longer use the shards of our people to power constructs."

Wailun smiled at me as a servant came around, pouring hot water into the waiting teapots. "Why not?"

My insides froze. Even Iloh had been grateful for the return of the shards. Was this a challenge? Something meant to test my intentions? "Because the people no longer wish to have their shards taken. It's a dangerous process, and those whose shards are used become sick and die."

"Yes," Wailun said. "But the process began as a way of defending against outside threats. We are now facing both a construct army and the rumored resurgence of the Alanga. How will you defend us from these without the constructs?"

"I'll build an army," I said. "I'm building one right now. If you pledge your guards' assistance in fighting the constructs, other islands will follow suit."

Servants began to enter the room with dishes piled high with sautéed mushrooms, fried bean curd and noodles. They placed both my plate and Jovis's with the maidservants for them to taste-test.

"I know you are new to your position," the governor said. She straightened the chopsticks next to her plate, gave them a swift, approving nod. "But is this not all a little too late? My sources told me the constructs have taken several islands now. Smaller ones, yes, but they're headed toward Gaelung. The next prize after that is Hualin Or. Will you be ready to defend us? Is that not your duty as Emperor?" The brightness of her gaze never dimmed; her smile did not fade. No one else spoke.

Jovis had laid his staff next to him, but he tapped it with his fingernails. I cast him a disapproving glare and he stopped. It was beyond rude to touch a weapon at a dinner table. Behind us, my maidservants rose and then set our dishes in front of us, taste-testing completed.

I picked up my chopsticks and everyone else at the table did the same, their gazes on their plates. The servants moved swiftly about the room and I judged their postures. Shoulders were tight, gazes low, steps close together. They were anxious, though I didn't know why.

The man next to Wailun sighed. His skin was darker than hers, his eyes narrower. Her adopted son was Chala, from my reports, barely old enough to sit at this table. He'd not yet picked up his chopsticks. "Mother, I'm sure the Emperor has a plan or she wouldn't be returning the shards."

I was returning the shards because I could do nothing less. Still, I shot him a grateful look. "That I do. Are you not happy?"

Wailun looked at me, unblinking. "Of course I am happy." Her expression never changed. She did not offer any gratitude before digging into her food.

I felt Jovis's gaze on my face, and I did my best not to look at him, keeping my expression flat. No need to let everyone know how uneasy we both were. I'd known I couldn't expect Wailun to welcome me with open arms, but this was not what I'd expected. Yes, I was a stranger to her, but she was just *strange*. It was as if I were looking at a book turned upside down. I could read it, but nothing was quite right.

I barely noticed the sweet-salty taste of the hand-pulled noodles, the crispness of the bean curd.

There was something Wailun wasn't telling me, and if I was to obtain the assistance of Hualin Or's guards, I needed to find out what that was.

30

Jovis
Hualin Or

Ylan is back. His family is gone.

I thought at first he'd come back as a pleasure visit, and though we hugged and greeted one another as old friends, his face was drawn.

He's older now, wrinkles forming at the corners of his eyes. I didn't expect that.

Philos and Viscen got into a disagreement over the allocation of caro nuts. A tsunami was the result. It wiped out the village where Ylan's parents lived. Aunts and uncles. Cousins. All gone.

"Dione," he says to me. "You're powerful. They respect (or honor?) you. Do something. Please."

—Notes from Jovis's translation of Dione's journal

Once, when I was fishing with my father, we'd hooked a juvenile sea serpent. He'd pulled it up into the ship, his face dismayed. In the Empire, juvenile sea serpents were sometimes eaten — a delicacy enjoyed by the wealthy. But the Poyer did not eat sea serpents. "They're smart," he'd explained to me. "You wouldn't eat a person, so we don't eat sea serpents." It writhed on the deck, the luminescent spots on its sides flashing, the frill on its neck standing on end. But as soon as my father approached, it calmed. He reached into its mouth, full of tiny, sharp teeth, and worked the hook free.

This palace felt like the mouth of a sea serpent, and without any assurance its jaws wouldn't close on my fingers. Even with the lamps lit, I thought I saw shadows around every corner.

Lin was silent as we followed the servants to the guest rooms where her remaining guards were waiting. Mephi and Thrana seemed unbothered, both their stomachs having been filled at dinner. But the dinner itself had been even more uncomfortable than the one we'd had at Riya. There was something odd going on here, and I wasn't sure what.

Lin waved me toward her room. "Jovis, with me. I need to speak to you a moment." Her maidservants exchanged a glance, one hiding a smile behind an upraised hand. I wanted to protest: it wasn't what they thought it was. But what was I going to do? Disobey an order from the Emperor? So I followed her inside. The room was spacious and beautifully appointed, but I didn't have the chance to admire the decorations. She rounded on me as soon as she'd shut the door.

"What was that? All the servants are afraid, the family is hiding something and Wailun herself doesn't seem to care at all what her people want. She seems content with the Tithing Festival as it is. Why?"

"I'm as puzzled as you are."

"Maybe she just doesn't care," Mephi said, leaning against my knees.

Thrana piped up eagerly. "A bad? A very bad?"

"More like a strange," I said.

"A strange," Thrana cooed.

"No," Lin broke in, "we don't say it like that. We say that the situation is strange. We don't just label things as 'a strange'." She threw up her hands. "Oh, what does it matter? What matters is that Wailun is hiding something. I don't know how to gain the support of Hualin Or if the return of the shards doesn't impress them. They're worried about the construct army – and they should be – but seem uninterested in helping. We'll need to make a stand at Gaelung, which is the only reason I brought Ragan with us."

I huffed out an uncomfortable breath. "You know, when we keep meeting alone – Mephi and Thrana don't count – people assume things. Your maidservants are gossiping."

She shot me a sharp look, though her cheeks were flushed. "What's more important here? The safety of my people or the idle chatter of my servants? Don't bother me about unimportant things."

Gossip could topple an Empire almost as surely as rebellion could. But I kept these thoughts to myself. "Then what did you want from me? Why am I here?"

Her expression turned pleading. She could keep herself so aloof, her thoughts so well-hidden. Yet she rarely seemed to do so around me. "I need your help."

"What do you need me to do?" The words slipped out before I could stop them. Maybe it was the way the lamplight caught the warm brown shades of her eyes. Maybe it was because, for the first time, I hadn't thought of them as Emahla's eyes.

I shouldn't be offering my help. She wasn't actually Shiyen's daughter and heir. I had no idea who she truly was. Did she?

"Tonight. When everyone is sleeping. I'm going to find out what the governor is hiding."

I raised an eyebrow. "Shouldn't you have . . . spies for that sort of thing?"

"I don't trust spies."

I held in a flinch. "So you're going to sneak around the hallways at night, running into the governor's guards, and then you'll explain yourself how?"

"No, not the hallways," she said, with a satisfied little smile. She pointed one finger up, just as Ragan usually did.

And then I realized her meaning was quite different from his. I let my gaze drift to the ceiling. Above us, the rain still pounded at the roof. "That's a terrible idea."

"I've done it before. I'll head to the governor's room and see what I can find. You, on the other hand, would have a reason to be patrolling the hallways at night."

"And you want me to . . . ?"

"Do just that – patrol the hallways and look for anything odd. Report back to me in the morning if you find anything. Wailun hasn't said so outright, but she doesn't seem keen on supporting my leadership. I need to find out why. We're running out of time."

I'd seen the similarities in their faces as clearly as everyone else must have. If Lin was not Nisong's daughter, whose daughter was she? She certainly looked like her mother's family. Or was she an illegitimate child, as this Nisong claimed to be, born soon before or after the legitimate one? But then why would Shiyen name her as his legitimate daughter?

And there was a thought I kept shoving away: if constructs could look like people . . .

No. She was far too complicated for that.

I'd written a letter to the Shardless Few the night after that discovery, had sealed it and then had broken the seal to read over the words I'd written again. In code: "Lin is not Shiyen's daughter and I have proof. I don't know who she really is." I'd told Gio not to expect any further letters. But this was information the Shardless Few deserved to know. It was information everyone deserved to know. I put it out of my mind for the moment, just as I'd put the letter away, unsure of whether to send it. "You'd think she'd be inclined to support a family member."

Lin pursed her lips, her gaze turning to the wall as if she were looking through it and to green mountains beyond. "She didn't mention my mother or our familial ties, not once."

I remembered my mother's words: *She's lonely.* Bah. I waved the thought away. It wasn't my problem to solve. It couldn't be. "I should go." Lin's gaze went to my staff. Damn it. I was tapping it against the floor again. I stilled my hand.

"Am I making you nervous?"

"Is that a question I have to answer, Eminence?" Stupid thing to say. Should have just denied it. Too many thoughts competing for space in my head for me to think clearly about anything.

She looked away. "You can go."

I left, taking Mephi with me. Kaphra's deadline was swiftly arriving. I'd have to take the sword and give it to the Ioph Carn tonight, when Lin was expecting me to be patrolling the halls. I knew where the Ioph Carn were stationed here in Hualin Or, a house where cobblestone streets turned to dirt roads. Out of the way, quiet.

"So . . . " Mephi said when I'd entered the room the servant had indicated for me and shut the door. "We are not doing what Lin asked." He eyed me, his head tilted to the side.

I could lie to anyone except for Mephi. "No, we're not. The thing I told you about before – the good-bad thing. We're going to do that instead."

Mephi sat at my feet, and I noticed, startled, that the top of his head nearly reached my waist. He'd still been growing; it'd just been so gradual lately that I'd not been aware of it. His brown eyes met mine. "Jovis. You can tell me what we're going to do. I trust you. It's why I chose you."

He'd been growing in more ways than one. "I'm not perfect, Mephi."

He scratched at an ear, his mouth in a grimace. He squinted up at me. "Oh, I know that too."

"I need to take Lin's sword to Kaphra. I'm going to replace it with the one we found and hope she doesn't notice a difference. In exchange, Kaphra will smuggle caro nuts to Anau."

"You're afraid of hurting Lin."

I rubbed a hand against my forehead. "Does she deserve to be deposed? Does she deserve to be executed?" I could barely force the words past my lips. Was it possible to start anew when the shadow of the old Empire still lived? "Everything is broken and I don't know how to put it back together in a way that makes sense."

"Have you thought about telling her the truth?"

I gave him a rueful look. "Have I *thought* about it? Yes. But have you listened to Lin at all? Where do you think that conversation goes? 'Hello, I sent information to the Shardless Few behind your back. I've stopped, but oh yes, I agreed to steal the strange sword you have for the Ioph Carn so I can make sure the people I care about still get the cure for the bog cough.'" I rubbed at my neck as though I could already feel the blade cutting into it. "That has a very poor end for me, I'm afraid."

Mephi wound around my legs, reminding me of when he was kitten-sized, his horns still just buds and his legs short. "I will be with you either way."

"I know. And I'll always keep you safe, Mephi. I suppose I am a smuggler at heart. I'll have to do what I've done so many times before."

"Which is?"

"Figure it out as I go along."

I set guards on rotation outside Lin's room and waited until I judged most of the household to be asleep. And then Mephi and I took a lamp and left the guest wing under the pretense of making sure there were no assassins lurking in corners.

The rain had lightened outside. Even now, Lin might be creeping over the rooftop, searching for a way into the governor's rooms. Easy enough for her — what could anyone do if she got caught? She was the Emperor.

The hallways of the palace were dark, my lamp casting wild shadows as it turned in my hand. Except for the rain, I heard nothing. It felt less like a palace and more like a tomb. No footsteps except for my own, no murmuring, nothing.

The courtyard of the palace was still, though out here I could hear insects and bird calls. The guards on the walls shuffled back and forth, keeping an eye out for intruders. The gate was closed.

That would prove a bit difficult. But I'd dealt with "difficult" before. The walls of the palace had been built before the founding of the Empire, and were bare stones — not plastered over like in Imperial. It would be easy to find handholds and I was quick enough that I was sure I could avoid detection.

I found a section of wall nestled next to the sheer cliff of a mountain. It was patrolled less frequently here, likely because few would attempt that climb.

"Come on, up you go," I said, patting my back. Mephi wrapped his front paws around my neck, and I winced a little at the claws on his back legs. He was heavier than he'd been even just several months ago, when we'd tried this last at Imperial.

But fortunately my bond with him lent me strength. We made it over the wall and then down the cliff with a few curses beneath my breath. When I looked up at the rooftops of the palace, I thought I saw a shadow pass over the tiles. I felt a tug at my heart and thought of the way I'd not been there for Emahla, not when she'd needed me the most.

Lin was not Emahla, and I had others who needed me.

A bit reluctantly, I turned from the wall and made my way toward the docks. Mephi trotted beside me, his tail swaying behind him, his step jaunty. Would that I could feel so carefree. It must have been nice, to be beholden just to one person and to know you would follow them to the depths of the Endless Sea. It must have been how people felt about the Sukais, back when they'd formed the Empire. How I felt sometimes about Lin.

Why did my mind keep circling back to her? I shoved the thoughts aside, trying to focus on the task ahead. They'd pulled up the gangplank, and a guard patrolled the deck. I waited for her to disappear behind the main mast before I made the leap onto the ship, letting my knees cushion my landing, keeping my footfalls light.

The door to below-deck was open and unguarded, which made me almost click my tongue against my teeth. If I could sneak past my own guards, someone else could too. I'd have to impress on them the importance of having eyes on all possible entry points. Lin's door would be locked, but the locksmith had only replaced the damaged hardware. My earlier charge into the room had loosened the wooden frame.

The stairs squeaked a little, and Mephi's claws clicked against the wood as we descended into the darkness. I went to my room, retrieved my sword from between mattress and frame and went Lin's door, gesturing for Mephi to wait. Just a push of my shoulder against the frame, a pull on the doorknob and the latch popped out of its resting spot. The door swung open. I stepped into her room quietly. The smell and feel of it nearly overwhelmed me. The scent of jasmine hung faintly over the bed.

Everything was neatly organized, not an object out of place. I couldn't help but remember the two assassins we'd faced down together, our bodies moving in tandem, as though we could read one another's thoughts.

Had I been bereft of romantic contact for so long? Was I now doomed to pine over stolen moments, the way I had as an adolescent – wishing for such moments to pass again? I might have grieved Emahla's passing, but I still missed the *solidness* of her presence, the familiarity of her movements, the sound of her breath at night.

Enough moping. I'd set my course for tonight, and I needed to sail it. I dug Lin's sword out from the bottom of the chest, replacing it with my own. They looked similar enough; even the wrapping around their hilts looked similarly worn. And this way, I was fulfilling both Kaphra's wishes and heeding Gio's warning about keeping hold of the sword I'd found in the hideout. If it did something terrible, I'd far rather it be in Lin's possession.

I strapped Lin's sword to my back next to the staff. "Let's go," I whispered to Mephi. He crept to my side like a shadow. I left the room and pulled the door back into place, turning toward the stairs.

Light flared, nearly blinding me. I brought my staff to bear, blinking as my eyes adjusted, my pulse pounding at my neck, already a thousand excuses running through my mind. I couldn't be caught. Not here, not now.

Someone had entered the hall, a lamp raised in one hand. The person's other hand lifted, one finger pointed up.

"Ah," Ragan said. "I do not think you are supposed to be here."

31

Lin

Hualin Or

Thrana wanted to come with me. I held her head between my hands. "I can get you up onto the roof, but how will I get you back down into the room? Please – the best thing you can do for me is stay here and to be safe."

"Just be careful." She agreed more quickly than I'd thought she might. She'd eaten a larger dinner than usual and her eyelids drooped as she spoke. She was asleep before I'd finished opening the shutters. Leaving her behind felt odd, like I was leaving a limb behind. Thrana had been a part of my life for such a short time, yet now she felt inseparable from it.

I reached for the roof and pulled myself up. It was easier now, the power thrumming in my bones and giving me strength. I'd eaten another of the cloudtree berries in my sash, and it boosted my strength further. The rain had abated to a light drizzle, thankfully, though the tiles were slippery beneath my feet. I'd left the oilskin cloak in my room in favor of tighter, more maneuverable clothing.

My father would have sneered at me. "An Emperor dressed like an assassin, climbing roofs? Beneath the dignity of the station."

But I couldn't care too much for dignity.

I'd noted the location of the governor's suites as the servants guided us through the palace, so I knew they were nestled up close to the mountain's base. Even through the rain, I could see a few lights still lit in city windows. From the jungle and the mountains came the faint calls of nocturnal animals, whooping messages into the darkness. Hualin Or was a beautiful place. There was a part of me that wanted to take Thrana, to venture into those mountains, to leave my responsibilities behind.

The tiles clicked beneath my feet as I made my way across the rooftop. Guards on the walls didn't bother to turn around, their gazes fixed on the outside world. I supposed, in this way, they were not too dissimilar from constructs. The governor's suites did not have a balcony, though when I peered over the edge of the roof, I could see large, shuttered windows and a wide ledge. I lowered myself over the roof and onto the ledge, clinging tightly to the shutters. I tested them. Locked, of course.

I'd noted the design of the shutters in my room, though. It was simple enough. I'd borrowed a knife from one of my handmaidens. Slipping it between the shutters, I felt for the clasp I knew was there. And then slowly, carefully, I jiggled the lever free.

The shutter swung open on creaky hinges, and I cringed at the sound – waiting, my breath held, for any cry of alarm. When it did not come, I let out my breath and stepped into the governor's sitting room.

There was something oddly clean and sterile about the place. There were no books lying about, no loose sheets of paper, no bottles of ink or errant pairs of slippers. Perhaps Wailun's maidservants were particularly meticulous, or she was particularly demanding.

The doorway between the sitting room and bedroom did not have a door; a screen with inlaid mother-of-pearl separated the two rooms, the polished wood gleaming by moonlight. I went to the screen, peeking behind it to make sure she still slept.

A shape lay in bed, on top of the covers.

I frowned. It was a bit chilly at night in the wet season. Perhaps she ran hot? I could barely make out the stirring of her chest as she breathed. I supposed I should be grateful she was a heavy sleeper.

I turned back to the sitting room and, squinting in the darkness, found her desk. The top was immaculate, a few books shelved above it. Nothing overly interesting. *Ningsu's Proverbs*, a book of maps, another on economics. I opened the top drawer.

A plain book lay there. I picked it up and held it to the open window. I couldn't be certain, but it looked green. It looked like the journal that had once belonged to Nisong. My heartbeat kicked up a notch. Nisong and Wailun were sisters; perhaps their parents had gifted them these journals at the same time.

I took a chance and lit the small lamp by the desk. I waited, but Wailun didn't stir. I'd been right — it *was* green, and the exact same shade as the journal I'd found in my palace's secret library. I flipped the book open.

Wailun was older than Nisong, and her writing reflected that. The entries were more focused on her relationships, on the subtle politics she was already a party to. There were large gaps of time between entries, but it looked like she wrote in it consistently.

And then, she'd stopped. The last part of the book was blank except for dates. She'd written in dates for every day yet nothing beneath them. I flipped back, to the last entry she'd written. It had been in the year 1538. Two years before my father had created me.

A chill crept up my spine, something pricking at the back of my mind. My father couldn't pull Nisong's memories from her blood; he'd burned her body before realizing he could attempt to reconstruct her. Where, then, had he pulled them from?

"What are you doing in my rooms?"

I whirled. Wailun, who had been fast asleep only a moment before, now stood in front of the wooden screen, very much awake.

"Who are you?" I said, unable to stop the question from slipping past my lips. "Are you still Wailun? What did Shiyen do to you?"

She scoffed. "Your father? He did nothing to me. Now answer my question. You may be the Emperor and here under my hospitality, but I did not give you leave to enter my rooms in the middle of the night, nor to look through my personal things."

Her voice was cold and angry. If I was wrong about her, about this palace, I'd be setting off a diplomatic incident. I supposed I already had. There was no easy way to explain away my presence. Everyone would hear about the Emperor skulking about in Hualin Or's palace in the middle of the night. No one would trust me. They'd label me mad, unstable. They'd depose me.

If I was wrong.

I pressed past the fear and stepped closer.

She retreated, pulling her robes tight about her with one hand. "What are you doing?" I reached for her and she whipped a dagger out from a hidden pocket.

There was no turning back at this point – she'd caught me in her rooms and I would have to answer for that. Unless I was right, then there was still a chance to fix this. I grabbed her wrist. She was surprisingly strong, the arm beneath my fingers warm and sinewy. Her face twisted into a grimace as she tried to pull free of my grasp. I reached for her torso and she ducked out of the way.

Before I could react, she switched her grip on the blade, ever so slightly, and dug the point into my wrist. I sucked in a breath but didn't loosen my fingers.

"Let me go!" she cried out too loudly.

"I'm sorry." She opened her mouth to shout again and I plunged my free hand toward her chest.

I should have been surprised that my fingers did not stop at her skin. Instead, I only felt a cold and certain dread as my hand entered her body. I'd been right. Shiyen might be dead, but the results of his actions still lived.

I felt around until I found the shards, clustered close to her spine. He must have invited them to visit at the palace, and then, once they were there – he'd murdered them. I thought of what I'd seen in my father's memories. So much blood burned in the memory machine brazier, along with witstone. He didn't have Nisong's blood, but he had the blood of her family.

And then he'd replaced the family he'd murdered.

I fished around, pulling a few shards free. I held them to the lamplight. The commands they held were complex, but still not at the level that Ilith's, Construct of Spies, had been. Write in your journal – he hadn't specified exactly what. Tithe regularly to the Emperor – that one referenced other shards. Sleep in your bed. He must have placed some of the memories back into their lifeless bodies, made them into constructs, and then counted his work done.

How arrogant, how foolish! To think no one would notice. To think no one would figure it out.

My hands stilled. But no one had. This was the governor of Hualin Or. She and her family might have come back from Imperial acting a little oddly, their mannerisms a little changed. But who were the servants to say anything? The guards? Who would have believed them or who even had the power to change things? Only the Emperor, and he was the initiator of this deception.

So Wailun adopted a son and everything continued as it always had – colder and stranger, but routine. The people of Hualin Or had been under the rule of a facsimile, and not even a very good one.

I thought I understood a little the need for rebellions.

I shifted the shards in my palm. My wrist was still bleeding, my blood dripping onto the floor. I needed to clean that up, put the shards back in and run.

Footsteps sounded outside the room. No time. I shoved the shards back into her body and made for the window, hoping she wouldn't spot me by the time she came to. She'd undergo a bit of a reset, forgetting everything that had happened immediately before I'd removed the shards.

I heard the guards enter the room just as I'd finished pulling myself onto the roof. The cut stung, but I knew from prior experience that it would heal quickly. My bond with Thrana would make sure of that.

The night air felt colder than it had on my way to the governor's rooms. I hurried back to my guest rooms, trying not to scrape my palms as I lowered myself from the edge of the roof and into the opened window. Thrana rushed at me, pressing her head beneath my palm. I rubbed the base of her horns, trying to reassure her. "I've returned. It's fine."

But I couldn't reassure myself. I thought about the shards in my hand, the order I'd had them in when I'd placed them back into Wailun's body. Had one of the shards slipped below another? I seemed to remember them jostling as I'd hurriedly thrust them back into place. A reference shard taking the place of a command shard. A cold dread wrapped around my chest. I'd interrupted the construct's logical balance. Wailun would fall apart. I still remembered the faces of Bayan and Ilith as their flesh melted from their bones.

I'd done the same thing to Wailun. They would find her with her eyelids gaping, her nose sloughing from her skull. Her dagger nearby and bloodied. By all appearances, a murder.

Someone pounded at the door. I jumped, my heartbeat fluttering. My wound was fast-closing, but it still oozed a little blood. They'd see it. They'd know.

"Quick!" I whispered to Thrana. She followed me to the window, where I leaned over. "Use my back."

The beast was heavier than I'd expected; only my Alanga-enhanced strength kept me from tumbling to the ground below. A shove and then the weight on my shoulders lifted. The pounding at the door increased. I pulled myself up onto the roof. Thrana's claws scraped against the tiles as she struggled to keep her footing.

Below me, I heard voices I did not recognize. "Eminence? Eminence!"

We fled toward the city.

32

Jovis

Hualin Or

Viscen is unrepentant. Philos, only a little. Viscen blames it all on Philos. The wet season is almost here, and the people on her island have suffered from bog cough each season. Philos isn't keen on sharing his supply of caro nuts. He needs them for his people.

I point out their disagreement killed twenty-three villagers.

"And what about the three hundred that died on my island from bog cough?" Viscen says.

"Destroying the village was unintentional," Philos says. "Or maybe Viscen did intend it; I don't know how her mind works." They're working up to another fight, I can feel it. Philos and Viscen have always hated one another and look for any excuse to bicker.

When I say we should all be more cautious with our powers, they shrug and turn away. How can they not

care? All these vibrant lives are more than a number. All
these vibrant lives winked out.
   Perhaps Ylan is right.
   Perhaps something needs to be done.

–Notes from Jovis's translation of Dione's journal

Of all the people I had to run into while engaging in sub-
terfuge, Ragan was the one I least wanted to encounter. I
couldn't pretend I wasn't here, there simply was no faking that.
But I could fake confidence, and Ragan was from a monastery;
how much did he really know about life outside of it? "Oh,
Ragan," I said, putting as much friendliness into my voice as I
could muster. I could still feel the pounding of my heartbeat, and
had to make an effort to keep my breathing even. "You're up late."

"And you are supposed to be at the palace with Lin," he said.
His ossalen, Lozhi, peeked out from behind his robes, blue eyes
wide. "She sent me back to the ship," I said. I worked through
a thousand excuses. She was angry with me, she wanted to
check on something at the ship, she was afraid someone might
have breached her rooms. As I studied Ragan's narrowed eyes,
though, I knew he would follow up with Lin about them. So I
chose something else. "She was having . . . " I lowered my voice,
leaned in conspiratorially. " . . . woman problems. She asked me
to fetch some herbs she left here on the ship."

But unlike many of the men I'd known, who would shift
uncomfortably and let the matter fall, Ragan wasn't deterred by
this revelation. "And she didn't send one of her maidservants
instead? She sent you?"

"Dione's balls, man," I said, and that at least made him flinch.
It gave me a moment to gather my thoughts. "Do you think

she'd send her maidservants alone into the streets at night? War constructs killed one of them on Nephilanu."

He blinked. "No, no, I suppose not. Well I hope the herbs help her." He stepped to the side to let me pass.

I made for the stairs, but as soon as my foot hit the first step, he called after me. "You carry a sword too?"

I'd strapped the sword to my back, and the cloak covered most of it, but the hilt still protruded above my shoulders. Endless Sea, did I need to murder him to shut him up? "Most guards do," I snapped, and then I lunged up the rest of the stairs before he could say anything else.

The drizzling rain cooled the heat of my face and chest. I wasn't sure what about Ragan bothered me so much. Maybe it was the way he'd inserted himself into Lin's confidence, making her think we needed him, making her think he could possibly be useful. He was youthful, he was annoying, he wasn't even a master among the monks. Maybe they'd sent him out into the world because they'd grown too irritated with him to let him stay.

I often had the feeling my mother wanted to do the same when I'd been his age. I crept past the guards and leapt from the deck to the docks without being seen. Ragan had already seen me, but the guards had not, and I didn't much want to explain how I'd gotten onto the ship in the first place.

"You don't seem to like him," Mephi whispered to me.

"Who? Ragan? He's a perfectly lovely fellow."

Mephi looked so startled that I couldn't help but to laugh. "I suppose I should teach you a little about sarcasm. It's when you say the opposite of what you mean."

He regarded me for a moment as we strode through the city streets. "His ossalen is very brave," he said in a fair approximation of my tone.

"Not bad," I said.

Mephi bounded in a circle around me as though chasing an invisible fly. I grabbed one of his horns as he passed and playfully wrestled him into place back beside me. "Enough fun for tonight. We're going somewhere dangerous. I need you to stay close and to do as I say."

It was a hopeless request, I knew. Mephi seldom did exactly as I told him to. The older he got, the more free he seemed to feel to make his own decisions. "I always do what you say," he said in the same sarcastic tone.

I bit back a sigh of exasperation. "The people we are going to see – Mephi, they are bad. I can't let anything happen to you. I'd never forgive myself."

He finally quieted and pressed his head against my hip. "I am bigger than I was, and stronger. I will be safe."

I'd thought so too, when I'd been a youth. It was only when I'd grown older that I understood the true extent of my mortality. More than a little apprehensive, I turned onto the street that would lead us out of the city.

I just needed this to work. Lin wouldn't notice her sword was missing, Ragan wouldn't bother me again, my family and the people I cared about would get the cure they needed for the bog cough. If I could get this to work, the rest – the Empire, the Shardless Few, the construct army – they might be manageable.

Just as the cobblestones turned to dirt and gravel, I found the house. It didn't look like a den of iniquity. It was a stately affair, complete with a manicured front yard and stone lamps. But Kaphra liked to count himself cultured. This was one of his many homes, used for Ioph Carn business when not in his personal use.

I tightened my hand around my staff and took the path of paving stones to the front door. I gave it a sharp rap. "It's Jovis," I said loudly, not bothering with any codes. They knew I was coming.

It took a while, but then lamplight shone through the shutters by the front door. Footsteps – more than two pairs – shuffled inside. A floorboard creaked.

At last, the door opened. Philine greeted me. She must have been asleep – it was the middle of the night – yet she was still wearing her leathers, was armed to the teeth and looked as alert as though she'd been awake for hours and had already taken tea. "Jovis," she said. "Someday I'm going to kill you and it will always have been long after you should have been dead."

I tilted my head, taking a moment to parse her words. I pursed my lips and nodded. "That's fair."

She jerked the door open the rest of the way. "Come in."

"Can't I just give you the sword and be on my way?"

She rolled her eyes in that odd way, never really looking away from me. "Kaphra wants to speak to you."

Every bone in my body felt lanced with ice. "Kaphra is ... here?" I knew it was a part-time residence of his, but I hadn't expected him to be here. Or to be awake.

"Putting the pieces together, are we? Your thirty days is nearly up, and we knew the Emperor's ship would be stopping in at Hualin Or. Yes, he's here and he wants to speak to you. That's why I'm inviting you in. Don't keep him waiting." She eyed Mephi, and I remembered the first time they'd met, he'd sunk his needle-sharp teeth into her leg. "He's a fair bit bigger."

"Bigger teeth now too," Mephi said, baring them briefly to show her.

Her eyebrows lifted to nearly her hairline, but she didn't jump back or even flinch. "Yes, well, keep them out of people's legs and we won't have a problem."

I tightened my grip on my staff and walked inside. When Kaphra wanted to speak to you in-person, you answered. I'd no doubt Philine and her lackeys would follow me straight back to the palace if I declined this invitation. And what did he want to say to me? It had been years since I'd last spoken with him.

"A moment," Philine said as she took the single lit lamp from the table and used it to light the other lamps in the room. The house had a spacious entryway, decorated with ceiling murals and lined with pillars. I imagined Kaphra entertained all manner of prestigious guests in his home. I wouldn't have been surprised if he'd entertained some governors here. It smelled of old, damp wood and green tea. "Someone is waking him up." Philine gestured to a couch.

I didn't sit. I wasn't here to get comfortable; Lin was still expecting me to be in my rooms by morning. I was here to deliver the sword he'd asked for and to leave.

Philine knew better than to try and command me to sit; she knew I wasn't good at following orders. At last, I heard shuffling from upstairs.

The door opposite me opened, and Kaphra stepped into the entryway.

Even though I'd arrived in the middle of the night, he'd taken the time to drape himself in a heavily embroidered robe with voluminous sleeves. He wore two delicate golden chains from which carved jade pieces hung, and several rings with various precious stones. Or perhaps he'd slept wearing them; that wasn't difficult for me to imagine. Kaphra was short and slender, a sapling of a man with a thin beard and thick brows. He looked younger than he was – a man of his mid-thirties rather than mid-forties – and I knew he often used his appearance to disarm his opponents, feigning ignorance or foolishness.

He wouldn't try such a tactic on me.

"Ah, Jovis. It's good to see you again. It's been too long." The man sounded sincere; he always sounded sincere. He spread his arms wide. "You refuse my invitations, you never send letters, you rebuff my emissaries … I might think you were avoiding me."

"Your emissaries gave me quite the beating."

"A misunderstanding," he said smoothly.

I knew what I should say: "Of course." Because when a man is as powerful as Kaphra, you just accept his version of reality to survive. But I was done with making myself less in order to appease people. My bones thrummed. He had power? So did I. "What do you want? I've brought the sword you asked for. When I spoke with your agent, she made it clear this was to be a one-time exchange. I was fine with that. I've paid my debts; I owe you nothing more."

I unfastened the sword from my back and held it out to him. "Take it and leave me in peace."

He didn't demur; he took the step closer and snatched the sword from my grip. A warning tingled at the back of my neck. Kaphra wasn't usually so direct. He wanted the sword, and badly. Was Lin's sword as dangerous as Gio seemed to believe his was? What exactly had I traded in for the safety of Anau?

Kaphra pulled the blade a little from the sheath. And then he took a knife from his belt and peeled back the wrapping on the hilt. Whatever he'd seen must have satisfied him, because he sheathed both knife and sword and looked back to me. "No," he said calmly.

"No what?"

"Leave you in peace. You see, Jovis, you're more unique than you know you are."

The tingle exploded into a full-fledged tremor of dread. Did he know I was Alanga? How could he know?

"I've collected many things over the years," he said. "Jewels, old Alanga artifacts, books … " He trailed off. He hadn't let go of the sword.

Did I hear hushed whispers outside? The creak of footsteps

from upstairs? My gaze flicked to Philine. She hadn't moved, but neither would she meet my eyes. It was a trap, but if Kaphra knew my abilities, what did he hope to gain?

"An interesting story, but I should be going." I took a step back.

Kaphra drew the sword and tossed the scabbard to the side. The strange white material glinted in the lamplight. "You think you know about the power that makes your bones thrum. The Emperor thinks she knows about the power that animates the constructs. But there is so much you don't understand." He shrugged a little, gave me a childish smile. "You and I both know you're not just walking out of here, Jovis. The house is surrounded by Ioph Carn."

I didn't know the limits of my power; I didn't think I'd ever stretched to my potential. I tapped my foot experimentally on the floorboards and felt a small, answering tremor. If I unleashed everything I had, I could collapse the entire place. But I was also standing beneath this roof, with Mephi at my side. I'd have to be careful. "I don't want to hurt anyone."

"Very noble of you. But I can't say I feel the same way."

I saw, from the corner of my eye, Philine drawing her daggers. No baton this time, then.

"So you want to kill me?"

"Too simple. When have I ever been simple? I have asked you nicely; I have practically begged. I want your power for the Ioph Carn, Jovis. Just say 'yes' and we needn't hurt anyone."

I answered by stamping a foot on the wooden floor of Kaphra's elaborate part-time home.

The walls shook, shutters breaking free from windows, tiles falling from the roof. The wood below my foot shattered into a web of cracks. Philine grabbed at an end table for balance, but Kaphra stood with the sword ready, riding the tremor like a wave. He kicked a fallen chair out of the way and advanced.

I met his blow with my staff. Kaphra was not a particularly skilled fighter or a strong one. I batted the blade away from me the way I might swat a branch away from my face. This was what he'd bargained for? As far as I could tell, he'd not been granted any special powers. The sword was just a sword. I gave him a knock in the ribs for good measure and turned to leave. "Come on, Mephi." I glared at Philine. "Move."

She shrugged and stepped to the side.

I opened the door and found a dozen Ioph Carn surrounding the yard, weapons drawn. Mephi growled, his sizable teeth bared. Kaphra and Philine weren't going to let me walk away from here; they wanted me cornered from all sides.

"I can destroy this house," I called back to Kaphra.

The Ioph Carn advanced. If I wanted to be clear of the walls, I had to get past them.

"With you and your beast inside it?" He'd recovered from my blow and was stalking toward me, Philine covering his right flank.

I didn't want Mephi in this fight; I didn't want him in any fight. But he was larger now than he'd been, and I knew from past experience he'd disobey me to help. "Keep Kaphra and Philine off my back," I told him. "I'll handle the rest."

"Very good," Mephi said, clacking his teeth together. I took a step toward the Ioph Carn and jabbed my staff at the nearest one.

It was like fighting a hurricane. They came at me from all directions, weapons buffeting my defenses like a storm-force gale. Mephi growled and snapped his teeth behind me. My staff connected, once, twice. Two of the Ioph Carn flew backward. I couldn't see their faces in the darkness, but I could hear their cries. Damned fools — only doing what Kaphra asked them to do. The way I'd once done, not caring for the consequences. I wondered if he had something hanging over each of their heads, if they had families at home that they cared about, or if they were simply motivated by greed.

I just wanted them to leave me alone. A knife grazed across my arm, and the glimpse of blood seemed to embolden the rest of them. They crowded me, blades flashing like teeth. I knocked a sword from someone's grasp, kicked another Ioph Carn out of the yard. Still too many of them.

And then I heard Mephi scream.

A sick feeling of shock froze my innards. I couldn't care about the Ioph Carn at my back; Mephi needed me. I whirled around and saw him bleeding from a gash above his shoulder. Kaphra stood over him, triumphant. Leaning down, he grabbed Mephi by one of his horns. The strange sword dripped blood onto the floor.

"Don't!" I cried out. The word felt ripped from me. If anything happened to Mephi, I would die. I wouldn't know how to go on. I'd lost Emahla. I couldn't now lose Mephi too. I couldn't take my eyes off of Mephi's wound, waiting for the bleeding to stop, waiting for it to heal.

"Don't what?" Kaphra said, raising the sword.

"If you hurt him, I'll never help you."

Kaphra only laughed. He shook Mephi a little. "All this power at your beck and call, and you cannot let this beast be hurt. Why is that?"

Oh, I hated him. I'd never cared for Kaphra before, but now all I wanted was to crack his head open with my staff, to shut his smug mouth for ever. "I think you already know."

"Your . . . ossalen. You are Alanga," he said. I'd already suspected that he knew, but hearing the word said aloud, from his lips, still shocked me into stillness. "Ossalen is what they used to call them. A bond that, once formed, cannot be broken."

"Then what do you want with him? Let him go."

Kaphra nodded to someone behind me – the Ioph Carn. "Collateral, obviously. Put down your staff, come with me quietly and I'll tell you how you can earn your freedom."

I dropped my staff because I couldn't do anything else. "The sword," I said, feeling a pressure against my chest, an ache. I'd done something very wrong here, and I wasn't sure yet what that was. "What does it do?"

"Allow me to demonstrate." Before I could move away, he lashed out with the blade. It wasn't like being cut with steel. I'd registered the earlier wound, and it had already begun to heal. This seared across my skin like ice and fire, sending pain crawling up my chest and into my throat. I bit back a shout. A small cut, and shallow, but more painful even than the beating Philine had once visited upon me.

I staggered back, pressing a hand to the wound.

Kaphra studied the edge of the blade, his hand still tight around one of Mephi's horns. "There are kernels of truth in stories, even the most absurd ones. When I was a teenager, I used to laugh at that play, *Phoenix Rise*. How could one special sword defeat the Alanga? It didn't really make sense. Even with witstone, it takes time to get from island to island. Are we meant to believe that one lone Sukai traveled the breadth of the Empire, searching out and hunting down Alanga? It's a fantasy that makes the Sukais sound more noble and intrepid than they actually are. In the end we are all animals, scraping by with what we can. None of us are noble."

I traced the carved ceiling beams with my gaze. "You are hardly scraping by, though I won't argue against labeling you as an animal."

"You were my best smuggler," Kaphra said, as though he hadn't heard me. I stared at the blade, the blood upon it, Mephi crouched and hurting. He might think he could keep me in hand with Mephi's life on the line, but my bones vibrated to an almost painful degree. Anger flooded hot in my belly. He thought he could control me? He thought he could cut Mephi with that accursed blade and get away with it?

"You could be so much more." He was still talking. Oh, he was worse than I was – he didn't just speak to fill silences, he spoke to hear himself speak. He wasn't selling me on anything, no matter how eloquent he thought he was.

I'd spoken an oath to Lin, and I'd made a pact with myself to help the Shardless Few. And now the Ioph Carn wanted to have me on a leash?

"I have a ship at the docks. We leave tonight." He pulled Mephi closer to him. The beast whimpered.

A breeze from the open door tickled my cheek. I could feel every tiny hair that it lifted. Something stirred within me. "I am not going with you," I said, not quite feeling myself. I felt like I was floating above my body, like I'd ceased to be Jovis at all. "And neither is Mephi."

"I think you are," Kaphra said, hefting his sword. He held it to Mephi's neck.

"*No.*" The word felt torn from me, ripping up my throat. But what could I do? I was injured and alone and I wasn't sure how many of the Ioph Carn behind me were still conscious. Philine took a loop of rope from a drawer and approached.

I was going to do this, wasn't I? Let her tie me up, let her take me with them. Be their obedient pet. I felt the crushing weight of it as though I were already surrounded by four walls and a locked door.

Kaphra's eyes widened. Before I could follow his gaze, a wall of water swept past me to slam into Kaphra and Philine. It hit them both at chest height. He lost his grip on both the sword and on Mephi. Not my water, not my attack. I splashed through it, reaching for my friend among the scattered furniture. "Mephi!"

The beast righted himself much more quickly than Kaphra and Philine did, swimming and limping back to my side.

The water drew back like a wave leaving the shore. I shivered as it sucked at my legs, my clothes drying as the moisture left them.

I whirled and had to squint into the darkness to make out a silhouette against the wall of churning water.

Philine rose first, staring out the door, grasping for her daggers — now strewn across the floor. The one remaining lamp in the corner of the room flickered. Kaphra scrambled to his feet behind her, his gaze casting about wildly.

A cloaked figure emerged from the night, hands lifted, water on either side of them, a beast at their side. Fingers extended and the water rose higher. Another Alanga?

I could hear some of the Ioph Carn I'd cast aside getting up, regrouping.

The wound Kaphra had given me still burned, still sent little jolts of pain to the tips of my fingers. I grimaced and gripped my staff, trying to take a fighting stance. Mephi was in no better shape. He let out a low growl, though he put no weight on the foot beneath the injured shoulder.

Philine hesitated only a moment before baring her teeth and darting toward me. I lifted my staff, hoping I could somehow fend her off.

"You will not *touch* him!"

Water whipped out in all directions, lashing at Philine, and by the shouts behind me, at the other Ioph Carn. It whirled around me, a miniature typhoon inside Kaphra's house. The storm needled my cheeks, blinding me. "Mephi?" I called out above the din.

He pressed a shoulder to my leg and I dug my fingers into his fur. "I am here," he said. He must have been shouting so I could hear, but his voice sounded soft and as though it were at my ear. My panic eased. Around us, wood groaned and furniture creaked as waves of water buffeted them. Cracks sounded as sundry items tumbled from their places inside the home, striking walls and pillars. I stood in the eye of the storm, untouched. The hooded figure appeared out of the storm in front of me, hands still raised.

I lifted my staff, trying to reach for that thrumming in my bones and feeling only a slight tremor. I couldn't make out the face beneath the hood. And then the Alanga let the water fall and she brushed the hood back. The lamp in the corner was miraculously still lit. By its light, I could make out Lin's eyes, her furrowed brow, her pursed lips. Thrana crept to Mephi's side, sniffing at his wound and curling her lip back.

I couldn't think of anything to say. My mind went blank, silent.

She frowned. "What are you doing here? You're supposed to be at the palace."

And then I found words, the panic from my near-capture still lingering in my throat. "So I'm your leashed pet? Waiting until you call on me?"

She was a slight woman, but she trampled the floorboards beneath her as she approached. The heat of her anger radiated from her as she jutted her face toward mine. "You are my Captain of the Imperial Guard," she hissed. "Or have you forgotten that? Is that why I find you in a den of Ioph Carn?"

"They were trying to trap me! I'm not here to work for them."

"I asked you to patrol the hallways, to look for anything odd. You left me there to handle things alone."

I gestured to the wreckage around us. "As you've stated before yourself, you're obviously more than capable. Were you following me?"

She threw up her hands, exasperated. "I ran into trouble at the palace. When I needed you, you weren't there. I checked back at the ship and Ragan told me you headed in this direction. After that, all I had to do was to follow the sounds of fighting. I wasn't trying to nose into your business; for once in your sorry life, acknowledge that a person can care about what happens to you!"

And then all of the implications fell on me at once, and I felt like such a fool. She could have sent my guards after me; she could have stayed in the safety of the ship. Instead, she'd risked her life to save mine. "Lin, I—"

Her gaze sharpened, and I realized my mistake. I was her Captain of the Imperial Guard. I was a commoner. And I'd called the Emperor by her given name. "Ah – Eminence, I meant—"

She seized the front of my shirt in her fists and pressed her lips to mine.

I couldn't breathe, my heart pounding in my ears. Fire raced along my veins. This wasn't the slow blossoming of love between two lifelong friends culminating in a soft embrace. In the time after accepting Emahla's death, I'd thought I would never find another woman I cared about. I'd thought I was done with that part of my life.

I shouldn't.

And then she tangled her fingers in my hair and I found my staff dropping from my nerveless palm, found myself wrapping her in an embrace, wanting to feel her body against mine.

"Lin," I whispered in her ear. Her name on my tongue tasted too sweet. I hadn't realized how long I'd wanted to say it until it slipped from my lips, making itself into a real thing instead of just a thought. And now all I wanted to do was to speak her name; it hummed in my ears with each beat of my heart.

Mephi coughed.

We broke apart, though her hand lingered over the wound on my chest. "You're hurt."

I checked her over and saw blood on her sleeve, though I

saw no wounds. "And you? You said you ran into trouble at the palace."

"We need to go back. Right away."

Wait. Kaphra! I cast my gaze about the dimly lit room. No bodies lay strewn across the floor. No Kaphra. No Philine.

And the sword, which he'd asked me to bring, and which had seared its way across my chest, was gone.

33

Lin

Hualin Or

I hadn't killed Hualin Or's governor. I'd merely incorrectly reassembled a construct. How willing would the people of Hualin Or be to believe that? They'd followed this woman, this facsimile, for years. Who would be the first to admit they'd made such a grievous error?

Either way, I had to go back to the palace. With Nephilanu and Riya against me, I needed Hualin Or.

And there was Jovis in front of me, the feel of his mouth still lingering on my lips. He hadn't asked me to kiss him. It wasn't something that was done – Emperors kissing their Captains of the Imperial Guard. He'd looked briefly about the room after we'd broken apart, his face the picture of consternation. Hadn't he kissed me back? Or had he kissed me simply because of my station? Who tells an Emperor "no"? And he was half-Poyer. The people accepted him as a folk hero, but what sort of pressures would he face if I dragged him into a relationship? Would the people accept him as Emperor's consort? I'd put him in a difficult position.

He frowned and opened his mouth.

"I'm sorry," I said, before he could tell me that what I'd done was wrong. "I shouldn't have done that. I'm the Emperor and you're the Captain of the Imperial Guard."

His mouth closed, his expression guarded.

Had I still said the wrong thing? "And you're half-Poyer. People can be cruel."

He took another step back, widening the distance between us. "Yes," he said, leaning over to pick up his staff. "A mistake, clearly."

I'd wanted to ask — could he possibly ever see past our differences? But his words trampled my feelings, folding in the walls of my heart. I wished to go back to the moment he'd said my name. To do everything differently.

He straightened his jacket as though that could make up for the tear in the front of it and the shirt beneath, the blood staining the fabric. "You said we had to return to the palace?"

I gathered myself. There were bigger things at stake than my hurt feelings. "Yes. Now."

He didn't ask me to explain as we made our way back to the palace. He fell in behind me, a familiar presence at my back. Why had he been in a den of Ioph Carn? I'd known he'd once worked for them, but I'd assumed he'd broken off all ties with them. He'd said they'd tried to trap him. What did that even mean?

But I had other things to worry about at the moment.

Though it was the dead of night, the palace was awake when we arrived. Guards marched the walls; the gates were partly open to allow people to enter and exit. I knew whatever assassin they searched for, they would not find.

They looked confused to see me striding up the street. I was supposed to be inside. "Tell one of our guards to go back to the boat and fetch Ragan. Quickly," I told Jovis before turning back to the gate. Jovis swept past the guards at the gates and into the courtyard before they could react, though he cast me a questioning look. I might need Ragan's help if what I suspected was true.

"Wailun is dead," I said to one of the guards at the gate. "And it's my fault. I need to speak to Chala. There are things I should explain."

"Eminence," the woman said, and then stopped, unsure if she should still be using the honorific. She considered, tried again. "Eminence, I'm not even sure where to put you. This is most unusual."

"I understand," I said, sensing her reluctance. She should put me in the dungeon if she truly suspected me of killing the governor, but I was also the Emperor and outranked the governor. "You can post your guards at my sitting room. Chala, Wailun's son, will want to speak with me when he's ready. There are things I should explain."

The guard nodded and waved three of her subordinates over to escort me back to my rooms. When you spoke with authority, people tended to cede to it, especially under difficult circumstances. It had been one of the first lessons I remembered my father teaching me. I had to know my place, he'd said, otherwise others would decide my place for me.

I had only one option left here: the truth. And I had to hope I could persuade Chala that the woman he'd always known as his adoptive mother was, in fact, a construct. I took a seat in my waiting room, the guards hovering over me nervously, and rested a hand on Thrana's head. Despite the tension in the room, she sank to the floor. "Tired," she said. And then she was out, as cleanly as though someone had blown out a lantern. I wished I could be so restful.

No one offered to bring me food or tea.

Ragan arrived before Chala sent for me, and though the

guards would not allow him to pass into my room, I spoke with him through the open door. He'd left his ossalen on the ship, for which I was grateful. The creature was too small yet to be of much use in this situation, and would raise too many questions. "I may need your help," I said.

Jovis stood behind him, looking steadfastly at anything but me.

Ragan glanced around the room, the guards standing over me. "I seem to have missed quite a lot."

"Please wait with Jovis. I have things I need to explain. To everyone." I knelt and dug my fingers into Thrana's fur, trying to calm the quick beating of my heart. Her skin was hot to the touch, her breathing labored. I frowned. "Thrana?" She didn't respond, didn't even flick an ear in my direction. I pressed my hand to her throat and felt the calm, steady beat of her heart. Had she caught an illness somewhere on Hualin Or? Something she ate?

The soft and steady thrumming I'd felt in my bones since we'd bonded was gone. I reached for it, trying to build the vibration. Nothing. Something was very wrong. I choked back tears. Riya and Nephilanu were against me. If I didn't play things here exactly right, I'd lose Hualin Or too. But none of that mattered next to Thrana. I'd give it all up just to keep her safe. "She's sick."

"Eminence," Jovis said from the doorway. He looked me in the eye for the first time since we'd kissed and his face was calm. "A little rest and she'll be fine. Mephi went through the same thing. Trust me."

I found, to my surprise, that I did. The swell of panic diminished until I could breathe again. I stroked Thrana's ears, hoping she somehow knew I was there.

At last, when light began to filter in through the shutters, a servant appeared in the doorway. "Chala wants to see her now," she said. "In the entrance hall please."

I rose to my feet, tucked a loose piece of hair behind my ear and waited for the guards to escort me. They should have taken me by the arms; instead, they let me walk freely. But I supposed there was nowhere for me to go. I'd come back here of my own volition.

The entrance hall lamps were lit this time, casting the walls in warm hues. Chala stood near the door to the dining hall, his family arrayed around him, each and every gaze settling on me. He'd taken the time to clean himself and to dress, and I made a poor contrast in my simpler clothes and the pants that were still a little damp at the hem from my climb.

"I suspect," Chala said, his voice bouncing from the pillars, "that if I executed you, I would have enough support from other governors to forestall a civil war."

I inclined my head as I approached. "That might be true, but would you then be able to forestall both the construct army and the Shardless Few? Both would gladly see you dead and deposed. We need one another, Sai. All the islands do. I have an explanation for my actions, though I warn you that you will not like it."

"My mother—" He stopped, his voice gone thick. He breathed in deeply, his gaze on the ceiling. "She was a strange woman. But she was good to me, she took me in from the streets and she named me as her heir. I owe her *everything*. I owe you nothing. Tell me why I shouldn't burn this world to the ground to give her the justice she deserves."

Wailun might have had real affection for Chala written into her bones. I could see the shard command in my mind. *When the timing is right (ref 3), adopt a gutter orphan as an heir.* Shiyen would have written in a subset of requirements to be met in order for the timing to be right. And then construct-Wailun would have done as commanded, and she might not have even realized why she was doing it.

"I did not murder your mother."

His eyes narrowed. "I find that hard to believe, given the blood on your sleeve. Do you deny that she struck you with her knife?"

"I don't deny it. I was in her room, yes. But Wailun was already dead."

"A ... dead woman struck you with her knife." He shifted on his feet, his patience already wearing thin. I had to be quick as well as thorough. Grief and anger would make it more difficult for him to hear me.

"In a manner of speaking. I regret that I did not realize this until last night – but Wailun is a construct of my father's making."

His jaw tightened and he waved to one of the guards. I felt them closing in on me, reluctantly, but ready to obey their new governor.

"We know now that constructs can look like people. There was a trip your family took; your whole family. This was before Wailun adopted you. My father invited them all to Imperial. Sai, they never came back from that trip. He murdered all of them and replaced them with constructs."

Chala raised a hand and the guards stopped advancing. "That's ridiculous. Why would he do that?" The rest of his family exchanged glances.

"Chala," an uncle said from next to him, "don't listen to this nonsense. She's telling you that we're not real. Do I seem like a construct to you?"

Another relative tittered.

And here was where I had to lie. I shook my head. "I don't know. My father didn't always let me into his confidence. But I sensed something strange about Wailun and I knew I had to investigate. Have you looked at her records, her journals? Eight years ago, the detailed record-keeping stops. Right when she returned with the rest of her family from Imperial."

I looked to the guards and servants surrounding me. "Have any of you been around long enough? Did Wailun come back changed from her trip to Imperial? Have you talked to the servants of her family members who live in other houses? Did they notice their masters don't seem the same?"

I saw them exchange glances. Of course they'd noticed. But none of them had the power to say or do anything about it.

Chala was looking at them too. "Please, do tell me if this is so." He spoke to them kindly. He'd lived nearly half his life on the streets; he knew what it was like to have no power.

One of the servants licked her lips. "We didn't think it was our place to say anything," she said.

"And she adopted you as heir — that seemed a step in the right direction," one of the guards said. "So what were we supposed to do after that if we wanted you to stay? Who were we going to tell?"

I studied Chala's face — the delicate curve of his jaw, the large ears, the trembling lip. He was doubting now. This was my chance. "I can prove it," I said, my voice cutting through the murmuring of the guards and the servants. I caught a glimpse of feet on the stairs, thinking I recognized Jovis's boots and Ragan's slippers. Good. They were close by. "My father taught me his magic. I can prove that what I'm saying is true."

I saw a thousand emotions flit through Chala's eyes. Fear, consternation, anger, sadness. He would want to think I was tricking him, that I'd done something insidious. But he had to know — I'd planted the seed of doubt and now he had to know for sure.

"Do it."

I approached cautiously, the guards still flanking me, coming to stand in front of Chala's uncle. The man regarded me suspiciously. "I know I'm real," he said, scowling.

Oh, so had Bayan. And so had I. And that thought made my

chest ache. I wasn't sure if what I was doing here was a good thing. I was stripping away reality from Chala, but I was stripping it away from these constructs too. They'd done nothing wrong; their only crime had been to exist, which meant they drained the life from living people. And it was my father's fault for creating them, not mine.

I plunged my hand inside of him and the world around me erupted into chaos.

The other members of Hualin Or's royal family reached into robes, pockets, sashes. They all pulled out weapons of various assortments – some more dangerous than others. They must have all had the command written into their bones: *When you are discovered, fight.* My father wouldn't let them go quietly into obsolescence. That wasn't his way.

They leapt to attack hesitant guards and servants.

"They're constructs," I shouted out to them, my hand still inside the facsimile of Nisong's uncle. "Don't hold back because they won't." I pulled free a shard near the top of the spine. They hadn't checked my sash for weapons, and I wasn't carrying any, but I *was* carrying my engraving tool – the one Numeen had once given to me.

I checked the command written on the shard. *You are Nisong's uncle.* Of course Shiyen would think that was of utmost importance. I pushed it back inside, pulled out another one, farther down. And then another. All commands relating to his place here in the palace, his personality. Had Shiyen truly not commanded these constructs to obey him? I supposed he'd never written that into Bayan's shards either.

An older woman darted toward me, a dagger held high in her hands. I froze, my hand still inside the construct. I didn't have anything with which to defend myself.

Ragan slid between me and the woman, lifting his sword to

intercept the dagger. He didn't quite make it in time and her blade grazed his arm before he batted it aside. Blood dripped from his shoulder onto the floor.

He plunged his sword into her chest and drew back, just as quickly. I saw Jovis behind him, swinging his staff. "Are you unharmed?" Ragan said.

Relief flooded my chest. "Yes, now go."

He gave me a swift nod, and turned back to the fight. I pulled free another shard. As I had suspected: *When you are discovered, fight*. This, I could work with. I wrote in two more words at the end: *other constructs*.

I pushed the shard back inside and turned to find the next construct I could coerce. Blood made the patterned tiles of Hualin Or's palace slippery, turned the elaborate beauty into something macabre.

I ducked beneath a knife, slid past a guard grappling with a construct, and pivoted to plunge my hand into that construct's body. From the corner of my eye, I saw the construct-uncle move again, his purpose now to fight the other constructs. I counted down the number of shards, pulled the correct one free. Swiftly, I carved the new words onto it and returned it.

This, this I knew. For a time, I was back in my father's dining hall, all of his palace's constructs called down upon me and Bayan, my only weapon the engraving tool in my hand. Another memory teased at the edges of my mind – one of Nisong's memories, all faded and indistinct. Old books in my hands, reading by lamplight late into the night, aching eyes and head, and in all of it the yearning to prove myself. I was no great beauty, but I was smart and clever, and that *had* to count for something. This was what I'd been made for. To write words of power onto bone shards, to manipulate the commands to my ends. It was what Nisong felt she had been made for.

I turned one more of the construct-relatives, and then, just as quickly as it had started, it ended.

One of the constructs I'd turned was sheathing a knife, the construct-uncle lay bloody on the floor, the rest of the constructs were dead and so were two guards. Both Ragan and Jovis wore stern expressions as they cleaned their weapons. Chala stood in the corner, his hands raised, blood spattered on the bottom of his robes.

"Sai," I called out. "The constructs are dead."

He lowered his arms, his face pale. He licked his lips and straightened, composing himself quickly. "I suppose this explains the state of my mother's body."

I tucked the engraving tool back into my sash and strode over to Chala so he needn't call to me across the entrance hall. "I didn't want you to find out this way," I said. "I had my suspicions and I wanted to verify them."

"You're a strange Emperor, to break into governors' rooms." I could tell he was still in shock, just saying whatever came first to mind.

"I had an unusual upbringing." It was as close to the truth I could ever get. Before he could blurt out anything else that might embarrass him, I pressed on. "This news should have been broken to you carefully, and in private. It was my sloppiness in returning the shards to your mother's body that caused things to play out this way. And for that I'm sorry."

"She was a good mother to me," Chala said. "Gather the bodies for burning," he called out to the guards. "Whatever souls they had, we'll send them heavenward." He gazed blankly out into the room. "Should we have a funeral? Does a person hold a funeral when their relatives turn out to be constructs?"

I started to reach out to him and then stopped. Neither my station nor his would allow it. I wanted to comfort him. The best

I could offer was my own truth. "Someone I thought was my friend – no, he *was* my friend – turned out to be a construct of my father's making." I'd burned Bayan's body in the courtyard with the cloud juniper, and had thrown a sprig of it onto the fire. I'd been alone, but I'd held a funeral for him in my own way. "I held my own funeral rites for him. I wouldn't think it odd if you did the same." I paused, thinking of my friendship with Bayan. "Everything you experienced with them was real. Just because they were constructs doesn't mean your feelings – or theirs – weren't real."

He met my gaze, and some small kinship passed between us. "Thank you for that." He looked so young. Once a gutter orphan, now the governor of Hualin Or and one of the most powerful men in the Empire. Yet all he could think of was the family he'd lost, the family that had never existed. I could work with someone like him, and it wouldn't be as hard as it had been with Iloh. "I can't make any decisions right now," he said, "but I'd like to continue the conversation you were having with my mother – with Wailun." He drew back, consulting with his Captain of Guard as men and women rushed to carry out his orders.

Now that the battle was over, I had time to think about Thrana. Jovis fell in behind me, as he always did. "You said she would be fine?" I said, just loud enough for him to hear.

"The same thing happened to Mephi," Jovis said. "He was hungry and lethargic the days before, and then he fell into a deep, feverish sleep. When he awoke, he was changed."

So Thrana was going through a similar change?

"Periodic hibernation," Ragan said, coming up from behind Jovis, making him jump. Jovis scowled at the intrusion. "Ossalen undergo this before growth spurts. My own has gone through one phase."

"What happens after the first growth spurt? You said Mephi changed?"

Both Jovis and Ragan shrugged. Ragan held up a finger. "Records from the beginning of the Alanga are very few. What happens next to your ossalen is lost to the ravages of time."

34

Jovis

Hualin Or

Speaking with my brethren failed. I should have known
it would. Ylan knows I keep the giant bones (? Could be
bones or some other word) in the depths of my cavern
home. I bring them out to him without him even asking.
Still, he continues to reassure me.

"If we have a weapon that can be used against your
kind, it will hold them in check." I give him what he
needs and let him do his work because I trust him.

I shouldn't have.

—Notes from Jovis's translation of Dione's journal

Mephi's soft fur beneath my fingertips steadied me. I'd
almost lost him to the Ioph Carn. I should have been tired
after two battles in just a span of hours; instead, I felt alert and
jumpy, my bones thrumming and my heartbeat fluttering against

my ribs. Philine and Kaphra had escaped with the sword – a sword that could hurt Alanga. I needed to find a way to tell Lin. Next to me, Ragan was droning on, explaining to Lin the ossalen hibernation process and how few records there were of ossalen in general. She was listening with half an ear, her expression troubled.

And then Chala approached to speak to Lin, and Ragan had enough good sense to shut his mouth. "Eminence, I'd heard about the constructs in the construct army that looked like people. I had no idea they could be so convincing." His expression was grim. "They fooled me, certainly."

"Don't be hard on yourself, Sai," Lin said, her voice warm and soft. "My father was skilled – one of the most skilled the dynasty has ever seen. He fooled more than just you."

I remembered what she'd said about befriending a construct of her father's making. After we'd chased the spy construct, she'd said her father had a foster-son. Was the foster-son a construct too? I'd forgotten that she'd lived in a palace staffed mostly by constructs. A lonely life, to be sure. She spoke to Chala with the compassion of someone who truly understood.

Yet she'd turned me aside for my station and for my heritage. That still stung. I supposed the wound *had* occurred less than a day ago. No quick healing from emotional devastation, it seemed. I'd spent so many years being reminded that I was half-Poyer, and then so many years alone on the Endless Sea, almost able to forget. And now, with the respect of the people and my guards, I thought I'd put all of that behind me. I'd thought it didn't matter anymore.

Apparently it still did – to the one person I wished it mattered not at all to.

I'd let myself grow too familiar with her, let myself believe that, in spite of everything, we could be friends. And in the heat of the moment, she'd kissed me. I wasn't sure if I wanted to forget the feel of her lips on mine, or if I wanted to hold the memory close, trying to keep it from slipping away.

They were still talking, and here I was, my expression as moody and thunderous as a wet season sky, my thoughts distant as the Poyer Isles. Some spy I was – derailed by one kiss.

"Committing my guards to help you fight the construct army won't make a difference," Chala was saying. "I've heard the reports. There are too many of them and too few in your army. Nephilanu won't send their guards to help and Riya is withdrawing. I'd be sending my people to their deaths."

"If not you, who will be the first to commit their guards?" Lin said. "The construct army is headed toward Gaelung. They'll commit their guards; they won't have a choice. If you help out, others may follow suit. It gives us a chance."

"Gaelung could agree to be ruled by your half-sister."

Lin's eyes narrowed. "She's *not* my half-sister. A convenient lie."

"You and I both know that doesn't matter. I spent a great deal of my childhood on the streets. Have enough muscle or enough money, and the other orphans tended to fall in line."

Lin did that thing again, where she looked at a person as though they were a puzzle she knew she could solve. "Did *you* fall in line, Sai?"

He held her gaze for a moment before looking away. I'd forgotten for a moment how very young the boy was. "No, I didn't. Too stubborn." He sighed. "It would be easier for me if I didn't help you. I'm young and becoming governor under unusual circumstances. Easy to criticize. But I don't like being bullied. I'll commit the guards. You have my support, and I'm not Iloh. I won't rescind it."

"Thank you." Lin inclined her head and Chala turned to tend to other things.

Ragan put a hand on my shoulder. "You're good with the earth shaking," he said, "but I have notes for your technique."

I gritted my teeth. "Has anyone ever told you to mind your own business?"

"Ah! In the monastery, everyone knows everyone's business; no one's business is their own," he said with his customary cheer.

Out of the corner of my eye, I noticed Lin kneeling by one of the bodies. Surreptitiously, she scraped something off the floor with her engraving tool before stowing it away again.

I focused my attention on Ragan again, flashing him my own obnoxious smile. "Ah well, it's a good thing we're not in the monastery then. How pleasant for us both." I pivoted and made my way up the stairs before he could expound on those notes.

The morning blurred into afternoon as we made preparations to leave. Thrana had to be carried to the courtyard and lifted into a covered cart. Mephi hovered by the side of the cart, making worried little noises in the back of his throat.

"She'll be fine," I told him as servants hurried past us. My gaze kept flicking to the door to the entrance hall where Lin lingered as she spoke with Chala, her long sleeves rolled up to the elbow. Neither looked happy. "You did this too, remember?"

He looked between me and Thrana lying unconscious in the cart. "I looked like that?" He sidled over to me, winding about my legs. "No wonder you were worried."

"I couldn't have woken you even if I had five fresh-caught fish in hand."

"Impossible!"

I laughed at his shocked expression. And then sobered as Lin approached, my heart leaping before sinking off the edge of a cliff. I found my gaze roving the courtyard, searching for a place to hide. I wanted to kick myself for even thinking it. It was my job to protect her; hiding from her would not only be a dereliction of duty, I'd look like a complete idiot doing so.

Not that I wasn't used to appearing foolish.

"Well, that unpleasantness is done with," she said, rolling her sleeves back down. "I had to dismantle the remaining construct. Chala wanted the chance to say goodbye. It's messy business, this." I opened my mouth to offer some words of sympathy, but she continued. "Now. I need to know. What exactly were you doing at a den of Ioph Carn? You disobeyed my orders." Chala's servants arrived, palanquin between them. Lin pursed her lips. "Thrana's incapacitated. Ride with me."

I couldn't very well disobey an order after she'd pointed out how poor I was at obeying them. "Ride with Thrana," I told Mephi, who readily jumped into the cart. "Keep an eye out." I ducked into the palanquin after Lin. The dark confines smelled of old, varnished wood. The bench was upholstered with a soft material that had begun to wear thin. It jolted as the servants lifted us, my thigh jostling briefly against hers. I scooted as far away from her as possible. It wasn't far enough.

She let us ride in silence for a while and I fidgeted. My staff didn't quite fit in the palanquin. I had to lay it across, each end jutting out from the windows. Mud stuck to the bottom of my shoes and I tried unsuccessfully to scrape it from one foot using the other. Now I had mud on the top of my shoes. I'd done a hasty patch job on my shirt and layered my jacket on top of it. Beneath, the wound Kaphra had given me itched. I scratched at my jacket and only made the itch turn into a burn. Was my jacket too tight at the collar? Warm air seemed to radiate from beneath it like smoke from a chimney, making my face hot.

Lin watched me, her gaze unrelenting.

"It was for my family," I blurted out. As ever, lies were easier to swallow when mixed with a healthy dose of truth. "I asked the Ioph Carn to smuggle caro nuts to Anau."

The furrow between her brows eased, though her voice was still sharp. "What did they want you to do in return?"

"I don't know – they attacked me before I could find out." The lie tasted sour.

"Are you sure they even smuggled the caro nuts then? You're not making sense."

"My father sent me a letter. I needed proof first." I rushed past this second lie, because she was giving me that studious stare and I could feel my facade cracking. The truth, the truth . . . "I didn't feel like I had much choice. I didn't want to be in debt to the Ioph Carn, not again. But . . . I'd do anything for my family. They've suffered enough. First the loss of my brother at the Tithing Festival, and then I left without a word. I couldn't let anything happen to my father. It would devastate my mother." I hated that my instinct had been to lure her in with vulnerability. I knew her well enough now to know this would work.

"You should have told me," Lin said, her voice pained. "I would have tried to help."

"You didn't have enough caro nut oil to spare. What were you going to do, come with me? The Emperor venturing into a den of Ioph Carn? No, that's a job for a lowly half-Poyer Captain of the Imperial Guard."

Lin flinched as I threw her own words back at her. "Jovis, it's not like that. It's——"

One of the servants carrying the palanquin stumbled, sending us jolting to one side. Lin threw up her hands to keep from tumbling into me. She only succeeded in getting her fingers tangled in the cloth-knot buttons of my jacket.

"Sorry, let me——" I started to help her untangle herself before realizing I was grabbing *the Emperor's* hands and that she thought me beneath her. I dropped her fingers as though they were spiders.

She straightened, steadying herself against the door, pulling away. It was a few more steadier steps from the servants before she spoke again. "Back at the palace. You said they set you a trap. Mephi."

I felt a twinge of panic as though I were back in Kaphra's house, Mephi beneath that sword's blade. The sword. "Yes, I needed to tell you. This is something that concerns you, me and Ragan. I don't know how or where Kaphra found it —" *a lie*. " — but he has a sword with a frayed hilt and a white blade. It did this to me." I unbuttoned the top of my jacket and drew the collar aside. The wound beneath was still red. "It hurt as badly as if he'd run me through and it still hasn't healed. Mephi isn't bleeding anymore, but he has a wound like mine beneath his fur. Kaphra meant to use the sword to threaten Mephi, to force me into serving him."

"A white-bladed sword . . . " Lin trailed off.

"*Phoenix Rise*," I said. "The play." A lie with some truth in it. How much truth, though? "Did your father ever talk about a sword, or how exactly the Sukais fended off the Alanga?"

She laughed bitterly. "I've had to uncover things myself. He didn't think me worthy of telling such secrets to."

"Am *I* worthy of telling such secrets to?" I wanted the answer to be "yes"; I wanted it to be "no".

Outside, vendors had begun setting up their stalls, shops had begun to open. Voices and footsteps sounded muffled through the palanquin curtains. We were cloistered in a hushed space. Her hands twitched toward mine, and then she clenched her fingers around the fabric of her sleeves. "I found something," she said finally. "In the cave we fought that beast in. It was a sword like the one you described. I brought it with me. And there's something you should know, too. I don't think Ragan is telling us everything."

The palanquin came to a stop at the docks.

I opened my mouth to ask her what she thought he was hiding, but she held up a hand to forestall me. *Later.*

When she'd implied later, she'd meant much later. She waited until after the ship had disembarked, the first meal aboard had been served and Ragan had retired to the servants' bunk to meditate. The crew hadn't brought out the store of witstone yet, and Mephi had taken the opportunity to go for a swim. I was taking my shift outside Lin's door when she opened it and beckoned me inside. I hesitated for a moment, knowing that anyone passing by would raise eyebrows at my absence. But I needed to know. So I slipped inside and let her close the door behind me. Thrana lay on the bed, her sides gently moving with each breath.

"The monastery he says he comes from – I asked after it," Lin said. "Unta sank, yes, but before that no one had been seen from that monastery in almost a year. The monks are reclusive, but they aren't *that* reclusive. Every so often, they send someone to the nearest town to pick up supplies. Why wouldn't he mention that?"

I tried to see past my dislike of the man. "He might not know. He could have been out of contact with them for a while."

"They're practically his family – why wouldn't he be in contact with them?"

I hadn't been in contact with mine. Although, to be fair, that *had* been for nefarious reasons. "So what do you want to do about it? Should I set one of my guards to tail him? They're not the best at that, but I've been teaching—"

"I have a better idea," she said, kneeling by her crate. She lifted her engraving tool. "He was injured during the battle. I collected some of his blood on this. I used my father's machine and some of Thrana's blood. I think it worked, but I'm not sure. I've never tried this before. If it did, I can look at his memories. That might tell me if he's being truthful." She lifted a small box of corked flasks out of the crate, tapping the one closest to her.

My spine stiffened; I could feel the grooves on the handle of my staff digging into my skin. "You would do that?"

"What? Why not?" No hesitation, no hint of misgivings.

"Taking someone's blood and then using it to glimpse into their mind? That's something you father would have done. The action of a tyrant." She recoiled at my words. It was the one thing she feared most, and I had used it against her. Because underneath my righteousness ran an undercurrent of terror: if she could do this to Ragan, she could do this to me. All it would take was my blood.

She could discover my connection to the Shardless Few.

"You don't even like him; how could you say that?"

Had I been that obvious? "Does it matter whether or not you like a person? Or when you said you wanted to make life better for everyone, did you mean only the people you liked? How many times will you taste other people's memories because you think you don't have any other choice?"

"Jovis," she said, her voice soft, and I hated the way my name on her lips made me feel, "he's done everything right so far, but what if he's just trying to get in my good graces so he can betray me?"

I closed my eyes. Didn't always know the right thing to say, especially when I was trying to get myself out of a mess. But this time I did. "Back on Haulin Or, he saved your life. Why would he do that if he was your enemy? Besides, most of us don't have magic to check on our friends. How do you think the rest of us manage to trust people? How do you think the blacksmith who helped you did it?"

Her gaze flicked to the bloody crane, perched on the edge of her desk.

Footsteps pounded on the deck above us. People shouted, though I couldn't tell what they were saying.

Someone knocked at the door. "Eminence, you'd best come see this."

She swept past me.

Thrana was asleep. Even before bonding with Mephi, I'd always been quick. I stuffed Ragan's memories between the mattress and the wall. That would buy me a little time. If she couldn't drink from it, she wouldn't know if she'd figured out how to properly work the memory machine. Mephi watched me with a quizzical gaze, but thankfully said nothing.

Then I followed Lin, leaving the door to her room slightly ajar. She couldn't blame me if she noticed the flask missing. Anyone could have taken it.

The Endless Sea was choppy, and I had to keep my knees bent to stop myself from hurtling into the wall. Lin gripped the railing, staring off the port side of the ship.

Another ship was passing us, filled to almost overflowing with passengers. Their captain shouted across the gap at ours.

"Survivors," one of my guards said.

I drew abreast of him. "Survivors of what?"

He met my gaze, the look in his eyes hollow. "Luangon. It sank. These refugees are on their way to Hualin Or."

Fear and dread mingled in my belly. Another island down into the depths of the Endless Sea.

The guard licked his lips. "They said their governor did not heed the moratorium on witstone mining. He redoubled their efforts. With Deerhead and Unta sinking, everyone is buying witstone just in case."

I watched as Lin dashed tears from her eyes, as she smoothed her hair back from her forehead and tried to regain her composure. Her two remaining maidservants flanked her, unsure of whether to try and offer comfort.

And I, asshole that I was, went back down below and to the kitchen. Everyone was above-deck, so this was my chance. I rummaged quickly through the cupboards and found a flask similar to the ones in Lin's collection. Swiftly, I poured in some water and added some cloudy rice wine to approximate the milky color.

Then I took it back to Lin's room.

"What are we doing?" Mephi said, so close on my heels that I nearly tripped on him. "Are we helping?"

We were helping ourselves. "Yes."

I slipped the flask into place in the chest. I reached for the flask I'd hidden by the mattress.

"Why aren't you above-deck?"

I pulled my hand back and whirled to find Lin in the doorway. Could she see the pulse at my neck, pounding as though the blood were seeking to escape my veins? Quick. Be quick, Jovis. I'd spoken to the guard above-deck. I couldn't lie about that. "I was, but then I came back down here."

"You came back down to my rooms."

I swallowed, and I didn't have to affect the tremor in my voice. "To wait for you. I've no desire to gawk at tragedy. Especially not after Deerhead."

Her expression smoothed with understanding. "It must be a terrible reminder."

It was. I'd been so focused on replacing the flask that I hadn't really considered what the sinking of Luangon meant. Now I could smell the dust from falling buildings, hear the screams of frightened people echoing in my ears, see the smoke rising from what once had been Deerhead. I'd left them all to die. I'd saved myself.

I'd saved Mephi.

I took in a deep breath. I was breathing air, not seawater. I wasn't trapped on Deerhead in a building, watching the water rise above my head.

Lin was going back to her crate, lifting the box of flasks. "You're right. Ragan did fight with us on Hualin Or. But I'm not convinced he's a friend. There's too much at stake here. I have to know."

She pulled the flask out, uncorked it and let the liquid slide past her lips.

I wasn't sure what bothered me more – my lies, or that she'd drank from the flask anyways. Gio had warned me she would justify the use of her power. I hadn't wanted that to be true.

Lin grimaced and stared at the wall. She blinked. She lifted the flask to her lips and sipped again. "That doesn't taste right at all," she muttered, peering at the liquid inside. "Did I miss an ingredient? Or maybe there was something to be said other than just the person's name? Or maybe I can't just add Thrana's blood. Maybe the machine does more to it than just pull it from her veins?"

"It didn't work?" I knew it wouldn't, but I put as much surprise into my voice as I could muster.

She corked the flask and set it back into the box. "The memories I see are at random. When I saw my father's memories of using this machine, I didn't see the entire process. I must have missed some crucial step." She eyed the box of flasks. "Did I?"

"You said you found a sword."

Lin shook herself. "Yes." She leaned over the crate again and lifted out a sword. A frown flitted across her face.

I'd tampered with too many of her things, skirting too close to discovery. Did she notice a difference between this blade and the one she'd found? And the flask was still jammed between her mattress and the wall. I'd have to come back for it.

But then she stood. "This is the sword I found. Does it look like the one Kaphra had?"

I took it from her hands, a ringing in my ears. Could a person die of their heart beating too quickly? I willed my hands to stillness, my breath to evenness, and thought about the attack at Kaphra's house. He'd lifted the bindings at the hilt to peer at something.

"Do you have a knife?"

She didn't ask me why, and I suppose that was a measure of her trust in me. She pulled a knife free from her sash and tossed it to me. I caught it, dug the point beneath the wrappings and tore them free. They were old and frayed already, so it didn't take much.

The hilt beneath was smooth and white as the blade. But it was not unmarred. Something was carved into its surface.

My blood ran cold. It was writing – the kind I'd seen in the Alanga book.

I held the blade out to her, my lips numb. "Look at this." My tongue didn't feel my own.

She frowned at me, stepped to my side, and took the sword. She held it up to the light. "It's a command."

"What does it say?"

Her gaze met mine, her eyes wide and frightened. "Die."

35

Nisong

An island east of Luangon

Light bled red through Nisong's eyelids. She cracked an eye open. Her nose and throat stung, her arms felt raw and her left ankle throbbed. Pain meant she was still alive.

She hadn't expected to still be alive.

She cracked the other eye open, feeling the crustiness of salt upon her cheeks. Experimentally, she moved a hand and found wet sand beneath her fingertips. How long had she been out for? Where was the ship? Where was Leaf?

It was the last thought that brought her fully to her senses. The smells of smoke and seawater washed over her. She pushed herself to a sitting position and found the world had turned into a nightmare. A dark cloud hung where Luangon had once been. Around her, the beach was littered with scraps of wood, sundry household items – both broken and whole, torn sails and bodies. So many bodies. They dotted the shore, lumps amid the sand, the waves gently licking at their limbs, carrying some in and out of the shallows.

There were fish among the bodies, farm animals, sea creatures caught in the last throes of a sinking island. The whole beach would begin to stink the next day. Already there were gulls, picking at remains.

Nisong coughed. Half the beads on her tunic had ripped away; one was embedded in her upper arm. She pried it free and tossed it onto the sands, pressing a palm against the wound and hissing at the pain. "Leaf!" she croaked out.

No one answered. After the cracking and rumbling of the sinking island, the beach felt eerily silent, only the call of gulls and the washing of the waves upon the shore. Disaster had come and gone and now she was alone in the aftermath.

She stumbled to her feet, testing her ankle. Not broken, just sore. She remembered knocking it on the side of the boat when she'd been tossed overboard.

"Nisong?"

She whirled and saw Coral in the trees where the beach ended, two war constructs at her side. Relief swelled within her. Coral hurried down the beach, picking her way across the sand and through the broken bodies. She caught Nisong by the elbows before she could fall. "Are you all right?"

How could she be all right? She would never be so again. The world had cracked open and swallowed Luangon. It had swallowed Grass. She let herself be held, unsure whether or not the water running down her cheeks was seawater or tears. "I tried to save Grass."

Coral rubbed her back. It was the same way her sister had once, when they'd been young and their parents had scolded her. Coral had known too, that juniper would help her concentrate, that she hadn't been able to concentrate when thinking of Shiyen. "You have some of Wailun's memories, don't you?" Nisong said.

"Yes," Coral said simply. "Not as many as you have of Nisong's, I think, but they're there. I'm still Coral. I'm not her."

Nisong wasn't thinking straight. Her head pounded and she coughed up more seawater, wiping her mouth on the back of one wet, salty sleeve. "Leaf," she said. "We need to find him."

Coral directed the two war constructs to search, helping Nisong along the sand. She shook off Coral's hand after a few steps, deciding she didn't need it. Her ankle still hurt and everything ached, but she could stand on her own two feet.

"There are survivors trickling in from Luangon," Coral said. "You said there was enough death for one day, and I agree. We've left them alone. Some are setting up camps in a clearing near the city. We've been consolidating food stores and have left some for them."

It was far, far more than Nisong would have done, because it was far, far more than any of those refugees would have done for a construct. But she let it go. She needed to find Leaf. He had memories of how to sail a boat; surely he had memories of how to swim. If she'd survived the wave from Luangon, she couldn't imagine Leaf hadn't. She'd been thrown clear of the boat, but maybe he'd been able to stay aboard. Maybe he'd sailed all the way back and was, even now, looking for her. She let hope bloom in her breast.

They found his body near the sea serpent.

She saw the sea serpent first, its torso winding down the beach like the root of some giant tree. Its green-blue scales shone dully beneath the cloudy sky, each webbed claw larger than Nisong herself. The prow of a ship had wedged its way between two of the broad scales on its belly. Its head lolled back, horns and frill half-buried. Blood seeped from the wound, staining the surrounding sand red.

Vague memories flitted through her mind, of being bitten

by a sea serpent when it was a baby, its coils no longer than her forearm, its teeth small, white and sharp. Few sea serpents grew into full-sized adults. Those that did rarely washed up dead – there weren't a lot of things that could kill a fully grown sea serpent.

And then she heard Coral's swift intake of breath, and she saw the frail figure curled on the sand next to the sea serpent.

Leaf had always been thin and gangly. His ribs pressed against his skin when he took in a deep breath; his cheekbones rose above his jaw like sheer cliff faces. She was kneeling by his side before she could remember moving, rolling him over, checking for breath.

His skin was cold, his lips blue.

Shell, and then Frond, then Grass. Not Leaf too. Not on the very same day. She struck his chest with her fist, willing his heart to beat again. He knew how to swim! He was supposed to be safe.

He didn't move, didn't breathe, didn't cough up seawater.

Coral hovered behind her. "Is Grass . . . ?"

Nisong closed her eyes. "No. She's gone too."

Coral knelt in the sand by Leaf's body. For a moment they just stared at him, as if hope and heartache could bring him back to life.

"It's just you and me now," Coral said.

"There are others—"

"You know what I mean."

Nisong did. If Coral, Leaf, Grass, Frond and Shell had been her family, Coral was now all she had left. "I told him I'd watch over him. I said I'd keep him safe." She'd lied to him.

"Nisong." Coral touched her shoulder, and the tenderness in her voice made tears prick at Nisong's already watering eyes. "We've come far enough already. We don't need to go all the way. You've done so much for the constructs."

It felt like most of what she'd done was to get them killed. There had to be a reason for it, she had to make their deaths worth something. If they retreated, she would have lost them all for nothing.

There was a sleeping Shiyen beneath the palace, waiting for her. That was her place. That was where she belonged.

She breathed in deep, thought of her sister and pushed her hand into Leaf's chest. The shards met her fingertips, clusters of them, trailing all the way into his arms. Her throat aching, she pulled them out in handfuls, waiting as Coral collected them in the bag at her side. Whatever memories Leaf held would be gone, but she could reuse the shards in new constructs.

Coral closed up the bag. "You can send out some of the spy constructs, have them tell the others to come home. We can build something from the islands we've already taken. You said Maila was a prison, but it's not. The mind-fog was the prison."

They'd taken four islands so far. Instead of sweeping across the Empire, they could stay here. They could dig in and fortify. Freed from their commands, they wouldn't have to engage in mindless tasks. They could all take the time to go through their memories, to figure out who they had once been and who they wanted to someday be.

Nisong set her sights on the horizon, toward where she knew Imperial lay. She'd started this campaign wanting justice. She'd wanted to make the Empire pay for its mistakes in blood. But there were so few of them left. She laid her hand on top of Leaf's.

If she continued on this campaign she'd lose the rest of them. Her place wasn't with Shiyen at the heart of the Empire. It was here, with the constructs. They didn't have the numbers to make it to Imperial. They didn't have the numbers to make it to the next island. She wiped the tears from her eyes. "You're right. Call the constructs back," Nisong said. "We'll stay."

Coral rose to her feet, brushing sand from the front of her dress. "We'll burn his body tonight. Just you and me."

A ray of the setting sun broke through the clouds, shimmering over the ocean and the sea serpent's scales. Nisong squinted against it. If they were to make this place a home, there would be a lot of work to do. It would take days to clear away all the debris and bodies. She sucked in a breath.

All the bodies.

People, yes, but monsters and creatures too. So much flesh just waiting to be used, to be animated, to be bent to her will.

"Coral." She reached back, seizing Coral's wrist before she could leave. "Wait. This doesn't have to be the end. We don't have to turn back."

Coral's voice was wary. "What do you mean?"

"Take the war constructs. Go back to the city. Gather all the survivors in the palace courtyard – all the ones that will fit."

"It's getting late . . . " Coral trailed off.

"Which is why I need to get started now," she responded. The deaths of Grass and Leaf would haunt her, but with stormy skies came much-needed rain. These bodies, monstrous and human, would be enough for her to storm the next islands. If she could take Gaelung, she would have a serious foothold in the Empire.

Shell, Frond, Leaf and Grass would not have died for nothing. They would have died to wreak vengeance on this Empire and to build the foundation of a new one.

Nisong rose to her feet. She needed a fresh change of clothes, to bathe the salt water from her limbs. And then the work could begin.

36

Phalue

Nephilanu Island

Phalue shifted on her chair in the entrance hall, always unsure of whether she should lean forward or lean back. She didn't feel like she was made for sitting, but she knew her height could be intimidating, and she wanted petitioners to always speak their minds.

She needn't have worried too much about that.

" . . . and what in all the Endless Sea am I supposed to do with them, Sai? I'm a good man; I fed them when they first arrived, but now they've overstayed their welcome. I've got my own family to feed and a living to make. They can't stay." The man in front of her was the last petitioner of the day, and had come from a village on the eastern side of the island. It wasn't a short trip, and he wasn't the only one to make the trek. Petitioners filled the perimeter of the entrance hall. Some she'd already dealt with, but she'd made a habit of making sure all petitioners received a good meal before they left — so they waited for the kitchens. It was the least she could do.

"They have nowhere else to go," Phalue said. A few scattered survivors from Unta had been arriving on the shores of Nephilanu, searching for a place to settle into. More than Phalue had expected given Nephilanu's distance from Unta. But Nephilanu did not have a witstone mine and she supposed that appealed to many.

"Isn't it the duty of the governor to enforce the laws? It's *my* land. Send some of your guards to remove the refugees."

She heard the creak of leather as the two guards behind her shifted on their feet. It had been a long day and no doubt they were eager for it to be over. Phalue remembered a quote from *Treatises on Economic Equality* — one of the books Ranami had asked her to read. "Laws tell us what we can and cannot do; they do not tell us what we should and should not do." These people hadn't chosen to leave their homes, their belongings and everything they'd worked for. "Yes, it is my duty. But it's not the fault of these people that they're on your land."

"Well, it's not my fault either." The man crossed his arms, his expression dark. "And yet I'm suffering for it."

Phalue thought about their list, reshuffling things in her mind. Ranami, seated next to her, touched her arm. Phalue knew exactly what she was trying to convey. They'd managed to send a few shipments of caro nuts out to the poorer islands, hiding them among shipments of fruit. The poorer islands didn't pay as much as Imperial did, but they still paid. Phalue could afford to be generous.

"I assume you're not the only one with this problem?" Phalue asked.

"There are more refugees on my neighbors' lands, yes," he said.

"I'll send workers to clear more land, to build shelters and to feed the refugees. Every refugee family will be granted their own land, so they'll be off yours. I'll have it done within the next ten days. Will that fulfill my duty?"

Ranami made a note in the book in her lap. She kept track of all the promises that Phalue made during these sessions.

His expression smoothed. "Yes. Thank you, Sai."

A hand squeezed her elbow. Ah. She was missing something – something Ranami could better see or understand. The man hadn't turned or backed away like the other petitioners. Now that Ranami had pointed it out, Phalue could see the tension remaining at the corners of his mouth. Best deal with it now instead of leaving it to simmer. "Is there anything else troubling you?"

He pressed his lips together as if trying to keep the words in, but then they burst forth. "If Nephilanu sinks, will you truly abandon us here?"

She felt like the floor had dropped out from beneath her chair. Someone had leaked the information about the escape route – and not just to the city below, but to the rest of the island.

The petitioners in the rest of the room shifted like waves lapping at the shore, murmuring among themselves. No one seemed exactly surprised.

"Nephilanu will not sink," Phalue said, trying to convey confidence.

"Then why plan an escape in case it does?" one of the petitioners called out.

Sweat gathered between Phalue's shoulder-blades. Ranami didn't grab her arm, but she could feel the tension of her wife's posture – a bowstring pulled taut by her ear. Anger and consternation simmered below the surface of the room, just waiting for something to knock the lid off and send it boiling over. Her father would have ordered in his guards, removed the petitioners by force. Her father would have never allowed petitioners in the first place.

She almost lifted a hand to order it so – just to buy herself a little breathing room, a little time to come up with a proper response.

The law would be on her side but her father had made the laws. Perhaps it was time to unmake some of them. She wanted her people to love her, not fear her. She was not her father, and she would keep it that way.

Phalue cleared her throat. "You're right. I did plan an escape. But the way I did it was wrong." Her voice rang through the room, silencing the mutters. "I didn't want anyone to panic, but I also wanted to plan for the worst just in case. It was an error on my part to keep those plans secret. The truth is – we shouldn't panic. The islands that sank had witstone mines on them. It's the only theory we have at the moment as to why they sank. Nephilanu has no mine. But we can prepare without panicking. I should have made my intentions clear. I shouldn't have kept this a secret. I thought by doing so I could lessen the panic, but instead I've made it worse. For that, I am sorry."

A chopstick dropping to the floor would have sounded ear-shattering, that's how quiet the room had become. Phalue supposed they'd never heard a governor apologize before. Certainly she'd never heard her father do so.

"Everyone should prepare," she said. "I'll take the guidelines we came up with and distribute them." She could feel Ranami staring at her. It took her wife a moment to remember to write this promise down. "Try to have witstone. Know which path you'd take to the ocean. Have a boat ready, or passage on a boat ready. Most likely we won't need these precautions. But these are trying times. We should all be careful."

"Do you think that's good enough? You lied to us." The woman who spoke had a rough look to her. Phalue's gaze flicked to the knife at the woman's belt. With Tythus and so many guards arrayed behind her, she'd never thought to check the petitioners for weapons. How many others had knives with them? Another thought occurred: how many had the Shardless Few planted among the petitioners?

The woman turned toward the crowd. "Am I the only one who remembers what it was like under her father? This is something he might have done."

A few of the others murmured in assent.

Phalue started running mental calculations. She'd unbuckled her sword before sitting down; she could get to it if she just leaned over. How much time would that take? The two guards at her back were younger recruits; she'd sent her best to hunt down the constructs.

Ranami's hand was warm on her arm. She would protect her wife with her life if it came to it.

The woman drew her knife and leapt forward.

Phalue rose to meet her. She ducked the blow and charged, wrapping her arms around the woman and carrying her to the floor.

A sharp sting across her shoulder told her she'd not ducked the knife completely. Around her, the world devolved into shouts, screams and stampeding boots. The woman beneath her squirmed, trying to bring the knife to bear. Phalue seized her wrist, slamming it on the ground once, twice, until the woman's fingers opened. She pried the blade from her and struggled to her feet.

Her guards had engaged with two other petitioners carrying knives.

"Don't kill them!" she called out. But they couldn't hear her over the din. It was over within moments, both the other petitioners slain by the guards. The woman she'd pried the knife from had fled; the entrance hall had emptied out.

Ranami hurried to her side, examining the wound in Phalue's shoulder. "Just a shallow cut," she said.

"Dione's balls!" Phalue swore. She dropped the knife and it clattered onto the tiles of the entrance hall. The cut was shallow but it still stung. What stung more, though, were the words the woman had spoken. She'd been trying to rouse the commoners against Phalue. "What a mess. I didn't want anyone to get hurt."

"I doubt they were real petitioners," Ranami said, echoing Phalue's earlier thought.

"They could have been. And now they're dead." Phalue could smell the food being prepared in the kitchens. A few petitioners had lingered in the courtyard but most had fled. She'd have to make some sort of statement about this, reassure everyone that they would be safe within the palace walls. "Take the bodies to the storage room," she told the guards. "If no one claims them by nightfall, burn them with juniper."

Someone scurried in from outside, still dripping from the rain. Another petitioner? But they shrugged off the hood of their oilskin cloak and Phalue recognized the messenger from the city. "A missive," the woman said as she strode toward Phalue. "Marked urgent, received just this morning."

She reached into her bag and pulled out a letter, the corner damp from her fingertips.

Phalue took it, turning it so that Ranami could also see what was written on the envelope. It was from Gaelung. Why would Gaelung be sending her an urgent missive? She broke the seal and opened the letter.

Ranami hovered nearby as she skimmed through the contents, her heartbeat kicking faster with each new line.

"It's not good," Phalue said. "The construct army is pressing toward Gaelung. The Emperor has promised aid, but I think we all know the state of the Empire's army. The new recruits will be only minimally trained. They won't know how to handle themselves in a fight. And there just won't be enough of them – not enough to make up for the lack of constructs. Another island has sunk."

"Another one? What?" Ranami leaned over the letter to read for herself.

"The good news — if we can count it such — is that this island had a mine as well. So if the Emperor was telling at least a version of a truth, Nephilanu may be safe. But this isn't a purely informational letter. The governor of Gaelung is asking us to send aid. It's separate from the Emperor's plea."

Ranami took the letter when she proffered it. "'If you do not send aid, Gaelung will fall, and the construct army will sweep across the Empire. She sounds desperate."

"If the construct army has grown as large as she says it has, and it's taken all the islands before Gaelung, I can understand her desperation." The rogue constructs had felt a distant thing to Phalue — clear on the other side of the Empire — made up of creatures who'd been cast aside at the change of a regime. She'd had so many other, closer things to worry about: Gio, the Shardless Few, the caro nuts, the sinking islands, the Emperor herself. Even dismantling the Alanga fountain had seemed more urgent. Phalue frowned. "Do we have any treaties or agreements with Gaelung?"

Her wife frowned. "I can't be sure. Your father didn't take any care to organize his documents, and neither did anyone who worked for him. It could have been informal, and he might not have written it down. You know how your father was."

"Him and his parties," Phalue said. She ran a hand through her hair, feeling the dampness of sweat at her forehead and at the nape of her neck. "Can you let the people who have stayed know there will still be food? Offer some comfort and apologize? I should go ask my father."

"You don't have to."

But Phalue was already making her way to the kitchen and the cellar. Noises and smells assaulted her senses as soon as she opened the door. Servants rushed back and forth, preparing food for the petitioners – mostly things that could be eaten by hand. Egg tarts, steamed buns, sticky rice dumplings, skewered pieces of chicken. Phalue took a step into the chaos and then froze.

A servant was stepping out of the arch that led to the cellar.

It wasn't time for her father's meals, nor had she ordered anyone to attend to him. She waited until the servant had returned to tending a pot before she stepped fully into the kitchen and made for the stairs. It was something Ranami would have done, not Phalue – was her wife's suspicious nature rubbing off on her?

The light from above gave way to lamplight as she descended the stairs, casting everything in an orange hue. Her father was where she'd last left him: sitting at his desk in his cell, reading and sipping a steaming cup of tea. He looked up when she approached.

"Someone was just here," Phalue said, trying to keep her voice neutral.

He lifted the cup. "I asked for tea; a servant brought it."

It was a reasonable enough explanation. She hadn't told the servants to ignore him, to treat him poorly or to shun any of his requests. "How's your health?"

He coughed into his elbow. "The same – but you're not here to ask after that, are you, dearest?"

Might as well be direct; she was good at that. "Do we have any sort of agreements with Gaelung? Your records aren't exactly in good order."

"Is there a reason you're asking?"

A prickle of unease lifted the hairs at the back of her neck. Why did he need to know? She tamped it down. Ranami was rubbing off on her. The man was imprisoned; he couldn't do much from a cell. "Gaelung is asking for aid. The construct army is on its way to their shores and the Emperor cannot provide enough protection. They want us to send our guards to help bolster their defenses."

He looked into his mug of tea as though staring at it could turn it to wine. "We have no such agreement with Gaelung. They must be desperate to imply that we might. I'll wager they've sent the same missive to as many other islands they could count, hoping that those that feel no obligation to the Emperor might feel some obligation to them. No one else will send aid; why should Nephilanu? We'd be sending our people to their deaths."

Sometimes Phalue wondered if she asked her father for advice simply so she could know what not to do or to test the strength of her convictions. "Gaelung is right, though – if the construct army takes the island, what's to stop them from going for Hualin Or next? Or Imperial? Eventually they will come to Nephilanu."

He waved a dismissive hand. "And we'll be ready for them then." He frowned at his mug. "Any chance you'll let me out? Even a locked room in the palace would be less damp." He coughed into his sleeve again, as if to emphasize the point.

Phalue clenched her jaw. "I'll have the servants bring you more tea."

At least she knew now they didn't have any agreements with Gaelung – though she wasn't sure how much that helped. It would have been easy to respond had they already been bound to. Without that, she was free to make her own decision.

She didn't exactly feel free about it.

"I just want you to be safe, dearest," he said. "Stay out of this conflict. No use helping others if it only gets you killed."

It felt like years of pent-up anger were surfacing. He'd always looked to his own pleasure first. Why had she bothered coming here and asking him for advice? Deep down, she already knew what was right. "No."

"No what?"

"No. You're wrong. I thought you understood politics better than me, but you don't. You have no understanding of it because you have no understanding of people who aren't like you. And you don't understand me. You don't understand me at all. Don't expect to see me again." She whirled, leaving him gaping, his mouth unable to form words.

Phalue ran into a child as she crested the stairs, the small body bouncing off her and nearly tumbling to the floor. Too much brooding and anger, not enough watching where she was going. She seized the girl's shoulders to steady her and—

Ayesh.

They'd received more than one report from the guards of Ayesh coming back to the palace and leaving again with what appeared to be a full sack. The girl had such a sack slung over her shoulder right now, her eyes so wide they looked in danger of swallowing her face.

"Hello," the girl said.

Phalue pursed her lips. "What's in the bag?"

Ayesh jerked away from Phalue's grip. "Just food."

"You know you can have as much as you'd like while you're here. Why do you need to take more?"

"I get hungry. Our training sessions . . . " She let out a breath. "I'm not just hungry here, I'm hungry at home."

Where was home to the girl? Phalue wasn't Ranami, but she could smell a lie when it slapped a wet fin in her face. "I'm sure you are." She lunged for the bag.

Incredibly, the orphan slid away from her grasp, leaving Phalue's fingers feeling only the whisper of burlap. Then she was darting away, out of the kitchen, faster than Phalue could follow.

She'd known the girl was quick, but not that quick. Desperation, it seemed, could lend one more than the ability to write presumptive letters.

Phalue dodged past the servants in pursuit, shoving open the kitchen door. "Ayesh, wait!"

The girl hesitated only a moment at the sound of her voice. And then she was running, sprinting down the hall, quicker than a gust of wind. It was like chasing a fish through the ocean.

By the time she reached the doorway to the courtyard, the girl was weaving between the few petitioners left and servants carrying food trays. She snatched a steamed bun from a tray before disappearing into the shadow of the gate.

"Ayesh!" Phalue tried one more time before slowing.

If Ayesh heard her, she gave no indication. And then Phalue noticed her wife standing between the pillars, in heated conversation with a man. With an eyepatch. Gio dared to show his face here? Now? Was he just here to check whether or not his rabble-rousing had succeeded? This was the last thing she needed in a day that had already gone from bad to worse. She felt like a wolf set loose in a well-kept home, shattering anything she came into contact with.

She understood the appeal that wine held to her father now.

Phalue marched over to them, wishing she'd taken the time to buckle her sword back on.

" . . . shouldn't forget where you came from, now that you live in a palace," Gio was saying.

"How can I forget I came from the gutters when people like you are always here to remind me?" Ranami snapped back.

"You've started to smuggle shipments of caro nuts out of Nephilanu," Gio said. "Don't think I haven't noticed. You've broken your side of the agreement. I've no incentive to continue mine."

"Is that why you sent people to assassinate my wife?" Ranami took a step closer to Gio, daring him to back down.

He shook his head. "I don't know what you're talking about."

Ranami scoffed.

Phalue made her body a wedge, forcing them apart. "I don't want a conflict with you, Gio, or your Shardless Few. I know you're gathering a force of rebels on Khalute, and I know you could do some real damage to Nephilanu if you wanted to."

"Then stop the shipments."

"When I took this position as governor, I did so knowing I wanted to rule differently than my father. I won't care too much about myself and not enough about other people. I can't be blind to the suffering my actions cause. What about you, Gio?"

He clasped his hands, his expression dark. "What do you mean?"

"No caro nut oil means people will die from bog cough. And it won't be the wealthy who will suffer. They'll find a way to get their medicine, one way or another. It will be the poor. The people who are already scraping by."

Gio let out a soft snort. "Is that what she told you?"

Phalue frowned. "Who?"

"The Emperor. I warned you about meeting her. If she's anything like her father, she knows the right things to say – but that doesn't mean she is right. You say you won't be blind to suffering. What about her? All she has to do is abdicate and this suffering will end."

Ranami's anger was like a living flame next to Phalue; she could feel the heat of it. "So we should set our ships to collide and shout, 'No, you turn your prow first'?"

Gio's scar pulsed with the beat of his heart. "Someone is always caught in the crush. You can't save everyone. But we can save more by making sure the Sukais are deposed. For ever! You would rather wait? Wait until she's gathered strength, until she erases her vulnerabilities? And then, when she chooses to use bone shard magic again or to enact some other harsh new laws, what then? We have no way to fight back. You have to harden yourself to fight against a hard enemy. It's the only way to win."

She'd been set on this path by Ranami, but now she'd claimed it fully as her own. And if Phalue followed it to the end, to the very heart of the matter, she found a truth she believed – that there had to be other ways. How could she condone the deaths of these people just because they were not her people? Happenstance had placed them elsewhere. It was easier to think of people she did not know or see as less significant, but that didn't make it right. "And what of Gaelung?"

His expression shifted. "Gaelung?"

"If you know about the caro nuts, surely you know about Gaelung. Or do you just not care about the plight of people far enough away? They've asked for aid. The construct army is headed to their shores and they mean to take the island."

Gio waved a hand. "Let the Emperor deal with it. That's her responsibility."

"She disbanded the war constructs and hasn't created any new ones. Her army is small, and though she's been recruiting, there just aren't enough soldiers yet. She's been asking the islands for their guards but everyone has been reluctant to commit. Now Gaelung is asking for aid too. They say the construct force has grown."

"Good. Let them fight among themselves. It'll weaken the Emperor if not take care of her completely."

Ranami's hand found Phalue's. They might have begun their relationship on two different ideological islands, but they'd found their way across to one another. And now they stood together. Always. "You could help Gaelung if you wanted to," Ranami said. "You have enough Shardless Few to make a difference. Isn't this what the Shardless Few is supposed to be about: helping the helpless?"

"No revolution is bloodless. No change comes without suffering," he said, his jaw set. "So many Shardless Few have died smuggling away children from Tithing Festival. They've died in raids against governors, trying to bring food and medicine to people who need it. Perhaps it is time for the people of Gaelung to do their part. In the end, we will all come out of this better for it."

"A coward is not a man who feels fear. A coward is one who would volunteer others for the suffering he would not take on himself," Phalue said.

Gio scoffed. "*Ningsu's Proverbs*? Please. The quote does not apply. I would gladly take on the suffering of the Shardless Few if I could."

Phalue's felt her heart grow cold. "You miss my point. The Shardless Few have volunteered for that suffering. The people of Gaelung have not."

How could a man stare that much venom with only one working eye? "When you have lived as many years as I have, you may finally understand. No progress comes without a price. If this is how you think of me, then we can never work together."

"I suppose not," Phalue said, her voice steady. She'd burned enough bridges today; what was one more?

"Don't think I won't bring the full force of the Shardless Few down on Nephilanu. Don't think I won't crush you the way I crushed the governor of Khalute. And I will crush you." He swept from the courtyard with the force of a storm gale, flinging raindrops from his cloak with each heavy step.

"Ah, Phalue," Ranami finally said once he'd disappeared down the path, "you really don't ever do things by halves, do you?"

37

Lin

Somewhere in the Endless Sea

Thrana awoke changed. She came around two nights after she'd entered her deep sleep, and I was desperately relieved to have her back with me. Right before her eyes opened, the thrumming returned to my bones, the preternatural strength to my limbs. If it came to it, if we had to make a stand at Gaelung, I'd have her strength. And I'd have Chala's guards. He was as good as his word, writing up the documents before I'd left, pledging his guards to support the army. He'd already begun to provision the ships that would carry them to Gaelung.

Perhaps more gutter orphans should have unexpectedly been made governors.

I watched Thrana napping in the corner of the galley, curled into a tight ball. Next to her, Mephi chewed on a bone the cook had given him. Even curled up, Thrana now took up a great deal of space. The most prominent change had been her size. She could now rest her head on my shoulder when I was standing, and she'd shed her horns, leaving fresh, black nubs at the base of her skull. I'd hefted the old ones in my hand, tracing the spirals, peering at the white cores. When I'd prodded at one, a piece had fallen out. The inner cores were fragmented.

"You can have them," she'd told me, her voice solemn. Feeling a little sad about how quickly she'd grown, I stashed the horns in the chest at the foot of my bed and tucked a couple pieces of the bone into my sash pocket. When I had the chance, I could have some memento carved from them, a reminder of when Thrana had been younger and smaller.

"Nisong *wants* you to go to Gaelung," Jovis was saying. "She wants you to engage in battle with her. You personally."

I rubbed a hand over my eyes. "I was on my way there already." We both picked at the food on our plates. But even the most elaborate of cakes would have tasted like dust to me now. Nisong. She mocked me by claiming to be my half-sister, aimed to demoralize me by kicking the supports out from beneath me and taunted me by terrorizing and murdering my citizens.

Jovis lifted a hand and began ticking off fingers. "In case you forgot, ships can be turned around. Yeshan, your general, is nearly there with her forces. Nisong is waiting for you and, whether or not she's a construct, she doesn't seem foolish enough to have no plan."

I speared a mushroom with one chopstick and wished it were Jovis's head. "If only my choices were as easy as you made them seem."

The boat swayed heavily to one side and I seized my bowl before it could go skittering off the table. Sailing in a wet season storm wasn't for the easily sickened. Most of the passengers, including Ragan, were laid out in their beds, waiting out the storm. I was lucky that it didn't affect me, though I also didn't have Jovis's easy gait across bucking floorboards. He'd kept a finger hooked over the side of his bowl.

He waited as I composed myself. "I could do as you suggest and turn the ship around," I said. "I could go back and hide on Imperial. But what does that say to the people of Gaelung? I'd be taking their folk hero with me and abandoning them to their fate. You can make a difference in that fight. Ragan can too. And if I can get Nisong to meet me, if she is a construct, I could end this all. I'm the only one who can. Taking this ship back to Imperial would be selfish and cruel. Is that what you expect of me?" Jovis looked startled at that and I sighed. "You can judge me all you want. I am *not* a tyrant." I threw my chopsticks down and did my best to rise from the bench with dignity. Instead, another wave outside swelled, sending me tumbling toward the wall.

Jovis reached out, caught my arm and steadied me. For a moment, his touch softened me. And then I got a hold of myself, shrugged him off and made for my room. Life and its morals were certainly easier when you were a smuggler. He thought he had all the answers. But when had he ever dealt with politics?

"Lin, wait."

I whirled, daring him to touch me again.

He lifted his hands, giving me space. "Maybe . . . " He sighed, pressed his lips together. "Maybe I just don't understand all of this the way that you do. I'm sorry I called you a tyrant. I've done questionable things that I thought were necessary at the time, and I think I might have even been right. At least, I rarely questioned myself. But I guess I thought – if you were Emperor, you wouldn't have to do the same. You could just wave a hand and make the right things happen."

The hallway was too small. "That's what the Emperor would have you believe," I said with a wan smile. "Because if we don't believe we have power, no one else will. Smugglers and Emperors – we are all just mortals in the end. I wish it wasn't true."

He frowned and opened his mouth to say something.

Another wave hit and I tripped over the hem of my pants. I put out my hands to stop myself, only to find them brushing against Jovis's chest and shoulder. He caught me again, his hands landing briefly at my waist before cupping my elbows.

"I know this must be frustrating for you – trying to keep the Empire from falling apart. There are too many things to keep track of, and the last thing you need is to be answering to a small-time smuggler."

"Small-time?" He hadn't let go, and I had to push the words past the tightness in my chest. He didn't want anything to do with me. I had to remember that. "I thought you were the greatest smuggler the Empire has ever seen. From what I heard, at least, that's what you told several of my father's soldiers as you left them in your wake."

He laughed at the tartness in my tone, his eyes met mine and then it seemed he couldn't quite catch his breath either. "Oh, Endless Sea take me," he said softly. "I am an idiot. And a liar."

His hands found my waist again, and he pulled me deliberately into him. All the lonely, wanting nerves in my body relaxed, soaking in his warmth, the feel of his breath tickling my scalp. I couldn't move, afraid to disturb this moment.

"Lin," he said into my scalp. "I don't really know who you are. There are so many secrets about you, so many locked rooms whose doors don't seem to have keys."

My heartbeat quickened. Some secrets could be told. Some had to be buried so deep I couldn't even admit them to myself. "I have told you more than I've told anyone."

He let that sit for a moment before saying, "I *am* sorry."

"You said that already," I said into his shirt.

He let out a warm breath. "So I did."

We stood there for a while in that embrace, the ship rolling around us. It was easier to stay on my feet. This close to him, I felt the rhythm and sway of his movements, anticipating each ocean swell as it passed.

He pressed his lips to my hairline, and then my forehead.

And though it hurt me to do so, I pulled away. "You said it was a mistake. As you've so often reminded me, I am the Emperor. I'm not a smuggler's plaything."

Jovis's lips curved into a rueful sort of smirk. "You have such an odd view of me. You think I had . . . playthings? Eminence, I had one wife, and when she died, I didn't know it, and—" He stopped. He reached up to tuck a piece of hair behind my ear. It was such a simple gesture, but done with such care that I wanted to cry. "Let me try again. I'm realizing that I cannot plan for all contingencies. And I don't know where anything will lead."

A part of me dared to hope, while the rest fled headlong into despair. Because the Jovis I'd kissed in the Ioph Carn den had been right. This couldn't lead to anything. I'd be breaking my own heart.

"How long does one of these storms last?"

I spun away from Jovis to see Ragan, his hand on the wall, his face pale and sweat-streaked. It took me a moment to orient my thoughts; they were still on the feel of Jovis's fingers against my cheek.

"Just a day or so," Jovis said.

"An entire day," Ragan said flatly.

"Why don't you just wave your hand and make it calm out there?" Jovis said. I was gratified to note he sounded more than just a little annoyed.

Ragan lifted a finger. "While my abilities can be augmented by cloud juniper berries, putting to rest an entire section of the Endless Sea would be beyond the grasp of anyone except perhaps

Dione. If the—" The boat swayed again, and he fell into the opposite wall, clutching his belly.

I grasped the doorknob of my room to stay upright.

"Are all the cloudtree monks like you?" Jovis asked, irritation seeping into his voice. "Ever think that perhaps Dione isn't a name you should mention in the same breath as your abilities? We've a thin enough veneer as it is."

"You should let people get used to the idea," Ragan said. "They'll have to be living with the reality sooner or later. We are not the only Alanga in this Empire."

Another wave hit the ship, and he fell to the floor.

"Can you help him back to his room?" I asked Jovis.

"Can I help him into the ocean?" he asked, his jaw tight.

"The servants' bunk, please," I said lightly.

Reluctantly, he went to help the monk to his feet. "Ginger tea helps," he told the man. "And just lying still. Try to sleep it off."

The click of claws against wood sounded behind me. Thrana had awoken from her nap. She blinked at me sleepily, her bulk filling the entire hallway. I cupped her chin in my hands and scratched the small beard there. It felt like dandelion silk between my fingertips. My heartbeat calmed. "If you get any bigger, you won't fit on a ship anymore," I said to her.

She blinked. "Then I'll swim."

I laughed at her matter-of-fact tone. "I'm not sure how you'd manage for that long."

She followed me into my cabin and settled by the window, waiting while I lit the lamps. She took up near half the space. It was like bringing a pony into a bedroom. I would have prepared better for this trip if I'd known she would grow so much.

But there were more pressing matters to attend to. I didn't have much time before we got to Gaelung. I needed to be prepared.

I went to the chest at the foot of my bed, unlocked it and pulled out the small box of flasks. I lifted the one that held my father's memories. Thrana watched me warily.

I returned her gaze. "You don't think I should."

"You come back not *you*," she said.

"Am I not me right now?"

She shifted, one ear flicking as she laid her chin on the floor. Brown, baleful eyes looked up at me. "You are you again, but it takes time. I feel like it takes longer each time."

I uncorked the flask and regarded the milky liquid in the bottom. I didn't relish the sweet, coppery taste, but I wasn't sure how else to get the information I needed. My father had kept copious notes, but they didn't address all of my questions. Each glimpse into his past gave me glimpses into my own past.

The windows were shut tight against the storm, but I could still hear the howling winds. "Be patient with me, Thrana," I said.

"Always."

I sat on the bed and lifted the flask to my lips.

Another wave hit the side of the boat, sending more liquid than I'd anticipated down my throat. I tried to cough, but then the room and all sensation vanished.

I was back in my father's body – a younger one again, without the creaking bones and subtle aches. I stood in a darkened hallway, a lamp held high in my hand. I could smell sandalwood oil each time I moved, clinging to the fabric of my clothes.

The lamp illuminated a door.

I knew this door, and not just as Shiyen – as myself. The library. Judging by the height from which I regarded this, I was Shiyen full-grown. My keys lay heavy around the chain at my neck. Why stand here with a lamp? Why not enter?

Through his eyes, I saw a thin bar of light from beneath the door, heard a soft creak.

Someone was behind the door. Someone who was not Shiyen.

I looked at my hands again. Not liver-spotted. Could it be an earlier version of Bayan beyond that door? Of myself? Footsteps sounded close to the door, and I covered the lamp with my robe, sending the hallway into darkness.

The door cracked open, the thin bar of light growing wider. A face peeked out from behind the crack – a face I would always know as my own. But there were slight and subtle differences.

Not my face. Nisong's.

She crept out of the door, shut it quietly and pulled a key from her sash pocket to lock it.

And I, as Shiyen, unveiled the lamp. "No need. I can take care of that part. That is my key, after all."

Nisong leapt back so abruptly that she dropped her lamp. "Dione's balls!" She knelt as the oil spilled out, lifting it before the floor could catch aflame. She did not shrink back, though by her back-planted foot, I could tell she wanted to. "What are you doing here?"

"It's my palace," Shiyen's deep voice rumbled from my throat. "I walk it as I please. When I please."

Nisong lifted her chin. "It's my palace too."

I felt my lips press together, my brows lower in a stern expression. "Some of the rooms are not. You may be my consort, and you may live here, but I made it clear from the beginning that the locked rooms are forbidden to you. And still, you disobeyed."

"I'm not a child!" Her voice rang out, echoing from the pillars.

Shiyen advanced, and I caught the glint of fear in her eyes. She took a step back and then held her ground. "No, you are not a child. You are a grown woman who has betrayed the trust of her Emperor. A child might be forgiven. A child might not be executed."

"And then who will you take for your consort? Who will bear you an heir?"

"Your position does not grant you immunity."

"Your position does not grant you the ability to do whatever you want without consequence."

Shiyen's gaze flicked to the door. "What were you doing in there? How long have you been using that key?"

She gave a one-shouldered shrug. "You always let me pour your tea, so adding some herbs for deep sleep was a small matter. I was researching."

A flicker of confusion – a feeling that was not my own. "Researching what? What use could you have for what is in that room?"

"Bone shard magic," she breathed out.

A moment, and then my belly shook with laughter. "You think you can learn bone shard magic? It has been passed from generation to generation within my family. Within *my* family. No one else has the ability to learn."

"You think it has to do with your bloodline? Anyone can read a book," she said, holding her lamp out in front of her like a weapon. "Anyone can learn."

"You? The third scion from Hualin Or? You never went to any of the Empire's Academies; you never studied under any of the great masters."

"No one ever *sent* me!" I could see the heat rising to her cheeks, and the odd thought arose: *She's not unattractive, just not beautiful.* Shiyen's thought, not mine. "I made my own studies; I'm not stupid or unlearned. Just . . . passed over."

"Except by me."

It was her turn to laugh. "Oh, you passed me over many, many times. My brother introduced you to me twice; you just don't remember. And I was not your first choice, don't pretend that isn't so. I had rivals."

Now I was intrigued. "Rivals you eliminated."

Her gaze met mine, and I forgot for a moment that she was so much shorter. "There is no proof of that."

Of course not. She wouldn't have left any. I made a quick, snap decision. "I'll give you use of the storeroom. The one where I keep the iceboxes with the construct parts. Thirty days."

She still held the library key in her other hand, and I didn't move to take it. Her fierce expression melted into confusion. "Thirty days for what?"

"You've never studied at any of the Academies, so here's a taste. This is how they do things there. You have a wild idea; I won't disabuse you of it. Thirty days to prove it. Prove to me someone not of the Sukai line can use the bone shard magic. Do that and I'll teach you everything I know. My knowledge will be your knowledge."

Confusion turned to consternation. "I've only been studying the books for six months. Emperors study these books for years before they even try to modify a construct. How can I build one from scratch in thirty days? There's too much information and not enough time."

"That doesn't sound like my problem." She'd dared to drug me, steal from me and now protested the limits of time on my already generous offer?

"What if I can't?"

I pulled a key from my chain and tossed it to her. She didn't react fast enough to catch it, and was left scrambling for it as it hit the floor. I turned, my robe sweeping the floor behind me. "Then I tell everyone what you've done. I execute you.

"And I find another consort."

38

Lin

Gaelung Island

He'd known what I would do.

I couldn't stop the thought from circling in my mind during every quiet moment before we reached Gaelung. I'd thought myself clever. I'd thought I was getting away with something. My father hadn't taken off his chain because he'd been afraid I'd attack him and take all his keys when we were alone in the questioning room; he was giving me an opportunity to take them. He'd instilled me with bits and pieces of Nisong's life and memories. He'd set Bayan against me as a rival and then waited, knowing what Nisong had done to her rivals.

How pleased he must have been, knowing that his experiment had worked! I clutched at the railing of the boat, watching the shape of Gaelung grow larger on the horizon, alone with my bitter thoughts. The wind brought it the spray of the ocean mingled with a few stray drops from above.

As if to remind me I was not completely alone, Thrana rested her head on my shoulder. "Close enough yet?" I rubbed at her cheeks, grateful for the contact. After coming out of the memory, she'd not wanted to be near me for several days. I'd found myself clutching for robes that weren't there, for a cane I'd never used, my words and tongue sharper than they normally were.

She'd feared my father, and she'd hated him. Anything I did in a way that resembled him made her shrink away, her limbs trembling. It had to be a terrible reminder of the suffering she'd endured for years beneath the palace. Trapped in the pool and in the darkness, hooked up to tubes that carried away her blood for use in my father's machine.

I still didn't quite understand that. How did her blood help hold memories in liquid form? I might have to delve deeper to figure that out.

"Yes, go ahead," I told her.

She launched herself from the railing and into the Endless Sea. I lost a little of my moroseness watching her swim and dive beneath the waves. Mephi, not wanting to be left out, soon joined her. Only Lozhi, Ragan's ossalen, was absent.

Ragan, however, was not. I thought at first it was Jovis, but then I heard him take in a deep breath next to me and knew it was not. His hands gripped the railing next to mine. "It'll be good to be on dry land again," he said.

"I take it the monks do not sail often," I said dryly.

"Not at all. We're mostly orphans, taken in by the monastery. Or children given over whose parents would rather never see their children again than to see them go through the Tithing Festival. And then we spend the rest of our lives there, caring for the cloud juniper trees and curating books."

"Sounds lonely."

He waved a dismissive hand. "It's worse than that. It's like being cloistered with family for the rest of your life, and they aren't always family you particularly like. The monks don't interact much with surrounding villages, and you never really get a day off to go into town."

"I never asked – how did you happen upon Lozhi?"

Something passed over his face – a grimace? I couldn't be sure. "Ah." He lifted a finger. "A good question." Was he stalling? "They do send monks to the villages for supplies and to trade. I drew the task once. There are so many acolytes that want to go, you see. I had a little free time, so I took a walk by the beach, and I found him there. I knew what he was because of my studies. Ossalen only appear every few hundred years, so I got lucky."

I mused this over. Was it luck to become one of the Alanga? Certainly there was power to be gained, but there was suspicion and scorn too. When the Alanga had fought one another, whole cities of commoners had suffered. Some people might have romanticized the stories about them, but more thought we were well rid of them. And always the Sukais had used them as a warning – this was why we had to complete the Tithing Festival; this was why we had to have the constructs. In case the Alanga returned.

I studied Ragan's face, the way his brows were drawn slightly together. He was holding something back. "Just luck?"

This time, I was sure it was a grimace. "Ah, that's not exactly the truth. I didn't draw the task. I was . . . running away. Trying to. It's an embarrassing story. Having potential isn't always wonderful. They pushed me hard. My masters did. Do you know what it's like to have someone expect something of you that you don't know you can live up to? So I ran away. And I found Lozhi."

I knew what it was like. I knew very, very well. "I found Thrana in the old mines beneath the palace," I murmured. I watched her play in the surf now, a far cry from the wretched creature I'd pulled from the water. "My father had been experimenting on her."

"They do have some very interesting properties," Ragan said. He added quickly: "Not that they should be experimented upon. No one deserves that, least of all these creatures."

"What else do you know about them? Where do they come from? Why do they bond with us? How do they choose who to bond with?"

"I didn't have access to all the books," he said, holding up his hands briefly before grabbing the railing again. "No one knows where they come from, only that they start to appear every few hundred years. Your father might have kept records – the Sukai family was very interested in making sure the Alanga did not return. As for why they bond with us and how they choose . . . " He squinted at the clouds. "I can't say I know that either. But I have guesses. They don't have this power on their own. Just as a cleaning fish will attach itself to a shark and they both benefit, I think the ossalen attach to people. We need one another. We receive these abilities, and they receive a way to influence the world."

"Lozhi doesn't seem to influence you much."

"I've a better control on our bond," he said lightly. "It's stronger."

I didn't feel like the bond between Thrana and me was weak; quite the contrary.

"Mephi!" Jovis came darting up from behind us, his hair in disarray. He searched the water until he found his beast, a shimmering form beneath one of the waves. "I think he took my comb. Someone needs to tell him that stealing is not the same thing as smuggling," he muttered. "What's it to be this time, Eminence? Never a dull stop on this trip."

It hurt me a little, to be called "Eminence" again, but I couldn't fault him for it in public company. Every time it felt like we were getting closer, I felt him pull away again. And maybe it was my fault – he was right, I'd never been honest with him. I had too many secrets. But I answered in his same light tone. "A battle, maybe two. Whatever it takes to keep Gaelung safe."

He let out a long breath. "So it's just to be us, then? Against her army?"

"If it comes to that, then yes. But I have one more play to make."

We arrived at Gaelung later that morning, when a rare bit of sun had begun to peek out from behind the clouds. Gaelung wasn't known for grand gestures. The governor there was relatively new – a little older than myself – though my father had never bothered to meet her. She greeted me at the docks, and there was no palanquin this time, but a covered wagon pulled by two oxen. Two other uncovered wagons followed for my retinue. I was bringing Ragan this time, and Lozhi joined him, the small, gray creature curling up at his side as he sat.

"Eminence," she said, bowing her head. "I'm glad you've arrived safely."

"Sai," I said, inclining my head in return. Urame was short by most standards, though taller than me and twice as broad. Her face was round and flat as a porcelain dish, her black eyes like two polished stones. She was dressed in one of the short-sleeved, heavily beaded tunics popular in the north-eastern isles, with a canvas cowl that looked like it had been oiled to keep out the rain. I noted her use of the word "safely". Nisong and her army must have been close.

Mephi and Thrana sauntered up, and Urame's eyes widened a bit as she took in Thrana, who followed me as easy as a pup, though she had the bulk of a pony.

"Your . . . pet is a bit larger than I've been led to expect," she said a bit breathlessly.

"They're harmless," I told her.

"We are *very* good," Mephi added as Thrana nodded her assent.

Urame's eyes widened even further. "Do they understand what they're saying?"

"I think they do."

"Remarkable," she said. "You'll have to tell me more about them if we ever have more leisure time." Again, that undertone of foreboding. I hadn't heard that Urame was a skittish woman; indeed, my envoys assured me of the opposite. So whatever she'd seen of Nisong's army had spooked her.

"I understand you're in a difficult position," I said. "And I'm here to help."

She gave me a tight smile, her gaze flicking to my ship and then back to me. "Forgive me, Eminence, but if you do not have yet another army with you, there may not be much you can do to help. The construct army is camped out on Gaelung and is much larger than it was when your soldiers last engaged with it. Please—" She gestured to the wagon. "The palace has a good vantage point and I have the use of a decent spyglass. I can show you."

I climbed into the covered wagon, signaling for Jovis to follow me. Ragan climbed into the uncovered wagon with the others.

Light streamed through the open sides of the wagon, illuminating Urame's concerned expression. "I am not Iloh, or Phaluc, or Wailun," she said.

"Chala," I corrected. "Wailun has unfortunately passed away." The full explanation, like Urame had said, was something for a more leisurely moment.

"Oh," she said, and I could see her readjusting all her mental calculations. "Regardless, I don't have many demands to make, no matter that my advisers press me to take advantage. I know you need the support of Gaelung. I know your rule is tentative. But you've ended the Tithing Festivals and that's a good enough gesture for me. You don't need to cajole me; Gaelung will support you."

A small relief. I'd set out on this trip with that being at the forefront of my mind. Now, with the sinking of Deerhead, Unta and Luangon, the growth of Nisong's army, the assertion that even more Alanga would appear and the whispers of rebellion still stirring in the south, I'd lost sight of the urgency of that support. What mattered now was keeping this Empire well and whole to face its next challenges. I'd thought for sure I was the one best suited to lead the Empire through those trials. Now, I felt like a rag wrung free of seawater, hung to dry in the sun. "I appreciate that," I said.

The palace at Gaelung wasn't near the docks, as it was on most other islands. It lay further inland, across the fields and atop a rocky hill. I supposed it reflected the more agrarian nature of the island. According to the stories, more than one battle had taken place on those fields, the hill giving a vantage point to the Alanga who'd resided there. Now, we passed a patchwork of farms, the blood having long ago soaked into the soil, the scars of battle faded. Oxen, pigs and goats dotted the landscape, grazing upon the greenery and rooting about in the dirt. I breathed in and, for the first time in a long time, couldn't smell the ocean. Only the musty smells of animal dung and damp earth.

A blur passed the window as Thrana and Mephi raced one another. Thrana was much larger now and thundered past, though Mephi did his best to keep up. I thought again about what Ragan had said regarding ossalen and their bonds. He might have thought his bond with Lozhi superior, but Lozhi also seemed to have a good deal less fun – always shut away and waiting for his master to return. I rarely saw them interact. I wasn't sure how Ragan bore being parted from him. Every time I left Thrana, it felt like exposing a gaping wound to the air.

The road began to slope upward, winding into switchbacks. When we arrived at the palace, Urame did not have servants show us to our rooms, or invite us to tea or to dine; she led us directly up two flights of stairs and then to the palace walls. "You should see this before anything else," she explained.

This high up, the wind had a bit of bite to it, wedging its way between my cloak and the back of my neck. On this side of the palace, in the distance, I could see thin columns of smoke.

"She's camped out on the eastern side of the fields," Urame said. She reached the easternmost end of the wall and turned to face me, her expression grave. "My guards can handle small skirmishes, and can do a fair job of defending the palace, but the farms are not walled in. She's been burning homes and killing villagers since she got here."

I didn't bother telling Urame that I had an army on the way. Both she and I knew there weren't enough of them and they were not battle-tested. "How many of them are there? Have you sent scouts?"

"I have, but after the first two did not return, I thought better of it."

"You said you have a spyglass?"

She knelt next to a basket and rummaged around until she pulled out a brass spyglass. "That's the other thing."

I took it and pulled the end out to its full length. "The other thing?"

She had the calm, grim air of a person about to pass the news that a beloved auntie had died. "Take a look for yourself. That's the best way to explain."

Jovis raised his eyebrows but I shrugged, pointed the glass in the direction of the construct encampment and put my eye to the lens.

I nearly dropped the spyglass.

I'd expected the human-looking constructs; after all, my foster brother had been one, I'd met Nisong's envoy and I'd taken apart the ones at Hualin Or. I knew my father had experimented with people's bodies. But the majority of her army was made of what looked like people.

"Are there people in her army?"

Urame spoke by my ear. "In a manner of speaking. Keep looking."

I focused on a group of them. They stood by a campfire but barely moved. There was something strange about the tilt of their bodies. Most wore tattered clothing, much of it stained with blood.

"We've been getting reports – they wouldn't have made it to you yet. But the isles on the edge of the Empire, the ones she's taken, have suffered more than just defeat and death and burned villages."

Some of the people had wounds that looked to still be open.

"She has been holding her own Tithing Festival. She has been taking shards."

The memory of Shiyen's I'd just seen floated to the forefront of my mind. She wasn't only killing villagers and taking shards.

She was filling her army with constructs of the dead.

I handed the spyglass back to Urame. "I'm going out there under a flag of truce. I've got something else to offer her."

"Not the throne?" Urame said, her face pale. "We've had tyrants enough."

"No," I interrupted her. "Never that. Can you ready a wagon?"

She seemed to remember then all the niceties of hosting. "You must be tired after your long journey. And you haven't eaten."

My stomach growled as though in response. "Just pack me something I can eat by hand. This is too important to wait."

Urame gestured to one of the servants behind her, and they leapt to obey. "I wish we had met under different circumstances, Eminence," she said. "I have the feeling our stories are not too dissimilar. No one knew who I was before I became governor either."

That fleeting sense of kinship made me ache for more. I wished we could sit down over tea together, to talk about our pasts, to find the threads that made us the same. But I was the Emperor and I didn't have a past I could speak of. "Someday circumstances will be different," was all I said.

I rode out to the construct encampment under a flag of truce with only Jovis, our ossalens running alongside the wagon. I couldn't trust anyone else with what I was about to offer Nisong. I glanced down at our hands, next to one another on the bench, yet not touching.

He cleared his throat. "So were we planning on eating or did the dirt beneath my fingernails dissuade your appetite?"

I shook my head, smiling despite myself. One of Urame's servants had handed in a basket from the kitchen. I uncovered the contents to discover flaky, savory pastries that smelled strongly of curry. I took one and handed the basket to Jovis. It was filled with beef and potatoes, the curry mild, the pastry slightly sweet. Brushed with honey.

"Those who say Gaelung is a backwater clearly have no taste," he said with a sigh. He gave me a sidelong look. "Do you actually have something to offer her or were you just going to . . . ?" He mimed thrusting a hand out, grasping, and pulling toward himself.

It wasn't the last secret that I had, but he might guess at the last one if I revealed this one. But he was right, I needed to start learning to trust the people close to me if I didn't want to end up like my father. "My father . . . he was growing something in the caves beneath the palace. A replica."

Jovis's eyebrows climbed toward his hairline. "A replica of what?"

I squeezed my eyes shut tight, took in a deep breath. "A replica of himself. Not a construct, a true replica. No shards. Don't ask me how it's done; I don't quite understand it myself. All I know is that he cut off one of his own toes to create it. But if my suspicions are correct, Nisong isn't just calling herself that out of some attempt to lend herself legitimacy. She might be my father's attempt to re-create his late wife. He'd told me he'd burned her body before he could use any part of it to make a replica, but he might have tried to put her memories into a construct. It would explain why he killed her family. He didn't have Nisong's blood to use in the memory machine, but the blood of her relatives might have worked. He would have needed a lot of it." Would he make the connections? Would he wonder about the daughter of the Emperor, rarely seen outside the palace walls?

He frowned and my heartbeat thudded against my ribs. "How did she get to the north-eastern reaches of the Empire?"

I let out my breath. "I'm not sure." And I wasn't, although I'd put together the pieces from my father's memories and Jovis's tale of his missing wife. My father couldn't bring himself to dismantle the constructs carrying my mother's memories. So he'd sent them far away, on that same blue-sailed boat that had taken Jovis's wife.

He lifted another pastry from the basket. "You want to offer the replica to her?"

"They loved one another," I said. "I meant what I said when I spoke to her envoy. Maybe there's a way to keep the constructs alive without draining our lives. I'm willing to take that time and effort if she's willing to wait. Shiyen might tempt her. It's that or try to get close enough to dismantle her."

"So you're hoping for romance to win the day?" He let out a bitter laugh that twisted a knife into my heart.

I wiped the crumbs from my fingers before we reached the

encampment. The constructs I'd seen from the palace walls were even more terrifying up close – their gazes empty, hands listless at their sides, blood staining their sleeves. They were barely held together by the shards within them. She must have figured out how few shards she could use – they'd still be a limited resource.

A woman with large, dark eyes met us. She put a hand over her heart in greeting. "Nisong will see you. If you'll follow me."

I left the wagon with Jovis on my heels, the thrum in my bones a welcome reassurance. Surreptitiously, I took another cloudtree berry from my sash and crushed it between my teeth. Strength flooded through my limbs. Mephi and Thrana stood back, their hackles raised, heads low. Both looked like spooked cats. Still, they fell in behind us, sniffing the air with lips pulled back. Mephi's head reached Jovis's hip, but Thrana was a solid presence, a wall of muscled beast at my back.

Nisong didn't wait for us in a tent, or surround herself with the niceties most rulers did. She met us in front of a bonfire, the smoke rising behind her, her constructs standing listlessly around her.

She was taller than I was, her face landing somewhere just short of middle age. Her hair was bound in a simple braid; scars marked her face and her bare arms. Two fingers on her left hand were missing. My father might have made her from disparate parts, but she stood the way the Nisong of my memories did – feet planted firmly in the ground, her chin raised as if asking for someone to challenge her. She stood the way I did.

A shiver tickled up my spine, digging in at the base of my neck. Nisong might not have looked like me, but it was like gazing into a dark mirror nonetheless. We both regarded one another, her head tilting to the side at the same time as mine. I was sure then: she was a construct and she was perhaps more Nisong than I was.

"We both know I have something you want," I said.

The fire glinted from her eyes. "You are so very like me, aren't you?"

I brushed past that reference, uncomfortable with the comparison. She was one of my father's discarded versions of me. A precursor, filled with memories she didn't understand. I wasn't sure what she knew about me. Did her memories show Nisong's real daughter? Was I what she'd expected? "I have terms to offer you."

"You heard my terms already. Are you surrendering?"

I snorted. "Hardly. But let me make this clear. Shiyen is dead. What your spy saw in the palace was not him, but a replica he'd made. I'm offering him to you in exchange for you ceasing your attacks. Turn over your army. I'll let you go – you and him, off to live out your lives together. And I'll look for a way for you to exist without the shards."

"And why wouldn't I just take him when I take the palace?"

"I could kill him before you got there, but most importantly – he is not finished."

Her eyes narrowed. "Not finished," she said flatly.

"Shiyen stored most of his memories but didn't have the chance to instill his replica with them. It's a true replica of him, not a construct, grown beneath the palace without the use of shards. Once his memories are in place, he will be Shiyen." I hoped the lies didn't show on my face. My father had instilled me with Nisong's memories and they hadn't made me her. But they'd also been secondhand memories, taken from the blood of her relatives.

"So you're offering me a chance to run away from all this, abandon the other constructs and live a normal life?" She said it scornfully, but I saw the tightness at the corners of her lips, the strain in her throat. She wanted what I offered. She wanted it very badly. "But I'd still be draining the lives of the people's shards inside my body until you found a solution, if you ever did."

"I can live with that, if you can."

She laughed. "You sound like Shiyen."

My spine stiffened. Did I?

"He always said that what we did – the Tithing Festival, the constructs – it led to less suffering than would occur than if we didn't. He said he could live with it, if I could." She shook her head. "Do you really think I care that much about reliving a past life? I'm not here to recreate the life I see in glimpses. Let that past Shiyen stay dead. Let that past life stay dead."

"Then what do you want?"

Her teeth flashed somewhere between a grin and a grimace. "I want you to suffer. I want all of you to suffer the way I have. The way those I love have. You never cared about us until we made ourselves heard in blood and fire. To you we were just made things to be disposed of. We were your mistakes, to be crumpled and burned like so many ink blotted pages. Give me your Empire or give me your deaths."

Now. I sprinted forward, my hand outstretched, the power from Thrana and the cloudtree berry mingling in my veins.

For a moment, I thought I would make it.

And then the shambling constructs closed in around her, my hand meeting only rags and torn flesh.

"I don't think so." Nisong met my gaze, and I read only determination in her expression. "This ends only one of two ways. You have until tomorrow morning to surrender."

39

Jovis

Gaelung Island

I thought once that age had made me wise; instead it made me foolish. I stopped paying attention to the smaller things. I stopped understanding the needs and feelings of mortals. Even after my friendship with Ylan, when I thought I understood, I didn't.

I went to see what he'd wrought from my gifts. I waited too long, perhaps, trusted too much.

He'd made swords. Seven of them. I knew he would make weapons, so it wasn't this that surprised me. He was evasive, trying to guide me away. At last, I pried his arm from mine and drew back the bindings to look at what he'd carved on their hilts.

"Die."

When I turned to protest — we had agreed on something to limit the Alanga, not kill them — he held a blade to my throat.

—Notes from Jovis's translation of Dione's journal

L in didn't say much on the ride back, and I bit my tongue for as long as I could. "So ... when do we go into battle?" I asked finally. "Death and glory and all that."

She sighed and looked at me. "This isn't a joke."

"Oh, believe me, Eminence, I know this is far, far from a joke. We're asking for a beating."

"We can do it," she said. "Her constructs are barely functional. I should know."

"Our army is too small. Yes, there's us three Alanga. I shake a little earth, move a little air, Ragan comes in with some water, you do ... whatever you feel up to doing. We can come up with a strategy or a plan, but I can count." I ticked off three fingers. "That's us."

"Perhaps you would do better to criticize less and remember your place more," she snapped back.

It felt like being physically struck. I knew I'd been pushing her away, and with good reason, but I'd thought we could at least be friends. I knew my place – half-Poyer, erstwhile smuggler, a man who had only been elevated by her good graces. I just wished she hadn't been the one to remind me of it. "Nisong was right," I said before I could stop myself. "You do sound like your father."

She didn't deflate, but she didn't get angry either. Instead, her expression turned brittle, like the slightest blow could shatter her, could scatter her to the four winds. "Maybe he'd have a better solution to all this. I just want to keep this Empire safe. From all threats."

I wished I could take back my words. Again, I wondered if she knew she was not the Emperor's daughter. Did she even know who she was? Perhaps she'd never intended to deceive anyone. I thought of the letter to the Shardless Few I'd still not sent. I could destroy her with a few words.

She suddenly straightened. "She thinks she's so superior now that she can make her own constructs. But she's not the only one who can do that. She's not the only one who can *modify* them." She reached into her sash pocket and pulled out her engraving tool. "We have shards," she was saying. "I can ask permission to use them. If I can get my hands on a body, I can make a construct to infiltrate her camp. It can alter the commands of her constructs. And then the numbers will be more in our favor." She finished, breathless. "We can still make this work."

She will use it again, if she feels she needs to. I remembered my bold assertions to Gio, that Lin was different, that she was foregoing bone shard magic. And here she was, proving him right and proving me wrong yet again. My throat felt raw, like I'd swallowed thorns. "So how do you word that so it's palatable, exactly?"

"Word what?"

"Permission," I said.

"Jovis," she said, "I'm not doing this to keep or maintain power. I'm doing this to save all our hides."

"Your father said the same thing."

"He was *afraid*."

"And you're not?"

"No!" she said, her cheeks flushed. "Not of the same things he was. I'm afraid of Gaelung falling to the constructs. I'm afraid of more islands sinking. I'm afraid that even with all the vast power of the Emperor, I won't be able to do anything to help. And I'm afraid that if I lose my position, there will be even less I can do. If I don't do this, who will? You?"

Words dried up in my mouth. Endless Sea, I wasn't meant for this! I'd rarely worried about ethics or morality when I'd been a smuggler. With Emahla gone, so went my singular focus. Now there were too many things to care about. First Mephi, then the Shardless Few, then my parents again, and now Lin. Every step I took seemed to be the wrong one, yet I couldn't seem to stop. I couldn't be sure I wasn't just making things worse. I'd arrived at Imperial hoping to bring an end to the Empire. Had Lin already done that? At least, in the form it had once known? Then what was I doing except undermining her?

I shouldn't be fighting with her, not on the eve of a battle and not when my position felt so precarious. I'd found a moment before we'd docked to sneak into her rooms. The flask of Ragan's memories, the one I'd hidden between her mattress and the wall, was gone. She'd not said anything about it. I could only hope that one of her maidservants had found it and, not knowing what it was, had dumped it out and returned the flask to the ship's mess.

The wagon rolled to a stop.

I fled as soon as the door was opened, barely listening as Lin explained to Urame that Nisong had not wanted to bargain, and that she had a plan that would buy us time. Mephi sidled up next to me, his face reflecting my own worry. He always hated to see me upset. "In a moment," I told him, knowing he wanted me to explain.

Urame's servants showed us to the guest rooms with the promise of a formal meal. I shut my door behind me as soon as I could and sat on the edge of the bed. What would Emahla say if she could see me now? If we were facing this together? I closed my eyes and tried to imagine her face.

I'd thought I would never forget her face, yet the edges of it were blurring, the exact texture of her hair uncertain. In my mind's eye, she looked my age, but I knew she'd only lived to nineteen. It was as though the person who had known Emahla, who had loved her – no longer existed. I wasn't the man now that I was then, and I wondered if she would even recognize me. Thinking of her had always centered me; now it sent me skittering along an unknown path, searching for answers in the dark.

Lin's face swam to the forefront of my mind unbidden. Hers

I knew clearly – the expressive eyes, the pointed chin, the secretive lips.

Mephi's head came to rest in my lap. "You are doing the best you can."

I cracked an eye open at him. "I'm beginning to think you may be a bit biased."

"Never," he said innocently.

"She wants to use bone shard magic again," I said. "And she wants us to fight." I pulled the letter I'd written to the Shardless Few out from my sash pocket. I should send it. I should. Then why hadn't I done it yet? "Mephi, she's not who anyone thinks she is."

"You don't know if she's a good or a bad," Mephi said slowly.

"She's not the Emperor. Or, at least, she shouldn't be. But she's trying." Like I was.

A knock sounded at the door. Before I could respond, Lin let herself in. I tucked the letter beneath the bed sheets, my throat tight and my heart kicking at my ribs. *Too close*.

"I need to tell you something," she said, her palms pressed against the door. "And I need to tell you before we go into this battle. You're right; I've been keeping things from you." Her gaze went to the floor, a loose piece of hair shadowing her face. "I've been asking you to trust me, but trust goes both ways."

"Wait—" Dread clawed its way into my belly. Some part of me knew that what she was about to say was irrevocable – too terrible and too secret.

But she was already speaking over me. "I thought I was my father's daughter, but she died when she was young."

I tried to form words, but couldn't, my mouth dry.

"He made me. I'm not a construct; I'm a replica, just like the replica of Shiyen I tried to bargain with. He tried to rebuild my mother, more than once."

I'd been young when Nisong had died – an unfortunate ailment, I'd heard. I hadn't understood until I was older the extent of the Emperor's grief. He'd shut himself away, burning all her portraits and putting her maidservants to death. It was a thing spoken of in whispers, tales told in drinking halls late at night. My lips fumbled one word: "Tried."

"By the time he discovered he could create replicas, he'd already burned her body, so he couldn't grow her anew like he did with himself." She took a deep breath. "Instead, he built her from pieces of his citizens. He built me. He sewed me together and placed me in the pool beneath the palace to grow. The water there has special properties; I'm not sure why. But he didn't need shards to bring me to life."

She lifted her gaze from the floor, and I *knew*. Her eyes didn't just look like Emahla's; they *were* hers. I couldn't breathe. He'd killed her. He'd taken her eyes and stitched them into another body. One I'd kissed. One I'd held, wishing circumstances were different. How . . . how was she any different than the shambling corpses out on the battlefield? I felt sick with horror.

And she was reading it all on my face.

"I'm sorry," she said. "This must be painful for you."

"You should have told me," I gasped out, even knowing as I said it that of course she couldn't have told me, that even telling me now she was risking everything. All because she wanted to be honest with me. Because she wanted my trust.

Mephi's head was still in my lap. I pushed him away and staggered to my feet. He made a small, sad sound but gave me space.

"Jovis," she said, and then stopped. "I didn't know. I didn't know until he told me. He tried to instill me with her memories, but it didn't quite work. The blood of Nisong's relatives didn't work the same way her blood would have. So all I get are glimpses. I'm not him, and I'm not her."

"And after he told you, you killed him." I'd never said it out loud, though I thought she knew. We'd met in the hallways of the palace soon after, when she'd still been tattered and bloodied.

"It was that or let him into my head again. He wasn't a good man," she said. "His daughter died when she was young. He hid that and told me I was his daughter; everyone believed it to be so. And I could change things for the better as Emperor."

"A fine job you've done." I wished I could swallow the words as soon as I'd said them.

She flinched back. "Yes, well," she said quietly, "it turns out that my father's legacy has stretched farther than I'd anticipated."

What was I doing? I was a liar and she was laying herself bare. "I'm sorry," I said, my head spinning, my chest hollow. Mephi was there beside me, propping me up. I dug my fingers into the fur of his neck, letting him steady me. "Give me a moment. I know it's not your fault."

She let out a long, shaky breath. "I don't have anyone. I have no real family, no friends except for Thrana. But I can't keep this all inside. I need to trust someone, to feel like I can still belong. That I'm still real and not just what he made me."

Mephi looked up at me. He'd seen past my smuggler's guise. He'd seen me as someone who tried to help. He'd seen me as someone who was good. It had been enough.

Who was I fooling? I'd never send that letter, no matter what she was. Gio might not be able to see it, but we needed Lin. We needed people like her. I took in a deep, shuddering breath. "If you were what he made you, you wouldn't have ended the Tithing Festival. You wouldn't have taken apart Bing Tai. You wouldn't be traveling to the islands and trying to gain the people's support." It felt like I was explaining this to myself as I explained it to her. "Your father never would have done any of that. Neither would Nisong. They certainly had the chance."

"Thank you," she said. She wiped at her eyes. "Urame approved my plan, and I have volunteers for the shards, and a body. This isn't me going back down that path, and I need you to understand that. This is me using the tools I have."

I found myself taking the few steps to stand before her, taking her hands in mine. "I trust you."

She sagged into me. I wrapped my arms around her; it came as naturally to me as breathing. Endless Sea could take the gossip. I might have been a smuggler and half-Poyer, but I was the Captain of the Imperial Guard and I had a song written about me — that had to count for something.

I was overthinking this.

The feel of her body pressed to mine did interesting things to my thoughts. I kissed the top of her head and heard her sigh. Her hands moved over my back, tracing the lines of my shoulderblades. I shivered, suddenly aware that we were alone in my room, that Mephi was staring studiously out the window and that the bed was three steps behind me.

"I don't know where this leads. I don't want you to have to suffer everyone's scrutiny." Lin's breath was warm across my chest. "But — " One hand ventured up to curl in my hair. "– do we need to think that far ahead?"

No, of course not, my body said just as my mind said, *Yes.*

She broke away, flustered. "You were married once, and I've never — you're the first person I've kissed, except in random memories that aren't mine. I can't tell what you're thinking. Just tell me — am I making a fool of myself? This is too much at once, isn't it?"

I remembered the beach, the breaking of the wet season, the water droplets on Emahla's eyelashes. I remembered blurting out that she was beautiful, the look of consternation on her face. "I think," I said, "it's often like this." And then I was pulling her in again, loosening the ties in her hair, pressing my lips to every bit of her I could reach. She responded eagerly, pushing me back toward the bed, her hands busy at the buttons of my shirt. I should tell her. Tell her everything.

But was this quite the time?

She gave me one last little shove and I sat on the bed. Paper crinkled. Lin frowned.

The world stopped. I opened my mouth to explain and found . . . I had no lies left. Not even one came to mind. And then she was reaching past me and I couldn't twist fast enough to stop her. "That's my seal," she murmured as she grabbed the letter.

"That's . . . that's important," I said, holding out my hand, hoping she'd give it to me.

She regarded me, and I knew she was reading my face, my body language. I tried to keep still, to project serenity.

Lin flipped the top of it open.

I knew it was in code, I knew it didn't look like it said anything incriminating. But my palms began to sweat, my heart ricocheting off my ribcage and landing in the vicinity of my stomach. The only person who would dare question the Emperor's seal on my letter was the Emperor herself.

She frowned, folded the letter back down and handed it to me. "Who were you writing to? Why use the Emperor's seal?"

The lies came back. I almost wished they hadn't. "It's not mine. Someone must have left it here."

"It's your handwriting."

Of course she'd know. But I'd already committed to the wrong lie. I flipped the top open, my pulse loud in my ears. "Looks like mine, but it's not." I should have reached for her again, did my best to make her forget, but I couldn't.

"The seal . . . " She trailed off, then shook her head and set the letter down. She froze and picked it up again. Her voice seemed to come from far away. "It's got too many feathers in its crest. It's a counterfeit."

She drew back as though burned, her gaze darting between me and Mephi. "It's in code. You're a spy." She studied my face again. "You're working for the Shardless Few."

All the words I couldn't find came tumbling out. "They're not who you think they are. They're not bad people. They just want a better Empire."

"So you *spied* for them? On me? You swore an *oath*."

I closed my eyes, wishing I could come back to a few moments ago when I opened them. No such luck. Not for me. "Funny thing about oaths," I said, my voice weak. "No way to actually enforce them." It was the worst time for a joke.

Her fingers curled into claws. "They want me to abdicate. They want to have no Emperor at all. Do you think their proposed council would be able to coalesce in time to face the construct army? To deal with the Alanga that are arising? You lied to me. You lied, over and over. You would have kept lying — don't deny it."

There had to be a way to fix this, to make it right. I grasped desperately for the right words, sweat prickling at my hairline, my heart trapped in the vicinity of my stomach. "No. I stopped working for them back on Nephilanu. I would have told you the truth when the time was right," I said. "I wanted to."

"But you didn't. When was the time going to be right? Never?" She snatched up the letter again. "What does it say? What were you telling them?"

No more lies. I'd fumbled this play; I'd fumbled it from the very beginning. Best to let the cards lie face-up. "I found the birth records," I said. "There was a part of the palace you hadn't repaired and I investigated. I knew you weren't his daughter. I didn't know if you knew."

She went still. "So you would give them what they needed to unseat me."

I lifted my hands, palms up, hoping for mercy. "I wrote it on Imperial. I haven't sent it."

For a moment, I thought she might relent. And then she crushed the letter in her fist. "You don't write letters you never intend to send. You couldn't decide, could you? I cannot believe I felt I had to justify myself to you, that I had to *earn* your trust and your loyalty."

I felt caught in a trap of my own making, my mind desperately searching for a way out and not finding one. This was the reality I'd wrought, and no wishing would change that. "*Please.*" It was the only thing I could think to say.

When Lin looked at me, I wondered if it was the same way she'd looked at Shiyen when she'd finally confronted him. Her brows low, her face an icy mask. She'd shut herself away from me, and somehow that hurt worse than her accusatory words. "Get out," she said. "Leave Gaelung before I change my mind and have you executed."

Mephi let out a whimper, creeping to my side, his brown eyes wide. "Not good," he whispered. Even the feel of his fur between my fingertips didn't soothe me. I couldn't be thankful for such mercy. "The battle – you can't do this with just the guards and Ragan. You need me there."

"No, Jovis. I know what I need. And I do not need a liar."

I went.

40

Lin

Gaelung Island

I'd thought nothing could hurt worse than my father's betrayal, learning that he'd never actually loved *me*, but merely the ghost I would never become. My heart was guarded against such things, I'd thought.

Time and experience make fools of us all.

And the worst was, I wasn't sure what hurt more – the fact that Jovis had lied to me from the beginning, or the way the door had shut behind him, leaving me alone. Somewhere in the time we'd spent together, I'd started to feel like I could rely on him, that we had a kinship. I thought the only thing that could make me feel better was an embrace, and the only hug I could remember receiving had been from him.

I ripped up the crumpled remains of the letter, my vision blurred.

Thrana was pacing by the door when I returned to my room. "Lin," she said when I entered. "Something is wrong. What happened?"

I buried my face in her fur, wrapping my arms around her neck. She waited patiently while I sobbed, my tears wetting her chest. I'd been so foolish – a child yearning for connection. And he'd taken advantage of that, letting me seek out his approval the way I'd sought my father's. I had to be stronger than that, better than that. "I sent him away," I told Thrana. "He lied and I told him to leave."

She let out a breath. It smelled of the ocean. A heavy paw came to rest on my back – her version of an embrace. I sagged into it, knowing that even though I loved her, it wasn't enough for me.

"You need other people," she said, as though reading the thoughts in my head. "This is not good."

"It was the only thing I could do."

"I know. But, Lin – we were both hurt. I trust you now. You need this too."

I drew back, wiping at my cheeks with the back of my hand. "How do I find the right people? I don't seem to be good at finding them."

She puffed up, as though proud to be giving me advice. "You make a mistake. You try again." Her tail lashed.

I let out a rueful laugh. I wished it were as simple as Thrana made it sound. Maybe for her, it was. "A matter for another time, I think. Providing we live through this."

A knock sounded at the door. I pressed my fingers to my eyes, willing the tears away. "Come in."

Urame entered, her guards carrying a corpse behind her, a bag in her right hand. "We have the items you requested," she said. "Sixteen of my household volunteered their shards, including me." She held the bag out to me.

I took it, feeling the trust they'd bestowed in me, the shattered pieces of my heart forming up. I could mourn the loss of Jovis later. Now I had people who were relying on me. I had an Empire to save. I had an army to defeat. Sixteen was not so many, but I was clever, and I had defeated my father and his constructs. I could make this work.

Ragan slipped into my room behind them. "Eminence, sorry to interrupt, but I saw Jovis leaving. Was that at your instruction?"

I felt a prickle of irritation at his intrusion, and the way everyone turned to await my answer. I'd have to tell them at some point, but I hadn't wanted to be pressured into it, not when my throat still felt raw and my eyes stung. "Yes, it was. He is no longer under my employ."

The guards shifted, exchanging glances. I knew what they were thinking. Jovis had quite the reputation in the Empire by now. Most people thought him a hero, and making him my Captain of the Imperial Guard had earned me quite a bit of goodwill. Everyone knew about the magic he wielded, the way he could make the ground shake. The numbers of my father's soldiers he'd defeated seemed to grow with each retelling. Doubtless they'd felt a little safer, knowing that Jovis was on their side.

And me? I was the Emperor's daughter, the wielder of bone shard magic, the one people were still uncertain they could trust. I'd had to fight for the support of the governors. Everyone thought I had more power than Jovis did, and worse, they expected more of me.

I was tired of fighting.

I chose my words carefully. "I would not have sent him away unless I could no longer trust him to do what was best for the Empire and his people. I need those in battle I can trust. We don't have a lot of room for error."

It was the truth – as close as I could get to it – though it seemed to bolster their confidence only a little. Naming the Shardless Few as my enemy would garner me little sympathy, no matter how true it was. Saying that he'd lied to me, that he'd been a spy, would only make me sound too self-involved.

"Better to have those you rely on by your side," Ragan said, his youthful face solemn. "It's for the best, I'm sure."

Urame pressed her lips together – she knew the odds better than most. "I hope this works," she said.

"Thank you for your trust in me," I said, the bag of shards still in my hand. "I did come here intending for none of your shards to be used again."

"And I intended not to be victim to a siege of constructs," she said lightly. "I'm ordering as many of the farmers inside the palace gates as can fit, and telling the rest to go to the harbor or a neighboring town. Yeshan, your general, has arrived, along with her troops. Keep your word, save Gaelung and I'll count it a fair bargain."

She bowed, I inclined my head and she left. A faint, musty smell rose from the corpse. However fresh it was, it couldn't have been that fresh. It was a middle-aged man, a bloody wound at his temple, his eyes closed and face slack. I went to the desk, took out a piece of paper and began to write out some basic commands, trying to figure out how to best use my sixteen shards. I paused, my pen above the paper.

Ragan hadn't left. His ossalen wound about his feet.

"Did you need something?" I said, twisting in my chair.

He lifted a finger. "Ah, it's not what I need. Not exactly. I thought we should discuss strategy. If the army attacks tomorrow, we may need your skills. Your Alanga ones."

There were too many things to hold in my head at once. I rubbed my temples. "Ragan, I appreciate your help and that you're here at all, I really do. But the fact of the matter is – I don't know much of what I'm capable of. I'm relying on you." I still remembered the guard spitting on Meraya's body, the word

"Alanga" like a curse. They wouldn't accept me if I revealed what I was.

"You should practice," he said.

I looked at him and then the pouch of shards and the corpse.

"When you have the time," he amended. "I'll draw up some of my own plans."

"Make your plans then," I said, turning back to the desk. "We can discuss later tonight."

He hesitated at the door, Lozhi on his heels. "I *am* sorry about Jovis," he said. "I know how hard it is to realize that you can no longer trust someone. Life in the monastery . . . it was not as easy as people think it is. I had to learn that no one would help me. I had to help myself."

Something in his tone made me turn back around, only to find the door clicking shut. I frowned. I'd have to ask him more about that later. If there was a later. I put my pen to paper.

One shard for obedience to me. Another three for basic combat skills. He'd have to be more sophisticated than her constructs in case he got caught. Twelve left. I wished I'd had the fortitude to examine Bayan's shards before I'd burned his body. I could have picked out the ones that gave him the ability to create his own constructs. But I hadn't thought I'd need those skills again.

Any commands I verbally issued could not be too complicated and would only hold for so long, so I had to rely on commands written into shards.

I could start with a command to rewrite any construct this one encountered, and from there add reference shards. But adding too many reference shards beneath a command often destabilized it, especially if the reference shards contained further commands.

Bayan had been written with the ability to learn. I couldn't do that with only twelve shards.

That left me with step-by-step directions. If I combined that with some reference shards, I might be able to make this work.

I pulled out some of the books I'd brought with me, scouring the pages for sophisticated commands – words that had the most meaning contained in the least amount of space. My head ached and I'd only just begun. If only I'd had more time and the full use of my father's library! Was there a word that described the calm state of mind one had to enter before reaching into a construct? Did a construct even need to have a calm state of mind if they didn't have much of a mind?

These sixteen people, including Urame, were bargaining away pieces of their life in the hopes I could save them.

I wrote down a few combinations.

If you see another construct and no other constructs are watching, reach into that construct. Too wordy – it would barely fit. *When you are two paces away from another construct, check if you are watched. If you are not watched, reach into the construct.* That would take two shards, but it didn't mention any state of mind. I could hope it wasn't necessary. And then there was the matter of the modification.

The enemy constructs would have an obedience shard near the top, telling them to obey Nisong, with the identifying mark carved into bone by her name as she held the shard to her chest. I'd changed the identifier on my father's constructs, making myself the one they should obey. But I wouldn't be there in the construct camp. That wasn't a strategy I could use.

They'd be programmed to attack. I wasn't sure how many shards Nisong had been able to gather or how complex her commands would be. I could have my construct go about and remove shards, replacing them in the wrong spots. Her army would begin falling apart. But it wouldn't be able to destroy many before someone noticed and it was caught, its work undone. I had to be subtle.

We were made to be similar, but Nisong's past had made her into a different person. My friendship with Numeen had changed me as well.

But at our cores . . .

I closed my eyes, trying to imagine what commands I would give constructs to fight when I had only a few shards. They hadn't seemed very aware. Their attack command would have to specify people, not constructs. But they hadn't attacked me or Jovis when we'd arrived at the camp to bargain with Nisong. So they were waiting for a command.

When a construct commands you to attack, attack people until asked to stop.

I remembered the modifications I'd made to my father's construct. The obvious solution would be to change "people" to "constructs," but the words weren't at all similar. I picked up the books again, flipping through them to try and find something that might jog loose an idea. Outside, the sky had begun to darken, clouds rolling in from the west. Thrana went to the window, closing the shutters. "Rain coming," she said. It would make it easier for my construct to sneak into the encampment. There was a small bit of luck, at least. "Do you think Jovis and Mephi are well?"

I pressed my fingers into the sides of my nose, drawing in a sharp breath. "I don't know." I'd been able to put them from my mind for a moment while I'd been concentrating. The pain rushed back in, a flash flood into a hollow basin. I'd spent far more time than I'd realized with Jovis, translating his book, discussing politics with him on the ship, learning how to use my Alanga gifts.

His book.

Had he left it with me? I went back to my locked chest, digging around in the bottom. There. He'd left it behind. I pulled it free, flipping through pages and notes as quick as I could read them.

A word caught my eye. I'd translated it as "neighbor". It was similar to "people" – though a bit longer. *When a construct commands you to attack, attack people until asked to stop.* If I had the construct change "people" to "neighbor," her army of constructs would attack itself when commanded. A less elegant solution than having them attack other constructs, and there still might be people caught in the crossfire, but it would work.

It had to work.

I wrote down other commands in a frenzy. A command to walk until it reached the camp and then to mingle. A command to search for the correct shard in each construct, referencing the words it would look for. A command to use the engraving tool to change the words. Another to replace the shard.

I still had several shards left, so I used those to address issues that might arise – hiding if it was caught, behaving like the other constructs to minimize suspicion, listening for nearby voices.

Finally, I was satisfied and began to carve. It was a crude construct, and would still be third-level by my father's reckoning. Yet even his third-level constructs could repair others. I'd forgotten what a joy it was, losing myself in this work, putting together the pieces like a complex puzzle. There was a logic and simplicity in it that didn't exist in politics and governance. I couldn't please everyone I needed to, no matter how hard I tried. This, though, bent to my will and my thoughts. I could understand a little why my father had locked himself away, why he had let his constructs control the Empire. People were fickle, confusing, disloyal. People lied to you. People betrayed you.

Constructs followed commands and any fault they produced was yours and yours alone.

Servants knocked at the door, brought me food and tea without speaking to me. I barely ate. The sky outside grew dark; rain pounding at the shutters and leaking onto the windowsill.

I finished pushing the last shard into the corpse by the time Urame knocked. "Is it done?" she asked when she entered. She handed me the engraving tool I'd requested. Not as elaborate or as sharp as mine, but the construct would still be able to use it.

Thrana sat behind me; I leaned into her fur, exhausted. "Yes. If you wait with me a moment, we'll see if I've done a good enough job."

Urame was much more surprised than me when the construct opened his eyes and rose into a sitting position. I knew I did good work; better than Bayan had ever done. If I were given time and the tools, I could be better at it than my father was. "We need to take him to the gates and set him toward the encampment," I said. "He'll do the rest."

Urame's fingers touched the scarred spot behind her ear.

"It will be only for one night," I reassured her. "It will shorten your life, yes, but only imperceptibly."

"And this is why my ancestors followed the Sukais," she said, more than a little awe in her voice. I wondered if Iloh would have shown me more respect if I'd demonstrated my power to him. He was an opportunist, and Phalue might still soften to me. If I could save Gaelung and defeat the constructs, there was a chance everyone would fall in line. I could save the Empire.

Urame and Thrana accompanied me to the gates, the rain soaking into my slippers as soon as I stepped foot from beneath the palace's roof. The guards watched from the walls; perhaps some of them had donated their shards. I felt the absence of Jovis then — always a familiar presence at my side or at my back. I hoped he'd at least found a place out of the storm.

I didn't trust him. But I couldn't bring myself to hate him.

I faced the construct toward the construct encampment and placed the engraving tool in his pocket. "Walk east until you reach the construct camp," I said.

We watched until his back faded into the night and the storm, our hopes written into sixteen shards.

41

Nisong

Gaelung Island

She gave command of the sea serpent to Coral. Even with all of Leaf's shards pressed into its body, it was not Leaf. But the beast could talk and follow complex orders. It burrowed into the mud of the jungle, its scaly body winding around the trunks of trees.

"How long am I to stay here after the battle begins?" Coral asked, her hand on the creature's nose. Rain trickled down from above, the sky growing darker. On days like these, it was nearly impossible to tell exactly when the sun had set. It might still be edging its way toward the horizon.

"With luck, you won't need to emerge at all," Nisong said. "I'll linger on the edges of the battle. If things get desperate, I'll send a gull construct for you. But until then, stay hidden."

"And if you do call for us?" the sea serpent asked. Its voice was deep and cold, the words enunciated as though by an orator. Nisong had never heard a sea serpent speak, though she'd heard stories that they could. When she'd been young, she'd doubted them. She didn't now.

"Storm the palace. Kill everyone from the opposing side who stands in your way. Follow Coral's lead."

Coral could sit astride the beast easily and speak into his ear. She'd be safe here, away from the battle. And if Nisong needed the sea serpent, Coral would be safest with him. It was the best she could do. She should have taken more precautions with Shell, Frond, Leaf and Grass. But she'd needed them.

She hoped she wouldn't need Coral.

Impulsively, she reached out, throwing her arms around Coral the way her sister had once thrown her arms around her. The hug was brief, and the woman didn't smell of juniper. But Coral had been there for her since the beginning. "Stay safe," Nisong said.

"You too," Coral responded.

Nisong turned away, her throat tight, and made her way back to the construct encampment. By the time she arrived, the sun had set, the surrounding plains a dark sea punctuated by fire and lamplight. She had to focus. She had to be the leader they needed – a leader who won battles and crushed her opponents.

Constructs had begun to stoke the fires for the evening, sparks and smoke rising into the sky. They'd brought some supplies and had pillaged the rest from the surrounding countryside. Gaelung was ripe for plucking, and the more intelligent of her constructs seemed to take great pleasure in the richness of the food they'd found.

The guards she'd placed around the perimeter only nodded to her as she passed. Leaf would have looked to her, waiting for some encouraging word. Frond would have been passing the time by carving and would have shown her what he'd been working on. But these constructs didn't really know her. She spoke and they obeyed. That was what she was to them.

She chose a spot by one of the fires, the stump of a tree making a decent enough seat. Through the flames she could make out the distant hill where the governor's palace waited. Her cheeks warmed and she held out her hands to feel the heat. When she'd first started this campaign, she'd only imagined herself at the palace, the people bowing before her. Maybe it was fitting, that she should now be alone this near to the end. Still, when she closed her eyes she could imagine Leaf at her side, Grass and Frond bickering over whether a fish should be fried or steamed and Shell sharpening his spear.

It was a pointless exercise. All it did was make her ache. She'd made her choices and she was still convinced they were the right ones.

Something caught the edge of her gaze. She squinted into the camp, scanning between the tents. Constructs ate their evening meals, a few speaking in low voices to one another. One shaped like a wolf idly scratched at an ear. Nothing out of the ordinary. Nisong shook her head. Had she imagined things?

And then she saw it again, and knew why the movement had caught her eye. It was one of the shamblers, slipping between tents, nearly out of view. Nisong frowned. The last command she'd given them had been to wait. She was constantly having to reissue commands to them since their shards were so unsophisticated. But this still seemed too soon.

She rose from her place by the fire.

Constructs nodded to her, moving to give her space. She had to maneuver around the shamblers, who had no spark of recognition in their dull eyes. Smells drifted up her nostrils as she wove through the camp: wet animal fur, smoke, boiled vegetables and rot. The grass had been trampled flat by her troops and it was slick beneath her feet. Nisong found herself creeping forward without meaning to, keeping her footfalls soft and silent.

The moving shambler ducked behind a tent. A middle-aged man with a head wound. She didn't think she would have recognized him – she'd created so many – but it still disconcerted her that she didn't. "Stop!" she called out.

Several other contracts halted in what they were doing. She gritted her teeth and waved them off, hurrying around the corner of the tent. The flap stirred gently in a breeze, but the construct she'd followed hadn't stopped. It strode quickly away, its back turned to her.

It wasn't one of hers.

The realization sent a thrill of anger through her. This was her domain, and this girl-Emperor thought to try and infiltrate it?

She beckoned to a nearby war construct – a hulking bear-like beast. "Pin that shambler down."

It lifted its head from its meal of fish and charged the shambler. Ah, she should have asked a different war construct. The shambler ran and the bear pursued, knocking down two tents in the process. A few remaining constructs from Maila shouted as they darted out of the way. The shamblers stayed put, tangled in the cloth.

Nisong stalked forward, throwing aside the tent cloth to find the bear and shambler tangled beneath. She didn't bother asking it any questions; she plunged her hand inside the body. There were more shards here than in her shamblers, confirming her suspicions. She pulled them free, holding them up to the light of a nearby fire.

The carvings were elegant, the commands smoothly written. She might have admired the craftsmanship if the circumstances had been different. But these shards were not without malice. Lin had given the shambler instructions – instructions to turn Nisong's constructs against her. She found an engraving tool in the shambler's pocket.

The anger turned very quickly to panic. How many of these infiltrators had the Emperor set upon her camp and when had they arrived? She'd thought Lin reluctant to use bone shard magic, but apparently desperation could force the girl's hand. Nisong cast the shards to the ground, grinding them beneath her heel. Every moment that she wasted now could be a moment where more of her constructs were turned against her.

She could go through the shamblers, line them up, examine their shards. It would take time – too much time. Time in which Lin could use them to attack, or to gather more defenses.

"We attack now," she said to the bear construct. "Line up all the war constructs."

She recognized the Maila construct closest to her – Waves. "You get everyone else. I'll handle the shamblers."

Attacking at night would hurt them in some ways. The shamblers were clumsy enough as it was, and couldn't see well in the dark. They'd lose some up the switchbacks. But most of the war constructs could see at night. She'd have to use this to her advantage.

She thought of Coral and the sea serpent, waiting in the woods. As if sensing her thoughts, the gull construct landed on the grass next to her. "Is it time? Shall I fetch them?"

"No," Nisong said. There was the chance that Lin's construct hadn't done much damage yet. They might still be able to conquer Gaelung without the sea serpent. Without Coral.

"Not yet."

42

Jovis

Gaelung Island

When the rain began to fall in earnest, all I could think was that I deserved it. Even in my oilskin cloak, it managed to seep into the crevices of my clothing, making me feel as though I were swimming on dry land. The things Lin had said about me were all true. She was right to send me away, and the rain was just yet another signal that I, Jovis of Anau, was Emperor of Fools. It was a more fitting title for me than Captain of the Imperial Guard.

My mother would be disappointed.

I could find a drinking hall to hole up in for a while, maybe even rest with some hot tea or mulled wine. I'd earned it, hadn't I? I'd broken with the Ioph Carn, failed the Shardless Few and betrayed someone I'd thought could become a friend.

Who was I fooling? I wanted more than just friendship with her. She was not Emahla. She was too sharp, too lonely, too clever. But when we weren't fighting, there was a part of me that felt she understood me. That I could sit in the quiet with her and not feel alone. Every bone in my body screamed the farther away from the palace I walked. Every bone told me to go back, to beg forgiveness again, to dare her to execute me.

But those were the notions of a young man, a romantic one, one who'd not already loved and lost a wife.

Endless Sea, I was tired. Lying for months on end could do that to a man, I supposed.

Mephi trotted next to me, not minding the downpour. Yeshan's army had just finished passing us on their way to the palace, row after row of soldiers, their expressions anxious. We'd waited on the side of the road for them to pass.

Mephi kept looking up at me, and though I didn't return his glance, I knew he was worried. "They are going to fight tomorrow," he said finally. The road to the harbor was unpaved, gravel crunching beneath my feet. The fields around us were still, the farmers retreated into their huts. A few passed us on the road on their way to the palace. They didn't bother glancing up from beneath their umbrellas and their hoods. "We should help," Mephi said.

"I already tried that," I said. "She doesn't want me there."

"But what about everyone else? They want you there."

"Lin can handle it on her own. Ragan will help too. They don't have a lot of soldiers, but she's clever – she'll figure something out." My voice was more confident than I felt.

"Jovis." He swerved in front of me, his paws firmly planted. "You and Lin had a fight. You need to make things right because she needs you there. Everyone does. You can't walk away." There was something odd about his voice, like he was choking on something.

I lifted my foot and darted around him. "This is me, walking away."

He slid past me, his body low to the ground, his ears flattened, jaw clenched. "Very funny. Jovis makes big jokes when he can't face big feelings."

Ouch. So maybe that was true. "Can't you be small again and talk less?" I said. "You were very sweet back then."

He clacked his teeth together. "Even ossalen grow up."

"Grow up into what?"

His ears flew forward, his eyes wide. He cocked his head at me. "Don't know."

I ventured to scratch his cheeks, though he swerved away from me, still not ready to forgive. "The right thing is to go dack – *back*."

He *was* speaking strangely.

"Mephi," I said, exasperated. "Not again. Not *now*." I seized his big head in my hands. "Drop it before you choke."

He narrowed his brown eyes at me, but his jaw shifted and I saw a bulge in his cheek.

"Drop. It."

He spat something onto the ground. "I found it. It's mine now," he said by way of explanation. I knelt to pick it up.

It was a clay flask, a small one, corked at the top. I knew what it held. The memories she'd extracted from Ragan, after taking a sample of his blood. That's why I hadn't been able to find it. Mephi had gotten to it before I had. "Where have you been keeping this?"

He ducked his head low. "Here and there."

Judging by the chipped clay, he'd been stuffing it wherever he could hide it. I wiped the flask clean and pocketed it. "For the very last time, just because you can take someone's things, doesn't mean that you should. I never see you just taking the food from food stalls."

He shook himself, the water spattering against my cloak. "If I did that, they would stop serving you food."

"So you *do* understand about not taking things."

He gave a little shrug as though he could barely be bothered to care. I should have requested a wagon – although I was sure Lin wouldn't have granted one. A few farmers gave me curious looks, though I waved them on when they started to stop. I was in too foul a mood to be decent company for anyone, or to play my role as the folk hero of the Empire. And with an army on their doorstep, no one wanted to press the issue.

At last, where the fields met forest, I found a drinking hall I could regroup in. It was one of those places that looked larger on the inside than the outside, the windows with broad enough awnings that they could stay open during the rain. Inside, it smelled of fish, charred wood and spices. Both Mephi and I shook ourselves off at the entrance, and I hung up my cloak by the door.

"We're closing up soon," said the man behind the counter, his head down as he butchered a goat leg. And then he got a good look at me and Mephi. "Though you're welcome to stay," he said quickly. "It's just – they say there will be a battle tomorrow morning. You . . . probably already know all about that."

If I could have lived without Mephi at my side, I might have left him behind more often just to get a taste of my former anonymity. I let the comment slide. It didn't seem the right time to let the proprietor know that no, I would not be fighting against the constructs – I would be headed to the docks and finding the first ship that would take me off Gaelung. I needed to get back to Imperial, to my own ship. If I could set my feet on its deck, I could figure out what I should do next.

I ordered some mulled wine, smoked fish and rice. There were no other patrons, all of them likely fleeing what would soon be a battlefield. The proprietor lingered after he brought my food, his gaze flicking to my rabbit tattoo as if looking for confirmation.

"They say the construct army is enormous," he said. Sweat beaded at his forehead.

He was looking to *me* for reassurance? I was ill-equipped for that. All of my ideals, my hopes that I could make this a life worth living without Emahla – dashed on the reefs. "Our Emperor is doing the best she can." I tilted my head. "Why are you still here? I'm glad that you are –" I gestured at my plate. "– but shouldn't you be inside the palace or down by the harbor?"

"My wife broke her leg a few days ago," he explained. "An accident while she was trying to retrieve some spices in the attic. She's not in much condition to travel, and we thought – we should be far enough from the fighting, and if we barricade ourselves inside we can stay safe."

No one was safe. I'd seen the size of the construct army. "Our Emperor has some tricks up her sleeve," I said, raising the mug of mulled wine. I hid my involuntary grimace by drinking a sip. Too many tricks, by my liking. I tried to put more cheer into my voice. "Constructs are no match for the men and women of Gaelung." And I'd told myself I was done with lying. Old habits died hard.

He gave me a quick, tight smile before returning to his kitchen.

I let out a breath and handed a piece of smoked fish to Mephi. This, it seemed, was enough for him to finally forgive me. The wine slid past the hollow in my throat, warming my belly if not my heart. What would this man think when he saw me leave and I did not return in the direction of the palace but instead fled toward the harbor with the rest of the citizens? I wasn't one of them, much as I might sometimes wish I was.

He might not know that Lin had Ragan – a replacement Jovis, as it were. Another Alanga with skills more refined than my own. Ragan's memories clicked against something else in my satchel. At the time, I'd condemned Lin's actions because

I knew where they might lead. She might decide to mine my memories, to see what secrets lay in my past, to see if I'd hidden anything from her.

I hadn't cared as much about protecting Ragan from intrusion. I'd wanted to protect myself.

Mephi was chewing the smoked fish thoughtfully, without his usual vigor. "None of this is right," he said.

I pulled the flask from my bag, setting it on the table next to my mulled wine. If I'd been righteous, I would have destroyed it as soon as it left Mephi's mouth. Maybe I didn't want to be a liar anymore, but I certainly didn't want to be a righteous man either. I'd leave that to men like Gio, so convinced of their morality that they'd sail straight into a reef if their heart told them it was ethical.

But did I really want to know what was going on in Ragan's head? Did it matter? He'd had more than one chance to turn on Lin, to turn on me – yet he'd helped both of us. But then, there was the matter of his ossalen. The way he treated the beast never sat right with me.

I spooned some smoked fish onto my rice. Every time Lin drank some of her father's memories, she seemed a little more like him. I wasn't sure if that was the memories or if it was just who Lin was. Did I really want to be more like Ragan – that pompous way he had of correcting facts or laying them out, his ridiculous grin, his sly admonishments? And I wasn't even part of the Emperor's entourage anymore. I wasn't anyone except Jovis, failed folk hero. What would I even do with what I found out?

Always had to know – even if that knowledge wasn't good for me. I broke the seal and pulled out the cork. "Watch my back, will you?" I asked Mephi.

He nodded, his gaze on my food. Well, I could always order more. I tipped the flask over my mouth.

The taste of the milky liquid was surprisingly sweet, but with a rich, coppery aftertaste that made me want to gag. I started to turn to Mephi — he had already slipped another piece of fish from my plate — and then I fell into another body, another place, another time.

Sweat stuck my shirt to my back, the bag of books slung at my side unwieldy and heavy. The hands that grasped at the rocks were mine and not-mine. Ragan's fingers, his bloodied finger-nails, the dirt caked on calloused palms.

"It's here, it's close," I muttered to myself. A trickle of his emotions reached me — frustration, hope, anger. The last loomed over the others, a mountain of anger that shadowed everything else. It rang true with my own anger, and I knew it had been born of similar experiences. Always being pushed aside, of being told I was not enough, of trying and failing to meet expectations that changed with the winds and the tide.

The sun beat down on the back of my neck as I climbed, half-dead shrubs scratching my hands and arms. They'd brought this on themselves. What was the point of having an archive if only a few were ever allowed to read it? So many pointless tests and lofty standards. Knowledge was meant to be shared; it wasn't dangerous. Now what they'd known would come to pass was happening — the Alanga were rising again.

And I meant to be one of them.

I hauled myself up onto a ledge, checking a map and the posi-tion of the sun. There, behind a ragged bush, I found the small opening. It was barely large enough for me to fit through, but the surrounding rocks were smooth.

I pushed the books in first to give myself courage. I removed the pouch of cloud juniper berries and bark and my belt, taking out just one berry and then hiding the rest beneath the bush. And then I crawled inside.

Time lost all meaning in the tunnel. I'd brought food and a lamp, but I didn't know how far I had to go, so both had to be used sparingly. The floor tilted down at times, sometimes so steeply I turned and felt for the bottom with my feet. More than once I wanted to turn back, to crawl back into the light, to return to the monastery.

But the monastery was gone, all the people there dead. I'd be returning to a graveyard. So I continued on into the dark.

After what felt like days, I felt a whiff of cooler air. And then the tunnel opened up into a larger chamber. If the books were right, if I'd found the right tunnel, then this was the place. With trembling fingers, I lit the lamp.

A cavern surrounded me, a pool hollowed out in the middle. Glittering stalactites and stalagmites protruded from the cave ceiling and floor, forcing me to pick my way across the floor. It took some searching to find what I'd been looking for. The pool was wide, though not deep, and there was more ground to cover than I'd expected. But just as I'd resolved to wade into the pool, I found it.

A tiny, curled creature, its eyes still closed, webbed paws twitching every so often and wiping across its face. It was the size of a kitten. Gray fur, long tail, whiskered face. Still young. Old enough to survive on its own, but malleable. My hands reached out to it and then stopped. I couldn't be impatient. There were other parts of the plan to enact.

The cloud juniper berry was bitter in my mouth, the sharp taste of it flooding my mouth and nostrils as I chewed. Strength flooded through my body. I went to the tunnel, took the little pickaxe from my belt, and tore at the rocks.

Some boulders pried loose easily from the surrounding tunnel. Others I had to pull at with all of my enhanced strength. But the tunnel filled. My heart beat wildly as my only means of escape closed off. If this did not work, I'd die down here. I could drink from the pool, and though that would keep me alive for longer than water would – eventually I would starve. The lamp would run out of oil. It would be a long, slow death in the dark.

"The greatest prizes are often born of the greatest risk," I muttered to myself. Was I quoting *Ningsu's Proverbs*? I was more than just a little shaken.

Waiting for the cloud juniper berry to wear off was more difficult than I'd anticipated. I paced the cavern, the light from my lantern casting wild shadows. All I wanted to do was return to the tunnel, pull the stones free of the entrance before I no longer had the strength. I wept, I dug my fingernails into my palms, I ran my hands over and over my close-shorn scalp. No one would care if I died here. But, then, no one would care if I died in the monastery either. They might look for the books, but they would not search for me.

When I felt the last of the strength leave me, I carried the lantern over to the pool. I reached in, cradling the creature in my arms. I lifted it free.

I waited a while for it to wake up. It took a shuddering breath and let out a mewling sound. I held it closer to my chest, hoping it could feel my heartbeat.

"We're in this together," I said to him, knowing the beast could understand me. I stroked the soft fur at the top of his head. "There is no one else."

He blinked, his eyes shining like pebbles by lamplight. He wriggled out of my arms and I let him go. The cavern was broad and took him some time to cross on legs still wobbly and unsure. Instinct guided him to the tunnel.

The way was blocked.

He began to mewl again, a screeching, plaintive sound that echoed from the cavern walls. His soft paws scrabbled at the stones, his nose nudging into every crack, trying to find an opening.

"There is no way out," I said.

The creature stopped at the sound of my voice, one ear swiveling back toward me.

"I am your only way out. Bond with me, and I will have the strength to clear the way."

It wasn't what the beast wanted to hear. He threw himself at the rocks with more vigor, wedging his way between stones, his cries pitiful.

I sat and waited until he'd tired, until his paws were raw and his breathing labored. And then I went to sit with him. He shrank away from me.

"Either we both die or we both live. Which one is the worse outcome?"

He lifted his trembling nose, the skin on the end rubbed free. And after a long moment, he placed a paw on my knee.

"Lozhi," I said, naming him.

He looked at me with sad, solemn eyes.

"You will grow to love me," I said, and I knew, from all the reading I'd done, that it was true.

The cave disappeared. I was not Ragan. I was Jovis, sitting at a table in a drinking hall, my hands shaking and my breath coming in ragged gasps. "He didn't get to choose," I said, and it felt like something made even more awful by saying the truth out loud. I ran a hand through my hair, relieved to find it loose and curly and not shorn short.

I downed the rest of the wine in one gulp, trying to steady myself. The monastery hadn't sent Ragan. He'd stolen from them, he'd taken the knowledge they'd deemed forbidden, and he'd used that knowledge to coerce his ossalen into bonding with him.

"Ragan isn't who he says he is," I managed. I reached for my plate, but Mephi had already eaten what remained. His head swiveled toward the palace.

"Lin and Thrana are in danger."

I rubbed at my temples. "She doesn't want me there." But she didn't know about Ragan, either.

Mephi put a paw on my knee, and I couldn't help but feel the echo of Ragan's memory. "What was your oath when you became Captain of the Imperial Guard?"

I remembered that day, the crowd singing the folk song about me, the solemnity of Lin's face, the feel of the uniform around my shoulders. "She had me swear my loyalty. To her . . . and to the people." I'd lied about my loyalty to her, but I'd gone to Imperial intending to help the citizens of the Empire. That was an oath I could still keep, and until Lin, I'd always kept my promises.

She might want to have me executed, but she'd risked everything to tell me the truth. The least I could do was return the favor.

I picked up my pack and tossed some money on the table to pay the proprietor. "Shut the doors and lock the windows," I told him. "It'll be a busy morning."

43

Ranami

Nephilanu Island

"I have to go." Phalue had spoken the words into the darkness, late at night.

Ranami had been awake, though, and she reached over to draw her wife close. She didn't need to ask where Phalue meant to go, or what she meant to do. "I know." And then they'd both drifted back to sleep.

Now, in the harsh light of day, the words didn't seem quite so noble. Now, they filled her with dread. Phalue sat with her sword on her lap, her armor strapped on, sharpening the blade with a whetstone. She'd always liked seeing to her own weapons and armor. It helped to ground her, she'd said. And Ranami had always watched, half-indulgent, half filled with wonder that this woman was her wife.

But that sword wouldn't be used in a friendly bout against Tythus, and the armor wouldn't be protecting her from blows that weren't intended to kill. Ranami was supposed to be writing a letter to Gaelung. She was supposed to be putting things in order in case the worst happened. In case she had to take over as governor. Every time she laid pen against parchment, her stomach churned.

She wasn't sure which was worse: to be the one who left or to be the one left waiting.

Phalue paused. "Any word on Ayesh? Has she come back yet?"

Ranami shook her head. "No. The guards haven't seen her either."

Phalue's shoulders slumped. "Ah. I'd hoped . . . since I'm leaving . . . "

"Perhaps she's found out all she was asked to," Ranami said before she could stop herself. It was an unkind thing of her to say, and she knew it. Phalue cared about Ayesh, had developed a bond with her. And Ranami had tried, but couldn't seem to help closing off pieces of herself whenever she spoke to the girl. Each time she'd spoken to Ayesh, she'd felt like a puppet, being pulled by distant strings. She should be kinder, more understanding. They'd come from the same sort of place, after all.

But maybe that was the problem.

"She's not the spy," Phalue said, frustration in her voice. "She might be a bit odd, but the girl is harmless. If taking extra food makes her feel a bit more secure, then let her do it. I know you saw her wandering the halls, but would you have done any differently had you been in her place? She's only known the streets."

And that was what Ranami kept circling back to. If she'd been Ayesh, she would have done anything. She'd been Ayesh, and she'd done things she now felt ashamed of: stealing from those weaker than her so she could live, lying, being selfish, keeping an apprenticeship where she'd been mistreated. She hadn't expected that bringing a street urchin into their home would bring it all back. Yet there it was — all the pain of a long childhood spent just trying to survive.

"I would have done worse than that," Ranami said, her throat tight. "I would have cut you for a piece of bread if someone had told me I could have one off you."

Phalue set down her sword and sheath and came to sit next to Ranami on the bench. "Ranami." She took her hands. "That's not your fault, you know. None of it is. If there's anything you've taught me — this is the first thing. You were a child, you were hungry, you were desperate. It doesn't make you a bad person."

Hot tears pricked at her eyes. She'd felt so angry about her past for so long. This was different, and she wasn't sure what it meant. "I don't know if that's true."

Phalue squeezed her hands. "I know it's true."

Why did crying make talking so much harder? She looked to the ceiling and took a few shuddering deep breaths. "Every time I look at Ayesh, I see myself at her age. I don't know how to trust her because I couldn't trust myself back then. I know you care about her. I know we said we would adopt an orphan, and she seems a good candidate. But how can I be a parent? Even you had a better example than I did. I don't know what I'm supposed to do, or how to do it right. I can help you take over Nephilanu, but I don't know how to talk to a child." She was talking in circles; nothing she said made sense.

Phalue's callused thumbs wiped the tears from her cheeks. "We'll figure it out together."

"If you come back," Ranami said.

"I'll come back," Phalue said. "What could keep me from you?"

Imprisonment, war, death. But Ranami didn't say any of this out loud. Giving voice to these fears would make them feel all too real. So she focused on something else. "And what of Gio? He'll try to take Nephilanu."

"I can't stay," Phalue said, running a hand through Ranami's hair. Ranami leaned into her touch, wishing it could last for ever. "You know that. If he takes Nephilanu, he takes Nephilanu. I'll leave some guards. If Gio comes for the palace, there's not much that can be done except closing the gates and hoping for the best. Take the back way out. Stay safe."

"So the Shardless Few get Nephilanu in the end?" It was the fate Phalue had unwittingly spared herself from when she'd convinced Tythus to free her from the dungeon. Now she walked into that fate with clear eyes.

"Watching my father and reading and listening to you ... if there's one thing it's all taught me it's that if I try too hard to hold on to power at the expense of everything else, in the end that's all I'll have: power."

"But that's like winning the battle and losing the war."

"I have to stand by my convictions. I won't pick and choose when it's convenient for me, not like Gio."

Ranami closed her eyes, focusing on the touch of Phalue's hand against her cheek, the leathery scent of her armor. When Phalue had finally come to understand, when she'd read all the books Ranami had asked her to, when she'd apologized and asked Ranami to marry her for the thousandth time – she hadn't foreseen this outcome. She'd thought their struggles were over. She'd thought they would tackle Nephilanu's problems as one and come out stronger for it.

Instead, they were being parted, the future and fate of Nephilanu in question. Phalue rose, as if to emphasize that point, picked up her sword, and sheathed it. "There. Ready."

Ranami wanted to ask for one more night together, one more morning, one more afternoon. There was never enough time. But the guards were waiting, the ship was at the harbor, and an army was fast approaching Gaelung. They'd need to use most of their witstone stores to get there in time. She took in a deep breath, held it, then let it out slowly. Wan morning light from the window limned Phalue's figure, catching in the scratches on her armor, highlighting her high cheekbones, her full lips, her fierce brows.

"You look ready to fight the constructs all on your own," Ranami told her. She'd sent letters to other islands, stating Nephilanu's intention to join the fray. Hopefully they would not be the only island to assist Gaelung.

Phalue tugged on the straps of her pouldrons and paused. "Could you look for Ayesh while I'm gone? See if you can find her? I shouldn't have grabbed for her bag. Tell her I'm sorry? Tell her I'll be back to finish training her."

"I'll look for her," Ranami promised. "I'll keep her safe, if she'll let me."

Some of the tension fled from Phalue's shoulders, a weight lifted. "And find the spy while you're at it?"

If it wasn't Ayesh, then who was it? Ranami had been forming theories, but the only other person that made sense was one she couldn't reveal to Phalue. Not until she knew for sure. "Should I add that to the list?" she said lightly.

Phalue touched a finger to her chin, considering. "Is there a cost associated with finding the spy?"

She couldn't help the bitterness that crept into her voice. "According to Gio, there is always a cost."

Phalue laughed. "Don't let him get to you, even if he does have an army at his back. Old men always think they know better than everyone else, even when the world has long since changed around them." She held out a hand and Ranami rose and took it.

In the courtyard, the guards had lined up. Some had already made their way to the ships and the supplies had been carted into cargo holds, but the remaining contingent of guards were meant to act as an escort. They'd make a bit of a spectacle of it – people loved spectacle. The rain of the wet season had died down to a drizzle this morning. Once in a while, the sun even peeked through the clouds. It was an auspicious day to leave for battle, Ranami could admit that.

Tythus waited at the head of the guards. His wife and two children stood off to the side. In the time since Phalue had taken over as governor, she'd had them to dinner twice at the palace. Ranami found the woman similar to Tythus: good-natured, kind, humble. It was a different sort of pairing than Ranami and Phalue, but worked just as well. Better, perhaps.

Tythus's wife had her hands on the shoulders of her two young sons, one of whom looked about to cry.

"You don't have to come with me," Phalue murmured to Tythus as they approached him. "There's a lot you're leaving behind."

"I'm not special," he said with a shrug. "We're all leaving loved ones behind. They're certainly safer here than at Gaelung." He looked to the sky. "Best be leaving soon, before the weather changes. You never know, in a wet season. There's always a storm around the corner. May the winds be favorable."

"And the skies clear," Phalue responded.

Ranami smoothed the turmeric-yellow skirts of her dress with her free hand. It was the same dress she'd worn when they'd wed, trimmed now to above the ankle to avoid the mud. It felt odd to wear a celebratory dress to see her wife off to battle. She didn't feel celebratory.

Phalue led them through the palace gates and onto the switchbacks. They'd turned two corners when Ayesh appeared from around the bend, shield strapped to her arm, bag in hand.

She froze when she saw them, her eyes darting from one side to the other. For a moment, Ranami thought she might dart into the bushes. There was no reason for her to run, but Ranami understood how this looked to a skittish street urchin — a contingent of fifty guards, all in armor, all marching in unison down the path, inevitable as an approaching tsunami.

"Wait," Ranami called out.

The guards behind them halted.

Phalue shifted from foot to foot. "You should go talk to her," she said. "I was the one who tried to take her bag. And you . . . you're both orphans. Can you, please?"

What could she say to the girl that Phalue couldn't? Ayesh had taken to Phalue like she was a treasured auntie. Ranami just felt strange and awkward around her. She'd been a child, once. Strange, how she no longer knew how to talk to them.

She took a step forward before she could convince herself otherwise. She came at the girl a little sideways, her gaze only glancing off of Ayesh's face, as though she were approaching a skittish cat.

"Where are you going?" Ayesh asked when Ranami was close enough.

"I'm not going anywhere," Ranami said. "But Phalue is going to help fight off the construct army at Gaelung. Surely you've heard?"

Ayesh pressed her lips together. "I don't always talk to the other orphans. I keep to myself. It's not that I don't like them, it's just—" She stopped herself, her hand tightening around the bag. Of course. Why hadn't Ranami considered this before? Ayesh was from Unta, had left any friends she'd had there to die so she could save herself. The same guilt that plagued Ranami had found its hooks in another orphan. Ayesh had lived. Ayesh had access to a palace. But she'd done things she regretted to get here.

"Phalue is sorry she tried to take your bag."

Ayesh only nodded. She peered around Ranami. "No more lessons?"

"One of the guards can teach you if you'd like."

Ayesh screwed up her face and Ranami laughed. For the first time, she felt a kinship with the girl. She could see a future where Ayesh came to live with them, where she became a mother to her. Not just another item added to a list, but a growing, changing person – one who needed both Phalue and Ranami. If she could learn to forgive herself for the things she'd done in the past, she could forgive Ayesh. Yes, the girl might be hiding things; yes, she might be a bit odd, but Ranami was no better. It had taken for ever for her to confess to Phalue what life had been like for her on the streets. She'd wanted to move past it by forgetting it. Instead it had lingered like a bandaged wound she'd never cleaned. Airing out her troubles had made them feel a little less painful.

This was something she could teach Ayesh.

The girl's stomach growled. Ayesh didn't seem to notice. Her hair had begun to grow longer, and her hollow cheeks had filled in a bit, but there was still a way to go before she would stop looking like she was on death's doorstep.

Ranami leaned down. "You know, you don't have to live on the streets if you don't want to. You can come live with us if you'll have us."

Ayesh frowned, as though she couldn't believe what she was hearing. "What? You want to adopt me or something?"

Ranami looked back at Phalue for confirmation. Her wife nodded. "Yes, exactly that."

"But I ... " Ayesh waved her shield arm around as though that explained everything. "What would you want with me? I'm twelve. You could find someone younger, someone with both hands. Someone who didn't steal things. Someone from Nephilanu, not Unta. I don't even belong here."

"You don't have to decide now," Ranami said.

Ayesh looked at her as if she'd grown a second head. "No, I'll do it. I mean, if you'll have me, yeah." She marched past Ranami to Phalue, craning her neck back to look the woman in the eye. "Don't die on Gaelung."

Phalue gave her a solemn nod. "Don't beat the guards too many times at sparring; it wounds their egos."

The girl's face split into a grin and she wrapped her arms around Phalue's waist in a brief hug before darting past her toward the palace.

There was one thing done, one thing taken care of. There were still the land grants for the refugees from Unta to be written, the unearthing of the spy and – oh yes – keeping Gio from overthrowing Phalue's place as governor.

The road to the harbor felt like both the longest and shortest trip Ranami had ever taken. She wanted to remember each moment that she held Phalue's hand in her own, each crease of her palm, each callused finger. People had come out onto the streets to see them off, leaving a narrow pathway for them to walk. The press of them, their curious faces, it was almost more than Ranami could take. She knew, better than anyone, how quickly they might turn if Gio found the right pressure points. Phalue smiled and pressed her hand over her heart in greeting as they passed. To her, they were a safe haven. She would always feel more assured of her place among them than Ranami ever would.

And she would be expected to rule them in Phalue's stead.

The boards of the docks creaked as they made their way to the ship, their weathered surfaces warped by years of salt water and rain. Phalue stepped to the side when they reached the ship, letting her guards pass her up the gangplank.

A small crowd of people had followed from the city, come to see off their governor. "You didn't have to go too," Ranami whispered as Phalue pulled her in for an embrace. "You could have just sent the guards. Tythus can lead them."

"Remember what Ningsu said about cowards," Phalue said into her hair. "My place is with them."

"You could stand to be a little bit cowardly," Ranami said faintly.

Phalue's chest rumbled as she laughed. "Look after our girl. Keep an eye on Gio. Stay safe."

And then she was gone, walking up the gangplank with Tythus, leaving the scent of cured leather in her wake. Ranami curled her fingers into her palm, aware of the emptiness there, the coolness of the air rushing in to fill the space her wife had been.

"I love you," Phalue mouthed to her as the crew set about pulling up the gangplank and hoisting the sails.

Ranami barely managed to mouth the sentiment back. She was watching her heart, her life, sail away on that boat. Even with Ayesh, even with the servants, the palace would feel empty tonight – a seashell discarded on the beach.

White smoke billowed from the brazier on deck, bringing with it a breeze that filled the sails. Three other accompanying ships set their witstone ablaze, and soon they were skimming forward across the Endless Sea, intermittent rays of sunlight turning the cresting waves to gold.

Ranami watched until she could no longer see the faces of those on board, and then she could no longer make out the people at all. Only sails and wood and an ache in her belly and in her chest. Finally, she turned to make her way back into the city and to the palace. There was still work to be done, no matter how much she wanted to just curl back into bed and smell Phalue's waning scent.

She passed the old flat she used to live in, above the merchant who sold steamed buns. He nodded to her and smiled. "Sai," he said. It still felt odd and uncomfortable to be referred to thus, though she smiled back.

This was where it had all begun, where she'd written to the Shardless Few, hoping to help them, hoping they could help her. She'd believed so stridently in their goodness, in their willingness to do whatever it took to make things right. When she'd turned down their plea to help them remove both Phalue and her father, she'd thought that was the end of it.

And then Gio had tried to have Phalue killed.

Ranami curled her fingers into fists. How could she still have faith in the Shardless Few or the man who led them? Gio was so single-minded, so focused on the idea of bringing down the Sukai Dynasty and installing a Council in its place. He would see Phalue removed not because they saw things differently, but because the paths they wanted to take to get there diverged. How utterly foolish!

It surprised her only a little when she found her feet turning onto the path out of the city, past the Alanga ruins, toward the Shardless Few hideout. She shouldn't go alone. Phalue had once told her that she saw Ranami as a soft, delicate thing she couldn't touch too firmly, lest she cut herself on the blades hidden beneath. She felt all the sharp edges of herself protruding now, like quills raised on a porcupine's back.

The way was farther than she'd remembered; it had been a long time since she'd visited. That assassination attempts against Phalue had broken her bonds with them. She marched into the forest, heedless of the damp vegetation slapping against her shins. Her wedding dress would be ruined, but she couldn't bring herself to care. She was a brazier of witstone burning, the wind at her back.

The cliff face was as she remembered it, though the vines climbing its surface were thicker in the wet season. It took her three tries to find the crack. "It's Ranami," she called into the crevice. "I'm coming in."

She slid through the crack, heedless of the stone ripping at the hem of her dress. A lantern swung about as the crevice widened into a cave, blinding her momentarily.

"Ranami?" The voice was hesitant, though she recognized it. Atash. A younger recruit of the Shardless Few, saved from the Tithing Festival at eight years old. The Shardless Few were all he'd known since then. "What are you doing here?"

She tugged at her dress, straightening and brushing at a smear of mud. That wasn't coming out without some work. "I'm here to see Gio."

"He's not expecting you," Atash said.

Just a boy, really. "That's unfortunate," Ranami said, sweeping past him.

"Wait," he called after her, dogging her steps. She didn't mind – he had the lamp and she needed the light, so she let him follow her. "He's not supposed to be disturbed."

"So he's in one of his secret rooms."

Atash's mouth clamped shut as he realized, too late, he'd given her exactly the information she'd wanted. Ranami snatched the lamp from his limp fingers and made her way into the Alanga tunnels. Mostly the Shardless Few used the surface-level corridors. But Gio was able to access some of the deeper rooms, the secret of which he'd not divulged to her or anyone she knew.

She took the steps down to the next level two at a time. The walls here looked smooth, but she knew better. "Gio!" she called out. "I know you're in one of these rooms." She wondered if he could even hear her through the stone – but if she were worried about making a fool of herself, she'd already done so. "Come out!"

And then she saw the seam of one of the stone doors. He'd left it ajar. She was dimly aware of Atash behind her, hands flailing around her as though unsure of whether he should try to physically stop her. Let him try if he dared. She marched forward and pushed the door open.

In her anger, she wanted it to fly open, but stone was heavy, and it rolled forward with the lazy precision of a tortoise. Still, Gio seemed surprised to see her, and that was gratifying enough. The room was lit with several lamps, though it was mostly empty. Gio stood by a shelf of old and weathered wood, sorting through books and objects she didn't recognize. Alanga things. His gaze flicked behind her, to Atash, an eyebrow raised.

"I tried to stop her," he said, though his voice sounded weak.

Gio put a book back onto the shelf. "It's not your fault. Ranami is still one of us, even if she no longer thinks she is."

His words didn't hurt in the least. She was not some pet, begging her master's favor.

"I just watched my wife sail away to Gaelung," Ranami said. "And here you are, cozy in your shelter, waiting out the storm."

He rolled his shoulders in a shrug. "Isn't that what the wise do: wait out the storm?"

"Not when there are people out in it that need your help."

He sighed, a weary sound, and Ranami remembered what Phalue had said about old men. "There will always be people who need my help. I can't heed all of them."

"So instead you just pretend they aren't calling out for it? Instead you'll bring your army to Nephilanu and attack us? What did the Sukais do to you, Gio?"

"They've subjugated the people they were meant to rule."

"No." She knew this went deeper than that. She should have realized it when he'd told them that all of the Sukais lied, but she'd not peeled back the layers of that statement until now. "Not what they did to the people of the Empire. What they did to you."

His lip trembled for a moment, then stilled. "I don't know what you mean."

"Is everyone defined by the legacy of their forebears to you? You want Phalue gone. You want Lin gone. Did you ever consider they could be different from their fathers? And what of me? My parents abandoned me. Am I now doomed to abandon any child I adopt? Why don't you think things can be different? What can't you let go?"

"If you knew the things I've seen—"

"Well, I don't!"

"They killed everyone I ever cared about," he snarled, his eyes wide. The scar over his milky eye pulsed with his heartbeat.

Ranami's anger swelled. "We've all suffered – but because you think you've suffered more, that gives you a right to dismiss what others are going through? Both the Emperor and Phalue are risking their lives to help Gaelung. I don't know Lin's motives, but I know Phalue is going because she can't turn her back on them. When the people of Gaelung are slaughtered, do you think they'll only see the construct army as their enemy? No. You think you're saving them, but you're the one who's wrong. You're not some hero, bringing them freedom and justice. You're the villain, Gio.

"They will know you could have helped. Instead, you chose to do nothing."

She whirled, shoving past Atash at the door and making her way to the exit.

If Phalue died, if she didn't come back from this, Ranami would make sure everyone knew – the whole Empire – what a fraud the leader of the Shardless Few was.

What a coward.

44
Lin
Gaelung Island

The soldiers Yeshan brought couldn't fit inside the walls of the palace; they arranged themselves on the plateau above the switchbacks, setting up their tents with impressive efficiency, their lanterns like fireflies in the darkness.

"You should sleep," Ragan said from behind me.

After I'd sent out the construct, I'd taken Ragan and met with Yeshan, going over the specifics of her plan – memorizing where she wanted to send her troops so whatever I did wouldn't interfere with them. And then I'd forced down a bit of food and had come up to the ramparts. Outside, the torrential downpour from earlier had slowed, my oilskin cloak keeping the worst of it out. Thrana sat next to me, her head now cresting mine.

Ragan's ossalen crept hesitantly behind him, his head low, looking around each corner as though it might hold some danger. I was glad Thrana had grown out of her timidity. Thrana lowered her nose to Lozhi's. The creature sniffed once before retreating back behind Ragan's legs. Thrana only rolled her shoulders before turning to look out over the fields again.

"I'll sleep when I can sleep," I said. "Why don't you take your own advice? And don't tell me the cloudtree monks never sleep."

He gave me a tight smile. "No, we are mortal, just like everyone else. I slept a little bit earlier; though you're right, I could use more sleep."

Somewhere out in the dark, my construct was moving among the enemy's camp, turning as many of their kind as possible against them.

I'd explained to my general and to a few others that Ragan had the same gifts that Jovis did, and I knew some of them were making the connection between the ossalen and the magic. They'd assume he had just the earth-shaking abilities, but as soon as he used his magic on water, there'd be more questions to answer. If only there were more time. I might seed the more positive Alanga legends back into the cities and towns of the Empire; I might remind people that the Alanga didn't just destroy – they had also protected. But my father's rhetoric still flowed among the islands like the waves of the Endless Sea, lapping up to shore and wetting the sand.

"With Jovis gone, you'll have to help me," Ragan said, as though he could tell what I was thinking. "If we want to win this."

"Do what you're able to for as long as possible," I said. "I'll help in the ways I can."

A shout went up in the dark, lamps waving around like scattering fireflies. I straightened. "What's happened?"

Both Ragan and I peered into the field below, trying to make out what had caused the panic.

The door into the palace burst open, a soldier standing with a lamp held high, her face fearful. I remembered then how fresh these recruits were, how they'd been rushed through the training. "The general says the construct army is approaching now," she said, her breath short. "They aren't waiting until morning."

"That doesn't make any sense," I muttered.

"Sense or not, it is happening." And then she seemed to realize who she was speaking to. She lowered her head and bowed. "Apologies, Eminence. But they are here." She whirled, her coat swirling behind her as she retreated back into the palace.

Attacking in the morning, when the light was better, would make more sense. They were laying siege to a palace on a hill, replete with its own defenses.

My construct. They must have caught him. Nisong wouldn't know how many I'd sent; she didn't understand my reluctance to use bone shard magic. She would have used all the shards at her disposal. She would have sent fifty constructs.

So she'd decided to take the losses and to attack now.

There hadn't been enough time. My construct would have turned perhaps twenty-five others at most. It would have caused more than just a small scuffle, but Nisong had so many constructs at her disposal. She would have been able to put down this miniature rebellion quickly and with force.

My plan had failed

There was only my handful of soldiers, Urame's guards, Chala's guards and Ragan and me standing against Nisong now.

My bones thrummed, and I felt each drop of water as it hit the backs of my hands. She wouldn't let me live if she won this battle. But that's not what worried me the most. I thought of the paper crane, stained with blood, lying tucked within Nisong's journal in my travel chest. I'd sworn to myself there would be no others like her — and though I found that promise harder and harder to keep, I knew Nisong didn't feel the same way. She saw the crown as her right, the way I once had. Anyone who opposed her, or even those who simply stood in the way, were obstacles to be crushed. She craved destruction the way I had once craved my father's love.

I couldn't let her rule over the Empire, not if I wanted to keep my promise in even the smallest part. "We have to get down there."

Ragan had already turned toward the palace, Lozhi in tow.

I rushed to catch up to him. There was something grim and forbidding in his face, the easy smile a memory as faded as the dry season after a wet season rain. Lozhi looked at his face and shrank back, ears low and tail tucked in. There was something familiar in that expression. I'd not seen Ragan and his ossalen interact much. They were consistently apart, and Ragan didn't often talk about Lozhi. I'd always supposed that Ragan's teachings had directed him to behave differently with Lozhi, and that this was superior to the way I'd interacted with Thrana. Was this why the Alanga had been depicted without ossalen? Had they kept theirs shut away the way Ragan did?

But there wasn't time to examine the bond between ossalen and Alanga.

The gates were open, and down in the crush of things I could hear the panicked voices, the captains directing their troops, the creak of armor and the sound of steel being unsheathed. Archers hurriedly strung their bows with trembling fingers. No one looked much to me, but then, I still wore the plain oilskin cloak over my finery.

Urame, however, noticed me. "They're marching here, Eminence," she said as she approached. "The full force of them. And they do not look much diminished. It will take them time to wind up the switchbacks, but your construct didn't work."

Even now, I wanted to bite back, to tell her it had – Nisong had just discovered it sooner than I'd anticipated. But what was the point? The end result was the same. We were facing down a force we couldn't win against. "Ragan can shake the earth," I said. "He's even more competent than Jovis. We can get through this."

I saw the despair on her face and knew it didn't matter. There were too many constructs bearing down on us, determined to make Gaelung the latest in their string of conquests.

"I'll stand here with you," I told her.

"Then you'll stand with me to watch my palace and our countryside burn." She opened her mouth, hesitated, but then continued. "Jovis is gone, then?"

I hardened my heart. "He is."

"He would have given them hope." And she left it at that. She would not countermand the orders of the Emperor. I'd already explained that I could no longer trust him to fight on our side.

Past the brightness of the lanterns in the camp, I began to see pinpricks of light in the distance. They moved like an ocean of stars, a high tide coming across the fields to drown us all. Perhaps Jovis had been right. Perhaps I should have stayed back on Imperial. Instead, I'd die here with the people I'd sworn to protect, and no one would mourn me.

A shout went up from the opposite wall. Urame whipped her head about. A guard ran to us. "Sai," she said breathlessly to Urame, "someone is coming from the direction of the harbor. A large group."

"More constructs?"

The guard shook her head. "I'm not sure. But they're approaching quickly."

A moment and then more shouts. I strained to hear. "Friendly!" someone was saying. "They're friendly."

I watched the wink of lanterns appear around the bend, my heart daring to hope as they climbed the switchbacks toward the gates. Both Urame and I went down to greet the new arrivals.

They were quicker than the constructs, and they made it to the gates with time to spare.

A tall, broad-shouldered woman led a disciplined group of guards, a man the same size keeping pace next to her. Someone held a lantern near her face.

Phalue.

"This doesn't mean I support your rule," she said gruffly as I approached, Urame on my heels. "I'm just not willing to let people die over my stubbornness." She nodded to Urame. "Looks like you could use some help."

I put a hand over my heart in greeting. "Sai."

"Eminence." Phalue shook the rain from her cloak and brushed a wet piece of hair back from her face. "Tythus here is my Captain of Guard, and he's trained these men and women well. We may not be as many as the constructs, but one of us counts for ten of them." Her guards straightened, chins lifting, the praise bolstering them. They'd follow her into the Endless Sea if she asked them to – I could read it on all their faces.

"My general will know where best to put them." I nodded in Yeshan's direction.

"To put *us*," Phalue corrected. "I may be governor now, but I train just as hard as the rest of them. And Tythus here knows my worth in a fight. If I die, Ranami will know what to do with Nephilanu."

"Thank you for coming," I said, and meant it.

She gave me an odd look, like she'd never expected gratitude from an Emperor. And then she shrugged and turned, leading her guards to where my general was directing troops.

Ragan appeared at my shoulder. "Tell me what I can do," he said.

"Can you send a tremor through the ground to them? Before they get here? Is that possible?"

He nodded. "I have a fair range. But I'll have to get closer. You should come with me."

Urame gave me an odd look, tossing her gaze between the two of us as though trying to catch the joke.

"Yes, I suppose I should," I said, past the uneasiness clawing up my throat. I was the Emperor; I should remain behind the soldiers and the guards. But if Ragan failed, he would need backup.

Urame didn't know that I had the same powers as Ragan did. "Eminence, do you . . . ?" She stopped, unsure of how to phrase the question. "Do you have some means to defend yourself?"

"I do." I put a hand on Thrana's neck, and she bared her teeth in response. It was all I would say on the matter. She would protect me with her life, and I would protect her with mine. I didn't care what Ragan said about ossalen relationships and the nature of balance. "We should go. Before they get here," I said to Ragan.

I felt the gazes of the soldiers as we strode through the camp. Most had finished readying themselves by now, and they stared at Thrana first before they found me. She certainly didn't look like any creature I'd seen before, and though I'd watched her grow somewhat gradually, I could see how her size could be intimidating.

We strode a little way down the switchbacks – just below the plateau on which the soldiers had set up their defense. Rain pattered against my cloak. I could hear my breath echoing inside my hood, warming my cheeks. At the front of the lines of soldiers, I felt alone. Thrana was at my side, but none of these people were here for me, not the way they were for Phalue.

I shivered as a trickle of rain made its way beneath my cloak. "On my word," I said. "When they're close."

I saw Ragan nod out of the corner of my eye. I wished I had more Alanga with me.

I wished I had Jovis.

His face swam into my mind – his haunted expression as he confessed he'd been spying on me. As he told me what he'd written in the letter. He'd seemed genuine.

But he was a liar. All the little encouragements, all the advice – little tricks to worm his way into my heart and my confidence.

So why did I still feel like I trusted him more than I did Ragan?

Ahead of us, the lights swarmed closer. "Get ready," I said.

Ragan lifted his hands, shaking them free of his oilskin cloak. Behind him, Lozhi cowered again.

It came to me in a flash. *I knew where I'd seen that before.* After I'd pulled Thrana from the water. She'd flinched each time I'd raised a hand. While she'd eventually gotten over that, she still flinched a little every time a man raised his hands around her. But while my love and dedication to Thrana had helped to pull her out of her shell, Lozhi remained in his. Ragan's ossalen wasn't shy; he had suffered, and almost certainly by Ragan's hand.

I focused on Ragan again just in time to see him lift his foot, that smile back on his face.

"You—"

The foot came down and the earth shook. I couldn't keep my balance on the muddy switchback. I tumbled down the path, slipping each time I tried to get my feet beneath me. It was too soon – I'd not given him the order. Part of me still dwelt in that confusion. But the rest of me knew, down to my bones, that Ragan had done it on purpose. My back slammed into something, nearly knocking the wind from me.

Thrana, stopping my fall. She curled her body protectively around mine, her hackles stiff as broom bristles as I grasped at her fur to bring myself to my feet. Cold, wet mud slid down my cheek. My hood had torn free and rain sluiced at the back of my neck. The scent of burning oil had faded, this far down.

I couldn't see the expressions on the faces of the soldiers, but

I could see them looking down on me. Ragan was following me down the slope, picking his way easily past the mud and the rocks. He spoke above the wind. "One thing the monks taught me was that history is not a line; it is a spiral." He lifted a finger and then traced a spiral in the air. "We don't repeat moments in time, but we come back around, echoing them. Your ancestors may have massacred the Alanga, but the Alanga are rising again. And here you are – from the bloodline of the Emperor and an Alanga yourself."

"I'm – I'm not," I said, though my denial sounded hollow even to myself. The soldiers were watching; they were listening.

He brought a foot down again, the earth shook, and I fell, barely catching myself on Thrana's side. "The evidence is there," he said. Again, he lifted that finger, as though teaching a lesson. He turned to the soldiers and guards. "Jovis has Mephi. I have Lozhi. We both have gifts. Your Emperor has Thrana. Does it not follow that she has the same gifts? The Alanga gifts? I know you've wondered. Let me give you proof."

This was why he'd chosen this moment to turn on me. If I fought back, if I used everything at my disposal, I'd reveal what I was. I was the very thing my father had taught us all to fear. And I was not a folk hero like Jovis.

Ragan reached into the pouch at his side, popping a cloud juniper berry into his mouth.

I reached into my sash pocket and found the last cloud juniper berry there. If I held out long enough, the construct army would get here, and he'd have other things to worry about. I crushed the berry between my teeth, feeling strength upon strength flooding my limbs.

A few of the soldiers stepped forward, which warmed me, but I held up my hand. "Hold your positions!" I couldn't have the defensive line falling apart just before the construct attack.

"Lin," Thrana said to me. "I'm steadier than you are." She held out a leg.

I realized then exactly how large she'd grown. Part of me would always think of her as the semi-hairless creature I'd pulled out of my father's cavern. I clambered onto her back. Her ribs moved beneath my legs, the muscles of her shoulders sinuous. It felt like the most natural thing in the world – like we were one being.

Ragan shook the ground again and Thrana dug her claws into the mud. We held steady. Still, I had no weapons. I wasn't a warrior. I was a politician, a practitioner of bone shard magic, an Alanga.

I was Lin. And that would have to be enough.

I watched his face, thinking about our prior conversations, about why he'd chosen to attack me. He didn't care about who held the crown. He didn't care if the governors or the Shardless Few deposed me and set no one in my place. At my back, Nisong marched, yearning for a place she saw as hers. Before me, Ragan sought to expose me. Why?

He held out a hand, and water began to gather from the air, from the ground. He watched me warily. "I don't want to hurt you," Ragan said. "Just tell them the truth. Show them."

"The monks will never take you back, but you never belonged with them." I was making guesses, gauging his reaction.

"And you don't belong with these mortals either."

I sucked in a breath. If I showed my people what I was, what I could do, if I was lucky they'd shun me. If I wasn't, they'd try to kill me.

Ragan cast his hand toward the soldiers. "Why are you even here, helping them against the constructs? What do their short lives matter when compared to ours? I read the books my masters forbade me. Lin, I could show you so many things. I could teach you so many things. You just have to be honest with yourself. You just have to be honest with them."

"I don't know what you're talking about." My voice sounded weak and small.

"I could be like Dione. You could be like Viscen. Look at you, fighting in the mud and the muck with the sort of weapons a mortal would use. Why be Emperor? Why rule among these petty beings when you are so much greater than they are? When you are Alanga?"

I could feel my world shrinking as he spoke. He meant to separate me from all the people I'd grown to care about, for it to be just me and him and the other Alanga. "Why can't you just go and leave me in peace?"

He scoffed. "As soon as you show them what you are, do you think they will follow you? They don't care about you. I've seen the way they treat you. Why are you standing up for them? Why are you trying to be like them?"

I wanted to tell him to go. I wanted to tell him to find other Alanga. I wanted to tell him that I would not stand in his way because I'd never asked to be one of the Alanga in the first place. I had enough to deal with just keeping the governors in line, trying to appease them, keeping the Shardless Few from sweeping across the Empire. Why would I want to take on yet another responsibility? Let Ragan serve as a beacon to the emergent Alanga, let him guide them.

But Lozhi stood behind Ragan's legs, tail curled about his tiny body, his blue eyes finding mine.

This was the relationship Ragan wanted between an Alanga and their ossalen. One of dominance and oppression. It was the same relationship my father had had with the citizens of the Empire.

I couldn't absolve myself of responsibility for this. I'd been putting my position as Emperor as a priority, determined to keep it so I could use that position for good. I'd told Jovis he was meant to be a servant of men because that's what I'd wanted for the Empire and the Emperor. For myself. But this was a truth I could not escape from: if I stood against the tyranny of the Empire, then I had to stand against all tyranny.

For Thrana, for Numeen, for Bayan, for all the ones who'd died and suffered.

I shook my head, my bones thrumming. "Because even if I am the Emperor, I am still one of them."

He lifted the water at his feet into a wave, casting it at me, hoping to wash me down the hill and into the approaching constructs. But I could *feel* that water, the same way I could feel the drops of sweat at my brow. I dug a knee into Thrana's ribs and she leapt aside.

Thrana growled, her body humming along with mine. Together we charged at Ragan.

He'd not been ready for me to fight back and was too slow to dodge. I kicked out at him with all the strength of the cloudtree berry and my Alanga magic, sending him tumbling a little way down the side of the hill. He grabbed a bush to slow his momentum. I swung from my perch on Thrana's back, needing to feel the earth beneath my shoes. "My people are on the brink of being overrun, you come to me offering to help and then you *attack* me?" I wasn't just angry at Ragan, it was Jovis too. It was the governors who saw me as no more than an extension of my father.

I was *not* him, and not even his memories could make it so. I softened my words. I might have been more like him if not for Numeen and his family. I'd have become Emperor without any thought for the consequences for the people I ruled. "You could help us. You could protect Gaelung from the constructs. You could have a permanent place at my side; I am not ungracious.

But what gives you the right to treat others even more poorly than your masters treated you?"

A flicker crossed his face; one I recognized – a deep and abiding loneliness, a yearning for love and acceptance in any form. "You don't know what I've been through."

"You could tell me."

He laughed bitterly, holding up a finger. "You try to give me pretty speeches, to inspire me, to *manipulate* me. I've had to claw my way into what I have, and you think what you're offering is appealing at all? I don't care about these *people* or what they think of me." He spat out the words. "I am one of the Alanga. I am above them."

He stuffed more berries into his mouth and slammed a hand into the ground.

The world shook. The palace rumbled, pieces of it breaking off and hitting the ground. Shouts went up from the soldiers, screams from servants somewhere inside. Thrana's head thrust beneath my arm, stopping me from falling down the slope after Ragan. I grabbed a nearby rock to steady myself.

And then another wave of water rose from the ground, hitting me hard in the knees. It swept Thrana's feet from beneath her. I clung to the rock like a shipwrecked sailor and watched with horror as she tumbled into the darkness.

45

Jovis

Gaelung Island

There didn't seem to be a good way to say: "I'm sorry for spying on you. Oh, also, I'm sorry I'm back even though you told me to leave – but Ragan is a serious asshole. Someone should tell you."

Would I even be let back inside the palace? She must have told them all by now that she'd sent me away in disgrace. And if they even let me back inside, would she hear what I had to say before she had me executed?

It didn't matter. I had to try. I'd clung to the idea of finding Emahla again like a lifeboat, and now I clung to the idea that I could somehow fix the mistakes I'd made, that I could still help the people of the Empire.

"She will be mad," Mephi said as he trotted alongside me. "Very mad."

"Not helpful," I said. I'd spent too long in Ragan's memory, and the proprietor of the drinking hall had been loath to disturb me. Night had well fallen by now, the moon providing barely enough light to see by. Most of the houses we passed were silent, their windows dark.

"I wouldn't let her execute you," Mephi said. He jostled my leg with his shoulder.

I almost halted on the path. I'd never thought about what might happen to Mephi if something happened to me. "If I did die, what would you do?"

He swiveled his head to consider me, and then looked out over the fields. "Run away. You are the only reason I'm here."

"And I thought it was the food."

He clacked his teeth at me, shaking his head so hard his ears slapped against his cheeks. "Maybe a little."

We fell silent as we walked. The rain hadn't stopped, and though the road had been laid with gravel, it was still muddy in places I couldn't see well enough to avoid. In the distance, I heard a faint roar. Mephi pricked his ears. "You hear that?" He swiveled his ears away and then forward again, as though checking his hearing.

"I did."

The palace glowed with lamps, though I couldn't see what was happening at this distance. The main gate lay on the other side. Mephi took a step forward, and then another, his neck stretched to its limit. "I think . . . I think there is fighting."

Already? Nisong had given a deadline of morning for Lin's response. Which only meant one thing: Lin's construct had been discovered. My throat tightened. If her construct had been discovered, it must not have gotten far in its task. Gaelung couldn't stand against an army of that size. Not without help. And I doubted Ragan was the help that Lin actually needed.

"We have to hurry." I picked up my pace to a run, Mephi trotting beside me. "Just don't go comatose to grow any bigger on me now. I need you."

"Can't control it," Mephi said. "But I don't think it's time yet."

A small blessing, at least, in a time when everything else was going wrong. The hill and the palace looked too far away; I'd never get there in time. My breathing was ragged in my throat, my feet numb from the rain and the gravel. I stopped twice to lean on my knees and to catch my breath, each time feeling like I was wasting precious moments. Even my Alanga-enhanced strength couldn't force me past my body's limits. And then I took the road around the hill and saw the lights from the construct army.

There were so many of them, all marching in an inexorable wave toward the palace. They'd started up the switchbacks but hadn't reached the soldiers yet.

Then who was fighting?

I started straight up the slope, foregoing the switchbacks. Mud slipped beneath my feet as I climbed, the rain in my eyes each time I looked up. Mephi climbed close beside me, bolstering my steps where he could.

I heard Lin speaking through the distance, though I couldn't make out her words. And then Ragan. Water sluiced over me; I had to cling to the brush to avoid being swept back down the hill. That hadn't been the rain.

All my fears were right: Ragan had turned against Lin. "We're too late," I gasped out, trying to find purchase.

Mephi dug his claws into the dirt, seizing my sleeve with his teeth, pulling me up until my foot met a rock. "Not yet," he said as he let go. "Still time."

I barely saw the next wave of water before it hit us. I clung to a rock, shivering, reaching for that trembling in my bones and feeling only fear. This was more than I'd been able to do with water. I simply didn't have that sort of power, and I wasn't sure if Lin did either. And still the construct army climbed the switchbacks.

Mephi seized my sleeve again, trying to force me to my feet.

"You don't get to give up," he said between his teeth. "What would Emahla say?"

She'd say I wasn't a fighter, and she'd been right, back then. I hadn't been. I'd only wanted to make my way through the world, to find a measure of peace inside it. I might have been shunned at the Navigators' Academy on Imperial, but I'd always had Emahla to return to – my own corner of the world I could build a life around.

She was gone, and I was beginning to find that I'd left her behind. The man she'd fallen in love with? The one who could be content with that measure of peace despite the suffering raging on around it? I could never be that man again. Emahla's death had helped to shape me, and it had shaped me into someone she wouldn't recognize.

Mephi tugged at my sleeve again, a growl low in his throat. "What would *Lin* say?"

Just the sound of her name shocked my heart back to life. Lin didn't know how to give up; that much was clear to me. Even with Ragan turned against her and the construct army on its way, she was still fighting. I felt the thrumming hit my bones, the power surging through me and amplifying each drop of rain that struck my face, making the earth beneath me feel like a living thing, waiting for my command. Lin didn't know who I'd been, but she knew who I was now.

And I *was* a fighter.

A despairing cry from above, and then a shape tumbled down the slope toward us. I recognized Thrana, her body limp.

Without even thinking, I gathered the water around me and used it to break Thrana's fall. She slid to a stop in the wave I'd created, a bush cradling her body. Mephi ran over to her as I found my feet again.

"She's alive," he said. "Go."

I ran up the slope, heedless of my slipping feet and the mud. Light crested the hill – the lanterns of the soldiers lined up on the plateau. I made out two shapes on the switchbacks ahead of them. One stood over the other, hands raised.

The magic gathered in my bones, demanding release. I lifted a foot and brought it to the ground with everything I had.

The entire hill seemed to move, dust rising from the palace as it shook. I kept running as my quake spent itself, and I made my way onto the path. Ragan fell to the ground just as I reached him, the water he'd been gathering flowing away from him downslope.

I took his water, using it to sweep him away like chaff. He fell down the hill. I tried to spare his ossalen but didn't have the control, and the creature tumbled after him.

Lin was already pushing herself to her feet, though I offered a hand anyways. She brushed it aside. "I need to find Thrana."

"She's alive," I said. "Mephi is with her."

She turned narrowed eyes on me. "I told you to leave."

"I . . . drank Ragan's memories," I said. "I came to warn you. He coerced his ossalen into bonding with him."

"Too late. I figured it out on my own."

"Am I too late or just in time though?" I pressed my lips together as she gave me a withering glare.

"I don't want you here," she said, each word a bite meant to wound.

Each word struck true, and I wished I could go back in time all over again. I wished I could take back what I'd done, to have trusted her sooner and to have told her the truth. I couldn't regret what I'd done; there was no way I could have known her intentions so early on. But this was about more than my betrayal. I lifted a hand to the soldiers behind us.

The cheer was deafening.

"*They* want me here," I said. "And if you want to hold this

Empire, if you want to help its people, you'll have to acknowledge that you need me." I reached for her hand but she pulled away. I swallowed past the lump in my throat. Here, standing in front of her, all I wanted was to hold her again, to close the distance between us. My mother had pitied her for how lonely she seemed, how isolated. "You may feel like you are, but you aren't alone."

Her expression softened, the pain in her eyes clear even in the dark. And then she focused beyond me.

I whirled to see Mephi and Thrana crawling onto the path. Both shook off the dirt and the rain. A scratch ran across Thrana's muzzle, and she looked a little dazed, but otherwise unharmed. Lin went to her, climbing onto her back.

There was something about seeing her up there that felt right. Again I wondered what had happened to the ossalen of the past Alanga. Why hadn't I seen them depicted in any of the tales or the artwork? Or had they all treated their ossalen the way Ragan did – coercing them into bonding with them and then hiding them away?

Thrana was getting a little difficult to hide.

I could make out the individual constructs now, shambling their way up the slope. I cleared my throat as both Thrana and Lin towered over me. "I know you meant to have me executed if I returned, but can we call a temporary truce on that? It's a little difficult for me to use my gifts with my head disconnected from my body."

She looked as though she wasn't sure if she should laugh or scowl. "When they're close enough, send them back down the hill. Try not to collapse the palace. There are still people inside."

"I'll do my best, Eminence."

She flinched a little at that. A small part of me hoped that perhaps she still felt something for me. But I had better things to do than to moon over the Emperor like a lovesick teenager. Like keeping myself alive. Like keeping us all alive. Everything else could wait.

My bones thrummed, a low note that only I could hear. I'd acted out of desperation when I'd seen Ragan about to attack Lin. He'd managed much better control than I had; I could learn to do the same. If the great Dione could drown an entire city while saving one fly, I could send my quake out in one direction.

My staff was covered in mud and water; I tried in vain to wipe it down with my cloak. I tapped a foot to the ground, felt the vibration run through the earth. Next to me, Mephi bared his teeth.

"Stay out of trouble," I said to him.

He snorted.

Lin clung to Thrana's neck, whispering in her ear. The constructs crested the last switchback. They wound around the hill like a luminous sea serpent, its body sinuous and never-ending.

My stomach tightened. I might be a fighter now, but I'd never get used to this. I'd much rather be in my mother's kitchen, helping her with her day's work as she scolded me over my studies. And that was saying something; she had quite the capacity for scolding.

I focused on the magic in my bones, the feel of my breathing. Now I could see the blank expressions of the constructs, their tangled hair, the killing wounds they'd received, stitched partially closed.

"Jovis, now might—" Lin said, a note of panic in her voice.

I stamped a foot into the earth.

The tremor rippled toward the constructs, the muddy ground turning into a wave of dirt and rock. None of the constructs tried to avoid it. They fell to the ground, some of them tumbling onto their fellows behind them.

Arrows whipped into the air behind us, metal tips glinting by lamplight as they arced toward the constructs. Another several lines of constructs died. I sent another quake toward the ones that followed. Some managed to hang on and to advance, but arrows, my staff and the teeth of our ossalen picked them off.

We could do this. We could manage to hold them off.

A howl sounded from somewhere behind me. I felt, more than saw, everyone go still. And then the beasts attacked.

They surged up from the surrounding slopes, teeth bared. This was no haphazard attack borne out of panic. Nisong had already laid out her strategy. The shambling constructs were a distraction, meant to pull our attention away. The war constructs were the true threat.

Bears, wolves, cats, giant crabs and spiders. I could only make out pieces in the flashes of lamplight.

Lin drew her engraving tool from her sash. "Kill the shamblers. Keep them at bay," she said to me. "I know how to deal with war constructs."

She leapt away aboard Thrana, and it felt like my heart was leaping away with her. I tore my gaze from the monstrous constructs, focusing on the army of shamblers climbing their way up the hill.

I sent another quake toward them, trying my best to direct it down the path and away from the soldiers behind me. The shambling constructs fell, their feet giving way, some pitching over the slope and onto the switchback below. Mephi darted forward, harrying the ones that made it through. He was the size of a large dog now, and used his horns to his advantage, plowing through constructs as though they were brush.

Something cold and sharp came to rest on my collarbone. "Ah, Jovis. You always should check, you know. Even when you're busy. Alanga are notoriously difficult to kill."

46

Nisong

Gaelung Island

Every blow she struck, every kill she made had a name. For Shell, for Frond, for Grass and for Leaf. Nisong waded into the thick of battle, surrounded by war constructs, putting the force of her anger behind each blow of her cudgel. They should have been here with her. Lin, the Empire, the world had conspired against her. Things would have been different with her friends at her side. Shell would have cooked something filled with hot peppers the night before battle. Frond would have finished his bird carving by now and would be whittling something new. Grass would have gone over her battle plans, sucking at her lip as she read them, age-spotted hands pointing out where improvements could be made. And Leaf would have been at Nisong's side, helping carry out her orders.

Lin spoke of peace, but she'd struck the first blow. Shiyen might have sent them to Maila, but Lin had put the bounty on their heads. The Emperor thought she could slap the constructs across the face and then hold that same hand out to be clasped in friendship. There was only one way this could have ended. Nisong had to remind herself the constructs from Maila had chosen to follow her; they'd chosen this path too.

She slammed her cudgel into a soldier's helmet, denting it and sending him tumbling to the ground. Blood spattered across her lips. For Leaf, with the thin, gentle hands and the narrow face.

She pushed through the soldiers on the plateau, trying to find a weakness in their lines. Already the war constructs were scattering them, sending some tumbling down the hill. They just needed to make it to the gates.

Several fell beneath her war beasts' claws and teeth. Another fell to Nisong's cudgel. For Shell. He would have led the way.

A break appeared in the lines to her right, near the switchbacks. She peered over the soldiers' heads. A woman stood on the path, facing off against a man in a monk's robes. Nisong squinted against the rain. Was that Lin? Down here, among the soldiers? She felt her teeth clench as her focus shifted. She wanted to smash her cudgel into that woman's skull. The crack and crunch of shattering bone, the wet sound of flesh beneath. If she could just make it there. One death to pay for four. For Shell, for Frond, for Leaf and for Grass. Nisong laid about with her weapon, urging her beasts to fight faster, harder.

And then the monk lifted his hands and the surrounding rain halted in its tracks, pulled toward him by some invisible force. He beckoned and it formed into a wave.

Everything seemed to shrink to just the taste of copper on her lips, the feel of water trickling down her neck.

Alanga. So it was true. They were returning. And one was here on the battlefield, fighting the Emperor. Speculation on his motives could wait. She redoubled her efforts. One of her war constructs whined as a soldier struck its flanks with his sword. Another one fell, shrieking, as its throat was slit. Nisong moved to fill the gaps, her hand with the two missing fingers slipping a little on the cudgel. She readjusted her grip. They could make it. Her shamblers were marching up the slope.

The ground shook.

Nisong struggled to keep her feet beneath her as the earth rippled. Mud loosened, making the ground liquid and viscous, sending gravel flying. "Forward! Advance!" she cried out. But words couldn't make it so. She pulled a foot loose from the muddy ground and nearly left behind a boot.

A soldier jabbed at her with his sword. Nisong swung and barely turned the blade aside in time. She'd lost another war construct during the quake.

Before she could recover, the ground shook again.

She dug her fingers into the fur on a bear construct's back, steadying herself, and dared a glance down the switchbacks.

Her shamblers were like flies stuck in honey. Many had fallen during the quakes, sticking in the mud or tumbling down the slopes. It doesn't matter, Nisong told herself. They were merely meant to be a distraction. The bulk of her war constructs were at the gates now.

If they took Gaelung, they could make a move on Hualin Or and then Imperial. Gaelung had a large population. So many bodies. So many bones. There'd be no stopping them. They'd bring the Empire to its knees.

And then what? Coral's voice spoke in the back of her mind.

Nisong shook her head, baring her teeth as she bore down on another soldier. And then they would have justice. And then they could rest.

She looked toward the switchbacks. The monk was gone, and so was Lin. Another man stood there. He brought his foot down.

This time, she seized the bear construct for support before the quake reached them. She let go as soon as the ripple had passed, launching herself at the soldiers. Shamblers began to pass her as they made their way toward the palace. The only things that seemed to mark the passage of time were the swings of her cudgel, the repeated names in her mind.

Shell. Frond. Grass. Leaf.

She wasn't sure exactly when she realized they were losing. Another of her war constructs fell; the shamblers had thinned. There was a mood shift in the soldiers ahead of her. They stood straighter, swung harder. It was a gradual thing, like night giving way to day. Her every push toward the gates was rebuffed.

Nisong knew: she had one last card to play. Yet she railed against it.

Shell. Frond. Grass. Leaf.

Not Coral too. She'd told Leaf and Coral she'd keep them safe. She'd broken that promise to Leaf; would she now break it to Coral?

But there was no one else she would have trusted with the sea serpent. And she needed that serpent to change the tide. She needed Coral.

Nisong slammed her cudgel into another soldier, feeling ribs crack beneath the force of the blow. Was this what vengeance cost? Was this the price of bringing justice to her enemies? She'd paid in blood already.

There had been other paths she could have taken, but this was the only one that made sense to her.

Before she could change her mind, she drew the red scarf from inside her tunic and lifted it to the sky. Her gull construct took flight from the trees.

She would crush the Empire and its Emperor and its people.

No matter the cost.

47

Lin

Gaelung Island

I skirted around the edges of the plateau, feeling the last vestiges of the cloudtree berry's power fading. But I didn't need that power for this. Thrana seized stray war beasts in her jaws, tossing them to the side so I could slide from her back and rewrite their commands. She stood over me as I carved, a solid, protective presence. I turned them as quickly as I could, the engraving tool digging grooves into my fingers, my hands sore. I barely had time for thought, but Bayan and our last fight against my father stood in the forefront of my mind. I wouldn't lose Thrana the way I had Bayan. The faster this ended, the fewer casualties we'd have.

So I pushed myself harder, faster. I ran downslope, Thrana on my heels, catching a war construct before it could rejoin the fray. The light from the lamps Urame had planted into the ground barely reached me; they swung with the wind, flickering. I caught a faint flash of teeth in the darkness before I plunged my hand into wet, stinking fur. The beast froze. Thrana's sturdy, clawed forelegs planted behind me as I knelt in the mud, feeling the indentations on the shard and carving the modifications I knew by heart. At my back, I felt the warmth of my ossalen, the vibration of a growl deep in her throat. I thrust the shard back into the construct, not waiting for it to awaken again and recover.

Some Emperor I was, covered in blood and dirt and cold, wet rain. My father never would have waded into battle alongside soldiers, but perhaps that was the point. He'd never have put himself in harm's way to protect his people. I hauled myself onto Thrana's back and she hurtled toward a war beast on the switchback. I glanced up at the gate and found it still holding, the soldiers there steady. Some of the constructs had broken through the front lines. Hastily, I modified the construct on the switchback, narrowly avoiding its claws.

"Be more careful," Thrana said.

"A bit difficult in a battle," I shouted above the din. She only snorted and dodged the blade of a shambler. "Go to the gates," I told her. "They need our help."

She surged forward, darting around constructs and knocking them aside with her shoulders and the nubs of her horns. Pride filled my heart as I wound my fingers around the fur at her neck. Beneath the coarse outer layer, it was soft, dry and warm. She was at least as formidable as any of my father's war constructs. And she was *mine*.

The first line of soldiers was beginning to falter, war constructs charging and breaking through. Men and women screamed on either side of me as teeth and claws tore into their flesh. Lamps at the walls cast the scene in stark orange and black. Thrana leapt through a gap in the lines and jostled one of the war constructs — a beast with the body of a bear and the face of a tiger — before it could bite into the face of a soldier it had trapped beneath its paw.

In one smooth movement, I slid from Thrana's back and reached into the construct.

Its growl stopped in its throat, the man beneath its paw gasping and writhing as he tried to escape. I didn't have time to help him up. I felt for the shard I needed, pulled it free and carved the modification. I thrust it back into the beast. Thrana yelped. I pivoted to find a pale, hairy beast sinking claws into her back. It opened its slathering maw to bite her neck. I clenched my jaw and felt grit between my teeth. I grabbed one of the construct's legs, pulled to boost myself up high enough and thrust a hand into its chest. It froze as I felt around inside it and dropped back to the ground with one of its shards in my fingertips.

Thrana screamed out a warning. Something slammed into my back before I could turn. A sharp and musky scent flooded my nostrils. Gravel dug into my palms and knees. Its weight pressed me into the earth. I could hear it growling and I reached desperately for the thrumming in my bones – knowing that revealing myself would mean my doom.

The weight suddenly lifted.

Phalue stood over me, pulling her sword free from the beast's back. She gave me a hand up. Beyond the line of soldiers, war constructs were fighting war constructs. "I see what you're doing," Phalue said, "and it's working."

Thrana crowded at my back, making sure no one else could attack me from that angle. My palms stung; I could barely catch my breath. Too narrow an escape.

Phalue nodded at the engraving tool. "Is that the only weapon you know how to use? Not a lot of range with that. Really should bring a sword into battle, Eminence."

The only defense I had right now was Thrana. "You'll teach me when this is through," I blurted out.

The woman laughed. "If we both live, yes. Why not?" She

pivoted, sword in hand, looking for the next fight. "Again, it doesn't mean I support you."

With shaking hands, I seized the fur at Thrana's neck. She ducked her shoulders a little, allowing me easier access to her back. Only the back of my head still felt dry; the rest of me was wet, muddy and bloodied. I could worry about a warm bath later. My bones thrummed, the water a living presence around me. I still had more to give. My stomach tightened at the thought.

Not unless I had to. Not unless I had no other choice.

Thrana and I plunged through the ranks of war beasts and constructs and my world shrank to stinking masses of fur, to shining teeth, to eyes flashing in the darkness. I barely noticed when the edge of a tooth caught at my shoulder, or a claw tore at my oilskin cloak. Nisong thought herself skilled with bone shard magic? Well, I had been up against Bayan, I had taken down my father's four greatest constructs, I had faced Shiyen Sukai himself and claimed his title. No matter that Nisong and I were meant to be the same person. I'd worked at this longer than she had.

I caught a glimpse in the sky, something white fluttering away from the palace. An owl? A spy construct, taking news of the battle to Nisong? Or was she here in the fray?

I turned Thrana toward the switchbacks, to where the fighting was the thickest and where they needed me the most. Gradually, I sensed a breaking in the ranks of the constructs, subtle as the stars winking out to give way to dawn. I found fewer war constructs to turn. The fighting around me seemed not so pressing.

We could do this. We could hold the army off at the gates. If we fought them to a standstill, I could convince the other islands to take our side. I could hold the Empire together.

A roar like a crashing wave emerged from the night. Trees groaned and cracked in the distance.

I found my fingers tightening. More constructs? Had she

held back a contingent of her army? Why? What sort of strategy was this?

A hush fell over the fighting as the sound of wood breaking stopped, replaced by a rushing sound, like wind or water, loud enough to hear over the clash of metal. Dread filled me, spilled over the edges. The sound grew louder, an approaching storm. A war construct leapt toward us and Thrana batted it aside. I was paralyzed on her back, waiting for the doom I somehow knew was coming.

What had Nisong done?

The rushing sound stopped.

The enormous head of a fully grown sea serpent rose from the slopes, each tooth as long as my arm.

48

Jovis
Gaelung Island

Ragan's blade hovered next to my throat. I felt it press against my skin as I swallowed. "I'll make a note of that for next time," I said. "The whole making sure you're dead thing."

The monk's lips didn't even twitch.

I kept talking, hoping to buy myself a little time. "I know about your old monastery. No one had heard from them in over a year before Unta sank."

"I don't like you," Ragan said, "but we don't have to be enemies."

"You attacked the Emperor. We are already enemies. What did you do to them? Did you murder them?"

"Their deaths were unintentional. A mistake when I dosed the drinking well. I only wanted to make them sleep. I only wanted what was my right." The blade wavered, parting my skin a fraction.

"Your right?"

"The restricted texts. I did everything they asked of me. I

excelled at every task. I should have been named a master a long time ago!" He shook his head. "But what does it matter? They're dead and gone, I'm an Alanga and you can either join me or die. I could teach you some things. How to fix the bond with your ossalen, for one."

Mephi darted in, seizing Ragan's leg in his teeth – much the way he'd once seized Philine. He was larger now, and by Ragan's shout, the teeth had a bigger impact than they'd had with Philine. The sword fell from my collarbone and all of Ragan's rage focused on Mephi. He lifted his sword.

I stamped a foot, sending a quake in Ragan's direction. At the same time, I brought my staff to bear and charged forward.

Ragan stumbled, the blow he meant for Mephi going wide. But he regained his footing before I reached him, shaking Mephi from his leg and meeting my staff with his sword.

I'd had no formal training, and now, as I fought against someone with the same Alanga-enhanced strength and speed, I realized my lack of it. Ragan placed his feet precisely, moving with ease and practice. I'd relied more on brute force and magic than I had admitted to myself. My blows, which had always taken out my opponents in one or two swipes, now felt clumsy, over-reaching. I took aim at Ragan's head but he ducked the attack, jabbing at my midsection in the same fluid movement.

Only Mephi saved me. He snapped at Ragan's heels, unbalancing him.

I wouldn't have been able to survive against Ragan without Mephi. We each harried him, taking turns, covering for one another. Ragan's ossalen lurked behind him, never daring to do more than to cower. I understood now that he'd only brought him to the battlefield so he could expose Lin as an Alanga. I pushed quakes in Ragan's direction, lashed at him with water. And Ragan gathered the water around him, making it into darts that stung my skin. He had more control than I did. My feet slipped on the mud and the slick grass.

But we were holding. All I needed was Ragan to slip up once, and I'd have him.

He leapt back, dodging the swing of my staff. He thrust a hand into the pouch at his belt and stuffed something into his mouth.

Of course. He was a cloudtree monk.

I could feel the exhaustion in my bones, a trembling that ran parallel with the tremor of power. I reached for the magic, tried to yet again shake Ragan off his feet. The quake I sent was weak; it didn't move the monk at all. He gave me that infernal smile as he swept forward with his sword, his movements so fast I could barely track them.

I blocked only on instinct, bringing my staff up to intercept blows I didn't see coming. My arms shook. Mephi snapped at his legs and he sidestepped easily. Ragan was stronger with the cloud juniper berries, stronger than I'd ever been. His sword sliced a line across my thigh, and then a cut across my shoulder. I could feel him forcing me back, circling around me so that my back was at the slopes. I couldn't seem to stop him. Rain trickled into my wounds, making them sting. They'd heal, but the next cut I didn't dodge could be the one that spilled my guts onto the ground.

Could Alanga heal from that?

In the distance, trees groaned and cracked. The battlefield grew silent. A rushing sound filled my ears, reminding me of the crash of waves against the cliffs at Anau. What fresh horror was being visited upon us?

Ragan stepped back, allowing me a reprieve. I could feel him studying me, judging the best way to kill me. My gaze flicked over the battlefield, over the soldiers, the guards, all doing their best to fight off shamblers and war constructs alike. I caught sight of a familiar face hovering at the edge of the plateau to my left and squinted against the rain. Was that Philine? Had the Ioph Carn joined the battle too? But then the woman, whoever it was, disappeared behind a tree. I readjusted my stance, tried to steady my breathing.

"We can't hold him off," Mephi gasped beside me. "We're not strong enough. Not yet."

"Run away," I said to him. "Get far away from here. You can still live, Mephi. There's still the Endless Sea to swim in and fish to eat, and morsels to be begged off street vendors."

"Jovis," he said, his voice clear above the din, "don't be an idiot." And then he darted past me, past Ragan's uplifted sword, to seize Lozhi between his teeth.

Ragan froze. He'd brought Lozhi to the battlefield to unmask Lin. But in doing so, he'd made himself vulnerable too. Lozhi didn't move, his body limp in Mephi's jaws. The creature was smaller than Mephi, but he still had teeth, claws and horns. He could have fought back if he'd chosen to. Instead, he whimpered. Pity filled my heart. The beast didn't deserve what Ragan had done to him. But I would use him as collateral if I had to.

"Leave," I told Ragan. "Leave, or your ossalen dies."

He scoffed at me, though I could only see his expression, the noise lost in the wind. "How do you suppose this works? I leave and you keep my ossalen? Why would I ever agree to that? I have no guarantee on my end."

Mephi wrapped a foreleg around Lozhi, his claws digging into the creature's fur. Ragan flinched.

"What happens to you if Lozhi dies?" I asked. "Do you want to risk that?"

Ragan peered at me, his expression odd. "You don't know, do you? So much power at your fingertips and you have no idea why or what it costs."

I opened my mouth to retort, sure something clever would drop out.

But a cold wind stirred at the back of my neck and the fighting around me went silent. Don't turn your back on an enemy, they always say. What they don't say is what to do if you're sure there's already an enemy behind you.

I turned.

The enormous head of a sea serpent rose from the slopes behind me, its mouth open. A woman sat astride its neck, her fingers tight around its horns. She leaned down to whisper into one of its ears. The luminescent spots on the beast's sides flashed, its wide yellow eyes catching the lamplight. Wide yellow eyes that focused on me.

I couldn't be sure if the wetness that fell on my head was rain or the saliva that dripped from the creature's mouth. When I'd pictured the ways in which I might die, being devoured by a giant sea serpent hadn't remotely been on the list. I sent a quake in the sea serpent's direction — a pitiful effort. I doubt the beast even felt it.

Its head darted down.

"Jovis!" Mephi cried out.

49

Phalue

Gaelung Island

The world became only blood, sweat and rain. Phalue gritted her teeth as she swung her sword, fending off war constructs. She'd sparred in the rain in the palace courtyard before. But never in the mud. Never with her arms bloodied and stinging. Never with men and women she knew dying around her. It had seemed a noble thing – the right thing – when she'd told Ranami she needed to help Gaelung fend off the construct army. She kicked a beast in its teeth, shoving her sword through the back of its mouth when it snarled at her.

There was nothing noble about war.

How long had it been? It felt like days she'd been fighting and killing and surviving. But it was still night.

The gates at her back were a solid presence. *Hold the gates*, the general had said. *Take out anyone who breaks the front lines*. Phalue wasn't used to taking orders; she was used to giving them. But she'd die before she'd disobey this one.

A construct leapt over the soldiers in front of them, landing on

Phalue's back. She ducked and heaved, tossing the beast over her shoulders. It landed in front of her but scrambled to its feet before Phalue could finish it off. It rushed toward her and she swept her cloak in front of her. Rows and rows of narrow, needle-sharp teeth sunk into the oilskin cloak.

She might very well die fulfilling this order.

Phalue jerked her cloak back, taking the creature sliding along the ground with it. Tythus, next to her, thrust his sword into the beast's chest.

"Thanks," Phalue panted out.

But Tythus was already turning, facing down a group of shamblers that had pushed their way through a gap wrought by the war constructs. On her right, another soldier died, his throat ripped out by a construct. Phalue swung her sword at the creature and it jumped back, snarling at her with bloody jaws. She cut a slash across one of its eyes and it screamed. One more thrust and the beast died.

She pivoted to help Tythus with the shamblers. They fought in lockstep with one another, all their years of sparring together lending them each insight into one another's movements. They swept through the shamblers like farmers cutting down wheat. She cut the last one down and found . . . no more enemies pressing at their flanks. There were more coming, but for now there was a lull and there was time to breathe.

"Are you hurt?" she asked Tythus.

He shook his head, shoving wet, loose hair back from his face with a gloved hand. "You?"

She glanced down at herself, unsure. "Maybe. I don't think so."

He laughed, the sound a bit manic. "Didn't think it would be like this, did you?"

"I don't know what I thought." She peered into the darkness, trying to judge numbers by lamplight. The constructs moved like mud loosened from a hillside, flowing inexorably toward the gates. "I think we can do this, though. I think we'll hold the gates." She thought she saw the dim light of dawn on the horizon, the stars winking out. It somehow seemed like it had been too long before morning and also not long enough. Time had lost all meaning. All that mattered was the ache in her muscles, the pounding of her heart. They meant she was still alive.

"Aye," Tythus said. "I think you're right. Long odds, but it looks like the Emperor has been changing them."

Had she really promised the woman she'd teach her how to swordfight? The Emperor? Phalue shook her head. A problem for a different dawn.

The crack of wood rose in the distance, from far across the fields below. It was followed by a loud, rushing sound. Something bad was happening, she was certain of it. "Form up!" Tythus said to the guards. They fell into ranks and Phalue couldn't help but notice there were fewer of them than they'd started with. "What do you suppose that is?" he said to Phalue.

"I wish I knew," she said.

The head of an enormous sea serpent rose from the slopes near the switchbacks. Its length coiled down the hill, disappearing into the darkness. Luminescent blue-green spots on its side flickered to life, lighting up the battlefield around it. Phalue had never had the cause to feel the sort of bone-deep, abiding fear that the prey animals feel before the predator. She'd always been one of the taller and broader people she knew. But now she felt the sort of terror a rabbit must feel when the talons of an eagle close around its midsection.

The serpent lunged, snapping at the people below. It half-ran, half-slithered up the slope, its short webbed legs finding purchase in the mud, heaving more and more of its body up onto the plateau. Everywhere, it knocked people to the side or trampled them, claws ripping torsos in two. Screams rose above the sound of clashing blades. The creature didn't even seem aware of most of the people it killed.

"Did you just shit yourself?" Tythus said. "Because I think I just shit myself."

Phalue struggled to find words, to find some way to make this less daunting. "A sea serpent wouldn't come out of the ocean to fight on behalf of the constructs. Which means it *is* a construct. We just need to give the Emperor enough time to change it to our side."

"If she can get close enough," Tythus muttered.

"We have to give her that time," Phalue said. "It's either that or lie down and let ourselves be eaten."

"The second one sounds like a tempting option, but I imagine my wife and children would have something to say about that." He turned his head slightly. "It's heading to the gates," he told the men and women behind them. He gestured as he spoke. "It won't break them on first impact. We split into two groups and step to the sides. If it gets past the soldiers and hits the gates, we converge. We box it in. Phalue and I will take point."

"We will, huh?" Phalue said. She was talking just to feel better. Her voice sounded so much calmer than she felt.

"We're the best fighters here, and you wouldn't stand for me protecting you. You take right. I'll take left. I can't be sure the sea serpent will hit the gates first, but it's a fair guess. Either way, we should flank it. I don't want to face that thing head on."

And then there wasn't any more time for talking. Phalue split off with her half of the guards, moving swiftly to the right of the gates. The sea serpent charged across the plateau and Phalue braced. The soldiers in front of her brought their swords to bear, lining them up like spears.

The creature slammed into the soldiers. The swords hit home

but the serpent didn't even seem to notice. It writhed from side to side, its head striking with the speed of a cobra. Blood, red and hot, slicked the gravel of the path. Phalue wasn't sure how much of it was the serpent's and how much of it was the soldiers'. The serpent seized a soldier between its jaws, the crunch of metal loud in the air. But before it lifted its head, Phalue caught a glimpse of someone *riding* on the serpent's neck.

"Tythus!" she called out.

"I see it!" he shouted back.

The serpent swiped one of its short, webbed feet across the ground. Soldiers flew, tumbling down the side of the hill. The creature charged.

As Tythus had predicted, it went for the gates first. It slammed into the wood, but did not break them, though it was a near thing. The wood at the enormous hinges splintered and the gates groaned. The beast was even more terrifying up close, the luminescent spots bright as lamps, the teeth long as Phalue's arm, the claws that could disembowel with a casual strike.

Sometimes, Phalue supposed, leading meant going first.

She charged.

How was a person even supposed to attack a creature so large? It was like an ant futilely squeezing its mandibles around the end of a person's thumb. This was so far from her sparring sessions in the courtyard. So far even from fighting two lone constructs on Nephilanu. She cut a bloody slice across the sea serpent's side and it rewarded her by batting her aside. The world tilted around her. Next she knew she was flat on her back, trying to catch her breath, an ache in her head. *Get up. Now.* She'd kept her grip on her sword. The beast's claws had scored deep gashes across her armor but she didn't think it had pierced her skin.

No time to check.

Tythus was shouting. Phalue shook her head, trying to clear the fuzziness from it.

"Hey, you big beast! Over here!"

Was he ... *taunting* it? The sea serpent struck out at him and Phalue understood then – by bringing the creature's head closer to the ground, Tythus could get a better shot at the rider on its neck. He rolled to the side as the serpent's jaws snapped shut, narrowly missing him. He couldn't know that taking out the rider would make a difference, but as he'd said before, it was a fair guess. Tythus recovered and swung his sword at the rider, the soldiers behind him rushing in. But all of them were too late. The serpent lifted its head, taking the rider out of range. It readjusted and slammed its body against the gates again.

Phalue shook the rain from her eyes, the taste of blood in her mouth. "Strike at the rider," she said to the guards with her. "Down here!" she called to the sea serpent. She thrust at the leg closest to her. The creature whipped its head about.

The focus of its flashing yellow eyes made her knees weak. Its head lashed out. She threw herself to the side, barely in time. Gravel crunched below her, water soaking through the back of her cloak. She heard its strike behind her. Its teeth snapped shut, barely missing her ankle. Phalue lifted her head. Her guards had run forward, but none of them had managed to get there in time.

Tythus was suddenly there at her side, lending her a hand up.

"What happened to flanking?"

"The rider is whispering commands to the serpent. We need to take them out. You and me – we can do this together," he said. Before waiting for her response, he rushed in. He shouted and thrust his sword at the sea serpent's shoulder. Phalue darted in after him. She had to be ready. The serpent struck and Tythus dodged. Phalue lifted her sword. The rider came into view. A woman, her head bent toward the serpent's neck. Phalue was bigger, stronger – she was going to make it.

The serpent's head diverted to the side at the last moment, its jaws closing around Tythus's torso.

Phalue's world stopped. She was screaming something, she wasn't even sure the words. All she could hear was her voice – a wrenching, wailing sound. The serpent's head lifted away, leaving a broken body behind on the gravel path. It swept past the guards and slammed into the gates for a third time.

With a crack, the gates gave way.

50

Lin

Gaelung Island

The crack of the gates sounded like the breaking of the world. For a moment, I thought we would hold them, I thought we could get through this with minimal casualties. I'd been doing my part, turning as many war constructs as I possibly could. This sea serpent had to be a construct too. Everywhere, I was stopped by constructs and fighting and saving soldiers who barely had a moment to offer gratitude. If I could just get close enough . . .

Where was Jovis? I could have used his help. I'd lost track of him after I'd left him to rewrite the war constructs.

"Quick, Thrana," I said in her ear. "Back to the gates."

She gave me a fresh burst of speed, darting around the fighting as best she could. We were almost there. Phalue and her soldiers had done what they could to buy time, but I needed to do the rest. If I could turn the sea serpent to our side, the battle would be over. We'd have won. If I couldn't turn it, if no one could kill it, we were doomed. With the gates broken, there was no place to retreat to.

Ragan stepped into my path, his sword at the ready.

"Step aside," I said.

"Is that an order from the Emperor?" he said. "Am I meant to tremble in fear, thinking about what you might do to me if I disobey?" He tightened his grip around the hilt and took a step toward me and Thrana.

He wasn't going to let me past without a fight. I glanced to either side of him. We were close to the gates now, and the fighting was thick here. I could take Thrana around him, but we'd have to turn back and go over the edge of the plateau, into the surrounding vegetation. We'd be slow enough that he could strike at us from behind. And there were his Alanga powers to contend with.

He gathered the rain around him, forming it into a wave at his back.

I had no more cloud juniper berries to lend me strength. All I had at my disposal were the engraving tool and a sword on my back I didn't know how to use. And Thrana. I knew he meant to expose me here, now, in front of all the soldiers. My bones thrummed but I tamped the power down. I opened my mouth, unsure of what I would say.

His face hardened. The wall of water rushed toward us. Thrana barely had the time to plant her feet before it smacked into us. I felt myself sliding from her back, my fingers slipping from her fur. He was trying to wash us down the hillside.

What could I do against him?

The wave passed and we stood, shivering, the rain still pelting us from above. Ragan laughed.

"Is this what you would use your power for?" I called to him.

"Better this than to pretend I don't have it at all." He lifted his foot and brought it down. The earth rippled below Thrana's feet.

And then he was there, in front of me, slashing with his sword.

Thrana darted away, though not quick enough. His blade scored both my thigh and her side. She grunted but gave no other sign of her pain. We'd both heal quickly, but perhaps not quickly enough. Ragan was already striking at us again, not giving Thrana time to bite back.

We couldn't hold him off for ever. And I needed to do more than hold him off. Even now, the serpent was crashing into the palace courtyard, reaching into corners to devour Urame's citizens and the archers atop the walls. Its body curled around the walls. We were going to lose this battle. I was going to lose the Empire.

My heart clenched. Either way I'd lose it. If I revealed myself as Alanga, these people would reject me. If I didn't do anything, these people would die. But I'd worked so hard for this position, for the ability to make a difference. I thought again of the bloody crane sitting at the corner of my desk. Of a little girl's smile and a blacksmith's strong, kind hands. Of the oath I'd asked Jovis to take – to be a servant of the citizens. Each person that was dying had families, people that cared about them.

It couldn't be about me and what I'd worked for.

I let the thrumming loose. It filled my body, a vibration that shook my bones, made my flesh feel more alive. I gathered the water around me, forming it into ropes that I whipped at Ragan, striking at the sensitive skin of his face. I used more of it to form a wall of water between me and the monk.

The damned man laughed again as he ducked away from my attacks. I threw the wall of water at him. With a wave of his hand, he moved it to the side. It splashed over constructs and soldiers instead, left them sputtering. But in that brief moment, I'd felt his will brush against mine. Somehow I knew: my will was as strong as his.

I could fight him. I could do this.

I slid from Thrana's back, tucking the engraving tool back into my sash. Power coursed through me, waiting to be used. I needed to move Ragan from my path quickly. I gathered the rain around me into two more waves as he advanced with his sword raised.

Thrana put herself between me and Ragan, her lip curled back. I could feel her growl vibrating through her body, an answering thrum to mine. She snapped at him when he tried to strike, raked her claws across his cloak, jostled him with her shoulders. And in turn I brought the waves crashing down on Ragan's head, tried to cover his nose and mouth and quaked the mud around him.

My efforts only unbalanced him a little. My will was as strong as his, but my skill was not. I'd spent my years learning bone shard magic; I didn't know much about the Alanga or their magic. I'd not had much time to practice. I stamped again, doing my best to direct the quake toward Ragan. It shook the ground beneath him but it was weak. Ragan smirked and sent his own quake back.

I had to seize Thrana's fur to keep myself upright. My hand came away bloody. How many injuries had she suffered on my behalf? "Get behind me, Thrana, you've done enough." She wouldn't move. I had to step out in front of her.

"They know what you are now," Ragan said. "Do you still want to stay here and protect them? Why fight me instead of coming with me? Let the constructs and the mortals fight. They'll turn on you as soon as the battle is over."

"You want me to follow you," I said to Ragan. "You want to lead the Alanga. At what cost? For all these people to die?"

"Better them than us. Why risk ourselves in this conflict?" he said, his brows low. He was the sort of Alanga my father had always feared, caring not at all for the people he crushed with each step he took.

His expression, his stance, his movements — they all spoke of a deep, abiding anger. The monks had held him back. I knew what that was like. I might have turned in his direction, in Nisong's direction, had my circumstances been only a little different. "I know the monks didn't treat you the way you deserved. I've been in that position too. My father never thought I was worthy, not until he died." I tried for soothing, though I had to shout. "You don't have to do this. If you help me fight back the constructs, as you promised, you'll still have a place in this Empire. You are worthy, Ragan. You don't need the monks to tell you that. You don't need me to."

The tightness in his shoulders eased. "Truly? We could reach out to the rest of the Alanga together?"

"Of course," I said. "You know more about them than I do. You're more skilled than I am. I need your help. We all do."

His shoulders slumped and then heaved. For a moment, I thought he was crying. And then he lifted his head. The monk was . . . laughing. "Do you think I want to live among the chattel of the Empire like I'm one of them? Are you so arrogant as to think you can cajole anyone over to your side? You sound like the monks when they first began teaching me: 'Oh, Ragan, you have so much potential.' But —" He lifted a finger. "— praise is cheap and empty. It can turn quickly to bitterness and scorn. I want more than words. I want obedience." Lozhi cowered behind his legs.

Ragan dug around in the pouch at his belt, pulled out a cloud juniper berry and crushed it between his teeth. He lifted his free hand and the rain above him stopped, swirled around his torso, coalescing into larger sheets of water. He spread these out, forming a barrier between me and the palace gates.

"If you won't leave these mortals behind, if you insist on protecting them, then we will always be at odds. We will always be enemies."

51

Jovis

Gaelung Island

Something large and furry slammed into me before the sea serpent's teeth could close around my head. I went tumbling down the hill, snapping brush in my path. If I lived through this, I was never going to climb a hill again. I kept my grip tight around my staff as I fell, as the world around me whirled and shook. When I finally came to a stop, I couldn't get my feet under me. The sky spun, rain falling into my eyes. And then a dark shape blotted out my view of the clouds. A wet nose touched mine, whiskers tickling my cheeks.

"Jovis, are you hurt?" Mephi snuffled my face, then my torso and hands. One of his horns snagged on the side of my jacket. How could he even tell it was me? I lay there, feeling like I was made of mud, twigs and loose bits of gravel.

A warm bath. I would murder everyone on the switchbacks for just one more chance at a warm bath and a hot meal.

Which meant I still wanted to live.

Which meant I probably should get up.

I groaned and heaved myself to my feet. Everything always hurt more once I got up. My knees throbbed; my shoulders ached. At least my head wasn't currently being chomped in the jaws of a giant sea serpent. Mephi had let Ragan's ossalen go in favor of saving my life. Ragan was on the loose again, wreaking who knew what sort of havoc on the battlefield.

I felt around in the dark. "Shit, where's the path? It's too steep a climb to the plateau."

Mephi took one of my hands gently between his teeth. "Over here," he said, tugging.

It was slow going. I was exhausted from my fight with Ragan, from the fall. But Lin was up there alone, doing her best to fend off an army. I could tromp through some bushes.

So I pushed myself forward, leaning on Mephi when my strength gave out or the grass slipped beneath me. He didn't complain, only kept pulling me onward, a silent support. The sounds of fighting grew louder. We passed several bodies on our way – constructs, shamblers and soldiers.

By the time we made it to the path, my legs were shaking. I knew – if I could just take a moment to catch my breath – I could recover. But over the trees I could see the sea serpent's raised head. It was inside the palace gates. The wood was shattered, our army in disarray. The screams of citizens who'd taken refuge inside the palace walls drifted through the air. I couldn't see much when I looked up the path at the fighting, but what I could see didn't look promising. Our soldiers were disorganized, fighting in loose groups that grew looser by the moment. I couldn't tell which war constructs Lin had changed to our side and which still fought on the side of the construct army. I steadied my breathing and found the thrum still there in my bones, waiting to be used.

When I'd decided to come back to the palace, I'd thought I might meet my end by Lin's decree. I hadn't thought about dying in battle. My mother always said I was short-sighted. But here I was, and I couldn't leave these people to die, no matter what it meant for me.

And I couldn't leave Lin to die. I peered over the switchbacks and foliage, trying to find her and knowing it was futile. As futile as this goddamned battle. Nisong and her constructs would crush us. Lin had done her best to bring the islands over to our side, to convince them to send their guards. She'd only been partially successful. I'd hoped that would be enough, but hopes couldn't spawn more soldiers. I could lie to myself all day long, but in the very back of my mind, I always knew the truth.

"Friends until the end?" I said to Mephi.

"Always," he said without hesitation.

I wiped the mud from the handle of my staff until I could feel the grooves of the metal beneath. I could see the edges of the fighting just ahead of me, the snarling constructs, the desperate soldiers. I'd make Nisong's army pay for my life at least.

The drum of footsteps sounded from behind me.

I whirled, and my throat went dry. An army was marching up the slope. *Another* army. Had Nisong held them in reserve too?

A lantern swung, its light catching the face of the man in front. I could make out a grizzled beard, low brows and a single, glaring eye.

"Gio!" I gasped out, though I knew he couldn't hear me from this distance and over the sounds of battle. "Gio?" What in all the known islands was *he* doing here? Was he here to crush Lin while she was low? Why bother? The constructs were already doing that for him. Did he just want to be sure?

I set myself in the path, reaching for the thrumming in my bones, my staff held at the ready, Mephi at my side.

Gio didn't slow, and neither did the men and women behind him. He frowned when he grew close enough to recognize me.

"Jovis!" he barked. "Get out of the way." He said it in the same tone my mother used when I was crowding her in the kitchen. I started to step to the side instinctively before stopping myself. Gio halted and so did his army of Shardless Few.

"She's trying to help the people here," I said. "The construct army is the enemy, not the Emperor."

Gio scoffed. "So the spy just hadn't stopped being a spy; he has become a turncoat. I should have expected as much. What did she do? Offer you money? A palace?"

I bristled. He'd managed to insult both Lin and me in one go. "You think my loyalty is so cheaply bought?" Never thought I'd hear those sorts of words coming out of my mouth. Used to be I could be bought just fine.

He peered at me through the darkness and the rain. "Really. So it's that. You. And the Emperor." At least he didn't laugh. He sighed, looking beyond me. "But that's not why I'm here. I'm here to help. So move, unless you want your Emperor dead and all the people here along with her."

He was here to help? That didn't make any sense. I knew Gio, and he wasn't the noble do-gooder he liked to make himself out to be. "Why would you come here? Why would you stick your neck out for the Empire with such long odds?"

"Jovis, this may not be the best time to ask these questions," Mephi said urgently. "The sea serpent has broached the gates."

"But what if he's lying? What if he's here to kill us all?"

The men and women behind Gio shifted, their expressions dark and angry. Great. So now I'd offended his band of loyalists. They'd never believe anything ill of Gio.

"I don't have time for this," Gio said. He lifted a hand.

I brought up my staff, realizing at the last minute that he wasn't holding one of his knives in his palm. His hand was empty.

A gust of wind and water slammed into my side. My upheld

staff was useless against it. I heard Mephi cry out as we were both sent falling farther down the slope. What in all the Endless Sea had just happened? The thought occurred almost at the same time as a memory came to mind.

Back when Gio and I had crept into Nephilanu's palace together, something had carried one of the guards off his feet and down the hillside. I realized now that it had been wind, aimed precisely at the guard. At the time, Gio had blamed it on me.

It hadn't been me. It had been him.

Gio was an Alanga.

And then I hit my head against something hard and the world winked out.

52

Lin

Gaelung Island

Water permeated every piece of my clothing, the fabric rough and heavy against my skin. Each time I thought I could catch my breath, Ragan sent another wave at me, forcing me to brace once more. Thrana did her best, but he kept her at bay with his sword. We were only just surviving and he seemed to effortlessly wield both his blade and his magic at the same time. I wished I'd brought more cloudtree berries and bark with me. Around us, the fighting still raged. A war construct broke away and came at my throat, only to be tossed away in Ragan's next wave. I barely brought my power to bear and knocked a portion of it aside. The rest drenched me, threatening to take me out at the knees.

I was farther from the gates than when I started. With each step I took, Ragan pushed me back toward the switchbacks.

Something seemed to shift in the fighting around us. At first, I thought it was merely dawn, chasing away the night. The darkness around us lifted in increments, the constructs and people around me more discernible, the blood streaking their faces more visible. But though the sky grew lighter, something else had changed too. I could feel it in the air, the mood of the people close to the us.

Someone was marching toward us. Many, many someones.

Ragan turned his head for just a moment, and Thrana darted past him toward his ossalen. I lifted the moisture around me, intending to stuff it down his throat. But then I made the mistake of looking to the sound of the footsteps as the first of the group made it onto the plateau.

I recognized the man leading them. It was the same man I'd seen at the refuse pile on Nephilanu and this time, I could place his face. The grizzled beard, the one undamaged eye, the perpetual scowl. I'd seen it on the posters the bureaucracy constructs had been painting.

Gio. The leader of the Shardless Few. And all the Shardless Few he could bring, by the looks of it. I'd heard he was gathering an army on Khalute, but hadn't expected it here, now.

Just my luck.

Constructs and humans alike turned to this new threat, unsure of whose side they were on. A war construct broke the tension, rushing at Gio. The man merely lifted a hand and the beast was swept off its feet.

Though my body was drenched, my mouth went dry. I'd never believed the rumors – that Gio had taken Khalute single-handedly. But what power was this? A breeze brushed my cheek and I remembered the tales of the Alanga. Mostly they focused on the Alanga's ability to control water, though there were a few that mentioned their ability to work the winds.

But I'd never heard of Gio having an ossalen.

Ragan had turned fully from me to face this new threat. "You have two choices," he shouted. "Swear your fealty to me or be destroyed."

Gio's mouth tightened. "*Boy*," he said, and I'd never heard the word infused with such contempt, "I don't have time for you."

Ragan created a wall of water between him and Gio, his lips pressed in concentration. "You have one more chance."

Gio merely lifted an eyebrow. He flicked a finger.

The wall of water shattered into droplets.

I'd never seen anyone look so lost. Ragan reached after the droplets as though he could physically pull them together with his hands. "How . . . ?"

"Move," Gio barked.

Ragan bared his teeth; he lifted a foot.

Gio waved his hand.

This time, through the gray dawn light, I could see the distortion of the falling rain as the wind whipped toward both me and Ragan. I didn't have time to dodge and I didn't know how to stop such an attack. Ragan threw his hands up and then we were both tossed into the brush on the side of the plateau, tumbling down past bodies and slick grass. I gained my feet before he did. He'd lost his sword somewhere in the fall. "Thrana!" I called out. She emerged from a bush, unhurt. I threw an arm around her neck, steadying myself.

Ragan took a moment to look for his ossalen and I stamped the ground, desperation making my chest tight. The sea serpent was still up there, ravaging the palace, killing citizens who didn't know how to fight.

The ground shook beneath my feet and Ragan stumbled. "Lozhi!" he called. The beast slunk out from the behind the corpse of a war construct, his head low to the ground. Before I could do anything about my momentary advantage, Ragan gritted his teeth and shoved another wall of water at me. He hit me from upslope, and I struggled not to slide farther down the hill. To the left of us, the grass and bushes disappeared over the edge of a precipice. I hazarded a quick glance and found the drop stomach-clenching. I tried to gather the rain around me and found the thrum diminished, my limbs aching, my head pounding. Only the presence of Thrana kept me from collapsing. How could she still have energy?

"Take strength from me," she murmured in my ear.

Ragan grinned, knowing I was nearly spent.

"And what do you plan to do after this is done?" I said. I couldn't help the bitterness in my voice. "There's still the construct army and the Shardless Few."

He only pulled a knife from his belt. "That's for me to worry about. You? You'll be dead."

All I had left were my wits and an engraving tool. *Take strength from me*. My breath caught. And a few shattered pieces of Thrana's horn inside my sash pocket. A suspicion grew in my mind, formed into a thought. Surely she couldn't mean . . . ?

"Yes," she said, as though she knew what I was thinking. "Do it."

Ragan advanced, knife up, his gaze on Thrana's bared teeth, his hand lifted to gather another wave.

I pulled a shard from my sash pocket and carved it. The bone gave way easily beneath my tool, as though this was what it was meant for. We moved as one. Thrana snapped at Ragan. He turned his knife toward her, distracted. And I, quick and small, darted beneath his guard. I slammed the shard into the flesh of his side, beneath the ribs.

It wasn't like stabbing him, not quite. I had the odd sensation of his skin giving way, and then he was falling back, his mouth wide. The wave he'd gathered splashed uselessly to the ground. He clawed at his side, looking for the bone, trying to dislodge it. But it was gone, disappeared inside him. "What did you do?"

I opened my mouth, tried to form some smug retort, but had

nothing. I wasn't sure myself what I'd done. Thrana breathed heavily beside me, blood soaking through her fur. Her feet, though, were firmly planted, the muscles in her shoulder tense.

Ragan's brows lowered. He struck out at me with his knife. I flinched back.

He dropped the blade halfway through his swing.

Something halfway between triumph and terror sung in my veins. What *had* I done? The monk lifted a hand, a wave formed upslope . . . and didn't move. He screamed out his frustration, clutching again at his side. "Tell me what you did to me!"

Finally, I found my words. "Only what you deserve. And you do not deserve death, not by my hand." I grabbed a handful of Thrana's fur and climbed atop her back. "Let's go rewrite a sea serpent construct," I said to her. "And defeat an army."

Muscles gathered beneath me as she launched us back up the slope, leaving Ragan behind, the piece of her horn embedded in his body and carved with one simple command: *Vu minyet kras.*

You cannot kill.

53

Jovis

Gaelung Island

I clawed my way back to consciousness with mud filling my ears and the taste of blood on my lips. The sky was turning a murky gray. Memory came back in increments. I remembered first that Lin had sent me away, then the discovery that Ragan was treacherous, then the battle and my unwanted trip down the hill's slopes. I smeared some of the mud from my ears and felt the back of my head. Wet and warm and aching fit to split my skull. I'd landed with my head on a log, rotting and water-logged from the rain. I was fortunate it hadn't been a rock. Seemed like I'd been out long enough for the bleeding to stop and for the wound to begin closing.

Something felt wrong.

"Not the best start I've had to a day," I croaked out. "How about you?"

No answer.

"Mephi?" I raised my voice, wondering if he hadn't heard me. We'd both been sent down that slope, and he carried himself lower to the ground than I did. Tended to fair better in falls.

I pushed myself up, the world spinning around me. Did my quick healing work for headaches? I tried to remember the last time I'd had a headache.

All thoughts came crashing to a halt when I realized: I didn't see Mephi anywhere. Panic flashed through me, my heart feeling like it was leaping into my mouth. I was on my feet, turning in circles before I could register that I was moving. I swept my gaze over bushes, grass, rocks, the bodies of fallen soldiers and constructs.

What could keep Mephi from my side?

Nothing, *nothing*.

He was there every morning when I woke up, his wet nose shoved in my ear, his whiskers tickling my cheeks. He liked to put his paws on my chest when he felt I slept too long, the weight of him making it difficult to breathe. He eyed every meal I ate, begged too many scraps off the ship's crew and seemed to think anything not nailed down was his for the taking.

He was my friend.

"Mephi!" I was calling his name, screaming it, tearing through bushes – half of me knowing he was gone and half of me expecting him to pop his head up, huffing out a breath in that amused way. *Were you getting this worked up? I've been here the whole time.*

I burst onto the switchback near the palace just in time to see Gio confront the sea serpent. It felt like I'd crossed into some odd nightmare world. Gio lifted his hands. A cyclone of wind and water formed in front of him. He thrust it at the beast, which roared as its body and limbs twisted in this miniature storm. It threw its head back. The person on its neck flew through the air, over the ramparts of the palace. I stumbled past bodies, past men and women turned toward the fight, their mouths agape. Gio whipped up the broken splinters of the palace gates, using hurricane-force winds to slam them into the underside of the serpent's body. It shrieked and tried to clamp its jaws on his head. But Gio was far too quick for it, moving with the strength and grace of a much younger man. A man with magic in his bones.

I paid the battle only half a mind. I wanted more than anything to wake up on the slope again. To find Mephi with me.

But Emahla had taught me I needed to keep moving forward. As the sea serpent and Gio made a ruin of the palace's courtyard, I traced my steps in my mind. I'd not seen Mephi's body. We'd fallen together, nearly side by side. I'd not seen him upslope or downslope.

There were only two possibilities here: he had left or he had been taken.

At the moment I realized he'd been taken, I knew who had taken him.

The Ioph Carn.

54

Lin

Gaelung Island

I made it back to the palace in time to see Gio engaged in battle, his strength beyond anything I could conceive. I couldn't whip winds into a frenzy like that, or have such precise control of water. The fighting had slowed to a standstill, the Shardless Few turning the tide. The remaining men and women had turned to watch Gio and the sea serpent, their eyes wide. How long had it been since anyone had seen an Alanga at their fullest potential? The stories gave an idea, but stories were distant things.

I was Emperor, and I was also Alanga. If everyone didn't know yet – they soon would. All this time and effort I'd spent becoming Emperor and now I'd made my position precarious, untenable. I'd given the governors even more cause to call for my abdication. They wouldn't be content to see me quietly retired to some distant island. There would be calls for my execution. I'd saved the people of Gaelung, but at what cost? I'd failed the Empire.

If I slunk away now, if I took Thrana and ran, I could find a living somewhere in the Empire. I was smart, resourceful. There were ways I could disguise myself. I could build a house on the edges of a town, where Thrana could go unnoticed. Just her and me, sunning ourselves on a beach somewhere, no one to care about except ourselves.

It sounded like a lovely life.

It sounded like a lonely life.

I'd told Numeen that I'd be a better Emperor. I'd promised him.

The serpent snapped at Gio, its long, sharp teeth barely missing him as he dodged. Whoever had been riding on its neck was gone. It struck out wildly.

He could handle the serpent on his own. He didn't need me. But I could be wrong, and then who would suffer for it? Everyone I'd promised to save. Perhaps I didn't need to be a better Emperor. Maybe just being a better person was good enough. I set my jaw. "We need to get close," I said to Thrana.

She'd already started moving before I'd finished talking. We shouldered past men and women fixated on the fight. A few turned to glance at me astride my ossalen, mouths agape once they recognized me, but apart from Thrana, I was indistinguishable from the wet and muddy masses.

The gate was rubble under the arch. Where was Urame? Phalue?

I didn't have time to look for my allies. Ahead of me, the sea serpent loomed, Gio dwarfed by its mass. "Distract it!" I called to him.

He scowled at me, only briefly. The sea serpent coiled, ready for another strike. Gio pulled the water around him into a swirling cyclone between him and the sea serpent, filled with rocks and debris. He sent it rumbling toward the serpent and I charged after it.

The beast screeched as the wood and stones struck its hide, embedded in the flesh between the scales. Before it could recover,

Thrana slammed into it, my thigh wedged between her fur and the slippery, scaled skin of the serpent. I centered myself and reached out.

I grasped only the massive spinal column of the serpent. It froze when my hand entered its body, but without manipulation of its shards, it would freeze only very briefly.

Of course. Nisong wouldn't have that many shards to begin with, so she'd have used them sparingly. They'd be wedged into the serpent close to the base of its skull. I looked up the daunting face of its sinewy neck. Well. I'd climbed more slippery surfaces in the past. Spears and arrows were embedded in its scales. They'd provide foothold enough. This was just a different sort of wall. A moving wall. With teeth.

I'd come this far.

Thrana whimpered below me as I grasped the first of my handholds and pulled myself upward. After only one handhold, the serpent began to move again. I looked down to see Thrana circling below and Gio with his daggers drawn. They looked laughably small next to the serpent. This was the most foolish thing I'd ever done. But it also felt the most right.

My muscles aching, I climbed as quickly as I could.

Not quickly enough. The serpent's muscles tensed beneath me. I gritted my teeth, trying to wedge my feet into the wounds made by the rocks. I locked my fingers around a splinter of wood above me. The coiled muscles released. My stomach soared into my throat as the beast struck out at Gio and carried me hurtling toward the ground. Both my feet slipped. I found myself hanging from that splinter of wood. Before I could decide to drop right then while the ground was close, it drew its head back into the sky again.

Endless Seas, I hoped this piece of debris was pushed in deep.

It stayed in place, and so did I. I almost wished it was still night so I didn't have to see exactly how far I'd have to fall.

Only a little farther. I could see the spot where the construct had sat, wedged between two webbed spines. I forced my screaming muscles to move, scrabbling for handholds. The serpent tensed again. I took in a deep breath, trying not to think about how I had no splinter of wood to hold this time, and plunged a hand into the creature's neck.

This time, I found shards.

I pulled one free and without even looking at it, shoved it back inside the serpent in the wrong spot.

The beast froze and I slid my way back down its neck. Thrana was there to catch me, supporting me with her shoulder. "It's going to collapse." Together, we limped away from the sea serpent. I heard its scales hiss against the paving stones as the creature unfroze. Gasps arose from the surrounding soldiers and fear made my shoulders rigid. I'd rearranged the shards. Hadn't that interrupted the logic of its commands? I whirled to find the serpent's head coiled to strike.

"Thrana!"

She pulled me, as fast as she could, to the side. We weren't going to make it. A rush of air as the sea serpent lashed out.

I'd done what I could. I had to make peace with that.

Its jaws closed just above me, its head throwing up dirt and paving stones as it crashed into the ground to my right. The ground beneath me trembled as the rest of its body tumbled to the ground. At last, the beast was still. Scales fell from its sides as flesh melted from bones. I ran a hand down the front of my torn and muddy jacket, surprised to find I was still in one piece. The beast was dead and I was not.

The rain had stopped at some point during my struggle with the sea serpent. The sounds of fighting had dimmed. I could see soldiers still standing past the archway, gray shapes in the morning mists.

We'd won. We'd ... *won?*

It didn't feel like winning. It felt like a long trek up an unforgiving mountain with no meal or hot fire waiting at the top. I closed my eyes and leaned into Thrana's side, trying to blot out the sounds of the stumbling, dissolving serpent. The world went silent.

Then footsteps began shuffling into the courtyard. I cracked open an eye. Civilians who had been hiding in the palace, behind pillars, behind broken pieces of rubble. Soldiers and Shardless Few stumbled beneath the archway, eyeing the sagging remains of the serpent as though unsure it was actually dead. People crowded the courtyard, though they gave Thrana and me a wide berth.

Urame's voice came from somewhere near the palace. "You and you, start looking for survivors. You, see if there's a physician somewhere in the palace. I know more than one took refuge here. And you – get as many of the servants as you can find. Start setting up the entrance hall as an infirmary."

So she'd survived. My relief only lasted a moment, because then I started to hear the murmurs.

"She made the water move with her hands too." "Saw her fighting the monk." "Emperor has one of those creatures too."

"*Alanga.*"

The word traveled through the crowd, each iteration filled with more fear, more terror, more anger. I grasped the fur at Thrana's shoulders, tried to haul myself onto her back. My fingers slipped, my hands aching, my arms too weak to support my weight. "I need to go," I said, even as I knew it was too late. There was no easy exit from the courtyard, nowhere I could slip away unnoticed. The circle of people around me closed in a little.

My bones thrummed, letting me know: I still had a little magic left. I reached for it, then stopped.

I hadn't saved these people just so I could kill them.

"All hail Emperor Lin Sukai!" a voice called out from the crowd. "She came to our aid when we needed it the most. She put her own life on the line to save us, like Arrimus defending the city from the sea serpent Mephisolou." I knew that voice. Jovis. The tale of Arrimus was one of the few positive stories of an Alanga, and he'd chosen the perfect comparison.

"All hail Emperor Lin Sukai!" he called out again.

Ever so gradually, the mood in the crowd shifted. Someone else took up the cry. And then others did. And then I was surrounded by people shouting my name, approving of me, of my actions. All the praise I'd never gotten from my father. All the acceptance I hadn't known I still wanted. Still needed.

Even though they knew who I was.

I was Lin. I was Alanga. I'd defeated the construct army and I was the *Emperor*.

Jovis broke through the crowd. For a moment we just stared at one another, and then he jerked his head toward the palace. *Can we talk?*

I found the last reserves of my strength, picking my way across the courtyard, bowing my head to the people who bowed to me as I passed, Thrana at my side. I followed Jovis through the entrance hall and into a small, empty side room.

"Watch the door?" I said to Thrana. She nodded, planting her feet.

I closed the door and we were alone, misty light streaming in from the half-shuttered window, the sounds from outside muted.

"Well," Jovis said, "I think that earns me a pardon from execution, don't you?" He was covered in mud, bloody from battle, his curly hair wet with rain and sweat – and somehow he still managed a cocksure grin. It was a bit wobbly at the corners, but there it was.

"A stay of execution," I said, tentatively returning his smile. There was a part of my heart that still felt tender from his betrayal. It would take time.

He sobered. "Did you see what Gio did?"

Was this why he'd wanted to speak to me? "Everyone did." My mind was already hurtling ahead, considering the implications. "He's Alanga too. I don't know where his ossalen is, but he has the same powers we do. Has he been hiding it this whole time?"

"I think he has been," Jovis said, his expression grim. "It would explain Khalute."

"The leader of the Shardless Few – an Alanga? It will mean trouble later." I winced at a sharp pain in my ribs. All my injuries began to throb at once, reminding me of their presence.

Jovis reached out a hand. "Are you hurt?" He brushed a clod of dirt from my shoulder with soft hands, noting the torn cloth beneath, the dried blood.

"Are you?" I reached hesitant fingers to the side of his head.

We checked one another over without speaking, cataloging wounds that had already begun to heal. Only the sounds of our breathing, the brush of cloth filled the small space.

"Lin," he said.

I froze as surely as though the word was his hand entering my chest, and I a construct. I didn't know what to say. I wanted more than anything to step into his embrace but I wasn't sure where we stood.

"I love you," Jovis blurted out into the silence. "Please don't execute me. Not even later. Ah shit. I'm no good at this. I mean – let me start over. I've made a mess of things. I don't care what you are. Whatever your father did to make you. I care about who you are. And who you are is a person that I care about." He pursed his lips, wrinkling up his nose. "I'm not even sure if – does that make sense?"

I laughed in spite of myself. "It makes sense, I promise." I lifted a hand to his cheek, wondering at the way he leaned into my touch, the feel of his warmth below my palm. I studied his face. There was tension in the lines at the corners of his eyes, his jaw set but not clenched. "But there's something else, isn't there?"

"It's Mephi."

My heart clenched. Mephi wasn't with him. Mephi was *always* with him. He was as much Jovis's shadow as Thrana was mine. "He's not . . . ?" I couldn't even finish the sentence. *Dead?*

"No," Jovis shook his head. "No. I'd know. I think I'd know. It's Kaphra. He was there that night you saved my life and he got away. I should have known. I should have been more on guard. He doesn't like to leave things unfinished, and when he wants something, he does everything he can to get it. I can't be sure, but it's the only thing that makes sense. He took Mephi. And I know where he'll take him to." He took his hands in mine. His fingers were cold, though mine weren't much warmer.

"Then you have to go." There wasn't anything else he could do. The thought of someone taking Thrana, of not knowing where she was, of knowing she was in unfamiliar hands – I couldn't bear it. "You have to find him."

He ran his fingers over my knuckles, his gaze on our entwined hands. "I shouldn't leave you. I'm your Captain of the Imperial Guard. You'll need me now, more than ever."

Now that the Alanga were returning. Now that we knew that their motives were as varied as the fish in the sea. "We both know Mephi needs you more. Take whatever you need from the ship. Money. Supplies. Witstone. It's all yours." I could feel the pull to be out on the open sea, away from the mess of politics, of trying to untangle the knots my father had wrought. "I wish I could go with you."

He sighed. "But you can't."

I tugged him in closer, reaching up to press my lips to his. He tasted earthy, like mud and rainwater. His clothes were heavy with moisture, as were mine. But I could feel the heat of him beneath, and it warmed me more than a roaring fire.

"Lin," he said, breathless, against my mouth.

To the depths of the Endless Sea with propriety. I seized his collar with mud-caked hands, pressing against him, knowing this could be the last time. The last kiss, the last embrace, the last time I ever saw him. It felt like drowning, but with no urge to come up for air. He caught me, one arm around my waist, the other lifting to cup my cheek, to dig fingers into the tangle of my hair.

I wished I could live in this moment. I wished it never had to end.

But for ever was a term for fools and poets. I was neither. I pulled away. "I don't care where you came from. I don't care about your heritage. Come back to me."

I didn't ask, but he offered it anyway. "I promise." He took my hand and held it over his heart. It beat, strong and steady, beneath my palm. "And I'll never break a promise to you again."

Before I could respond he was gone.

55

Nisong

Gaelung Island

Nisong should have been grateful that Coral was light. She found her among the bushes on the hillside, thrown there from the sea serpent's neck. She wrapped the woman's arm about her shoulder, lifting her by the waist and dragging her away from the battlefield. Everyone was more focused on the fallen serpent than on the woman who'd been riding it.

Nisong couldn't blame them. The creature's coils wound around the palace walls; its claws digging into stone. Its head lolled into the courtyard.

Gaelung had won. Lin had won. It seemed impossible. But she hadn't counted on the Shardless Few arriving to help, and their numbers were too great. Her army was scattered, crushed. But Coral – Coral was still alive.

The ground was still soft from the rain; it must have broken her fall. Nisong dragged Coral into the foliage, half climbing, half falling down the slope. The edges of the grass cut at her skin and free hand as she did her best to slow their progress.

"I'll get you back home," Nisong said.

Coral stirred. "To Maila?"

Maila – this was home to Coral, and she'd taken her away from it. She'd taken them all away from it. And for what? Nothing.

She ducked beneath the leaves of a nearby bush as soldiers ran about on the switchbacks, and laid Coral across her lap. Lin's army would be chasing down stragglers, looking for their own wounded, cleaning up the battlefield. Nisong had no intention of becoming the Emperor's prisoner.

At least she still had Coral. They could start over, figure things out together. There were still the scattered constructs she'd sent out to wreak havoc on the Empire. She could still build up an army again. With bone shard magic, the possibilities were open to her.

"To somewhere safe," she amended.

Coral looked up at her, sweat and blood plastering the hair to her forehead, her soft brown eyes wide and wet with tears. "We lost, didn't we?"

"No," Nisong said. "Never."

Something warm trickled on her leg. Nisong's heart pounded in her ears, her mouth suddenly dry. Trying not to panic, she lifted Coral a little, felt her back. Something sharp protruded from between Coral's ribs. A broken arrow shaft.

She hadn't seen it when she'd lifted Coral from the ground, as she'd carried her away from the sea serpent's body. Had she damaged the woman even further, dragging her away? "We need to get this out," she said, even as she felt the blood seeping from the wound. "If we find a fire, I can cauterize it, get the bleeding to stop."

"Sand," Coral said, and then blinked. "Nisong."

"You can call me Sand." There was a part of her that knew how this ended, that had accepted it the moment she'd called

Coral into battle. But the rest of her raged against this outcome. She had given everything she had to this cause. There was still a way to fix this; there always was.

"Take me home. Please." Coral's lips were pale.

Nisong tried to lift Coral, to sling the woman's arm around her shoulders again. But the woman's face locked into a grimace of pain, and Nisong let her slide to the ground again. She reached for the arrow; it was broken too deep in the wound for her to get a decent grip. Back at the construct camp, there would be tools. It would be swarming with the Empire's soldiers though. If they even made it that far. Everywhere she turned, she ran into a wall.

Nisong found herself speaking. "You were right. Maila is not the prison. The mind-fog was. I'm giving up. We're going home."

Some tightness in Coral's face relaxed, her lips curving into a faint smile. "Giving up isn't always the wrong thing to do."

"We'll go back to Maila," Nisong said. Her breath felt like a solid thing in her throat; her chest ached with the weight of it. "I'll tell the remaining constructs to spread the word that the island is our home. We'll tell them how to get past the reefs. We'll all build a life there, together."

Coral's fingers grasped weakly at the hem of Nisong's shirt. "You don't have to gather mangoes, you know. You can do something else."

Nisong choked out a laugh in spite of herself. "I know."

It was the last thing Coral said.

The sky was light by the time Nisong let the woman slide from her lap. She covered Coral with branches from nearby trees, wishing that at least one was a juniper. Did constructs' souls ascend to heaven? Did they have souls?

Coral had a soul.

Nisong did not. She rose to her feet and picked her way down the slope, keeping out of sight of the soldiers on the switchbacks.

Her tears dried on her cheeks as she walked. She was alone, but she didn't have to be. If there was anything this battle had taught her, it was that she was not the only one who opposed Lin.

She remembered watching the cloudtree monk flee the battlefield. He'd had the same sort of powers that Lin and Jovis had. He'd almost beat them. She made a mental map of the surrounding area, trying to extrapolate where he might have gone, where he might have ended up.

And then she set her feet in that direction.

There was always a way to fix things. There was always a way to come back.

56

Lin

Gaelung Island

When he turned to leave with his swords, I tried to stop him. We fought. Ylan was a scholar, not a warrior, but I've never felt such pain as when one of those blades parted my skin. He left me there in the dark, half-blinded.

And then he went to destroy my kin.

He found six others to bear the swords, and together they swept across the islands, hunting the Alanga, wreaking their own disasters. How can anyone ever forgive me for what I've done? How can I ever forgive myself? The younger ones with families — he's killed the children too. He won't leave anyone alive to seek vengeance.

Someday he will be back for me.

—Notes from Lin's translation
of the last pages in Dione's journal

J ovis had forgotten to take the Alanga journal again when he
left. Or perhaps it just wasn't that important to him, given
everything else. Books and mysteries seemed to be my purview
anyway. Even in the aftermath, in the cleaning and the envoys
and the promises I had to make, there was time, late at night,
for reading.

To my surprise, the Shardless Few didn't immediately demand
my abdication or retreat back to Khalute. They stayed to help,
clearing rubble and lending their own physicians to assist with
the injured. Urame was ceaselessly grateful to me; I would
have found it embarrassing if I hadn't needed exactly that: her
gratitude. She showered me with praise, insisted I commandeer
her study and made certain her servants asked to assist me at
least twelve times a day. Slowly, in the days after the battle,
word trickled out of what had happened. And then word began
trickling back in. The other islands would fall in line. Even Iloh
rescinded his demand for abdication, doing his best to paint it as
a terrible mistake made in the throes of fear for his people.

I could afford to be magnanimous, so I let it pass.

Phalue came to see me in Urame's study. The remains of the
sea serpent had finally been cleared from around the palace walls,
the dead burned, the injured all tended to. Thrana was recovering her energy and good humor, spending more time in the
palace kitchens than was necessary, where the servants lavished
her with praise and food.

"Eminence," Phalue said, when she walked through the door,
"it's time I go home." She stood in the pose that reminded me
more of a soldier than a governor – hand resting on her sword,
feet planted apart, knees soft and ready to spring into action. Her
leather armor bore a fair number more scratches than it had when
she'd arrived, and her face looked drawn, her eyes red-rimmed.

I snapped the Alanga journal shut, having finished reading it for the third time. I'd finally deciphered the last few words I'd had trouble with. "You don't need my permission, Sai. You're free to come and go as you please. You may not support me, but the Empire owes you for your help here."

"And I owe you. I didn't forget I made you a promise."

"Made in haste. On a battlefield. I won't hold you to it."

She only shook her head, her lips pressed together. "I have matters to attend to at home, but I'll be back when I'm done. And I'll teach you. Ranami can handle Nephilanu for a few months."

"A few months? That long?"

Phalue smirked, and I could see what Ranami saw in her – the devotion and the charm. "Eminence, you may be smart, and you can climb like a monkey, but swordplay is another matter entirely. You're strong, and you're Alanga, and those are the only reasons I think bringing you up to competency will take so *little* time." And then the smile disappeared, a mere glimpse of the sun on a rainy season day. "Thank you for ensuring a proper funeral. For Tythus. His wife and sons—" Her voice broke on the last words. She gathered herself. "They would have approved."

It didn't take the sharpest mind in the Empire to make these connections. "He was not just your Captain of Guard. He was your friend. I'm so sorry."

She gave me a long, piercing look. "An Emperor who actually gives a shit. Well," she said, and her voice wasn't the least bit mocking, "that's a wonder indeed." And then she clapped her heels together and bowed. "I'll take my leave then, Eminence. But I'll be back."

Well, there was an island I wasn't exactly sure would fall in line. But whatever ice had existed between us seemed to be thawing. And I'd take whatever victories I could get.

I needed to leave too – to return to Imperial. Ikanuy had been taking good care of the island and the palace in my absence, as far as I could tell. She shouldn't have to do so for ever.

But there was one more matter I had to attend to. One more thing that had been nibbling away in the back of my mind, a mouse searching for an exit in a maze.

I went to the door and found a passing servant. "Send for Gio. Ask him to meet me." I paused, thought for a moment. "Tell him 'please'."

You may carry a sword, my father had once told me, *but tread lightly when you're in the tiger's den.*

I strode back to Urame's desk, sat and waited. Gio arrived – not soon, and yet not late enough to provoke insult. He didn't bring any of his Shardless Few with him. He came unaccompanied and unadorned. "Emperor Sukai," he said as he entered. I noticed his judicious avoidance of "Eminence". "You asked for me?"

"I owe you thanks," I said, "for coming to our aid."

He stared at me, and I couldn't help but to stare right back – right into his scarred, milky eye. "And that's why you called me here? That's why you pulled me away from helping the citizens of Gaelung?"

We both tiptoed around the subject that loomed between us. He was Alanga. So was I. But I knew something else. "I must admit the Shardless Few helping to save the Empire puts me in a difficult position, Gio. Or should I stop calling you that? Should I call you by your original name?"

Everything in his demeanor shifted, went tense and jittery. He was an alley cat with his back arched and ears flat to his head. "What do you mean?"

I closed the trap. "Dione."

He stood stock still. Opened his mouth as if to dissemble and then, deciding better of it, shut it. I lifted the journal. His gaze flitted to it and his face told me that I'd hit my mark. "You translated it."

"Yes. You survived the massacre of the Alanga." I judged his bitter expression. "No. He spared your life."

Dione's mouth twisted. "He thought he was being merciful, leaving me alive and with only one damaged eye. But it's no mercy to live on – year after year after year – when all those you've loved are dead."

A thousand questions swirled in my mind. I couldn't stop them from escaping. "What do you want? Why stay hidden for so long? Where is your ossalen?"

He scoffed at me, his nose wrinkled with contempt. "I don't have to answer your questions. I am not beholden to any Emperor."

I pitched my voice low, soft. "What about a fellow Alanga?"

For a long time, he didn't speak. He stared at me, and then turned his face to the window. "It's taken me years of work. So many years. Another identity, another life. All just to bring them back."

Another identity, another life. Was he speaking of his work with the Shardless Few? And then everything in me went still. I felt as though I were beneath the surface of the Endless Sea, water filling my ears. I reached a hand up to where I'd so often watched others touch. That spot on my skull. A spot that was unmarked. The Sukais didn't tithe their own. And Jovis – he'd told me the story of his Tithing Festival, of the soldier who'd taken pity on his family and had only left him with a scar. Ragan – a cloudtree monk in a monastery, monasteries that were not under my father's jurisdiction.

And the Shardless Few rescued children from Tithing Festival.

All of Gio's lofty ideals, the insistence that the Shardless Few were here to bring about a better life for the people – had he ever meant them? Or was it just a front for what really mattered to him? To Dione?

"Those with shards taken can't bond with ossalen," I whispered.

He fixed me with a level gaze. "And you've just opened the floodgates by ending the Tithing Festival for good. So I should thank you for that."

I wasn't just drifting beneath the surface of the Endless Sea; I was sinking in it, searching for something I could hold on to. "We don't have to be enemies. Isn't that why Ylan Sukai massacred the Alanga in the first place? Too much infighting and too much collateral damage. We can work together. We can find a way into a new era – a peaceful one."

I was rambling and he stood there, as cold and disapproving as my father. He let me finish, let my words die in the ensuing silence. "You owe me nothing. I came here to defend the people of the Empire from the constructs – another Sukai abomination. I didn't come here to help *you*. This is the last time we will meet peaceably." He turned on his heel, not even waiting to be dismissed.

"Wait," I said, scrambling for words. "Isn't there anything—?"

He jerked the door open. "You're a Sukai," he said simply, his back to me. "We can never work together."

The door slammed shut behind him. I was left alone with a book and the echo of Dione's presence – the greatest of the Alanga, and my freshly made enemy.

57

Ranami

Nephilanu Island

News from Gaelung arrived in pieces. The most sensational items arrived first, borne by eager retellings and quick tongues. Ranami wasn't sure what to believe as truth, and what were the tales told by those seeking attention. The battle had been almost lost, the constructs had a fully grown sea serpent on their side, Jovis had been cast out of the Emperor's favor, the Shardless Few had arrived just in time to turn the battle, the dead walked the field.

How was she to make sense of these pieces? The life or death of one governor from Nephilanu was unimportant to most people in comparison. She sifted through the gossip like a desperate woman sifting for a lost earring on the beach.

Ayesh's anxiety was nearly as keen as her own, and in that way they had found common ground. The girl had only just found a mother, and now had to wonder if that relationship had been severed.

When news had finally arrived that Phalue had indeed lived

through the battle, Ranami had felt sick with relief. She and Ayesh had celebrated with an elaborate dinner where they'd both eaten past the point of feeling full, clinking mugs of water as though they were wine and the two of them visiting dignitaries. The waiting became easier, knowing that her love would return to her.

It was almost enough to distract Ranami from everything she was supposed to be doing while Phalue was gone.

Almost.

She kept a hand to the wall as she descended the cellar stairs, a leather satchel in hand. She'd had her suspicions before, though she'd not voiced them. It had taken her writing down every piece of information that had leaked and who might have known to narrow down her suspects. One judicious questioning of a kitchen servant whom she'd immediately dismissed – and she had her answer.

The noise from the kitchens gave way to the cool, oppressive silence of the cellar. Only the crisp turning of pages and the drip, drip, drip of rainwater met her ears. Phalue's father sat in his cell, reading, his broad shoulders hunched over the tiny desk. He started to cough when he heard her footsteps.

"There's no need for that," Ranami said. "Phalue isn't back yet. It's me, and I know you're not sick." She approached the bars.

"Any news about my daughter?"

Her heart softened a little at the concern in his voice. That was genuine, even if the cough wasn't. Phalue was right – he was a decent father, if not a good one. "She's safe and on her way home. It was a near thing, but she's unharmed."

The man sagged with relief. "I thought for a while . . ." He cleared his throat. "I'm glad she's safe, even if she will no longer speak to me." His dark eyes studied her, bushy brows drawn low. "Is that what you're here for? And I *am* sick – I don't know who told you otherwise."

Ranami hefted the pack. "No, that's not what I'm here for." She took the keys from her pocket. "I'm here to set you free."

For a moment, wild hope filled his face. He stood so abruptly his chair nearly fell over. "Did Phalue order this? Has she finally come to her senses?"

"No. I have."

She might have felt sorry for him, the confusion clear on his face, if she hadn't known what he'd done. "I don't understand," he said. "You never wanted to set me free."

"You're right. I didn't. I was angry – too caught up in wanting you to be punished, in wanting you to pay for what you did to the people of Nephilanu. I've had a lot to be angry about. But when I finally let go of that, I started to see things more clearly. I came to understand that leaving you in a cell does nothing. It doesn't help the people of Nephilanu; it doesn't help you. You don't care about what you've done. You don't want to make amends. Instead, you've used your position here, your closeness to your daughter, to do harm. You've been feeding information to the Shardless Few."

Phalue's father scoffed. "That's absurd."

"I dismissed your liaison. She admitted to it."

As she'd suspected, he didn't take much to break. "They said they could get me out of here," he said. "You don't know what it's like, being caged like an animal."

Oh, she knew. She'd known what it was like most days of her life. "You betrayed your own daughter."

He grabbed the bars of the cell. "They weren't going to hurt her; they just wanted her out of the governor's seat."

People were willing to believe all sorts of lies if those lies served their interests.

She didn't bother responding; she only went to the door, unlocked it and swung it open. She held out the bag. "Here are your things. I've had the servants pack you some clothes; there's a package of food in there, plus money — enough to set you up in a flat and pay for your living until you find a place to work."

He stopped on the threshold of the cell and didn't reach for the bag. "You're . . . throwing me out?"

She'd not had the chance to discuss this with her wife, but how could she tell Phalue who she suspected the spy was, especially just as she'd been about to leave for battle? Phalue might be estranged from her father, but she loved him. Ranami hadn't been able to convince her wife that Ayesh might have been a spy — how could she convince Phalue that her own father was spying on her? She wouldn't have believed it. Not without proof. But the longer the man stayed in the palace, the more harm he might do.

Now who was acting impulsively? Phalue might be rubbing off on her.

Ranami sighed and thrust the bag into his chest. He grasped it reflexively. "What did you think would happen, old man? I'd set you free and you'd live in the palace again? Your ex-wife lives in the city; you can manage the same. I don't care anymore about punishing you; that's not justice. I care about keeping you from harming the people of Nephilanu. I care about keeping you from harming my wife. Here, you are still in the seat of your power. There, with the rest of the people, you have none. And maybe living among them will teach you things that Phalue and this cell could not."

"I can't get a job." He sounded so panicked, Ranami might have almost felt sorry for him. Almost.

"You were smart enough to pry secrets from your daughter and sell them; you'll figure something out. Now get out before I have to make the guards escort you. It would be embarrassing for us both."

He had enough dignity to heed that warning. And while she no longer felt any satisfaction for keeping him in the cell, there was a measure to be had from knowing that she, an erstwhile street urchin, was kicking the former governor out of the palace. Life had a way of balancing the scales every so often.

Ranami watched his retreating back and felt a little bit pleased with herself. The construct army was defeated, her wife was on her way home, Ayesh was safe within her keeping and Gio hadn't tried to take Nephilanu. Oh, she wasn't foolish enough to think she was fully responsible for each victory, but she'd had a hand in them all.

Now, if only she could tackle all the items on the list – then she might start thinking she was truly gifted.

She climbed the steps out of the cellar and stopped just as her line of sight crested the kitchen floor. Ayesh was in the pantry, stuffing food into a bag. The shield was strapped to her arm; Ranami had difficulty sometimes getting her to take the damned thing off. The girl was a fixture in the palace now, so the servants paid her no heed. Ranami pressed herself to the wall as she watched. She'd promised herself she'd give Ayesh space, and discovering that Phalue's father was the spy had alleviated all her concerns about the girl, but she had to know. Had the girl made friends outside the palace? If so, they didn't need to scurry about, waiting for Ayesh to bring them food. Ranami could organize a way to get the orphans meals on a regular basis. It was on the list of things they'd intended to accomplish.

Ranami waited until Ayesh had finished packing her bag and had left the kitchen before following her. She hadn't been cautious enough the last time. This time, she used all the skills she'd picked up after years on the streets – keeping close to the walls, keeping her footfalls soft, staying in the shadows. She didn't bother with her cloak by the door. Ayesh, for her part, seemed much more relaxed than when she'd first arrived at the palace. Living there had done much to fill out her sharp edges – both emotionally and physically. The news that Phalue was still alive had done even more.

A light rain pattered on the palm fronds laid above the court-yard. Ranami crept to the gate after the girl, waiting until she'd made her way onto the switchbacks and then ducking into the surrounding brush. She didn't follow the path this time; she cut straight down the slope, making sure not to disturb the plants too much. Her dress was green and blue and blended into the vegetation. With a little luck . . .

Ayesh didn't seem to notice she had a shadow. Her step was jaunty, her head high, the bag slung over one shoulder. She swung her shield-arm with abandon, jabbing out once in a while as though fighting an invisible enemy, shouting, "Hah!"

Ranami could see why Phalue had taken to the girl.

Ayesh became a little more furtive once she reached the city, checking side streets before she passed them, slowing before she turned corners. She'd probably been jumped by other orphans more than once. Ranami remembered doing the same.

But the girl didn't turn into any of the alleyways. She didn't disappear into any sort of hidey-hole, not like Ranami expected. She marched straight to the harbor and then turned westward down the beach. Why the beach? Did the girl have crab traps set up? Did she mean to use the fish as bait to catch . . . more fish? Every possibility that ran through her mind was equally absurd.

She hid in the trees and bushes and walked in parallel with Ayesh, feet sinking into the sandy soil, moisture seeping into her shoes. Phalue would scold her for doing this, she knew. But Phalue trusted so easily and so unequivocally. Ranami could do her best to be more open, but she'd never be like Phalue. She could move on from her past, but she'd always carry pieces of it with her. And she found she wasn't displeased by the prospect.

Ayesh finally stopped when the city disappeared behind a

bend, and then she walked into the forest. Ranami had to take a few steps back to avoid being seen.

She waited as Ayesh passed.

And then she heard voices.

"Sorry it took me so long," Ayesh said. "It's hard to get away these days. I'll have to figure something else out."

"Fine, fine, fine," said a reedy voice Ranami didn't recognize. The rain that slicked her hair to the back of her neck felt like ice. Had she misjudged again? Was Ayesh still a spy? Ah, it would break Phalue's heart. She knelt into the brush and edged closer, her breath held.

"Here." The sound of the bag rustling, then the sound of someone eating.

"You'd like them, I think — my new parents. Phalue is so nice. I don't think Ranami liked me much at first, but she's all right."

"I come with you?" The voice sounded plaintive.

"I don't know," Ayesh said. "I'm not sure that's a good idea."

Ranami pulled a branch out of her line of sight and froze.

Ayesh wasn't speaking to a person.

A creature with mottled gray and brown fur sat in front of the girl, a fish in one paw. It was the size of a large cat, with a long, curling tail, tufted ears, and the nubs of horns at its brow.

She'd only seen two creatures before that resembled it: Mephi and the Emperor's pet, Thrana. This one was more gray than brown, with eyes the color of the jungle in a wet season, but it was the same.

"Why not?" the creature said.

A talking pet was more than Phalue and Ranami had bargained for when they'd adopted Ayesh, but it wasn't as though Ranami could be angry. She was more relieved that Ayesh wasn't a spy than anything else. An odd pet? That was an eccentricity that could be dealt with.

She imagined Phalue, beside her, a wry smile on her lips. "Add it to the list?" Phalue would say.

Ranami rose from her hiding spot, her hands raised to show she meant no harm. "Yes," she said, and Ayesh nearly jumped out of her skin. "Why not?"

The girl very quickly turned from surprise to contrition. She rubbed at the wrist her shield was strapped to, shyly meeting Ranami's eyes. "I . . . uhhh . . . " Her face screwed up. "I found her after Unta," she said. "I helped her aboard the ship I was hiding on, at night. When the sailors caught me, they threw me overboard and she helped me get to shore. I wasn't . . . I wasn't going to just leave her after that."

Ranami waited.

"I didn't know who to trust!" Ayesh burst out.

That was something Ranami could understand. Her heart softened. "She shouldn't be out here in the forest by herself, and neither should you. There's space in the palace. Does she have a name?"

The girl's relieved smile could have parted the clouds. "Yes. Shark, meet Ranami. Ranami, meet Shark."

"Shark!" said the creature, baring sharp white teeth.

Well. That would take a little getting used to. But Ranami was willing to try.

The story continues in . . .

THE BONE SHARD WAR

Book Three of
The Drowning Empire

Acknowledgements

Whew! It's odd to be doing this again. I wrote another book? How and when did that happen? I suppose the answers to that are "one word at a time" and "during a pandemic". Even though we are all socially isolating, I fortunately did not do this alone. So without further ado, the people I owe a debt of gratitude to:

Megan O'Keefe, Marina Lostetter, Tina Gower, and Anthea Sharp/Lawson: THANK YOU for listening to me whine about second books and for helping me brainstorm fixes to my revision problems. I really appreciate you taking the time to read my notes and to speak with me on Zoom. I know you were all probably pretty tired of Zoom by then.

My agent, Juliet Mushens, and her (former, now promoted!) assistant, Liza DeBlock. Juliet, I honestly don't know how you do it? I can always count on you for a quick answer to a question. Liza, your assistance with all of those tax forms was invaluable. Because wow, I would not have known what to do with those all on my own.

And again, the team at Orbit: James Long, Brit Hvide (and thank you to Priyanka, who took over while Brit was out!), Joanna Kramer, Ellen Wright, Nazia Khatun, Nadia Saward and Angela Man. James, I so appreciate you pointing out spots where

I could improve this story and strengthen motivations. Joanna, I am in awe of your sharp eye for repeated words and consistency errors as well as places where I just . . . didn't make sense.

My sister and my brother-in-law, Lei, who offered a place where I could work and not be constantly distracted by my baby (she's very cute, okay?).

My parents and my brother, who have been constantly and consistently encouraging, even if my parents cannot seem to believe this may never be a movie. And Mom and Dad, letting us stay with you after the baby was born was so kind. We had a rough go of things and you made it easier.

John, I would not have been able to get this done without you. Through an exhausting pregnancy and a fresh new colicky baby, you made sure I had the time and space to write. Even though you have your own demanding career, you were constantly asking, "How can I take some of this burden from you?" I will always strive to be the sort of person who deserves you.

Sasha Vinogradova and Charis Loke, for respectively providing such beautiful cover artwork and such a gorgeous map. And Lauren Panepinto at Orbit, whose cover design skills are unparalleled.

I would be remiss if I didn't mention everyone who has read the first book. Your enthusiasm and reviews have made my day repeatedly. I spent years (and years) writing books knowing that a lot of what I wrote would not see the light of day. You've made all of that worth it a thousand times over. Thank you.

extras

orbit

meet the author

Photo Credit: Lei Gong

ANDREA STEWART is the daughter of immigrants and was raised in a number of places across the United States. Her parents always emphasized science and education, so she spent her childhood immersed in Star Trek and odd-smelling library books.

When her (admittedly ambitious) dreams of becoming a dragon slayer didn't pan out, she instead turned to writing books. She now lives in sunny California and, in addition to writing, can be found herding cats, looking at birds, and falling down research rabbit holes.

Find out more about Andrea Stewart and other Orbit authors by registering for the free monthly newsletter at orbitbooks.net.

if you enjoyed
THE BONE SHARD EMPEROR

look out for

THE FOXGLOVE KING

Book One of
The Nightshade Empire

by

Hannah Whitten

From the instant **New York Times** *bestselling author of* **For the Wolf** *comes a brand-new adventure filled with dark secrets, twisted magic, glittering palaces, and forbidden romance.*

When Lore was thirteen, she escaped a cult in the catacombs beneath the city of Dellaire. And in the ten years since, she's lived by one rule: Don't let them find you. Easier said than done, when her death magic ties her to the city.

Mortem, the magic born from death, is a high-priced and illicit commodity in Dellaire, and Lore's job running poisons keeps her in food, shelter, and relative security. But when a run goes wrong and Lore's power is revealed, Lore fully expects a pyre, but King August has a different plan. Entire villages on the outskirts of the country have been dying overnight, seemingly at random. Lore can either

extras

use her magic to find out what's happening and who in the King's court is responsible, or die.

Lore is thrust into the Sainted King's glittering court, where no one can be believed and even fewer can be trusted.

It'd been three years since any of them had paid rent, but Nicolas still thought to send his most unfortunate son to ask at the end of every month. Lore assumed they drew straws, and assumed that someone cheated, because it was always the youngest and spottiest of the bunch. Pierre, his name was, and he carried it nearly as poorly as he carried his father's already overfull purse.

A dressing gown that had seen better days dripped off one shoulder as Lore leaned against the doorframe at an angle carefully calculated to appear nonchalant. Pierre's eyes kept drifting there, and she kept having to press her lips together not to laugh. Apparently, a crosshatch of silvery scars from back-alley knife fights didn't deter the man when presented with bare skin.

She had other, more interesting scars. But she kept her palm closed tight.

A cool breeze blew off the harbor, and Lore suppressed a shiver. Pierre didn't seem to spare any thought for wondering why she'd exited the house barely dressed, right at the edge of autumn. An easy mark in more ways than one.

"Pierre!" Lore shot him a dazzling grin, the same one that made Michal's eyes go heated and then narrow before asking what she wanted. Another twist against the doorframe, another seemingly casual pose, another bite of wind that made a curse bubble behind her teeth. "It's the end of the month already?"

"I—um—yes." Pierre managed to fix his eyes to her face, through obviously conscious effort. "My father...um, he said this time he means it, and..."

Lore let her face fall by careful degrees, first into confusion, then shock, then sorrow. "Oh," she murmured, wrapping her arms around herself and turning her face away to show a length of pale white neck. "This month, of all months."

She didn't elaborate. She didn't need to. If there was anything Lore had learned in twenty-three years alive, ten spent on the streets of Dellaire, it was that men generally preferred you to be a set piece in the story they made up, rather than trying to tell it yourself.

In that regard, Pierre didn't disappoint. From the corner of her eye, she saw his pale brows draw together, a deepening blush lighting the skin beneath his freckles. They were all moon-pale, Nicolas's boys. It made their blushes look like something viral.

His eyes went past her, to the depths of the dilapidated row house beyond. It was morning, though only just, and the shadows hid everything but the dust motes twisting in sun shards. Not that there was much to see back there, anyway. Michal was still asleep upstairs, and Elle was sprawled on the couch, a wine bottle in her hand and a slightly musical snore on her lips.

"Is there an illness?" Pierre kept his voice hushed, low. His face tried for sympathetic, but it looked more like he'd put bad milk in his coffee. "A child?"

Lore's brows shot up. In all the stories she'd let men spin about her, *that* was a first. But beggars couldn't be choosers. She gently laid a hand on her abdomen and let that be answer enough. It wasn't technically a lie if she let him draw his own conclusions.

She was past caring about lying, anyway. In the eyes of the Bleeding God, Lore was damned whether or not she kept her spiritual record spotless. Might as well lean into it.

"Oh, you poor girl." Pierre was probably younger than she was, and here he went clucking like a mother hen. Lore managed to keep her eyes from rolling, but only just. "Do you know who the father is?" He raised his hand, settled it on her bare shoulder.

And every nerve in Lore's body seized.

It was abrupt and unexpected enough for her to shudder, to shake off his hand in a motion that didn't fit the soft, vulnerable narrative she'd been building ever since she opened this damn door. She'd grown used to feeling this reaction to dead things—stone, metal, cloth. Corpses, when she couldn't avoid them. It was natural to sense Mortem in something dead, no matter how unpleasant, and at this point, she could hide her reaction, keep it contained.

She shouldn't feel Mortem in a living man, not one who wasn't at death's door. Her shock was quick and sharp, and chased with something else—the scent of foxglove.

Her fingers closed around his wrist, twisted, forced him to his knees at the edge of the doorframe. It happened quick, quick enough for him to slip on a stray pebble and send one leg out at an awkward angle, for a strangled "*Shit!*" to echo through the silent morning streets of Dellaire's Harbor District.

Lore crouched so they were level. Now that she knew what to look for, it was clear in his eyes. All poisons worked differently, and foxglove was one of the riskier ones. Pierre's gaze was bloodshot and glassy; his heartbeat under her hand, slow and irregular. He'd gone to one of the cheap deathdealers, then. One who didn't know how to properly dose their patrons, one who only gave them enough to make them sick, not bring them to death's threshold. Stupid.

The Mortem under Pierre's skin throbbed against her grip, thumping and meaty, a second, diseased pulse. Mortem was in everyone—the essence of death, the darkness born of entropy—but the only way to use it, to bend it to your will, was to nearly die. To touch oblivion, and for oblivion to touch you back, then let you go.

Most died before they got there. More never got close enough, earning only a sour stomach or blindness or a scattered mind for their efforts. And some didn't actually want the power at all, just the euphoria, a poison high that skated you near death, but not near enough to wield it. It took a closer brush with eternity to use Mortem than most were willing to try.

The Bleeding God and Buried Goddess knew Lore wouldn't have, if she'd had the choice.

"Here's what's going to happen," she murmured to Pierre. "You are going to tell Nicolas that we've paid up for the next six months, or I am going to tell him you've been visiting deathdealers."

That was enough to make his eyes widen, glassy and poison-heavy or not. "How—"

"You stink of foxglove and your eyes look more like windows." Not exactly true, since she hadn't noticed until she'd sensed the Mortem, but by the time he could examine himself, the effect would've worn off anyway. "Anyone can take one look at you and know, Pierre, even though your deathdealer barely gave you enough to make you tingle." She cocked her head. "You weren't after it to *use* it, I hope, or you were completely swindled. Even if you only wanted the high, you didn't get your money's worth."

The boy gaped, the open mouth under his window-glass eyes making his face look fishlike. He'd undoubtedly paid a handsome sum for the pinch of foxglove he'd taken. If it wasn't so imperative that she lie low, Lore might've become a deathdealer. They made a whole lot of coin for doing a whole lot of jack shit.

Pierre's unfortunate blush spread down his neck. "I can't—He'll ask where the money is—"

"I'm confident an industrious young man like yourself can come up with it somewhere." A flick of her fingers, and Lore let him go. Pierre stumbled up on shaky legs—Buried Goddess and her plucked-out eyes, she should've *known* he was on something; he stood like a colt—and straightened his mussed shirt. "I'll try," he said, voice just as tremulous as the rest of him. "I can't promise he'll believe me."

Lore gave him a winning smile. Standing, she yanked up the shoulder of her dressing gown. "He better."

Eyes wide, the boy turned down the street. The Harbor District was slowly waking up—bundles of cloth stirred in dark corners, drunks coaxed awake by the sun and the cold sea breeze. In the row house across the street, Lore heard the telltale sighs of Madam Brochfort's girls starting their daily squabbles over who got the washtub first, and any minute now, at least two straggling patrons would be politely but firmly escorted outside.

Soothing, familiar. In all her years of rambling around Dellaire, here was the only place where it really felt like home.

"Pierre?" she called when he was halfway down the street. He

557

turned, lips pressed together, clearly considering what other things she might blackmail him with.

"A word of advice." She turned toward Michal's row house in a flutter of threadbare dressing gown. "The real deathdealers have morgues in the back."

Elle was awake, but only just. She squinted from beneath a pile of gold curls through the light-laden dust, paint still smeared across her lips. "Whassat?"

"As if you don't know." There was barely enough coffee in the chipped ceramic pot for one cup. Lore poured all of it into the stained cloth she used as a strainer and balled it in her hand as she put the kettle over the fire. If there was only one cup of coffee in this house, she'd be the one drinking it. "End of the month, Elle-Flower."

"Don't call me that." Elle groaned as she shifted to sit. She'd fallen asleep in her dancer's tights, and a long run traced up each calf. It'd piss her off once she noticed, but the patrons of the Foghorn and Fiddle down the street wouldn't care. One squinting look into the wine bottle to make sure it was empty, and Elle shoved off the couch to stand. "Michal isn't awake, we don't have to pretend to like each other."

It was extremely obvious to anyone with the misfortune of being in the same room as the two of them that Lore and Elle didn't like each other, and Elle's older brother knew it better than most. But Lore just shrugged.

Elle pushed past her into the kitchen, the spiderweb cracks on the windows refracting veined light on the tattered edges of her tulle skirt. She peered into the pot. "No coffee?"

Lore tightened her hand around the cloth knotted in her fist. "Afraid not."

"Bleeding *God*." Elle flopped onto one of the chairs by the pock-marked kitchen table. For a dancer, she was surprisingly ungraceful when sober. "I'll take tea, then."

"*Surely* you don't expect me to get it for you."

A grumble and a roll of bright blue eyes as Elle slunk her way toward the cupboard. While her back was turned, Lore tucked the straining cloth into the lip of her mug and poured hot water over it.

Still grumbling, Elle scooped tea that was little more than dust into another mug. "Well?" She took the kettle from Lore without looking at her. "How'd it go?"

Lore kept her back turned as she tugged the straining cloth and the tiny knot of coffee grounds from her cup and stuffed it in the pocket of her dressing gown. "We're paid up for six months."

"Is that why you look so disheveled?" Elle's mouth pulled into a self-satisfied moue. "He could get it cheaper across the street."

"The dishevelment is the fault of your brother, actually." Lore turned and leaned against the counter with a cat's smile. "And barbs about Madam's girls don't suit you, Elle-Flower. It's work like any other. To think otherwise just proves you dull."

Another eye roll. Elle made a face when she sipped her weak tea, and sharp satisfaction hitched Lore's smile higher. She took a long, luxurious sip of coffee.

Another knock, shivering through the morning quiet and nearly shaking the thin boards of the row house.

Elle rose up on her tiptoes to look out the small window above the sink, head craned toward the door. She raised her eyebrows. "Your boss is here."

Swearing under her breath, Lore plunked her mug on the counter with a dangerous *clink* of porcelain and strode toward the door.

"Hey," Elle whined from the kitchen. "There was *too* coffee!"

For the second time that morning, Lore wrenched open the door, the squealing hinges echoing through the row house. "Val."

Green eyes glinted beneath a faded scarf, white-blond hair a corona around pale cheeks sunburned to ruddy. Val always wore the same scarf and the same braid, and she never wasted time with pleasantries. "You and Michal need to be headed for the Ward in fifteen minutes."

"Good morning to you, too."

"I'm not playing, mouse." Val gave a scrutinizing look to Lore's dressing gown, her mussed hair. "This could be a hard job. You need to be ready."

"I always am." In the ten years since Lore had been running poisons for Val, she'd never had the woman herself show up like this, right before a drop. A confused line carved between her brows. "Is something the matter, Val?"

The older woman shifted on her feet, her eyes flicking away for half a heartbeat before landing on Lore's again, steadied and sure. "It's fine," she said. "This is just a new client. I want to make sure everything goes off without a hitch."

"It will." Lore nodded, channeling confidence she didn't quite feel. "Don't worry."

Val stood there a moment longer, mouth twisted. Then, whip-quick, she leaned forward and pressed her dry lips to Lore's forehead. She was off the stoop and headed down the road before Lore's teeth clicked shut, chasing the shock off her face. The old poison runner might be the closest thing Lore had to a mother, but she still wasn't one for affection.

Lore's brows stayed furrowed as she went back to the kitchen and collected her coffee again—though the look on Elle's face said chances were high she'd spit in it—then drifted toward the stairs.

Could just be nerves. It'd been a while since Val picked up a new client. Most of the deathdealers they ran poison for were well established, dug into the underbelly of the city like rot in a tooth. Mari, Val's partner, was historically picky about who the team took on. The two of them had raised Lore on tough love and hard choices, and *be careful about who you let in* was high on their list of lessons.

Maybe the collective coffers were low, though Lore couldn't imagine why. It seemed to her like more and more people were gobbling down poison every day, stuffing their mouths with petals to chase power or death or a few hours of kaleidoscopic high.

Whatever. She'd never had a head for the business side of things. Just the running. Lore was good at running.

The stairs of the row house were rickety, like pretty much everything else, and the fourth one squeaked something awful. Lore made sure to grind her heel into it. Fifteen minutes weren't much, and Michal needed the job with Val's team. Even with rent taken care of, they could use all the coin they could get. She didn't want him in the boxing ring again.

Michal had apparently heard the squeak. He was sitting up when Lore pushed aside the ratty curtain closing off their room, sheets tangled around his waist and dripping off the side of the mattress to pool on the floor. The light through the cracked windows caught his gold hair, so like his sister's. He ran a hand through it and squinted at her. "Coffee?"

Lore leaned against the doorframe. "Last cup, but I'll share if you come get it."

"That's generous, since I assume you need it." He grumbled as he levered himself up from the floor-bound mattress, holding the sheet around his naked hips. "You had another nightmare last night."

Her cheeks colored, but Lore just shrugged. The nightmares were a recent development, and random—she could never remember anything about them, nothing but darkness and the feeling of being trapped. Usually she could trace her dreams back to a source, pick out a piece and see how something she'd thought about that day had alchemized as she slept, but since the nightmares were so vague, she couldn't figure them out. It made them more unsettling. "Sorry if I kept you up."

"At least you didn't scream this time. Just tossed and turned." Michal took a long drink from her proffered mug, though his face twisted up when he swallowed. "Damn, that's bitter."

She didn't tell him that the taste was probably not improved by his sister's spit. "Val came by. We need to leave in fifteen minutes."

Another squint. His eyes were blue, also like Elle's, but deeper and warmer. If Elle's eyes were morning sky, his were twilight. "Guess I'll be late, then." He leaned in and kissed her, mouth hungry and as warm as his eyes.

She kissed him back, just for a moment, before pushing him away. "If we don't make it to the rendezvous point in time, it'll be *crawling*."

Michal frowned, concern cutting through the haze of heat and sleep. "I wish Val didn't make you watch the drop point," he said quietly. "It isn't safe."

The solemnity in his voice made her stomach swoop, for more reasons than one. Lore poked his shoulder, and her lips bent the corner of a smile. "I can take care of myself."

"Doesn't mean you should have to."

Her wry smile flickered.

But Michal didn't notice, running a hand through his hair to tame it while he bent to pull clothes from the piles on the floor. The sheet dropped, and Lore allowed herself an ogle.

"I don't get why she always gives you the most dangerous jobs," he said, voice muffled by thin cotton as he pulled a shirt over his head. "Didn't she and Mari *raise* you? They act like your mothers, and then they send you to be the lookout. It doesn't make sense."

Lore just shrugged. She'd only given Michal her history in broad strokes, an outline she had no intention of ever filling in. He knew it, too, though sometimes he prodded. "Yes, they raised me, but that just means I know my shit," she said, turning to slip her feet in her well-worn boots. "And we need to get a move on. Val won't tolerate lateness, even if the guilty party is my..."

She didn't finish the sentence. She wasn't quite sure how.

The mischievous curve to Michal's mouth said he noticed. Now dressed, he crossed the room, hooking his hands languidly on her hips as she turned away to hide an answering smirk. He leaned forward, chest against her back, brushing his lips over the shell of her ear. "Your what?"

Lore turned, flicking his collarbone, biting her lip to keep it from turning up. "*Mine*," she finished decisively, and let him kiss her again.

Still, cold clawed into her chest. She could feel Mortem everywhere, now, like her realization that it was somewhere it shouldn't be had sharpened her perception of all the places where it *should*—the cloth of Michal's trousers beneath her hands, the stones in the street outside, the chipped ceramic of the mug on the windowsill. Here on the outskirts of Dellaire she didn't feel it as intensely as she would near the catacombs, near the Citadel, but it was still enough to make her skin crawl.

The Harbor District, on the southern edge of Dellaire, was as far as Mortem would let her go. She could try to hop a ship, try to trek out on the winding roads that led into the rest of Auverraine, but it'd be pointless. She was tied into this damn city as surely as death was tied into life, as surely as the crescent moon carved into her palm.

All of it, reminders—she shouldn't linger too long. She shouldn't get too close. It wasn't safe.

Michal's mouth found her throat, and she arched into him, closing her eyes like it might shut out the cold in her chest and the itch of so much death. Her fingers clawed into his hair, and his arm tightened around her waist like he might lift her up, carry her to their mattress on the floor, and forget all about running poison for Val. Forget about everything but safety found in skin.

She wanted to let him, and that was the decision-maker, in the end. Lore had to stop using people like fences, like moats, like things to wall herself in with.

Masking it as playful, she pushed Michal away. "*Go.* Val won't wait."

Blue eyes hazy, Michal pulled back. "Will you?"

He asked every day. Neither of them knew if it was a joke. But today, there was something newly apprehensive in his face, as if for the first time he knew the answer was *no.*

So Lore kissed him again instead of speaking.

He lingered at her lips a moment before stepping back. "I'll see you at the Northwest Ward, right?" He switched into reciting the plans for the drop-off instead of asking her anything further. Smart man, not to push. "Right at the bell, when the guard is changing. Leave the cart at the old storefront. And you'll stay with it until it gets picked up from the catacombs' entrance."

A tiny shiver slunk over Lore's skin at the mention of the catacombs. "Shouldn't take long," she said, trying to sound reassuring. It wasn't so bad, the outer branches of the catacombs—outside of the city center, they were little more than tunnels, the dead were all kept under the Citadel—but being close to them still made her feel twitchy.

Lore knew the catacombs. Not just in the sense of someone who remembered the twists and turns of a place—Lore felt them, a part of her, like if you turned her skin inside out, a map would be printed on the wet, bloody underside. And because of that uncanny *knowing*, she'd be able to tell if someone was coming through them.

Another handy side effect of a dark, strange childhood.

She'd been the watchdog for the crew since she was thirteen, when Mari first found her wandering the streets with blank eyes, and brought her back to Val's headquarters at the docks. Val, thankfully, didn't ask why or how Lore had acquired such an odd skill. She just put it to use.

And if Lore stayed with Michal, who was increasingly vocal about his objection to her dangerous position, things could get precarious for him.

She closed her eyes.

A calloused hand on her cheek made them open again. Michal kissed her, sweetly this time, without heat. "Be careful," he murmured. Then he slipped out.

Alone, Lore took a deep, ragged breath. Despite the chill outside, the sun through the cracked window was warm on her skin. She rested her forehead against the glass and counted her breaths, an old trick from childhood to calm her heart, calm her nerves.

They'd still be looking for her. Lore knew that. And the longer she stayed in one place, the easier she'd be to find.

She could move in with Val and Mari again, if she wanted. That door was always open. But having someone who tried to control her comings and goings never sat well with her, after... after what her life had been like before.

So not with Val, then. But staying here wasn't an option.

It'd be awkward to end things, with both her and Michal on Val's team. Val would intercede where she could once she knew the situation, but it would be impossible for them not to see each other at all. Val had warned her as much, when Lore first took up with Michal. Lore had thrown it back at her, saying that Val and Mari had obviously made it work, so why couldn't she? But both of them knew it wasn't the same, that it was an argument for the sake of arguing. Lore wasn't looking to be settled. Lore was always running, always moving. She just liked to rest sometimes.

She sighed, forehead still pressed to the glass. It'd be easiest if she could make Michal hate her, probably. And though the thought was an ice pick, she knew she could do it. She could make Michal glad she'd decided to leave, hurt him so badly that he'd never try to get close again.

That would be easiest.

Lore opened her eyes, straightened. She pushed aside the curtain that served as a door and walked down the stairs.

A flounce of tulle on the couch indicated that Elle had resumed her pre-breakfast position. Lore huffed a laugh. "Bye, Elle-Flower."

Elle groaned in response.

At the threshold, Lore paused, placing her hand along the weather-beaten wood of the lintel. She'd stayed here longer than any of the previous places—with Michal, with Elle. He was a good man, one of the first she'd encountered. He cared about her.

She'd miss him more than the house, more than the safety. *That* was new.

Another pat against the doorframe. "Goodbye," Lore murmured, then she slipped out to lose herself in Dellaire's streets again.

if you enjoyed
THE BONE SHARD EMPEROR

look out for

THE STARDUST THIEF
Book One of
The Sandsea Trilogy

by

Chelsea Abdullah

Inspired by stories from One Thousand and One Nights, The Stardust Thief *weaves the gripping tale of a legendary smuggler, a cowardly prince, and a dangerous quest across the desert to find a legendary, magical lamp.*

Neither here nor there, but long ago....

Loulie al-Nazari is the Midnight Merchant: a criminal who, with the help of her jinn bodyguard, hunts and sells illegal magic. When she saves the life of a cowardly prince, she draws the attention of his powerful father, the sultan, who blackmails her into finding an ancient lamp that has the power to revive the barren land—at the cost of sacrificing all jinn.

With no choice but to obey or be executed, Loulie journeys with the sultan's oldest son to find the artifact. Aided by her bodyguard, who has secrets of his own, they must survive ghoul attacks, outwit a vengeful jinn queen, and confront a malicious killer from Loulie's past. And in a world where story is reality and illusion is truth, Loulie will discover that everything—her enemy, her magic, even her own past—is not what it seems, and she must decide who she will become in this new reality.

1

Loulie

When Loulie al-Nazari was told by the One-Eyed Merchant to meet on a small and humble dhow, she expected, quite reasonably, a small and humble dhow. But the dhow was not small, and it was not humble. It was, in fact, quite the opposite.

The *Aysham* was a behemoth of a ship, with full sails, a spacious deck, an impressive assortment of rooms, and a lofty crow's nest. It was, by any measure, a very nice ship. Had she been here as a passenger, she would have enjoyed exploring it.

But Loulie was not here as a passenger. She was here as the Midnight Merchant, an esteemed magic seller, and she had come to meet with a client who was keeping her waiting long past their scheduled meeting time. *I will call for you the first hour of moonrise,* his message had said. Only, the hour had come and gone, and Loulie was still waiting for him on deck, dressed in the star-patterned merchant's robe that made her stick out like a sore thumb.

She turned her back on the gawking, well-dressed passengers and focused on the horizon. There were no familiar constellations in the sky, and the night was dark and gloomy, which hardly helped her mood. For what was probably the dozenth time that hour, she sighed.

"I wish you were in your lizard shape," she said to the man standing beside her.

He angled his head to look at her. Though his stony expression barely shifted, Loulie perceived a very slight height difference between his brows. He was most certainly raising one at her. "And what good would that do us in this situation?"

"You could sneak belowdecks and find our client's room. You're useless in your man shape."

The umber-skinned man said nothing, but his silence was easy to decipher. Loulie had known him for nine years—long enough to understand all his mannerisms and magics. She was no longer surprised by his shapeshifting or by the fire that danced in his eyes when he grew emotional. Right now, he was quiet because he knew she would not like what he had to say.

"We're offering the man magic," Loulie said. "The least he can do is be on time for a meeting *he* proposed."

"Don't think too hard on it. What will be will be."

"Sage advice, oh mighty jinn," she mumbled beneath her breath.

Qadir's lips twitched into a brief smile. He enjoyed toying with her—he was the only one who got away with it.

Loulie was considering breaking into the ship's interior when she heard approaching footsteps and turned to see a man in a white thobe.

"Midnight Merchant." He bowed. "I have been sent by Rasul al-Jasheen to bring you to the designated meeting place."

She and Qadir exchanged a look. His deadpan expression said, *I told you not to worry.*

"It's about time." She gestured to Qadir. "This man is my bodyguard. He shall accompany me."

The messenger nodded before leading them through crowds of colorfully dressed nobles to an obscure back door on the other side of the ship. He rapped on the door in a specific fashion until it was opened by a burly man, who guided them down a dimly lit corridor. At the end of the hallway, the man rapped on a different door in a different pattern. There was the sound of a lock and a key, then the messenger opened the door and beckoned them inside.

Loulie looked at Qadir. *After you*, his silence said. She smiled before ducking inside.

The first thing she noticed upon her entry was that there were mercenaries—three of them, each positioned in a different corner of the small room. Unlike the nobles on deck wearing brilliant robes, these men were dressed mostly in weapons.

Her mind filled with images of bloodshed and murder. Of her mother, waving frantically at an empty jar, telling her to hide. Of her father, lying in a pool of his own blood.

She took a deep, steadying breath and looked to the center of the room, where a merchant dressed in hues of green sat on a cushion behind a low-rising table. True to his title, Rasul al-Jasheen had only one muddy-brown eye. The other was a glossy white orb half-hidden beneath layers of scarred skin. He had a nose that looked as if it had been broken and reset many times, and a forehead that was at once impressive and unfortunate in size. He was vaguely familiar, and Loulie wondered if maybe she'd passed his stall in some souk before.

The merchant's lips parted to reveal a shining smile composed of gold, bronze, and white teeth. "Midnight Merchant. What a pleasure to see you in the flesh. I apologize for the late summons. I was entertaining important guests." His eyes roved over her.

She imagined what he was seeing: a short, seemingly fragile woman dressed in layers of blue velvet shawls dusted with soft white. Stardust, she called the pattern. Appropriate, for it had belonged to her tribe. The Najima tribe. The Night Dwellers.

As was usual, the merchant stared at her half-covered face longer than at her robes. Most of the men in this business tried to intimidate her by looking right into her eyes.

It never worked.

"Please." He gestured to the cushion on the other side of the table. "Have a seat."

She glanced over her shoulder at Qadir, who had not budged from his spot by the door. Though the merchant had not acknowledged him, the mercenaries eyed him warily. Qadir showed no sign of being perturbed. But then, he rarely did.

Loulie sat.

The merchant offered his hand. "Rasul al-Jasheen. It is an honor."

She clasped it. "Loulie al-Nazari." She pulled her hand away quickly, wary of the way his eyes lingered on her iron rings.

"I must confess, I was not expecting you to be so . . . young."

Ah yes. Because twenty is so young.

She smiled at him pleasantly. "You are exactly as I expected. One eye and all."

Silence. Then, remarkably, the merchant started laughing. "That is where I get my title, yes. As you can imagine, it is also the reason I called you here tonight. I assume you have the magic I requested?" Loulie nodded. Rasul cleared his throat. "Well, let's see it, then."

She reached into her pocket and withdrew a coin. The merchant watched skeptically as she vanished it between her fingers. From his side of the table, he could not see the face on either side: a jinn warrior on one and a human sultan on the other. Every time the coin reappeared, it sported a different face.

Human, jinn, human, jinn.

"Must I remind you of our deal?" She held up the coin between pinched fingers.

Rasul frowned. "I already paid you in advance."

"You paid in advance *once*. Now you must pay the other half."

"I will not pay for a magic I have yet to see with my own eyes."

Loulie did her best to ignore the stares of the armed men around her. *Nothing can happen to me. Not while Qadir is here.*

She shrugged, feigning nonchalance as she reached into her merchant's bag. The bag of infinite space, Qadir called it, for it had a seemingly endless bottom. "If seeing is believing . . ." She withdrew a vial. It was a small thing, no bigger than one of her fingers. The minute the One-Eyed Merchant beheld the sparkling liquid inside, he tried to snatch it from her hand.

She tucked it away, into her sleeve. "I'll take the other half of my payment now."

"That could be water, for all I know!"

"And? If it is water, steal your gold back." She gestured to the human weapons lining the room. "That is why they're here, isn't it? To make sure this exchange goes as planned?"

The merchant pressed his lips together and snapped his fingers. One of the men set a pouch in Rasul's hands, which he offered to Loulie. She scanned the coins inside and, just to make sure she wasn't being scammed, flipped the two-faced coin. It came down on the human side. *Truth.*

She offered him the vial. "Your requested magic: the Elixir of Revival."

The merchant snatched it from her, and Loulie smiled beneath her scarf as he fumbled with the stopper. He was so excited, his hands were shaking.

If only he realized how easy this magic was to find.

Her eyes slid to Qadir. Though his expression was stony as always, she imagined a smug smile on his lips. She recalled the words he'd spoken the day she shared Rasul's request with him: *One jinn's blood is a human man's medicine.*

There was a reason humans called it the Elixir of Revival.

That reason became apparent as the One-Eyed Merchant blinked the silvery contents of the vial into his eye. Loulie watched as sparkling tears streamed down his cheek, making his skin glow. But while this effect was temporary, something more permanent was happening to the merchant's blind eye.

Darkness bloomed in the center of his iris like an inkblot spreading on a scroll. With every blink it spread, growing wider and wider until the blackness lightened to a dark brown.

Medicine indeed.

Soon it was not just the so-called elixir that fell from his eyes, but real tears. Even the mercenaries were unable to mask their shock as Rasul fixed both of his eyes on them.

"Praise be to the gods," he whispered.

Loulie grinned. "Worth the price?"

"Such a miracle is priceless." Rasul rubbed at his tearstained face, carefully avoiding the newly revived eye. "A thousand blessings upon you, Loulie al-Nazari."

Loulie dipped her head. "And a thousand upon you. May I offer a piece of advice?" Rasul paused to look at her. "I suggest you come up with a new title. One-Eyed is a little melodramatic."

The merchant burst out laughing. Loulie found, much to her surprise, that she was laughing with him. Once Rasul had finished heaping praises upon her and insisted on treating her to a stupendous feast later that evening, she left.

She and Qadir shared a look as they walked back down the corridor. The jinn lifted his hand to showcase the healing scab from a self-inflicted wound he'd made mere days ago.

She mouthed the words *Shukran, oh holy, priceless miracle.*

Qadir shrugged. He looked like he was trying not to smile.

—⊶—

Mama and Baba are dead. *The words kept cycling through her mind. Every time Layla buried them, they resurfaced, a reality she could not escape.*

Had the jinn not been dragging her through the desert, she would have succumbed to the weight of her sorrow days ago. But even when her body grew heavy with fatigue, he pressed forward. At first, she despised him for this—even feared him.

But the fear eventually faded. First into reluctance, then defeat. Why did it matter where the jinn was taking her? He'd told her that the compass her father had given her would lead them to a city, but she did not care about the city.

She did not care about anything.

Many sunrises later, she collapsed. She wanted to cry, but her chest was too heavy and her eyes too dry. The jinn waited patiently. When she did not rise, he picked her up and set her atop his shoulders. She was forced to hold on to him as he scaled a cliff.

That night, after the jinn had started a fire with nothing but a snap of his fingers, he took a coin from his pocket and set it on his palm.

"Watch." He curled his fingers over the coin. When he next uncurled them, his palm was empty. Layla was intrigued despite herself. When she asked if it was magic, the jinn clenched and unclenched his fingers, and the coin was again on his palm.

"A trick," he said.

Layla looked closely at the coin. It appeared to be a foreign currency, with the face of a human sultan on one side and a jinn wreathed in fire on the other. "There are two lands in this world," Qadir said. "Human and jinn. And so there are two sides to this coin."

He made the coin vanish and reappear between his fingers, moving so quickly she could not track the movement. "This may be a trick, but the coin itself is magic. It will tell you the real or moral truth of any situation."

He set the coin down on Layla's palm. "See for yourself. Flip it, and if it comes up on the human side, the answer is yes. If it comes up on the other, the answer is no."

Layla would not have believed it was truly magic had the coin been given to her a few days ago. But things had changed. She was no longer so naive.

"My family is dead," she whispered as she flipped the coin.

It came up on the human side.

She breathed out and tried again. "A jinn saved my life."

Human.

Tears sprang to her eyes as the coin continued to come up on the human side, confirming her new reality. Truth. Truth. Truth.

"I am alone." Her shoulders shook with sobs as she threw the coin into the air. It bounced off her knee and rolled away, back to the jinn. For a few moments, Qadir said nothing. Then he silently reached for her hand and set the coin on her palm.

Jinn.

He curled her fingers around it. "Not alone," he said. "Not anymore."

—⁓—

Loulie was lost in her memories and absently making the two-faced coin vanish between her fingers when she returned to the *Aysham*'s deck the next morning. The crowds from the previous night had dispersed, and the sailors paid her no mind as she wandered past them in her plain brown robes. She had traded the scarves obscuring her face for a light shawl, which she wrapped loosely around her head and shoulders to better feel the sun on her cheeks. It was a relief, as always, to doff her merchant apparel and bask in anonymity the day after a sale.

Also a relief: the familiar, hazy shape of Madinne in the distance. Loulie smiled at the sight of the city. "Qadir, do you see that?"

The jinn, now in his lizard form and humming softly in her ear, shifted on her shoulder. He made a sound of confirmation.

She drew closer to the ship's railings. Even through an orange veil of sand, the sun was bright enough she could make out the tiers of the great desert city of Madinne. At the top was the sultan's palace, made up of beautiful white domed towers and minarets that reached for the sun. It was surrounded on all sides by colorful buildings—stone and wooden constructions both domed and flat, tall and squat. And somewhere in the midst of those buildings, nestled in a nexus of crooked, winding alleyways, was home. Their home.

"I wonder how Dahlia is doing." Qadir's voice, made much softer by his smaller form, was directly in her ear.

"However she's doing, she'll be much better when we drop by with our rent."

Qadir made a clicking sound—she still wasn't sure whether he did it with his teeth or tongue—and said, "Yes, because our rent is equivalent to all the coin in our bag."

"I won't give her *all* of our earnings."

"That last exchange was for my blood, you know."

Loulie suppressed a smile as she looked over her shoulder at the sailors. Though the men were far from graceful, she could not help but think they resembled dancers in the easy way they went about their docking preparations.

"Would you like me to keep your blood money, then?"

Qadir hissed. "I do not need your human gold."

"Ah, what a shame. And here I thought you'd enjoy spending it on wine or women. You know the dealers won't take your commemorative coins." She glanced at the two-faced coin between her fingers.

"Loulie?"

"Mm?" She slid the coin into her pocket.

"I overhear talk of the sultan."

Suppressing a groan, Loulie turned and surveyed the deck. Other than the sailors, she spotted a few scattered groups of people. She walked between them, keeping her expression blank as she eavesdropped. As little interest as she had in the sultan, she could not afford to ignore the gossip. Not when she, a criminal, always tried to avoid his men.

But while she caught two sailors trading profanity-laden opinions, heard a couple confessing forbidden love to one another, and was audience to a strange riddle game, she overheard nothing about the sultan.

She had just given up hope when she spotted Rasul al-Jasheen speaking with a man wearing the uniform of the sultan's guard. Loulie quickly glanced away and slowed her pace as she approached them.

"The sultan's councillors are beside themselves," the guard was saying.

Rasul snorted. "Why does he not send the high prince to search for the relic?"

The guard glanced in her direction. Loulie grabbed hold of a passing sailor and asked him in her most pleasant voice if he knew where they were docking. The sailor responded, but she was not listening. Not to him, anyway.

"Could such a treasure really exist?" Rasul said.

"The rumors are that the sultan's late wife brought up the artifact in one of her stories."

She thanked the sailor and angled her head to catch Rasul's response.

"Poor man. Does he truly believe Lady Shafia's stories were true?"

The guard shrugged. "They had power enough to stop the killings, so perhaps." There was a mournful pause. All desert dwellers knew of the sultan's wife killings, just as all knew of Shafia, who had stopped them with her stories. She was as much a legend as the tales she'd told.

"His Majesty believes there is something in one of her stories that will help him claim a victory over the jinn."

"Against the jinn? They are like flies; surely you cannot kill them all." Rasul's voice died down to a murmur. By the time the wind brought the conversation back to her ears, they were speaking about something else.

"But tell me about this miracle!" the guard said. "I hear the Midnight Merchant herself delivered the elixir to you? Do you have any idea how she obtained it?"

"None. But I suppose it wouldn't be much of a miracle if we knew the how of it." Rasul laughed. "Regardless, I bless the gods for my good luck. I did not think she would so readily accept my request."

Qadir sighed in her ear. "Why do humans thank the gods for things they do not do?"

"Because they are fools that believe in fate," Loulie said bitterly. If these gods existed, they had not batted their lashes when her family was murdered.

She glanced over her shoulder at the looming city. They were close enough now that she could make out people on the docks waving at the ship. She turned and made her way toward the bow for a better view. Behind her, the guard was still talking.

"What a shame she disappeared! I would have liked to see this legendary merchant."

Rasul sighed. "She had a sharp tongue, to be sure, but what a rare gem she was. Had she not disappeared last night, I would have convinced her to have dinner with me in Madinne. Can you imagine it? Having the Midnight Merchant on your arm?"

Loulie thought again of how relieved she was to have slipped out of her merchant's clothing and rubbed the kohl from her eyes this morning. For if the formerly one-eyed merchant had invited her to dinner with the intention of flaunting her, she would have punched him.

"So." Qadir spoke in her ear. "The sultan is looking for a relic. Do you think we can find the magic before he sends his hounds to track it?"

Loulie paused at the ship's bow and stared wordlessly up at the city. She stretched out her arms, allowing the wind to push and pull at her sleeves. Qadir had the sense to stop talking. Later, they would speak of relics and gold and magic. But for now, all of it disappeared from her mind. The world folded into a single, simple truth.

She was home.

orbit

Follow us:

/orbitbooksUS

/orbitbooks

/orbitbooks

Join our mailing list
to receive alerts on our
latest releases and deals.

orbitbooks.net

Enter our monthly
giveaway for the chance
to win some epic prizes.

orbitloot.com